FREEING HOOK

THE LOST GIRL SERIES
BOOK TWO

T.A. LAWRENCE

This one's for me
at twenty

PREFACE

This is a dark fantasy book, in which the following themes are addressed: murder, addiction, sexual assault, trafficking, and suicide.

CHAPTER 1

WENDY

*T*he best part about flying is the nothingness. Nothing but the weightless hum of the empty air. No ground to tether me. No gravity to shove me downward and chain me to the earth.

The sweet taste of honeysuckle and powdered sugar still lingers on my tongue, sparking in clusters throughout my weightless limbs. The feeling lasts for but a moment before my spine scrapes against something hard. Faintly, I can feel a splinter puncture my shirt, lodging itself into my skin.

A moment later and the faint pain is gone, lost to the vast array of colors speckling my vision.

I'm not sure how long I stay like that. Forever and a second are synonymous when your body obeys the tick of a clock not of another realm, but a different plane of existence entirely.

"Get. Her. Down." Rage suffuses the growl, making the hairs on my arms prickle. I don't mind. Even gooseflesh feels pleasant at the moment.

"Captain—"

"I said get her down. Now."

There's a shuffling like flapping parchment against my ears. Labored breaths as someone climbs. Perhaps once they reach my heights, they'll stay up here with me. I'm not sure whether I'd prefer that. On the one hand, I'd love nothing more than for every creature that roams the earth to soak in this pleasure. On the other, part of me worries that having someone else join me in the nothingness will make it...well, less like nothingness and more like somethingness. Cause the pool to overflow at the edges, chase the warmth away.

The skin that grasps my wrist is calloused, but the hand itself is small. Almost like a child's. My thoughts threaten to go to Michael, but he's far off, and I don't want to think of my brother right now. Not when fingers wrap around my wrist like my fingers wrapped around Michael's throat...

No. No, I'll just drown in the nothingness for a while longer.

A gentle tug, and my body drifts. Down, down, down. Like a feather freed from a recently shredded pillow.

The hand weighs me down, and I soon worry it'll steal me from the flecks of riveting color that mask my surroundings. We're above the clouds, and this hand will drag me through their soft embrace, only to stake me to the ground. To the world below, where death and suffering reign.

I flail, and though my movements are weak, like kicking through sludge, the grip around my wrist loosens.

"Captain." The voice is both warning and panicked. Female, I think.

"Out of my way." That one's the deeper voice, the voice I'm trying to escape. The voice that would tie me down, shear my wings if I had them.

I thrash, digging my fingernails into the nearest flesh they can find, and whoever's detaining me lets go with a cry.

Finally, I'm free.

I hang suspended in the air, just for a single breath of exhilarating freedom, when another hand fastens around my wrist.

This grip is not so gentle. It digs into my skin like it intends to imprint itself there, and yanks. A whoosh of air, and I find my body pressed against something hard, something warm, something pulsing, no—heaving.

This is not what it feels like to fly. This is what it feels like to be had. Seized. Owned.

I kick at my captor, but each successive blow only strengthens his fortitude. And then he yanks me down.

I WAKE to the caress of plush bedsheets, my captor's warm but rough grip replaced by the icy sting of metal around my left wrist. I gasp, flailing, mussing the sheets, but all that serves to do is get my arm tangled up in the chain securing me to the bedpost.

"I see you've come back down from your little excursion. Tell me, Darling, did you soar?"

A chill, colder than the shackle's kiss, trickles down my spine as I turn to face my captor.

Captain Nolan Astor is perched on the bedside facing me, swathed in shadows, though none of them consume him. Not with the lantern sitting atop the bedside table illuminating his harsh features. The sharp slant of his jaw, the black tips of his hair razoring across his forehead. His ivy green eyes glow in the darkness, pinning me to the bed.

When I don't answer, Astor's throat bobs. He digs his fingers into the mattress, like he's restraining himself. "I offered you freedom. I would have thought you clever enough not to toss my generosity overboard."

The past few days swarm the edges of my memory, but I try to hold them back. Better to keep them from assaulting me all at once. Still, they break through my measly fortifications. Nettle confessing to the murder of three Lost Boys. Captain Astor stealing me from the cave I'd used to imprison him. Peter bargaining me away on the onyx beach in exchange for the Lost Boys' safety.

I'd thought the captain would throw me in the hull of his ship, but to his credit, he'd been a man of his word. Back in Neverland, he'd told me he wouldn't stuff me in a barrel when he took me. Instead, he'd provided me with my own room—a small, dingy chamber, but it was mine and it meant there was a lock between me and the rest of the crew.

I'd huddled in the small cot, wrapping myself in blankets that smelled of mildew and salt, unable to sleep with how violently my body was shaking from the events of the day.

It soon became evident that terror wasn't to blame for the shaking.

I'd made it three hours, judging by the clock on the wall, before I tiptoed out of bed and slunk into the belly of the ship. The ship that, according to the captain, was powered by faerie dust on occasions when the wind failed to drive the sails. I'd only meant to take just enough to calm the tremors, to keep the shadows from encroaching on my vision—the same dosage Peter's been giving me to keep me sane. To prevent me from waking in the middle of the night in a panic and strangling my brothers. Once the faerie dust touched my lips, however, I'd craved more than a disciplined alleviation of my symptoms.

I'd wanted to erase myself from my own body. Just for a while. Or forever. I'm not entirely sure which.

"Do you often call it generosity when you kidnap women?" I ask, deflecting if only because I can't bear to admit my loss of control to the captain.

Captain Astor turns those piercing green eyes on me, the golden ring looped through the pointed tip of his left ear glinting. "Do you know where we found you? While you were off enjoying your little jaunt?"

"In the rafters of the bunker, I assume." I clutch the interior of the blanket someone's wrapped around me, so the captain won't sense my nerves.

He offers me a close-lipped smile. "If only. No, Darling. We found you tangled up in the anterior moonsail."

My heart plummets out of my chest, my mouth going dry. "I'm assuming that one's on top."

"Very good, Darling."

"But I took the faerie dust in the bunker."

"It appears as though someone, in her drugged state, decided on an outing."

Sweat breaks out on my forehead, though I can't tell if it's from fear of the captain, or what could have become of me, or if it's just the effects of the faerie dust refusing to wear off.

There's a predatory stillness to the way the captain watches me. An intentionality that betrays a learned restraint. "Tell me, do you enjoy the idea of falling?"

I bite my lip, memories wafting over me. Peter dancing with me through the sky. His challenge to let him drop me. The "yes" escaping like a ravenous plea from my lips. "Only with someone around I trust enough to catch me," I say, hoping the words will cut. It's a foolish notion, given I'm the one who's made myself look like an idiot tonight.

The laugh the captain lets out has to press through his teeth. "If I were you, I wouldn't be so reliant on the assumption that this someone cares enough to catch you."

His words twist at the already lodged splinter in my chest, one I've tried to claw out, only to snap off the tip instead, leaving my fumbling fingers helpless to remove it. Peter's voice returns to my mind. *What's in it for me?* That's what he'd asked when the captain wanted to steal me away.

But Peter doesn't feel pain. I'd realized that was the curse the Sister had placed upon him. So that if he needed to eliminate any of the Lost Boys for going mad, he could kill those he loved without the burden of pain.

"It's not his fault he's the way he is," I whisper under my breath.

I'm not sure the captain would gaze upon a slug with more disgust than he casts at me.

"You're lucky one of my gunners couldn't sleep and happened to be on deck at the time. Though you'd have been less lucky if she hadn't called for help. Couldn't quite keep a grip on you with you flailing like a surfaced fish. Not when she was trying to hold on to you and sidle down the mast at the same time."

I roll my eyes, and though the movement is foreign to me, I find it cathartic. "And I suppose I have you to thank for rescuing me."

Astor shifts on the bed, and I can't help but notice how my muscles tense when his hip grazes my thigh, even with the blanket separating us. "You do have a tendency to idolize those who put you in harm's way. So no, I wouldn't be surprised if thanks found its way out of your lips."

My stomach curdles, anger threatening to add to my trembling, but I worry the captain will interpret it as fear, so I dig my free hand further into the mattress underneath the sheets to steady myself and say, "I'll thank your gunner should I get the chance to meet her."

At that, the captain's lip twitches upward. "Good. I'm fond of Charlie, though I'd appreciate it if you didn't mention as much to her."

Something stings in my stomach at his words, but I refuse to acknowledge the implications of such a reaction. Instead, I roll my head toward the chain shackling me to the bed.

"This doesn't seem necessary now that I'm no longer floating, don't you think?" I ask.

The captain snorts, crossing his arms and revealing a muscled divot in his forearms, bare up to the cuff where he's rolled his sleeves. "I gave you a chance to walk freely about my ship, and look how that turned out."

"I won't do it again. Believe it or not, the idea of floating away and finding myself tumbling into the depths of the ocean isn't exactly palatable."

"Is it not? I wasn't sure, given your affinity for danger."

The curve of my rounded ears heat, which the captain must notice, because he offers me a smirk.

"The point is, I've learned my lesson," I say, settling numbly against the headboard of the bed. "I won't be taking more of the faerie dust, I promise."

"You're such a terrible liar."

I go to protest, but even now, my tongue is parched, the memory of faerie dust still fresh on my tongue. My body craves it like it should crave water.

"If you keep the faerie dust locked up with a guard, I won't be able to get to the lock," I admit, shame that such measures are even necessary warming my cheeks, the back of my neck.

Captain Astor shakes his head, and when he speaks, I can't tell if it's annoyance or admiration tinging his voice. "Something tells me you'd find a way."

"I wouldn't have thought you believed me brave enough to go after what I want. Always letting life happen to me and all." The immediate urge to swallow my words overcomes me when the captain raises a thick, black brow. I wait for him to mock me for keeping his insult— the one he tossed at me so haphazardly the night of the masquerade— so close to my already bruised heart. I'm sure to him it's a sign of weakness, allowing his words to linger in my head. The captain had likely forgotten them as soon as they reached my ears.

But Astor doesn't mock me. He doesn't even address the insult. "Is this what you want, Darling? Never to feel?"

The words are almost tender, and I might believe them if I weren't so used to him setting me up for cruelty. But we're no longer in the cave. He's no longer my prisoner. There's no reason to disarm me, to rile me, so I'll forget to drug him.

"What I want is to go back to Peter."

I wait for the captain's lips to break into a mocking smirk, for his sharp laughter to clang against my ears. Instead, he just stares at me, a blankness in his expression, then stands from the bed. "I have business to return to on deck. Believe it or not, commanding this ship demands too much attention for me to be wasting my time trying to talk an addict out of her vices. Don't bother missing me. I always retire to bed by ten."

My body freezes in place, and I inspect the room. I'd been so caught up in my conversation with Astor and the dread of what could have happened if I hadn't been snagged by the sails that I hadn't noted my surroundings.

The cabin is dark, but it's much larger than the one the captain initially gave me. It's more decorated too. There's a finely carved desk in the corner, one with mermaids carved into the legs. In the center of the room is a broad table with maps spread about it. Trunks and wardrobes line the sides of the rooms, and there are more well-preserved maps hanging on the walls.

The rug on the floor is ornate. Kruschian, probably—the type even my parents, with all their wealth, would have struggled to get their hands on.

I wonder if the captain stole it, or if he simply has that kind of money at his disposal.

"This is your room," I whisper, then grasp at the sheets, recognizing for the first time that rather than mildew, they smell of teakwood and pipe tobacco... just like the captain. "And this is—" I hate the way my voice goes high, betrays my panic, but I can't help it. Instinctively, I tug at the cuff shackling me to the bedpost, but even if my limbs weren't weary from the faerie dust, I'd still be too weak to do any damage.

"Astute observation," the captain says dryly.

"I'm not sleeping in the same bed with you," I cry, my voice scaling the mast itself.

The captain whips around, and it's the first time I've seen him lose his composure. "Then," he says through gritted teeth, "you might have considered that before you broke into my bunker, drowned yourself in faerie dust, and almost killed yourself for good measure."

"So what?" I say, panic amplifying my voice so that I'm almost screaming. "I thought you said what my mother did to me by making me..." I trail off, my mouth going dry as the incense of the parlor wafts into my nose from the past. "I thought you said that alone excused you for her murder. I thought you said I shouldn't let men touch me," I say, feeling the ghost of hands on me, remembering the slimy Lord Credence who danced with me at my masquerade.

The captain is facing away from me now, but I glimpse his shoulders lift, then settle as he lets out a deep exhale.

"Sleep well, Darling," he says, before slamming the door behind him.

CHAPTER 2

WENDY

There are certain words the men who drank of my body called me when my mother abandoned me to their whims in the parlor. Nasty, dreadful words that taunted me hours, days, years later. Words I always assumed would feel slimy coming from my lips, should I ever choose to use them.

Over the next few days, I unleash the store of them. I can't unleash them on Astor, because he hasn't graced his room again after I first woke chained to his bed. Instead, I fire them at the human woman Astor sends to tend to me.

Charlie is her name, though I'm certain it's short for something more feminine, certain she curtails it to convince herself she's more capable of being a pirate than her sex allows.

I hate Charlie, and I let her know as much.

She hates me, too. That's why she won't give me any faerie dust, why she looms over me as I writhe in agony, sweat pouring off my forehead as I grapple with death. Because she enjoys watching me suffer.

"He'll kill you when he knows you're the one who let me die," I seethe as Charlie dabs my forehead with a frigid wet cloth, each dab an icepick to my cracking skull. I lunge at her, going for the scarlet

9

claw marks across her neck where I got her this morning. This time, she's prepared and catches my free wrist just before my fingernails scrape her flesh.

Charlie just offers me a wink. "Nah. He likes me better than you. At least, at the moment he does, now that he's fuming at you for almost getting yourself killed."

Again, I throw my body weight into lunging at her, but it's little use. I'm weak, and I can't use my left hand because of the shackle anyway.

"I bet you get a kick out of torturing women who are prettier than you, don't you?" I ask, the aching in my temple throbbing.

It's not true, of course. Charlie is much prettier than me. Her face is round and soft, a perfect set of dimples framing her parchment-colored cheeks. Her deep brown eyes tilt upward at the edges. Shiny black hair frames her face. When she first visited me, it cascaded in straight locks down to her waist, but she's gotten wise and started braiding it behind her back so I can't get a grip on it.

Charlie must know she's breathtaking, because she offers me a deceptively kind, closed-lipped smile as she continues to blot the sweat from my brow. "You are quite pretty," she says, though there's a hint of amusement in her voice.

"He wants me, you know," I say, every word feeling as if it's scraping against my throat. "He might frequent your bed because you're the only woman onboard, but don't think he'll look twice at you now that I'm here."

I wait for the words to land, but Charlie seems unfazed. "I imagine that's more true than you know. Except the part about the captain frequenting my bed." She snorts, and the way her expression softens when she speaks of the captain makes my head feel as if it's going to explode.

"I'm so thirsty," I say, the words coming out in a subtle whine. I sound like the beagle puppy my mother adopted when I was a child.

Charlie rolls her eyes, then offers me a chalice. When it hits my mouth, I gag at the metallic taste, the bile sting of the liquid within. "You're poisoning me," I choke.

"If you're intolerant of water, then I suppose I am."

Did I mention that I hate Charlie?

Before I can tell her as much again, the door bursts open and in strides the captain. He surveys me, from the tip of my toes to my forehead. It's the type of glance that makes me feel naked, though I'm buried underneath a bundle of clothes and wrapped in a wool blanket.

"What are you looking at?" I snap.

"I see we're making progress," the captain drawls, as if he's bored by my presence.

"I seem to remember telling you that this process tends to go more smoothly if we progressively wean the patient off the dust," says Charlie.

I wait for the cruel captain to strike her for her brazen statement, but he doesn't. "You also said it wouldn't kill her if we did it this way. That faerie dust withdrawal isn't lethal. And that it would be faster this way."

Charlie flashes the captain her set of pearly teeth, the first hint of annoyance I've detected from her slipping through them. "Yes, well, had I known you were going to assign me to sit with her all hours of the day, I might have kept that tidbit of knowledge to myself."

Captain Astor punches Charlie in the shoulder lightly, the sight of which has my ribcage twisting in on itself in knots.

"Really, Captain. I have duties on this ship, you know. I would have reconsidered taking this job had I known you'd have me attending to addicts."

Astor actually frowns apologetically at that, then lowers his voice. "I know, and I'm sorry. But I already told you why I can't have any of the others watch after her."

Charlie lets out a little sigh, then shrugs. "Those heartstrings of yours are going to get you in trouble one day, you know. You might just find yourself in need of a new gunner."

The captain clutches his chest, groaning. "You wound me so."

Charlie awards him with the most stunning smile I've ever seen, and because my position prevents me from punching her in the mouth, I say, "You might enjoy being his little whore now, but just give me a few days and he won't look at you twice."

The captain spins toward me slowly, mouth slightly agape. As if he's just now remembered that I'm still in the room. "My, aren't we pleasant today? I promise you," he says, turning to Charlie, "Darling's exceptionally more timid when she's in her right mind."

I chuck my chalice full of bile at the captain, but he catches it in one hand without even sparing me a glance. Water sloshes over the side and onto his hand, dripping over his ruined Mating Mark.

Something cruel and wonderful slithers from my heart and up my throat. "What would your wife think, knowing you're lusting after me? Think she can hear your thoughts from the grave?"

The chalice in the captain's hand bursts, shards of clay shattering across the floor.

I grin.

WHEN I DREAM, it's of a glass window carved into the wall of the cabin. Outside, the waves lap against the window, begging to be let in. Water drips in through the cracks between the window and the sill, saltwater turning black as ink as it spills down the wall and into the floor. At first, I think it's Peter, and I gasp in delight, tears streaming down my cheeks at the realization that he's come for me.

But the ink never dissipates into shadow, nor does it coalesce to form the figure of my Mate. Instead, it coats the floor, burying the rug in inky sludge. Thick tar bubbles up from the floorboards, and as the water level rises, it creeps over the edge of the bed, coming from underneath the sheets.

It's not long before it covers my thighs, the heavy weight of it pinning me to the cot. I fight at the manacle securing me to the bedpost, but it's dripping of tar too, melding itself to my wrist.

"Peter," I call out, beg, but it's not Peter. Or if it is, he's too far gone to hear me. "Peter, stop."

The black sludge is heavy, bearing down on my muscles. It's as if I'm trapped underneath a pile of cement, the weight of it crushing my bones. Pain presses my ribs as the sludge reaches my chest, my lungs fighting desperately against the pressure for breath.

A moment later, and the sludge has reached my lips. I brace myself for its bitter sting, but it tastes of the dew of honeysuckles.

"I can take away your pain," a voice whispers from nowhere and everywhere at once.

"You're hurting me," I cry.

"You're mine, Wendy Darling. Mine to hurt," the voice whispers back.

When the shadows force themselves down my throat and drown me, I let them.

CHAPTER 3

JOHN

*I*f I had it to do over, I'd chop off my left forefinger instead of my pinkie. I'd been uncharacteristically emotional the night Peter brought us to the reaping tree—hadn't been thinking straight. Watching your parents slit their own throats tends to do that to a person.

I'd gone with the pinkie because I read once that it's the least utilized finger. Had my parents not been slaughtered in front of me that night, I might have recognized the flaw in this logic. The human body is so much more complex than that.

A fool thinks about which finger is employed the least. A wiser man would have considered the hand as a whole. Would have known that the hand can compensate much more efficiently for a missing forefinger than a missing pinkie.

This mistake has been bothering me for months. Perhaps more than the loss of my finger itself.

As it stands, the grip strength in my left hand is significantly diminished. I can hardly lug a basket of onions back to the Den, much less climb like I used to. The night Michael and I met Wendy at the storehouse on the edge of the cliffs in an attempt to escape Neverland, I'd had to go the long way around. Trek up a path on the sea-facing bluffs that I'd spent weeks clearing of brush. Secretly, of course.

It's getting more difficult to hold on to Michael, too. It still sets me on edge—thinking about how for the past day, he's been under the watch of Victor and Benjamin while I've been asleep, knocked out cold by Nettle's somnium oil.

We'd been so close to getting out of here. Wendy had been so close.

I would have left weeks ago, once I cleared the sea-facing path up to the storehouse. I could have taken Michael and run—rather, soared —into the sky and left this horror novel of an island behind.

But that would have meant leaving Wendy behind.

My sister has changed during her time in Neverland, and not for the better. She thinks I don't notice the bags under her eyes, the way she licks her dry lips when it's been almost an entire day since her last dose of faerie dust. Peter says it's to prevent the shadows from torturing her. To keep her from mistaking a nightmare for reality and strangling us like she did to Michael that one night.

But Wendy doesn't need faerie dust. She needs help.

Wendy's needed help for a long while now.

I can't blame her; not really. Having Peter visit her from the shadows as a child messed with her psyche. The alienist my parents hired didn't help much either. I used to listen in on their discussions from the vent in the library; it was big enough for me to crawl into before their sessions and camp out. I watched as he showed my sister charcoal sketches—dead, mutilated bodies, from what I inferred, though I never saw the depictions. I watched that familiar glassy emptiness wash over her expression.

The alienist had called my sister cold. Unnatural.

That's because he never stuck around to hear her screams in the middle of the night. When we were older, she used to stuff her sheets into her mouth to muffle the sound. She didn't wish to wake me.

My sister isn't cold. She's broken. Used. Has spent half her life fattened like a heifer, her owners hoping that instead of being led to the slaughter, she'd be bought and caged and paraded.

But my sister isn't livestock to be bred.

I struggle with whether to fault my parents for their obsession with finding her a husband. To them, optimizing her chances of marriage was the logical decision to make. My parents only failed Wendy by not being clever enough to devise a better alternative.

And perhaps for being too inattentive to realize that a suitor had gotten her alone in the smoking parlor that one night.

I can't exactly condemn my parents, as I'm guilty of a worse sin than ignorance.

We'd come so close to getting out of here. I'm not sure what had Wendy waking up to the danger of Peter. What dragged her out of his glamour for long enough to spook her and have her scrambling for a way to get us out of Neverland. But the window of time for escaping closed the moment she told Simon about our plans.

Cold-hearted, the alienist had said.

Unlike her, I'd have left the Lost Boys. Not out of malice. I even like some of them—Benjamin with his bluntness and affinity for whittling, and Smalls in his blustering innocence. But my duty belongs to my siblings first.

There's no telling what lie Peter has woven to keep Wendy here with him, to keep that ring on her finger, claiming her. But whatever he's told her, she's his for good now.

I fear what I'll have to do to get her out of this place.

I never want to force my sister into anything. Not after all she's been compelled to do in her life. But Wendy has a tendency of letting others push her into things, and I fear that if I'm not the one to do it, someone else will. Someone who doesn't have her best interests at heart.

Victor came by and explained the situation to me when I woke in bed an hour ago. After Wendy alerted Simon that we were escaping, he'd told Nettle about our plan to leave Neverland. Nettle, who, as it turns out, was telling the truth about remembering his past, though Victor didn't know the details regarding how that was possible. Just that his memories had turned him paranoid, convincing him that Thomas, Freckles, Joel, and I were all killers at heart. Nettle had murdered the others. Thomas, Victor's brother, was his first victim. I was supposed to be his last.

Apparently, Simon killed Nettle to save my life.

I'll thank him when I'm convinced that's the entire story.

I hear Michael humming from down the hall. Victor must be bringing him to visit me. That's unnecessary. With the fluids I've been pushing thanks to Smalls keeping the jars of water next to my cot brimming over, my muscles should have recovered enough from the somnium oil to walk by now.

I'm pushing myself out of my cot when Victor reaches the doorway and pulls the leaf curtain aside. Michael rushes to my side and parks himself cross-legged on the bed, rocking back and forth, causing the rickety beams to creak.

Victor's face is a shade paler than his usual bleached eggshell.

"What's wrong?" I ask.

Victor swallows. It annoys me when people do that—pause before they deliver bad news, like they think they're sparing you.

"Just tell me," I say, though I have a sneaking suspicion I already know.

"Wendy's gone."

MY FIRST THOUGHT is that *he* killed her.

That's the most logical explanation. The story practically writes itself.

Woman who's only ever been bred to be a wife falls in love with a dangerous fae, thinking she sees the good in him—and she probably does, for what it's worth. She agrees to marry him, because again, that's all she's ever been told that she wanted. Then she gets spooked. Discovers something that frightens her. Tries to run.

Jilted, he makes her disappear.

It's the type of story that's easy to paint, but it's unsupported by evidence as of the moment. So when the fear of what Peter might have done to the one person in the world who's ever really understood me threatens to eat away at my bones, I tell it to come back later. In case I have use for it.

There's no use in hurting over something I'm not confident has happened. It won't help me, and it certainly won't help Wendy.

"Where was she last seen?" I ask.

Victor shakes his head. "I don't know. She came to visit you a few times while you were out. She told me goodnight before she went to bed last night."

Clearly, he's not going to be of any use. "Where's Peter?"

Victor blinks, stunned, but not by my question, then nods for me to follow him into the hallway. When I stand, I instinctively reach for Michael with my left hand.

He grabs for my pinkie. When he was young, he used to hold on to it. But of course, it isn't there. Self-loathing wriggles its way into my chest. I should have considered that too, before I chopped off that finger. Should have remembered it was the finger Michael likes to hold on to.

I don't like having him on my left side anymore, anyway. Not when I can't keep a hold of him if I need to. So I maneuver him to my right side and we take off down the hall, following Victor.

Voices clamor through the tunnel as Victor, Michael, and I approach the living room of the Den.

As soon as we enter, all noise muffles to silence, the sound absorbed by our presence. Five sets of eyes avert themselves from our general direction and to their plates. This matters little to me. I've never kidded myself into thinking the Lost Boys are my friends. Besides, it's Peter I need to speak with.

As if my thoughts summoned him, roots descend from the ceiling, depositing Peter in the center of the room before unfurling from around his body. He stretches his wings behind him. I search them for scratches, wounds.

As if Wendy would have fought him. As if my sister would have struggled.

Even if she had, Peter heals at a faster rate than humans. Unless she managed to get a blade in his flesh, there'd be little evidence of a struggle left behind on his body.

"Where is she?" I demand.

Peter, back facing me, turns slowly, and I mark the deliberation of his movement. The way he gives himself a moment longer to perfect his response. It must be an impressive lie he has to tell if he didn't have time to shave off the rough edges while I slept. Especially for a master liar like Peter.

"Taken," he says, and the hairs on the back of my neck stand on edge.

I tap my foot and have to grit the next question out. "By whom?"

Peter's jaw pulses. "Pirates."

Imprinted in my memory, blood drains from my parents' self-inflicted wounds. It took my father minutes to bleed out, my mother longer. I'd watched as their pulses slowed, trying to remember if the adrenaline brought on by the night's events would have tempered their pain.

I still can't remember.

"I take it at least one of these pirates has a name," I say.

Peter nods, rubbing his forehead. "Astor took her."

"So your story is that Captain Astor somehow tracked Wendy all the way to Neverland, a realm separate from all realms. What—did he just snatch her off the beach?"

At the breakfast table, the rest of the Lost Boys' heads dart back and forth, following our conversation.

"It seems that way."

"It seems, or it is?"

A cool indifference that I've come to loathe overcomes Peter's features. "It is."

I bite the inside of my cheek. "I see."

I don't buy Peter's story. Not for the tick of a pocket watch. The only way Peter would know that it was Captain Astor who came to steal Wendy away would be if he saw Captain Astor. And if he truly witnessed Captain Astor kidnapping Wendy, wouldn't he have stopped it from happening? Surely he could have managed it with those shadow powers of his.

"Well, how do you intend to get her back?" I ask, only because it would be less than wise to challenge Peter openly. He has the Lost Boys in his pocket. They'll defend him no matter the evidence against him, just like Wendy did. If I cause trouble, I don't trust that Peter won't find a way to silence me.

Another thing the Lost Boys won't question.

Benjamin taps the fork he carved himself against his plate, his knee bouncing at the same rate.

Simon looks as if he's going to be sick. I'm shocked the other boys let him eat with them after he killed one of their own. But Peter calmed their apprehensions about Simon, too. He's an expert in that arena.

Where I expect Peter to scoff at me, to confront my challenging of his care for Wendy, he doesn't. Instead, he strides over to me and puts his hand on my shoulder.

I have to fight my instincts to squirm out from under his touch. I hate being touched. If someone's incapable of communicating their thoughts and feelings with words, that shouldn't have to be my problem. I shouldn't have to submit to their proximity.

But I don't pull away. Something tells me Peter knows I won't be placated by a pat on the shoulder, so I'd better face his power flex instead of cowering from it.

"Trust me, John," he says, his voice all brotherly affection. "I'm as worried for Wendy as you are. There's not a night I'll rest before I find her. I'll scour the realms to get her back, I assure you."

His promise isn't worth much, especially since many of his nights are already spoken for by the Sister and her errands. But we both know that, so I don't bother mentioning it.

"And if the captain slaughters her first? Like he did our parents?"

Peter examines me carefully. "I think we both know if he wanted her dead, he would have killed her that night."

"If he wanted her dead *yet*," I correct.

Peter sighs, then pats me on the shoulder before finally removing his hand and giving me space to breathe.

"Just let me know what I can do to help," I say.

Peter nods, as if he'll let me anywhere near any evidence of what might have happened to Wendy. I don't buy for a second that he's telling me the entire truth, but it's not as if I'm going to be able to pry it out of him.

Before Peter leaves, he makes his rounds about the table, patting the Lost Boys on the shoulders. I hear their whispers, though just fragments. Mostly I hear words like Winds and safe and okay.

The Lost Boys might be blind to Peter's manipulations, but at least they care for my sister.

Michael wriggles out of my grip and dashes to Peter, who rustles his hair and offers him a smile that my brother returns with a whistle. My gut writhes, and I can't tell if it's from hatred for the fae who ruined our lives and is now hiding the reason behind Wendy's disappearance, or if I'm simply being petulant about Michael favoring him.

The only person Peter doesn't clap on the back is Simon. The Lost Boy who supposedly saved my life from Nettle and typically worships Peter stares at his barely touched meal. Victor must notice, because he glances at me and cocks a brow.

When Peter leaves, Simon slides his onions onto Smalls's plate.

LATER, someone grabs at me as I'm leaving the Den, the reaping tree having just deposited Michael and me outside. I flinch at the touch, but the grip remains firm. When I turn, I'm met with shaggy black hair and empty eyes framed by dark bruises.

"Walk with me," says Victor, sliding his hand off my shoulder and gesturing for me to follow him.

Michael hums to himself as we accompany Victor into the woods. If he'd asked me to follow him down a dark path alone only a few days ago, I would have found an excuse not to. Or outright refused. But now that we know that Nettle was the killer, I'm less inclined to mistrust Victor.

That's not accurate. I still have a blade inside my belt—I found it in Thomas's old rooms when I was digging around there for information on his disappearance—but I don't anticipate having to use it. Besides, I'm fairly sure I already know what this is about.

"You don't think Peter's telling us the truth about what happened to Wendy," I say as soon as we reach a clearing.

Victor cocks a bushy black brow at me. "How'd you know?"

Seems obvious enough, but I don't mind explaining. "Peter deflected attention away from your brother's murder. Made the Lost Boys feel as if it wasn't actually a murder, even though all logic pointed otherwise. If he wasn't forthright about Thomas's death, why would you believe what he claims about Wendy's disappearance?"

Victor harrumphs and plucks a twig off a nearby tree, rolling it between his forefinger and thumb. "You're a know-it-all. You know that, right?"

"I suppose if I didn't, I wouldn't be a know-it-all, would I?"

It's meant to be a joke, but Victor hardly pays me attention. He just scans the area.

"You think Peter's listening?" I ask.

Victor shakes his head. "Not Peter. Something else, though. I get the feeling this island's always listening."

I frown, and Michael says, "It's time to use our listening ears."

"I guess you're always listening too, aren't you, buddy?" Victor asks Michael. He goes to rub the top of my brother's head, then must think better of it because he retracts his hands to his sides. Strange. It's the first glimpse of tenderness I've ever witnessed in the guy.

"Always," I say, offering a faint smile down at my brother. Michael squeezes my hand. It's about the only comfort I have at the moment, so I cling to it.

"So what do you think happened to Wendy?" I ask. Hopefully, Victor will recount the events that occurred while I was drugged. He's already told me some down in the Den, but now that we're away from prying ears, I'm hoping there's more to the story.

Victor paces, thinking. "She was snooping around, your sister."

Wendy wasn't the only one, but I don't mention as much.

"She had a sketch of Thomas in her pocket the day we all wrestled," Victor says. "She had to have been looking into what happened to him."

"And Wendy figured it out," I say, thinking. "You said Nettle was the one going around killing people. Wendy confirmed as much before she went missing, didn't she?"

Victor works the corner of his lip. "Yeah, she, Peter, and Simon came back and told all of us what happened. That Nettle had gone mad, thinking you were the killer. And that Simon killed him to defend you."

I snort. "Why would Simon do that?"

"Man, you really haven't taken to us, have you?"

I shrug. It's always been difficult for me to get close to others. Getting close to the Lost Boys has been at odds with keeping my siblings safe. No need to attempt something that's both difficult and counterproductive. Sure, I've spent time with them since arriving in Neverland, but that doesn't change that we're more acquaintances than friends.

"You know what? That's not important," Victor says, one hand on his hip while he waves the other in front of him. "It's not Simon killing him to save your life that seemed odd to me. Not even how shaken up he was. I'm sure anyone would be shaken up after killing their friend. It's how he's been acting around Peter."

This piques my interest. "Simon's always been Peter's biggest fan."

"Exactly." Victor flicks a low-hanging tree branch. "And now he breaks into a sweat every time Peter enters the room."

I stroke the bridge of my glasses. "You think Simon knows something about Peter? Something that frightens him?"

"That, or Peter knows something about Simon," says Victor.

I tuck that thought away for the time being. "And what does that have to do with my sister?"

"Whatever it was that happened that night, your sister witnessed it. What if she was lying to us when she told us about Nettle? What if there was more to the story, and Peter told her to keep it quiet?"

My mouth goes dry. Something had spooked Wendy the night she tried to get us to run—something about Peter. Obviously, by the time she came back to the Den, her fears had been assuaged. I'd assumed it was because Nettle was found to be the killer.

"Simon was there the night we tried to run," I say. "Wendy tried to get him to bring the rest of the Lost Boys to run with us. When he showed back up, he said the other Lost Boys refused to run away with us." I grit my teeth, annoyed that I don't remember anything after that, Nettle having dosed me with somnium oil.

Victor runs his hands through his hair. "Well, I can confirm that was a lie. Simon didn't alert us that you were leaving."

I frown. "Unless you were the only one he didn't try to save."

"Thanks," says Victor, but he's too self-aware of his standing with the other Lost Boys to dispute me.

"You're probably right, though," I say. "I doubt Simon told the rest of the boys about the escape attempt."

"Yet Nettle somehow found where you were and attacked you," says Victor. "Then Simon was conveniently there to save the day."

"Leading us back to the beginning. That the only people who know what happened that night are Peter, Simon, and Wendy." I have to admit, it's all a bit suspicious. I don't at all like where this train of thought is headed, though.

Apparently Victor doesn't either, because he says, "You don't think they would have killed her, right?" There's desperation in his eyes. Strange. He's the most cynical of all the Lost Boys after what happened to Thomas. But there's still hope there. For Wendy. For my sister. "It's just hard to imagine anyone wanting to hurt her, that's all," says Victor.

My head aches. "I suppose it's possible that Peter has her tucked away somewhere. I agree with you; it seems more like him to make her disappear than to kill her." I tell myself I'm being logical, that this has nothing to do with what I want the truth to be. "He stalked her for years. If it was all just to kill her in the end…"

I can't finish that sentence, because I know it's not intellectually honest. Stalkers murder their victims all the time. Especially when it becomes clear that the love they feel for their victims is unreciprocated.

And Wendy had just tried to escape the island. To escape Peter. The thought raps against my skull, refusing to let me ignore it.

"I know you have a brain where you should have a heart," says Victor, "but I'm glad you're here."

"Why's that?" I ask, unable to fathom a reason.

"Because," says Victor, "you're the only other person on this island who Peter doesn't have in his pocket."

Before I can respond, Michael starts humming. It's a song our father used to sing to him before bed. Totally inappropriate for a child, now that I understand the lyrics. It's a song about a man who keeps his ex-lover's ring-finger bone in his pocket after hunting her down when she refused to marry him.

I suppose Victor saying pocket was what made Michael think of it. Or...

The rusted wheels in my head begin to crank. "You know, Victor, I don't think that's entirely true."

CHAPTER 4

WENDY

*W*hen I wake, it's to a dreadful cocktail. A pounding headache, a clear memory, and a vibrant recollection of every horrible thing I said when the faerie dust was working its way out of my system.

Charlie perches on the stool beside the bed, chin tucked into her palms, elbows docked on crossed knees. Her braid swings behind her as she shakes her head to the tune she's humming quietly under her breath. She looks as if she might perish from boredom.

My mind recounts every awful word I called her over the past few days, my stomach turning over at the obscenities.

"I'm sorry," I whisper, my throat dry. It still feels like sandpaper, and though the desire for faerie dust still haunts the back of my mind, it no longer feels like going without it is going to rip my skull in half from the inside out.

Charlie flinches, like the sound of my voice is the agreed-upon signal to fling her hands in front of her face to protect herself from an oncoming projectile.

"Oh," she says, blinking a few times as she examines me. "You're you."

I nod, embarrassment wafting over me as I curl the blanket, damp from how I sweated through my clothes, around my reddening neck. "I called you some awful things."

Charlie shrugs, her carefree demeanor returning. "The name-calling wasn't all that bad. It was the spitting I could have done without."

When my eyes go wide with mortification, Charlie hesitates for a moment, then, still balancing cross-legged on the stool, extends her hand. I take it hesitantly, and when she shakes it, it's like a shark shaking a wet fish in its clamped jaw.

"You're going to have to work on that handshake if you want to make it as a privateer," she says, and I don't miss how she rubs her palm on her pants like it's a nervous tick. I'm not sure what's more mortifying—that she's wiping my sweat off her palm, or that she is kind enough to hide that she's doing it.

"I don't think offering me an apprenticeship is what the captain has in mind," I say, propping myself up against the cedar headboard.

Charlie whistles. "The captain was right about you."

I crane my brow in question.

She offers me a teasing smile. "He said you were lacking in the humor department."

Pain trickles down my chest, and it must show on my face, because Charlie immediately retracts her words. "To be fair to you, though, the captain's sense of humor is the acquired sort. Like drinking coffee black."

I crinkle my nose. I've only had coffee once. The beans don't grow anywhere close to Estelle, and though my family lived in a harbor city, the tariffs in the tropical countries were too high for the ships to bother venturing that far south very often. The only reason I've tried it at all is that my parents invited a potential suitor from the island of Kalawai to stay with us the summer after my sixteenth birthday. He'd smuggled his own stores of coffee into Estelle, insisting he couldn't be expected to live without it for an entire month.

Charlie stretches her legs out on the stool. "It's not so bad once you get used to it."

I'm no longer sure if we're talking about coffee or the captain's sense of humor. "I really am sorry for the horrible things I said. And the scratching."

Charlie bounces up from her stool, her long braid slapping at its wooden seat. "And the spitting?"

I cringe. "Especially the spitting."

She places her hands on her hips, then grins. "Consider it in the past, then. Just—please don't continue to bring it up. I know how aristocrats are about that sort of thing."

"I'm so—" I blush, then swallow, chuckling nervously when she offers me an I-told-you-so sort of look.

"So..." Charlie says. "Cap says I'm supposed to orient you to the *Iaso* once you've, you know, recovered."

"The *Iaso*?" There's something about the name that rings in my memory.

"Name of the ship. Well, and the captain's wife, but I wouldn't bring her up again if I were you. She's dead. But I guess you already know that."

I cock my brow. "How do you know I know that?"

Charlie bites her tongue and juts her jaw out to the side like she's considering her words. "You might have mentioned it while you were in an...unfortunate mood."

Oh. Right. My mouth goes dry as I remember my last words to the captain. I can't decide if I'm more ashamed of being so hateful about the captain's dead wife, or that I accused him of lusting after me.

"Yeah, if that were me, I'm not sure I'd be able to look the captain in the eyes again," says Charlie with a commiserating grimace.

"Avoiding him is going to be a tad difficult," I say, glancing over at the shackle on my wrist.

"Ah, that," says Charlie, tapping her hands against her thighs. "Well, the problem with that is that the captain has the only key."

I swallow. "I don't suppose you could ask him for it, could you?"

Charlie just laughs. "I'll have to tell Cap that you have a sense of humor, after all."

· · ·

THE FAERIE DUST might have left my system, but the memory of it remains. The ghost of its taste lingers at the back of my tongue, haunting in the way that though I can recall it, I can't quite replicate it in my memory.

There's nothing that I want more, and that's what frightens me the most.

I berate myself with images of John discovering that I'm gone. The fear he must have experienced learning I'd been taken. I castigate myself with the guilt of leaving him to tend to Michael alone. The fact that my youngest brother won't understand why I'm gone.

Part of me believes that if I remind myself what I've done to them, leaving them to fend for themselves in Neverland, I'll crave reunion with them more than I'll crave the taste of faerie dust on my tongue.

It doesn't work.

There's a hole in my chest that the dust lets me forget. A hole that should echo the emptiness of missing my brothers. Instead, my heart has been devoured by the agony of being rejected by my Mate. The scene replays in my mind, over and over, until I've memorized every rise and dip of Peter's tone as he traded me away.

As he let the man who killed my parents borrow me for a while.

Because Peter is a boy who feels no pain, and I'm a toy that was prettier in the shadows of my dusty shelf.

The next time the door opens, I'm biting my lip, hoping it's Charlie, back with the key.

It's not.

Captain Astor strides in, dressed in black sailing clothes that are hemmed to accentuate his broad shoulders and chest. I'm unsure whether it's his posture or the new attire that makes him appear more formidable than usual. Either way, I find myself shrinking from his presence, though I can't tell if it's from fear of his wrath or mortification at the rather crude comments I made when I was not myself.

I open my mouth to apologize, but Captain Astor holds up his palm. "I swear, Darling, if I catch you apologizing to your captor, I'm afraid you'll tempt me to say something I'll regret later."

Affronted, I suddenly no longer feel quite as guilty. "Why do you assume I was going to apologize?" I say, pulling my blanket over my chest with one hand.

He gives me a casual smile that dimples at the edges and knocks the breath out of me. "Well, were you?"

I avert my gaze.

This time, he doesn't sit on the edge of the bed with me. In fact, he grabs Charlie's stool and sets it across the room before resting atop it. I can't help but wonder who the distance is for.

"I'm going to ask you some questions, Darling," he says, folding his hands between his sprawled knees as he twists a wedding band I've never seen around his finger. His crew must have held onto it while I had him trapped in a cave in Neverland. "It would be for the best if you answered honestly."

The sheets bunch between the crevices between my fingers and palm as I grip them. "I'm not going to betray Peter, so don't waste your breath."

The captain sighs, his eyelids shifting downward ever so slightly, eyelashes serving as onyx window slats for his ivy green irises. "We'll address that slight issue later. And you will tell me what I want to know, one way or another." A shiver runs the course of my spine as I wonder how he intends to pry the information out of me. "But for now, I need to know how long you've been a slave to the faerie dust."

I blink, taken aback. "I can't see why you'd care."

"I can't see why you think I'd tell you."

I sigh, leaning my head against the headboard and letting my elbow hang from the shackle. There's not really any harm in telling him. Not when he already knows that my affinity for faerie dust has become...problematic.

"The first time was when I was almost attacked by a nightstalker. The shadows on the island were paralyzing me, so Peter gave me a small dose so they couldn't get to me. I wasn't as affected by it then. It wasn't all that bad the second time either. I liked the way it made me feel, but Peter gave me just enough so that..." I trail off, realizing how ridiculous this sounds considering where I've ended up.

The captain taps his fingers together. "Just enough for what?"

"Just enough that I could dance with him in the sky."

Astor's eyes narrow to slits. "A justifiable reason to risk lifelong addiction."

I shake my head. "He didn't give me enough to get me addicted. He knew what he was doing." I get lost in my head a little, remembering how it felt to dance in the swirl of color in the air, how it felt to fall, over and over. "It was the third time that did me in. I was having nightmares. After I killed the man who attacked Peter."

"Ah, yes. The child murderer," says the captain. "As evidenced by possessing a cheap bracelet."

I nod, hesitantly, and it feels like the worst sin I've ever committed, but I can't bear to tell him the truth about Thomas and Victor's father. That I killed a man whose only crime was searching for his children. Not with the way the captain's posture makes his rickety wooden stool look more like a judge's bench.

"I was having nightmares. They were making it dangerous for me to be around my brothers at night." Memories of choking Michael assault me, filling my stomach with nausea as the ship rocks. The chain holding me to the bed clatters. "So he gave me another dose. It was supposed to help. It did help," I correct myself. "So he kept me on a low dose, just to keep me safe. To keep everyone around me safe."

"I'm certain it was all with noble intent," says Astor in a tone that would suggest otherwise.

I don't fight him on it, not when I'm remembering the day I wandered off to the storehouse and ended up in the rafters. Nettle murdered Joel that night, and I'd unwittingly handed him the opportunity. The only reason Joel was outside the Den was because he was searching for me after I didn't show up to help him with kitchen duty. I'm afraid if I respond to the captain, the truth will burst out of me, just like the night I told the captain about the men in the parlor.

"And the nightmares?" Astor asks. "What were those about?"

The question takes me off guard, like I was expecting the captain to dig up my worst secrets, not the content of nightmares I couldn't help.

"Mostly just nightmares about the Lost Boys' murders. My imagination running away with me," I say, but then reconsider. "Rather, the shadows running away with my imagination, I suppose. That night, I saw visions of Thomas's murder." My heart stutters as I remember the scene the shadows played out for me—the silhouette of a man choking Thomas from behind.

I hadn't realized until now how accurate that vision was. Had the shadows replayed for me the event exactly as it had happened, with Simon choking his friend on accident?

"Mmm," says the captain.

"What?"

"Nothing."

Before I can press him, the captain shifts topics, which I'm secretly grateful for. "Tell me about Peter."

My mouth goes dry, but I remind myself that I'm the one in control of the narrative here, not Astor. As much as he'd like to make me doubt Peter, as much power as he has over my whereabouts, he doesn't get to dictate my thoughts, my feelings.

"There's something you have to understand about Peter," I say.

The captain flicks at a beetle that's just landed on his knee. "I know Peter. Or have you forgotten that I knew him before you did? The boy who refuses to grow up. The boy who would rather fly than land."

I shake my head, unable to hold back the gentle smile tugging at my lips. If it were up to me, my voice would remain cold, harsh. But it's not up to me, not when I'm talking about Peter. "No, but that's just it. Peter doesn't just fly. He soars."

Astor takes a golden coin out of his pocket and runs it sidelong up and down his knee. "And what about you, Darling? Do you soar?"

"Don't call me that."

"Call you what?"

I grit my teeth. I'm not sure why it bothers me so much. Perhaps because Darling feels like it should belong to my parents. "You know what."

"Darling?" Astor's scrunching brow is all innocence. "That is still your name, isn't it? Or did you end up wedding Peter after all and taking his? What is the winged boy's surname, by the way?"

The question hangs in the air between us, a taunt I have no response to.

"I see," the captain drawls, returning to playing with his coin, glistening in the lamplight. "My apologies. I didn't mean to offend."

When I don't answer, he gestures for me to continue. "You were talking about Peter."

"Life's been difficult for him, you know." A dampness settles over my heart when I consider the torment he must have endured at that wretched orphanage where he grew up.

The edges of the captain's lips lift in a close-lipped smirk. "Has it?"

"If you're going to laugh, I..." I hug the sheets to my chest, like I think they'll keep me restrained, prevent me from telling the captain more than he deserves to know. Peter's trauma is his own; it's not my place to share. "You know what? Never mind."

The captain shifts his stool, dragging it closer to the bed so that his knees graze the mattress, almost touching my thigh through the blanket. When I instinctively pull my knees to my chest, Astor looks me up and down, then props his chin in his hands expectantly. "Alright, alright. I'm finished laughing now. Promise."

I level him a glare. "I thought you said you didn't make promises."

"That one was clearly sardonic. Still, you should explain why you believe life has been harder on Peter than the rest of us."

I sigh, averting my eyes from the captain's glinting eyes. If I look at him too long, my neck warms, and I don't want him mistaking my reaction for anything other than loathing. "I don't know. It's just... That's the thing about soaring. I'm sure it seems great for a while. But when you're the only one who can fly, it's got to get lonely up there in the stars."

"Seems like a proper reason to come down."

"No. That's another thing you have to understand about Peter." Even now, locked to the captain's bed in the dim belly of this wretched ship, I can almost taste Peter's exhilaration, his contagious craving for adventure, the kind that was palpable as he twirled me among the stars. "He can't stay down for long. It's not in his nature."

"But you're down."

My breath catches. "Pardon?"

"You. Are. Down."

And Peter doesn't want to be where I am goes unsaid, but it's written in the way the captain leans forward, placing his elbow on his knee to examine my reaction. It's in the way he sweeps my lower lids with his gaze, searching for the tears that are clawing their way out.

Peter left me. Traded six months of my life away to the man who slaughtered my parents. He'd left me helpless on the ground as he soared away. As the tears grow too weighty for me to hold back, Astor's eyes trace their path down my cheeks, but they snag on the faint golden speckles of my Mating Mark, then bounce to the emerald betrothal ring on my finger.

Captain Astor and I realize at the same moment that we're both twirling our rings.

"I think I'm done with questions now," I say, breathless.

The stool squeaks as the captain jolts to his feet, returning it to its place by the wall. "Perhaps next time you'll have an answer for me," he says.

"An answer for what?"

"For my question. Do you soar?"

Before he leaves, he tucks a metal key into my hand and closes my fingers around it.

CHAPTER 5

JOHN

*G*etting Michael up to the storehouse is about as arduous as last time. The only reason we were able to make it to the top of the cliffs the night Wendy told me to pack our bags and get out of Neverland was because I'd been working for weeks on a roundabout path to the top. The loss of my little finger has made climbing problematic.

In the night, I'd been sneaking out after Wendy went wherever she was going—I assume to Peter's rooms, though I choose not to dwell on that—and working on forging a path up the cliffs from the long way around, on the north side.

It had been an anxiety-inducing task, mostly because it meant leaving Michael alone in our room. But Michael is an expert sleeper, and he'd always been fast asleep when I returned.

Of course, after Joel's death, I'd started waking Michael in the middle of the night to come with me. It wasn't as if I could leave him alone in the Den when I was suspicious of the Lost Boys. The disruption to his sleep pattern had been difficult for Michael.

My stomach still twists in knots when he melts down, especially if he manages to scratch himself and draw blood. I know there's a possibility he'd do this anyway, but there's always the thought lingering in the back of my mind that it's my fault. That if I weren't waking him up in the middle of the night and disrupting his sleep schedule, his body wouldn't be so dysregulated.

But I remind myself that it's better Michael be dysregulated than dead. And if I want him safe, I need to get him off Neverland.

Of course, I plan to find out what happened to Wendy first. But it would be preferable if I had a pouch of faerie dust on hand already when I find her. Or in case Peter finds out I've been snooping.

At the end of the day, if I need to leave Neverland before I find Wendy in order to save Michael, I will. Not because I love him any more than I do my sister. There's simply an unspoken understanding between Wendy and me that Michael's needs come before our own.

Still, were I a better protector, I might have been able to save both of them.

Can still save both of them, I remind myself.

Assuming Wendy's not dead, the voice in the back of my mind whispers, quite dry and with little empathy. There's a logical path that leads to that conclusion, but I'm choosing not to follow it at the moment. Instead, I work my way through the brush and make the steady climb up to the cliffs, Michael's hand in mine.

If I was alone, it would be easier to ascend, but with Michael everything is more complicated. Part of the problem is that guiding him uses up my good hand, as I don't want him wandering off toward the edge. The other issue is whether Michael decides coming with me is something he wants to do.

My brother can be quite determined.

Still, we make it to the top eventually; me sweating and heaving, though Michael doesn't seem at all fazed.

Unfortunately for us, the storehouse is empty. Cleaned out. Swept, even.

That answers my question about whether Peter knew we were coming.

. . .

"You're looking especially thwarted today," says Victor, sweat forming on his brow as he watches over a pot of boiling water at the stove. Today's my day to cook, but he volunteered to help, claiming fear that dinner wouldn't actually make it onto the table if the "cripple" was the only one working on it.

As much as I don't appreciate being called a cripple, I at least can acknowledge that it's wise for Victor to come up with a reasonable excuse to help me. One everyone else will believe, especially Peter. Victor isn't the type to offer to help with chores out of the goodness of his heart.

Besides, I really do hate kitchen duty. There might have been a time in my life when I enjoyed it. Cooking is basically just chemistry you get to eat, and both are activities from which I derive great pleasure. But between the fact that I still can't grip well with my left hand and trying to keep Michael out of the furnace, it really does take me hours to get anything accomplished in here on my own.

"Thwarted is accurate," I say under my breath, thankful that Michael is banging cast-iron pans together as if he's experimenting on which combination is the absolute loudest. Michael usually isn't fond of loud noises. Unless he's the one making them. "Peter's cleared out the storehouse. Moved all the faerie dust."

"I was under the impression you were going after Tink," says Victor. "Had I known you were planning on skipping out on me—"

"I wasn't skipping out on you," I say, which is technically true. I omit the fact that I will gladly skip out on Victor if given the chance. There are some things that are just better left unsaid. "Having faerie dust on hand would have been nice. Just in case."

Victor grunts, but he doesn't argue, the knife in his hand glinting. "Just don't double-cross me and we'll be fine," he says.

The potatoes crunch underneath his blade.

"Anyway," I say, taking careful note of Victor's knife and trying to ignore the skitter of gooseflesh prickling my arms. "That leaves us back at the original plan of finding Tink. Seeing if she knows anything about Wendy's disappearance."

"I'm still confused why you think she'd know anything."

"She has a habit of stalking my sister. Probably Peter too. It's possible she saw what happened."

"Or *was* what happened," Victor says casually.

I adjust my glasses, though they're fogging up in the steam from the pot—another reason it takes me so long to cook. Really, I should get rid of these, but I can't bring myself to part with them. "All the more reason to start with her."

There's an additional reason I want to find Tink, but I keep that to myself.

No one knows how faerie dust is collected. The traders keep that secret locked down. But Peter has an abundance. It's possible he steals it from traders in the other realms, but unlikely. I have a theory for how he gets it, though. I have ever since Wendy told me that the faerie who attacked her had shredded wings. At first, I assumed it had been Peter's way of keeping Tink from escaping the island, but what if there's more to it than that?

"So how are you planning to catch her?" asks Victor, plopping the potatoes into the boiling water.

"You're good at traps, aren't you?"

Victor glances at me sidelong. "Who told you that?"

"Wendy."

Victor actually blushes a bit, which catches me off guard, though it shouldn't. Objectively speaking, I am capable of acknowledging that my sister is the type of girl that boys might develop a crush on. Even if the thought makes me want to writhe out of my skin.

"I'm good at trapping animals. Faeries tend to be just a smidge more intelligent than hare, though. It's not like she's going to walk over a hole covered in sticks just because we put fish innards in the middle of the circle."

I nod, focusing on chopping the onions in front of me. They make my eyes water, and when I wipe my eyes, dislodging my glasses, they sting. "The Twins were trying to trap something the day Freckles died."

Victor snorts. "Good luck recruiting either of them. You think you're a hermit..."

"Do you have a better idea?"

Victor shrugs. "We could follow Peter. If Tink's stalking him, and we're stalking him, we're likely to cross paths."

That's actually not a horrible idea, except for the bit about having to follow Peter, who I'm still not positive didn't hurt my sister.

"You really think we can trail him without him noticing?" I can't help but glance over at Michael in the corner, who is now humming along with his pot-banging.

"Surely you're not thinking of bringing him along with us, whatever we do," says Victor, pointing his blade in Michael's direction.

"I'm not leaving him alone. Not when we're still not sure what happened the night Nettle died."

Victor sets his knife down on the counter, tapping his fingers against the wood. "That does complicate things, doesn't it?" I'm a bit taken aback when I don't detect any mocking in his voice. What's even more shocking is when he says, "I could stay behind and watch him."

Suspicion instantly creeps up my spine. "And why would you offer to do that?"

Victor rolls his eyes. "Why do you assume there's nothing I can do out of the goodness of my heart?"

"It's not that. It's that you're not the trusting type. You're the type who likes to see things done yourself. Why would you offer to stay behind and leave everything in my hands?"

Victor groans, wiping his slick hair from his forehead. I really wish he wouldn't do that while he's cooking. At home, the cooks with hair that long would have been required to pin it back.

"When we catch Tink, we need her to cooperate, right? If we want to get information out of her?" asks Victor.

"And?"

"Well, that's going to be a bit problematic if I'm around."

I narrow my eyes. "And why is that?"

Again, Victor runs his hands through his hair. I guarantee he's not going to wash them before touching the food. "Because Thomas and I used to make a sport of hunting her."

I snort. "Excellent."

"Yeah, well, nothing that can be done about it now."

"When you say hunt—"

"I mean, we used to track her down and blow darts into her wings."

I don't much like Tink after what she did to Wendy, but the thought of darts puncturing her wings makes me a tad sick.

Victor's no longer looking at me. He's just staring at a knot on the countertop like it's the most interesting thing he's ever seen. "Like I said. Can't go back and change it now."

"And you think I'm going to let you watch Michael after admitting that?"

Victor whips his head toward me. His face is red, and not from the heat of the stove. For a moment, I think he might yell at me, but he must swallow it because he says, "I wouldn't let anything happen to your brother, okay?"

Despite all rationality, I believe him.

"Michael's not always easy to watch," I warn.

"I'll manage."

I glance at my brother, then back at Victor. There's an earnestness in Victor's eyes I haven't often seen. He might be rough around the edges, but he isn't cruel, and he hurts for the loss of his brother.

"Fine," I say, knowing instantly I'll come to regret it. "But tell me: whose idea was it to hunt Tink?"

Victor pretends not to hear me.

As I'm clearing the plates after dinner, I count and realize I'm missing one. When I go to the table to search for it, I find it empty. Strange, one wouldn't expect a dinner plate to go missing between the dinner table and the kitchen.

I'm pondering where it could have gone when the roots on the ceiling descend, dumping Smalls onto the floor with considerably less care than they did Peter. Smalls huffs as he shoves himself to his feet, his pale face flushed red and his dusty brown hair disheveled. He wipes the dirt off of him until he looks up and spots me, at which point his hands stop mid-sweep.

The child salutes me, whistles, and bounds off.

I frown, and once he's gone, signal the roots to sweep me away.

THE PLATE IS HIDDEN POORLY. I only had to circle halfway around the reaping tree's base to find it, covered in pine needles atop a stump. After picking aside a few of the pine needles, I realize Smalls has left over half of his portion on the plate. I'd be tempted to be annoyed by this, given Smalls whined to me about needing extra, except something rustles near the tree line.

Instinct has me slipping around the curve of the reaping tree, just in time for the sound of footsteps to approach. It's dark out, but when I peek around the trunk of the tree, the glowing orbs on its limbs illuminate the stranger well enough.

And the fact that her wings are glowing.

THE NEXT NIGHT, when Smalls leaves a plate of food for the wild faerie, I'm already waiting.

Unfortunately, the boy waits around for a while, whistling with his hands in his pockets. I wonder if he's developed a crush on the faerie, if he's ever seen her, or if he just makes up a beautiful female in his head.

Well, if a beautiful female is who he's picturing, he's certainly not wrong.

I'd been a bit dumbfounded last night when I first laid eyes on her. It didn't really matter how many times I recited to myself that her beauty was simply a glamour meant to entice her prey.

It had been an exercise in self-control not to go out to her.

I'm beginning to think I might have given Wendy too hard of a time for falling so easily into Peter's clutches. Still, my sister was ensorcelled by the fae, and now she's missing. In the end, that had been enough to keep my wits about me until Tink disappeared into the woods and out of sight.

Several minutes pass before Smalls's attention span comes to its inevitable end. He yawns as he kicks over nearby rocks. One of them he punts with such force, it almost strikes me in the throat and I'm only just quick enough to dodge it. Eventually, the younger boy gives up on getting a glimpse of the rumored faerie and raps three times on the side of the reaping tree before it swallows him.

I waste no time sprinting to the stump. I'm not sure how long it will take Tink to get here. I'd wanted to carry out this part of the plan before Smalls got the plate outside, but he'd watched his leftovers like a hawk.

If I'm going to do this, this is my only shot. When I reach the stump, I stuff my hand into my pocket and pull out a parcel. Inside the piece of fabric is a baked onion, seasoned just like the one on Smalls's plate. Except for one extra spice.

Tonight was Victor's turn in the kitchen—his actual turn—so he'd helped me bake this onion separately. We'd chosen onion, because we figured it would hide the taste of rushweed the best.

Quickly, I swap the onion on Smalls's plate for the one Victor and I enhanced, then slip back around the tree. I'm only hidden for moments before the footsteps return, and out of the woods prances a beautiful faerie with cropped blond hair and twinkling butterfly wings as sheer as a dragonfly's.

Like last night, she stuffs the food into a makeshift satchel made of burlap, just like her clothes. She's about to turn around, when her ears flick in my direction.

I startle, yanking myself behind the reaping tree and out of view. Heart pounding, I hold my breath lest she hear that too. Once my head feels as if it's about to explode, I finally hear footsteps pad over the leaves and fade away.

Once I'm sure she's gone, I glance behind the tree again.

And make eye contact with the feral faerie.

She offers me a smug look. She must have engineered the footsteps to make it sound as if she was walking away. Sure she's about to rip me to shreds, I go for the dagger at my side.

But then the faerie does something I'm not prepared for.

She winks.

CHAPTER 6

WENDY

I fiddle with the quaint metallic key, turning it over in my fingers. I unshackled myself as soon as the captain left the room, but now that I'm free to roam about, I don't seem to know what to do with myself. After stretching my sore wrist out, I lift myself to my feet, wary of my balance. I'm somewhat lacking in the coordination department at the moment—a mixture of having been bedridden for days and the unpredictable sway of the sea below the ship.

There's a nervous energy wound up in my chest, a constant ticking, except I'm unsure what the clock is counting down to. Whatever the captain needs me so desperately for, I suppose.

I should be doing something. Devising an escape. Finding a way back to my brothers. But I'm paralyzed by the daunting task of figuring out where to start. It would be foolish of me to think I'll be getting off this ship a moment before Astor wills it. Even if I wander up to the deck, it's not as if I can simply toss myself overboard and swim to shore. I could try to get my hands on more faerie dust and fly away, but I'm painfully aware of my limitations when it comes to my ability to control the quantity I consume.

Flying away won't do me much good if I have no concept of where I am in space.

So I pace about the captain's chambers, a poor attempt at tricking my body into thinking it's at least doing something.

John is likely frantic right now. At least, in the way he gets frantic —a frenzied sort of focus, undeterred by his environment until the problem is solved. But I'm gone, and he won't be getting me back anytime soon. I've gone and left him, just like our parents did. Left him to care for Michael on his own.

My chest throbs as I consider all the choices I could have made that would have prevented me from being separated from my brothers. I should have told Peter that I'd found Astor washed up on the shore. Should have trusted him with my secret. In the moment, I'd worried he would act impulsively and end Astor, carried away by a drive to keep the Lost Boys and me safe. As I'd hoped to discover the reason behind my parents' deaths at Astor's hand, I couldn't afford that.

Maybe that's why Peter left me. He'd come to the beach to save his Mate, but he'd found a version of me he didn't know. I try to consider how I would have reacted if I'd discovered that Peter had been hiding another woman from me, going to meet her at night.

No. I shake my head like it will somehow clear the lies out of my mind. Peter doesn't know I'd been hiding the captain from him. When he let Astor take me, it had nothing to do with my betrayal.

I twist the emerald ring around my finger. It's even looser than it was the day Peter proposed, likely from how little I ate while the faerie dust was working its way out of my system, how much water I lost as I sweated it out. Still, I cling to it like the topmost rung of the ladder in my parents' clock tower. The proof that Peter is real, not some conjured figment of my imagination. That my Mate's love for me is real.

It's just inaccessible at the moment. Locked underneath the calloused exterior the Sister crafted for him so that he can accomplish her will without too much resistance. You can't love without pain. Not really.

That's why he'd left me on the beach. Bargained me away. It had been both a logical and impulsive decision, a combination irresistible to Peter. He can't feel the agony of wondering what the captain might be doing to me while he has me trapped away in the hull of his ship. He can't feel my absence like a phantom limb, like I feel his.

And I *feel* his.

Now that I'm sober, it's worse than before, clawing its way into my chest and plucking out my ribs one by one. I close my eyes and cling to the cool metal band on my finger.

Peter can't feel pain, but he knew to protect the Lost Boys. Even without the pain to urge him on, he knew he needed to save them, protect them from the pirates. Which means he also knew he needed to protect me.

I spend the next hour obsessing over that last conversation between Peter and Astor, trying to extrapolate meaning from every insignificant detail. When Peter had struck his deal with Astor, what had he been careful to leave out? How exactly had he worded it?

What's in it for me?

Six months with Wendy.

You'll grow tired of her before then. Trust me, six is a mercy.

I search his words for clever games, clues left behind by a boy in love with adventure, but I'm either too weary or too dull to crack it.

But I know this much.

Peter is nothing if not calculating. And if he left me in Captain Astor's clutches, he had a reason.

I just need to figure out what that reason is.

Warm salt air coats me like a blanket when I reach the deck. The wind is rambunctious tonight, tossing ocean spray my way. I wrap my shawl around my face to protect myself from a portion of the sting, but it feels nice to be outside of the wretched cabin. To breathe fresh air for the first time.

I'm not sure what I'm doing up here, just that I couldn't stay in the captain's cabin any longer and I didn't know where else to go.

My head still hurts. I wonder if it'll ever stop aching until I get a taste of faerie dust again. Mercifully, breathing in the ocean air helps some. Hearing the waves lap against the side of the ship—it's grounding, strangely enough.

The captain must have told the crew not to bother me, because though a few of them look up from their duties as I cross the deck, no one approaches me or asks what business I have up here. I meander about for a while, trying to find a place I can curl up with my thoughts. I feel trapped, crowded on this vessel. Charlie's been with me most of the past few days, and when she's been gone, Astor has been there to pester me.

My soul craves a moment alone, so I search the deck until I find a pile of crates I can perch on near the edge of the ship and watch the moon's rays dance across the waves, situating myself between the crates and the railing so no one can see me. I stare up at the sky and search until I find a pair of twin stars, offset by the night, watching over me. They wink, taunting me. Reminding me that I have no way of getting back to the man I love. No way of getting back to my brothers.

After a few moments, though, my aloneness feels less satisfying than I imagined it would. There's an aching in my bones, a longing to be held by no one other than Peter. But Peter isn't here.

Peter left me.

"What were you expecting?" asks a female voice. The unexpectedness of being snuck up on makes me jolt, but it's the way the voice is so eerily familiar that has the hairs on the back of my neck standing on end. "No one has ever wanted you."

I glance around, hands fisted at my sides like that's going to help anything, but I can't see the origin of the voice in the dark.

"Oh sure, they wanted you for a while. For a moment. For a few stolen touches and a host of wicked things." Someone steps out from behind the crates. A woman, my height, of slender build. I can't make out anything else about her in the dark, but there's something so familiar about her, her voice crawls up my arms like spiders. Like I should know that voice intimately, but don't. "Maybe they wanted the excitement of something forbidden. Or maybe it was the thrill of touching a girl with a Mating Mark—how many of them will ever get that chance again? How many of them have already divulged every detail of what you let them do? Tell me, do you ever wonder how many of your suitors came to meet you just because they'd heard from a friend how easy you were? Have you ever wondered how many of them have sat around a table, drunkenly sharing their stories of conquering you? Just how far you let them go?"

My skin goes cold, clammy. The humid air turning to ice against my gooseflesh. "How do you know about that?" I ask. For a moment, I wonder if Astor told the entire crew about what happened in the parlor. If he took what I foolishly told him in confidence and laughed at me with his crew over drinks as soon as we arrived.

"It doesn't take much to figure it out. It's written all over your face. It's in the way you tremble around anyone who intimidates you. It's in the way you can't seem to manage a clever response, how you freeze under the slightest commanding touch. Really, I can't tell what makes you more dull-witted—that you never have anything clever to say or that you thought you of all people could keep Peter's attention. You couldn't even keep the attention of those dull human men for more than a night. None of them even came back for seconds. And yet, you thought Peter, a fae, a perfect specimen longed for by even the Fates, would not tire of you."

"Peter's my Mate," I say, stepping backward until the base of my heel hits the crate behind me.

The woman laughs. I still can't distinguish her facial features in the dark, not with the way she keeps to the shadows. "Of course he is. Why else did you think you managed to keep his attention as long as you did? Really, you should have known the second he looked twice at you that something supernatural was going on."

Tears sting at my eyes, a burning swelling in my throat. I want to tell her she's wrong, but all I hear are Peter's words ringing in my ear.

You'll grow tired of her before then. Trust me. Six is a mercy.

"Why can't you see that no one wants you? Are you really just that dull, that you can't piece the evidence together? Perhaps if you were half as intelligent as your brother, you might see it. John sees it. He's seen it for a long time. He's just too bound by his loyalty to tell you.

But his life would have been better without you. Michael could have had his mother, if it weren't for you. And now you've gone and traumatized him for good."

I glance at the stars, but this only feeds the woman's antagonism. "You keep looking toward the sky, but tell me, do you see anyone coming?"

My mouth works, but no sound comes out.

"What are you going to do?" the woman asks. "Just wait until the captain gets what he needs out of you? Wait around until time passes, and he's forced to give you back to Peter? Do you think Peter will be glad to see you? It only took him a handful of months to lose interest. What do you think half a year will do? And Michael, he might have healed of what you did to him by then. Can you imagine how far it will set him back to see you again? It's selfish, really, to try to go back to them. You've only ever made everyone's lives worse by your presence. Well," the woman laughs. "Except for those men in the parlor. You did them the favor of providing them a story. Why don't you just do the people you love a favor and…" The woman gestures toward the railing.

I stand, hardly able to face her. I'm not sure I want to make out her face. Put skin and eyes and hair to the voice that makes me writhe inwardly. She should be hideous, a nightmare, but I have a feeling she is not, and that will only make things worse.

The boards of the deck are slick against my feet, damp from being so close to the railing, unprotected from the stray wave that makes its way over the edge. When I reach the railing, I have to support myself on it, my hands trembling as much as my legs.

Below, the dark waves almost look kind. Playful. Inviting.

They look as if they'd be warm.

I fidget my engagement ring around my finger and feel its cool kiss around my skin. It stings, but part of me clings to the feeling. A part of me died on this deck the moment we crossed the warping out of Neverland. It ripped me in half, being separated from Peter, though he felt none of it.

I've already died alone once.

"I could endure it, you know—the pain," I whisper to the strange woman, now quiet behind me. "I could hurt forever if I thought I could keep John and Michael safe."

"But you know better than that." The woman almost sounds sad, the bitterness in her voice drained.

"I never wanted to, but I've only ever caused them trouble…" I say. "John—he would have gotten out of Neverland with Michael. He would have found a way, but he stayed for me. Because I wanted to stay."

"And if you were gone?" asks the woman, her question as steering as the lower lights guiding a ship in the fog.

"If I were gone, John could take Michael and move on. They could live out their lives in our realm. Where they belong. John's clever—he could make a life for himself and Michael. They could be safe. Happy."

Below, the waves lap against the hull of the boat.

"You love them very much," says the woman, as tears stream down my cheek. I watch them, like I'm going to be able to tell when they hit the water.

In the end, that pursuit is vain, too.

When I climb over the edge of the rail and jump, I can't help but wish I had made my last climb just a little higher. That I could have had further to fall.

CHAPTER 7

JOHN

*W*hen Tink disappears into the cover of the shadowed forest, I hesitate.

This wasn't the plan. I had hoped she'd eat her meal outside of the reaping tree. I knew that was a long shot, but not having to follow her would have made this simpler.

Second best option was that she wouldn't notice me, and I could follow her to her hideout and wait until she consumed her meal and the rushweed.

As it is now, I don't know what I'm supposed to do.

She knows I've seen her. If I follow her, she'll know what I'm doing. It's likely I'll be part of her meal, and that's probably her intention. Lure me into the woods so she won't have to depend on Smalls's generosity for a while.

I almost return to the Den, sure this is the only option at the moment. But then it occurs to me what might happen if I allow Tink to get away.

She'll go back to her hideout. Whether she'll eat Smalls's meal, I'm not sure, but she has no reason to expect that I poisoned it. Unless she saw me switch out the food on the plate, in which case I'm already in trouble.

But if she eats the meal and becomes temporarily paralyzed, she'll definitely know that I poisoned her. And when she regains control of her limbs, it's likely she'll hunt me down. She attacked Wendy unprovoked—well, unless you consider Wendy being in Peter's room reason enough for an attack. If Wendy being in close proximity to Peter was enough for Tink to try to kill her, I can only imagine what she'll do to me once she realizes I poisoned her.

I won't be able to leave the Den safely. Even then, Tink has been known to sneak into the Den before. Ideally, I'd like to wait to follow her until she's paralyzed, but I have no idea where she stays on the island, and I'm not confident that I'll be able to find her in a day, the time it should take for the poison to run its course.

That means my only option is to follow her now and hope that she lures me all the way to her hideout. As long as she eats before she kills me, all should be well.

I am aware that my odds are less than optimal.

But Tink strikes me as the type of creature who likes to play with her food first. Not ideal, but at least that would buy me some time to think.

I feel a bit queasy, but I follow Tink into the woods all the same.

BRANCHES and brush crackle underneath footsteps ahead. Tink's a faerie, meaning she could be imperceptibly stealthy if she wanted, but she's choosing otherwise.

That doesn't exactly relieve the churning in my intestines.

On one hand, that she's letting me follow her is essential for my new plan. On the other, it means she has the upper hand. I'd been counting on the element of surprise, mismatched as I am with my human strength.

Okay, so I'm not all that strong anyway, even for a human.

Yet another way I'd failed my father.

As Wendy's brother, I was supposed to be able to protect her. Instead, my father had gotten a bookish son with gangly limbs. I'd tried to use what I had to protect Wendy, studying up on the fae, gathering all the information I could on magical bargains.

In the end, it hadn't been enough.

I'd never been enough.

My father had taught me that as a man, I was supposed to be a protector, but I'd failed drastically in that endeavor. I've been failing to protect my siblings long before Neverland.

I'm going to get Wendy and Michael to safety, or die trying.

The path of crackling footsteps leads me through the dark forest, moonlight peppering the ground, providing just enough light for me to sidestep fallen branches, though I have to prop my glasses on my head to see with as smudged as they are.

Yet another embarrassing secret.

I don't actually need them.

I had the misfortune of never being taken seriously growing up, at least, with everyone except for Wendy. My father was taken seriously. But that was for his intense ability to woo people, to influence.

I look like him, just a smaller version.

Everyone expected me to be gregarious, but when they found me awkward, they simply dismissed me. Saw me as unintelligent because I couldn't find my place in their conversations.

Wendy and I are alike in that way. People think we're not clever because we lose the ability to be coherent when we're nervous. And we're nervous. A lot.

I would have been better off if I'd just kept quiet in groups. People always think quiet people are intelligent. But my father had pushed me to cultivate connections, and I'd consistently made a fool of myself.

Still, there was a young nobleman who spent time with my father's group of confidants. I hated him and his round spectacles, not because everyone listened to him, not because he was drowning in accolades for his wisdom despite his youth, but because he was an idiot, and no one saw it.

The first time I wore spectacles to one of my father's functions, it was meant as a cruel joke that only I was party to.

But then people had started questioning me, not to mock me, but because they thought I had answers. In a way, they'd freed me of my shackles, the tether that had hindered my tongue.

So the spectacles had stayed.

Even Wendy doesn't know they're made of ordinary glass.

The pattern Tink is making ahead of me is a bit circuitous. She wants me as disoriented as possible by the time we reach wherever we're going. That way, if I get away, I won't be able to find my way back.

But I've been marking every curve and turn, keeping careful location of where the moonlight in the canopy is coming from. As it is, we're on the east side of the island.

Eventually, Tink leads me to a cliffside I've never seen. As I peek through the dense brush, I notice the opening of a cave. It looks about ready to swallow me whole, and I steel myself.

I'm doing this for Wendy. I will find out what happened to my sister.

Something rustles from behind.

I spin around, only to find Tink has circumvented me. Silently. She's staring at me with hungry blue eyes, her face consumed by craving. The faerie flashes me a sharp grin, then nods her head, gesturing toward the cave, now behind me.

Though I recognize that she's herding me into her dwelling, into a place that will be easy to contain me, I step backward in the direction she indicated.

I can't tell how much of my compliance is part of my plan, or how much is due to my *wanting* to do as she says.

Even as she corrals me toward death, I can't help but notice her beauty. There's something ethereal that shines past the grime on her skin, the burlap sack covering her. Her smile is cruel, but I can't help but want to keep her smiling at me forever. Can't help but wonder how her lips would feel against mine...

No. No. I'm here for Wendy. And this is fae glamour, preying on my humanity and influencing my thoughts. Knowing that's all it is helps. It doesn't stop her beauty from rapping on my mind, but it does assist me in tuning it out.

It feels like I've only taken a few steps before my spine scrapes against the cliffside wall. My pulse is accelerating much too quickly, my mind not accounting for time and space.

Feeling is what gets you killed.

I try to turn it off, the sharp allure, the tether tying me to the idea of pleasing this faerie, but I'm not used to having to combat these emotions.

I fear I might walk over barbs if she asks me to.

Tink is close now, and she extends a long fingernail, scraping it down my cheek. Forceful enough to sting, to break the outmost layer of skin, but not hard enough to draw blood. My limbs are paralyzed. Ironic.

But then the casual cruelty on Tink's face warps into something else. Confusion flashes across her delicate features, then something more poignant. Fear. Anger. She goes through an array of them before she slumps to the ground before me.

When she does, her satchel spills open, littering the ground with a half-eaten meal.

There's no onion among the mix.

CHAPTER 8

WENDY

I'm not sure what hurts worse—knowing deep down that my brothers will be happier without me in the world, or knowing that this last time I fall, Peter's arms won't be waiting to catch me.

My stomach drops as I plummet, the dark waves lashing underneath me, suddenly no longer as peaceful as they appeared just a moment ago. I realize too late that what I mistook for invitation was actually just hunger.

I'm about to loose a scream when warm arms envelop me. The scent of amber and pine strikes me just as the waves splash against my bare feet. Before I can think of what to do, my body reacts, curling into the firm and familiar chest.

"This game isn't nearly as fun to play by oneself, Wendy Darling," says a voice so familiar it makes me ache.

"Peter." I shut my eyes against his chest, memorizing the feel of him against my clutching hands, the press of his weight against my palms. Steady pulses of air bat at my cheeks, his wings maintaining our position close to the waves, below the view of the deck.

Tears pour from my cheeks and into his shirt, and I have to swallow the sobs lest we be overheard by the crew on deck.

"Did you miss me, then?" he asks, so playfully I get the urge to slap him. Or maybe that's just from how quickly I become irritated now that I don't have the faerie dust to calm me. When I peer up at him, I expect to see his beautiful blue eyes, but of course, that's foolishness. The Sister forces him to morph into his shadow form when he visits anywhere other than Neverland, and though he can take a solid form by touching me, it takes time for him to regain complete control over his shadow self.

What I get aren't the cool but kind blue eyes that I'm hoping for, but cruelly amused black pits, looking to devour me.

My heart hammers, my panic dissipating and giving way to the betrayal that's been tearing me apart the past few days. "You gave me away."

I mean it as an accusation, but it comes out more pitiful than that.

"Is that why you decided to take a plunge?" Peter tsks. "Really, you should consider bolstering your emotional fortitude."

Sparks flare within me. Peter's one to scold me about my emotional fortitude, when he has the option of not feeling the most unpleasant of them. But I swallow my anger. It's no use anyway, not when this version of Peter isn't him.

Not when the version of Peter I love isn't really him either.

"When we get back, please don't tell John about this," I say.

"I won't," Peter muses. He smirks, then with a beat of his wings, pushes me up against the hull of the boat and presses his mouth to mine.

Dizziness overwhelms me at the way he claims me with his lips. "You came," I say, my voice almost lost under the hunger of his kiss. "I thought you wouldn't come for me."

Peter responds with a playful bite at my ear. "I'll always come for what's mine."

"As much as I'm enjoying this," I say, nudging my head up against the side of the boat and blushing. "We'd better leave before they realize I'm gone."

Peter brushes my hair from my face and tucks it behind my ear. "You know I can't do that."

My heart stops in my chest. "But—"

"I wanted to see you. Make sure he hadn't touched you. He hasn't touched you, has he?"

I shake my head.

"Good," Peter says. "And it's a good thing I came too. What had you despairing, my Darling pet?"

My throat hurts, still reeling from the disappointment that Peter didn't come to take me away. Though now that the adrenaline of the past few moments has subsided, I understand why. Peter made a binding bargain with Astor. He might be able to bend the rules by visiting me, but he can't whisk me out of Astor's clutches.

"There was a woman on deck," I say, though even as the words come out, I recognize how strange they are. "She knew about..." I catch myself, remembering I haven't yet told Peter about the parlor. I doubt it would deter him from wanting to marry me, but now isn't exactly the time. "Some things from my past. And she told me that John and Michael were safer without me. I don't...I don't know how she knew. Or why I even believed her." Panic rises in my chest as the gravity of what I'd almost done slams into me. "Peter, Peter, if you hadn't been here..." My lungs tighten, and I can't breathe.

Peter's inky eyes examine mine. "When was the last time you had faerie dust?"

I blink. "Astor cut me off. It was awful for a few days, but it's out of my system now."

Peter nods. "It wasn't a woman on deck with you. It was a wraith."

I frown. "I thought you said wraiths were made when someone experiences pain strong enough that the nearby shadows drink it up and come to life. If that's so, why did she know about...Oh." My jaw works. "When we left Neverland, it felt like I was being ripped in half. I guess that was my end of the Mating Mark knowing we were being separated. That's why her voice seemed so familiar, but not. The wraith came from me...from my pain."

Finally finding logic, I school myself not to expect Peter's pity. Not when he can't feel pain, and especially not when his eyes are still inked over. "Peter," I say, meaning to tell him that I know what the Sister cursed him with. Before I can get the rest of my sentence out, he puts a hand over my mouth and nods toward the deck. I can't hear anything, but his ears swivel, homing in, so I assume someone is nearby.

After a moment, he takes his hand from my mouth. Before I can resume, he plucks a pouch from his pocket and tucks it into my hands. My heart skids to a stop.

"I want you to ration this for yourself," he says. "I'm limited in the time I can come keep an eye on you. I have to time my visits around the Sister's errands so she doesn't grow suspicious. I don't want any wraiths convincing you to off yourself while I'm gone."

I open my mouth to protest, to tell him I don't have the self-control to ration it for myself, but already my mouth is watering. I can almost taste the honeysuckle flavor on my tongue. Almost feel the pain being washed away for a moment.

"Now," says Peter, tucking me against the hull again, and pressing his mouth into the crook underneath my jaw. "Where were we?"

Sparks go off in my head, but it's short-lived, because above us something rustles on deck.

"Did I ask where you last saw her? Or did I ask *where she is?*" Astor's voice booms from above.

Peter lets out a quiet groan of annoyance against my neck, then presses his finger against his mouth, his other hand still firmly steadying my waist against him.

My heart races, not so much that the captain will catch us—Peter's not foolish enough to get caught. But I anticipate Peter's gentle ascent before his wings even beat us upward. The path he courses around the curve of the hull, his ears locating the footsteps of the shouting crew members on deck, searching for me. They're no match for his stealth, and I spend my last few moments in his arms drinking in the scent of amber and pine, trying to memorize it before it flees my mind for good. Before I'm left with nothing more than a fading memory.

When Peter deposits me on deck, he doesn't waste time with a goodbye kiss. He disappears into the shadows so quickly, I'm left wondering if I imagined it all. If his appearance was nothing more than the ravings of an addict, the same one who believed her own wraith.

My heart aches. Not just from my separation from Peter, but the knowledge of how easily I'd let the part of me that hates myself talk me over the edge. I'd almost left John grieving his sister, Michael without an understanding of why I never came back for him.

It feels like the moment after you almost caused a tragic accident, yet were subverted by something equally as coincidental. Like almost stepping into the street and being distracted by a flittering sparrow, only to realize had you not delayed to marvel at it, the carriage rounding the corner would have trampled you.

My legs tremble violently, and I have to sink onto the nearest crate, cradling my face in my palms as I shake.

"Cap'n, she's over here!" someone cries. I don't bother to lift my head and look at his face. It doesn't really matter who found me. It's not as if I ever left.

Astor comes barreling over, though I actually do look at him. He's heaving. It's only when he lays eyes on me that his shoulders sag in relief. His sharp eyes rake over me. "You're wet," is all he says.

For a moment, I'm confused. Peter caught me before I hit the water, but as I glance down, sure enough, the hem of my trousers is soaked. I didn't realize how close I'd been to the water swallowing me. "They're too long, and the deck is soaked. Maybe if you actually found me some trousers that fit."

Astor glares at me, suspicion all over his face. But he doesn't contradict me. "You could have called out. Unless I'm mistaken, you're not deaf. Surely you heard the crew shouting for you."

I stare up at Astor and give him the blankest expression I can muster. "You tracked me down all the way to Neverland. I figured it would be no trouble to find me on your own ship."

Astor presses his lips together. "You're shaking."

It's warm, even at night, so I can't blame it on the cold. "I'm told addicts do that sometimes," I say.

Addicts. The word hurts coming out of my throat. But it's no use trying to deny what I am. Not when I sense the lover's touch of Peter's sachet of faerie dust at my hip, hidden between my rolled trouser waistband and my belly.

If Astor was considering punishing me, he must decide better of it, because he opens his mouth, then immediately clamps it down. When he finally speaks, his voice is all business. Before he walks away, I think I hear him murmur, "I'll get someone to hem your pants."

CHAPTER 9

WENDY

There's a guard outside the door to the bunker.

To be honest, I don't even remember wandering here. It's ridiculous, given I have Peter's stash of faerie dust tucked into my waistband. I don't need what's in the bunker. But I've been roaming around the deck, my fingers fidgeting at the cord tying the pouch. Just a daily dose, I've been telling myself. I can handle that.

In truth, I wandered down here to escape the scolding voice in my head telling me I should throw the faerie dust overboard. Or perhaps I just wanted a reminder that if I do throw it into the sea, more will still be down here in the bunker waiting for me. That I won't have to abandon it forever.

The bald, burly man waiting for me at the doorway flashes me a metallic grin and says, "Cap's up the stairs and on the right if you're looking for his attentions."

My face colors, and I shake my head violently. "No, I'm not looking for him. I was just with him…"

The burly man only grins wider, and I exhale forcefully, scampering up the stairs and to the right as he told me.

On the way, I take note of the strange nature of the ship. When I first glimpsed the *Iaso*, I thought it was made entirely of shadow, but now that I'm inside it, I realize it's only cloaked in shadows. At least, it was when we left Neverland. Now that I think about it, I hadn't noticed the shadows when Peter backed me up against the hull. Astor must have some way of keeping them contained. I peer at my feet. The floorboards and walls are made of wood, probably oak, if I had to guess.

That morsel of knowledge reminds me with a pang of John. He went through a ship phase as a child, which I suppose is only natural for those who grow up in a port town. He used to tell me all about them, begging me to sketch diagrams with him and help him gather materials for his miniature boat models.

Oak is hesitant to rot, I remember. My chest stings as I think of John, of the worry that must be nagging at his protective soul right now. John's always considered it his responsibility to protect me.

And now I'm gone.

I'm not sure what the captain wants from me, but I have the sneaking suspicion that by the time he returns me to Neverland, I won't be the same girl I was when I left.

Will Peter still want me then?

I shake my head, dispelling the thought. Of course he will. I'd let my despair at being given over to Astor undermine my trust in Peter. But he's been watching over me, hasn't he? When I needed him, when I was falling, it was Peter's arms that caught me. Irritation with myself prickles at my ribcage—I should have asked him what his plan was in handing me over to Astor instead of letting my passion for my Mate overtake my senses as he kissed me up against the hull of the ship.

Warmth spreads its fingers between the divot of my shoulder blades at the memory.

Still, Peter's proven that whatever his intentions are, it was never to leave me to the captain's devices. For now, that's enough for me to trust that he knows what he's doing.

I let my fingers trail the treated wood as I wander the hallway, following the faint echo of voices. When I reach the door at the end of the hall, I find there's a natural knot in the wood that's left a crack larger than most of the slats. When I press my face to it, I get a decent glimpse inside, if not a bit shadowed at the peripherals.

Inside looks to be some sort of council chamber. At least, that's the impression I get from the massive round table at the center of the room. Parchment dangles over the edges, likely a map of the world based on the islands I glimpse scattered at its corners. Several of the crew stand around the table, Captain Astor in the center.

He's scowling, his black sleeves cuffed just below his elbows, his fists atop the map in the center of the table.

"What do you mean Cortland Rivers is married?"

"Worse than that," says Evans, the slight young man who danced with me at my masquerade ball. He's wincing, his dark brown skin wrinkled at his forehead. "He's a newlywed."

Captain Astor squeezes his eyes shut and digs into his temples with his Mated hand.

"I don't see what the problem is," says another—a fae man with golden hair and skin just a shade darker. He looks like the type of being an artist might choose as a muse if they were going to carve a likeness into the side of a mountain. Some people are just the sort of attractive that you know is going to withstand changes in fashion. "Can't you just tell the Carlisles that you left your wife at home? That she's afraid of the sea? Or that she fell ill? Or better, that she's expecting?"

Charlie pipes up from across the table. "We could, Maddox, except that Cortland Rivers is Delphian."

Maddox folds his tree trunks for arms across his chest. "And?"

"The Delphi have a custom that newlyweds aren't to leave each other's sides for the first year of marriage."

A spindly red-headed man who looks as though he might have given away his serving of fruit one too many times, judging by his rotten teeth, whistles in disbelief. "Hate to be Delphian, then. The men have to give up the brothels for an entire year."

Charlie rolls her eyes. "Yes, Teeth, what a tragedy that a man might be expected to remain faithful to his wife. For an entire year, no less."

Teeth nods in agreement, Charlie's sarcasm falling on rather dull ears. Though even I have to admit, Charlie's voice is so cheerful, it's difficult for me to tell she's being sarcastic sometimes.

"Sorry to break it to you, Captain," says Evans, "but we're going to have to find another lead."

"Or," says Charlie, swinging herself onto the table—and the map—until a sharp glance from the captain has her swiftly hopping back onto the floor, "you could give up this quest altogether."

A hush falls over the crew as Captain Astor rakes Charlie with his scowl. "I don't anticipate hearing you mention that again," is all he says, to which Charlie purses her lips, planting a hand on her hip.

Evans glances back and forth between them, the lantern light giving his deep brown skin a warm glow. "Charlotte has a point, Captain. I'd be amiss not to point out that there's little in this for the crew."

The captain sneers. "There is for anyone who wishes to remain on my crew." He gestures toward the door. "You all know you're free to leave anytime we port."

Evans glances around at the others, like he's trying to muster up support. I remember Evans seeming young when I first met him. Shy. I'd felt compelled to pay him attention because of how awkward and timid he was.

That was before he helped the pirates slit my guests' throats.

When it's clear that no one in the room wishes to take their chances on another crew, Evans stands down. He sighs and rolls up the map they had laid across the table. Then he glances at Charlie. "You'll have to play the part of the captain's wife then."

Charlie snorts. The captain grunts. Maddox says, "That, I'd pay a thousand silvers to witness."

When the captain gives Maddox a withering stare, the handsome man just smiles. "What? You might as well pour cement on a wet rag for all the spark you and Charlie have between you."

Charlie nods emphatically.

Astor rolls his eyes. "We'll play it off as an arranged marriage."

Evans shakes his head. "It's well known that Cortland Rivers would settle for nothing less than a love match."

The entire crew, all but Charlie, groan.

"I could go with Charlie," says Maddox, offering her a wink. Charlie actually flushes, her cheeks a sheet of parchment attempting to conceal a flame in a dim room.

Evans shakes his head. "The coloring of those golden locks of yours is too fair, Maddox. They'd know you weren't Delphian."

Charlie wilts, and Maddox narrows his golden brow. "Except my hair is only this color because I spend my days in the sun."

"Yes, but perception is more important than reality when it comes to the aristocracy, isn't it?" says Evans.

"We'll just have to make do," says the captain. Though his hands are still supporting his weight on the table, the space between his shoulder blades has sunken in. It seems his plan is slipping through his fingertips. Maddox glances back and forth between Charlie and the captain, looking as if he's about to say something, but in the end, he keeps his mouth shut.

I HIDE in a hall closet while the crew file out of the room. Captain Astor and Maddox are the last to leave. Judging by the whispered tones of Maddox's voice, I'm guessing that wasn't accidental. Footsteps come to a halt right outside the closet door, and I calm my breathing so their fae hearing won't sense me.

"Is this really worth it?" asks Maddox, his previously carefree voice twined with concern.

"I don't embark on quests that aren't worth my time. You know that better than anyone."

"Nolan..." My ears perk at Maddox's use of the captain's given name. I expect the captain to scold him for impropriety, but he doesn't. "Iaso is gone."

"I'm aware."

Maddox sighs. Someone's tapping their foot on the floor planks. "You at least have to acknowledge how this looks to the crew. Dragging us all over the world just to get rid of a Mating Mark."

My heart skips two beats as I fumble with Maddox's words in my head. I press my ear against the door, fearing I'll miss out on any tidbit of information I could potentially use.

"There are plenty who understand why one might want to rid themselves of a Mating Mark," says the captain. Something about the words sounds rehearsed.

Maddox's response is infused with a wariness he's not bothering to conceal. "One that's decayed?"

"I can't bear to look at it anymore." Again, the floorboards creak underneath the captain's shifting weight.

Maddox goes quiet for a moment. "I'm not sure this is going to help you get over her."

"It's not your choice to make, is it?" says the captain coldly.

Footsteps sound against the floorboards as someone—I'm assuming the captain—makes to leave. I have to clutch my heart to convince it not to ache for him, though I'm unsuccessful. As much as I hate the captain, I can't imagine the pain that would rip through me if I lost Peter. I'd felt a portion of it when the ship had left Neverland, and even that had been unbearable.

The idea of Peter dying…

I believe I'd want to rid myself of my Mark, too.

"It's not going to work," says Maddox, calling after his captain. "Not if you need to convince the Carlisles that you're in love with Charlie."

The captain's voice is distant, like he's already made it down the hall. "I'll make it work."

"You're such a stubborn fool."

The captain laughs, but there's a brotherly sort of affection in it.

"What if they don't have the information you need?" Maddox asks.

"The Carlisles make it their business to know everything. I assure you, if there's someone out there with the ability to remove a Mating Mark, they'll know."

I bite my lip, my mind whirring. I've heard of the Carlisles before, though I know little about them. John and I used to hide underneath the wheeled serving carts and spy on my parents' dinner parties.

People spoke of the Carlisles the way they spoke about serial murders, feigned horror disguising the elation of twisted intrigue. From what I gathered, if you had a question, the Carlisles could answer it.

For a hefty price.

If the captain has enough faith in the Carlisles' hoard of knowledge to believe it's worth impersonating this Cortland Rivers to learn how to rid himself of his wife's dead Mating Mark, then maybe the Carlisles could tell me how to rid Peter of his curse, the magic that makes it so that he can't feel pain.

My feet move independently of my will, and I shove myself out of the closet, mouth blurting, "I'll do it."

The captain whirls around to face me, aggravated surprise limning his sharp features. Maddox, on the other hand, looks to be teetering on the edge of laughter.

"Why, you must be Wendy Darling," he says, taking my hand and pressing a kiss to my knuckles with a wink. "I'm Darian Maddox, First Mate."

My stomach flips over. He really is quite handsome, his eyes a steely gray, exuding warmth despite their cool tone. I can see why Charlie was disappointed when the opportunity to play the part of his wife was snatched out from under her.

"You'll do what?" drawls the captain, glancing back and forth between me and Maddox. Maddox smirks and drops my hand.

I do my best to assume a more confident posture to make up for the trembling in my voice. "Be your wife."

"That's a tad presumptuous of you, don't you think?" says the captain, and rather blandly.

Maddox snickers, but I'm undeterred.

"You need someone to play your wife, don't you? And you know no one is going to believe that you and Charlie are involved. So why not take me?"

The captain tucks his fingers underneath his chin, like he's thinking. "Oh, I don't know. Perhaps because I abhor your very existence?"

I don't expect the pain that goes barreling through my stomach, but I'm too motivated by the hopes of saving Peter to let my trampled feelings get in my way. "Hate? Love? All the Carlisles need to sense between us is passion. Doesn't matter which type," I say, fighting not to bite my lip in embarrassment.

"Oh, I'm liking this plan," says Maddox, mischievous dimples appearing at his cheeks.

I expect the captain to argue, but he doesn't. Instead, he says, "And what do you presume is in it for you?"

I bite my lip. I'd rather not tell the captain about my desire to cure Peter's inability to feel pain. It feels like handing him fodder to mock me.

When I don't come up with an answer quickly, Astor stares at me. "Spit it out, Darling."

Maddox shoots him a disapproving look, but I wet my lips and let my mouth run away with me, hoping it'll come up with something good while I'm talking. "Well," I say, stalling. "You didn't travel all the way to Neverland for nothing, did you? There's something you need me for, and I assume it has to do with getting rid of that Mark of yours." I try to read the captain's face for any sign that I'm on the right track, but his hardened face betrays nothing. "You wouldn't have gone to all that trouble to kidnap me, just to pivot to a completely different goal." My mind races, and it lands on my and the captain's conversation earlier. "You kept asking me about my nightmares. You've been suspicious that I'm a shadow soother," I say, remembering Peter's speculations that I might have fae blood in my ancestry. "That's it, isn't it? You need a shadow soother to help you get rid of that Mark."

The captain's expression shutters, but Maddox's doesn't. The First Mate runs his hands through his hair.

I can't help the satisfied smirk that taints my lips.

"There we are," the captain finally says, realizing his First Mate's inability to suppress his reaction. "Wendy Darling, finally showing some cleverness."

The cruel words threaten to sting, but I've come to realize it's the captain's sole strategy for distracting me from whatever's at hand. His only card trick when his opponent has the upper hand.

I think I might enjoy having the upper hand.

"So the sooner we get that Mark off your hand, the sooner you'll take me back to Neverland," I say. "You kept trying to bargain for more time, in case the search took you ages. But as it is, we only have six months. One would think you'd want to make the best use of your time."

The captain snorts. "And you think you're the best use of my time? That's assuming you're even trainable."

"I think I can help convince the Carlisles that you're Cortland Rivers," I volley back.

Maddox shrugs. "She is an aristocrat's daughter. She'll know how to play the part of a nobleman's wife."

I huff. "Believe me, if there's anything I've been trained for, it's just that. And I'd be willing to be trained further."

Maddox opens his hands, palms facing the ceiling. He's angled himself toward the captain now, so that his body is aligned with mine. It almost feels like having an ally.

"What do you say, Captain?" says Maddox. "It could work."

Captain Astor looks over the two of us for a moment, shooting daggers at Maddox with his green eyes.

Then he strolls away.

I let out an exasperated huff. "Well, what does that mean?"

Maddox nudges me in the shoulder. "I'll let you in on a little secret about the captain."

I arch my brow, and Maddox offers me a full set of perfect teeth, as well as a set of dimples for good measure. "Render the captain speechless, and you've as good as wrestled a yes out of him."

"And how often do you manage to do that?" I ask.

Maddox peers down at me, notching his chin between his fingers and scratching his sun-touched beard as he contemplates. "Considering the brief time you've been here, I'm afraid your average is more impressive than mine. And that's saying something."

"Because you and Captain Astor are friends?" I pose the question as innocent, knotting my fingers behind my back in a posture my mother used to encourage because she thought looking girlish would make me more endearing to suitors. I'm not looking to attract Maddox, but it's in my best interest if he feels at ease talking to me. Maybe I can coax out some information about why the captain hated my parents so much.

"What makes you say that?" asks Maddox.

"You called him by his given name earlier. From what I've observed about the captain, that seems like the type of thing that would end with any other subservient hanging from the mast."

Maddox clicks his tongue, though playfully. "If that's what you believe, then you're not as observant as you'd like to think."

Okay, so maybe I'm not going to get much out of the First Mate. Which makes sense, now that I think about it. Maddox might look like the kind of man who's never had to develop his brain to get what he wants, but I don't see Astor trusting a man who is dull or easily influenced.

"The two of you don't seem like the type to become fast friends," I say.

Maddox appears amused. "Why not?"

"Your dispositions seem…" I try and fail to come up with the word I'm looking for. In the end, I settle on, "incompatible."

"Why?" Maddox says. "Because he's the murderous sort and I'm all innocence?"

There's nothing sinister in his voice, only a reticent sorrow, but it raises gooseflesh on my arms all the same. "Were you there?" I ask. "The night my parents were murdered?"

"I don't prefer the connotation of murdered, but to answer your question, yes, I was there."

Dozens of bodies crash to the floor in my mind's eye.

"I'm not sure I like the way you're looking at me," says Maddox, his jaw firm even if his voice is soft.

"The guests at my masquerade were innocent." And I condemned them to death by penning their invitations myself, I don't add.

"No one's innocent, Miss Darling." There's a pang of regret in Maddox's voice. "Not after a certain point, at least." For some reason, Simon's face comes to mind.

Anger bubbles up in my throat. "And that gave you the right to slaughter them? Just because you assume that at some point in their life, they did something wrong? I bet you don't even know the names of the people you killed."

Maddox's hands wriggle in his front pockets. "I only killed one that night. And, as a matter of fact, I do remember his name. Lord Credence, I believe."

I hold in my gasp, recalling the revolting man who tried to coerce me into marrying him the night of my masquerade, incorrectly assuming my desperation was due to my being with child.

"Nolan asked me to pay careful attention to make sure he didn't leave," says Maddox, a slight smirk at the edges of his lips. "As for why, you probably know more than I do."

When I don't answer, Maddox says, "Everyone needs a prickly friend, Miss Darling. If I were you, I'd use this opportunity to vie for Nolan's loyalty."

"How long have you known him?" I ask, wishing to deflect away from any talk of my relationship with the captain.

Maddox tucks his hands into his pockets. The way it causes his shoulders to slump gives him a boyish air. "Sixteen…no….I guess it's been almost seventeen years now."

My heart pounds rapidly. "Did you know Peter?"

Maddox examines me skeptically. "No. Peter was before my time."

I blink. "They knew each other as youths, then?"

Maddox doesn't attempt to hide the way his gaze dips to my finger. More specifically, the loose ring that I'm now twirling. "I'm assuming you didn't get that from Astor."

I snort in answer, but Maddox only says, "Your fiancé didn't tell you?"

It's not as if I haven't been asked the question before, by Captain Astor even, back when he was trying to get a rise out of me in the cave so that I would forget to give him his dose of rushweed. Still, it stings all the more coming from someone as seemingly genuine as Maddox.

"Tell me what?"

"They grew up together. Lived in the same village. The three of them were as tight-knit as an iron wire cord."

I frown. "The three of them?"

Maddox nods. "Yeah. Peter, Astor, and Iaso."

My heart stutters in my chest. "Peter knew Astor's wife?"

CHAPTER 10

WENDY

*P*eter knew Astor's wife.

That information shouldn't shock me. I knew that Peter and Astor were acquainted. It stands to reason that Peter would have known Astor's wife as well.

So why does that knowledge bother me so?

Perhaps it's what the knowledge implies about Peter's age that unsettles me. I've never asked him his age. Deep down, I probably knew he was older than he looked. I'd gotten the impression that the Lost Boys hadn't aged since being transported to Neverland. It stands to reason that the same would apply to Peter. If he was close friends with Astor and Iaso, he's likely in his mid-thirties as well.

How he's managed to evade the curse that made the fae mortal, I don't know.

There's a lot about Peter I don't seem to know.

Perhaps this new information is just another reminder that I've only scraped the surface of who Peter is. There's so much left to discover about my Mate, so much he hasn't told me. Not that I can blame him. Our relationship has been a bit of a whirlwind—a lovely, exhilarating whirlwind.

But now that the whirlwind is over, I'm afraid to open my eyes and witness the destruction in its path. Afraid to gaze upon that which I chose to ignore when I was wrapped up in the sky.

Still, I remind myself this new information isn't a reason to distrust Peter. As much as a thorn pricked at my heart when Maddox told me such a tender part of Peter's childhood, one that he hadn't shared with me—that he, Astor, and Iaso grew up together—it's not as if this changes who Peter is. Iaso is dead, and if Peter knew her for years, it would make sense that he'd have little motivation to bring her up.

And it's not as if I don't have painful parts of my past that I've kept from Peter. No, not kept—held onto for later.

Granted, Peter doesn't feel pain, so it's possible that he doesn't even register the importance of sharing that kind of intimate detail with me. I'm not sure if that's comforting or unsettling.

I've already opened the door to the captain's room before my brain can process the shuffling sound coming from inside.

When I left Maddox in the hallway, my feet carried me back here, my mind buzzing. Not only did the news of Peter's childhood friendship with the Astors rattle me, I'm also invigorated by the idea that I'm so much closer to freeing Peter of his curse than I ever would have thought possible after being taken captive on Captain Astor's ship. Sure, I'm nervous about impersonating a woman I've never met, but that's a small anxiety to pay for what's before me.

I've been visualizing it, playing coy on Captain Astor's arm while we siphon information out of the faceless but extravagant Carlisles.

Perhaps that's why I don't think before I barge into the captain's rooms.

Well, he's not naked. So I have that to be thankful for. But he's clearly just gotten out of the bath, his black hair slick like it's wet with dew, his tanned skin red from the hot water someone must have fetched him from the ship's boilers. A towel's wrapped around his waist, but that only slightly soothes the embarrassment. Astor's cheeks heat. With anger or embarrassment or a mixture, I'm unsure.

I just stand there like an idiot. Instead of averting my eyes like a respectable person, I fixate on the scar on his chest, just over his heart.

It looks as though he was burned once, deeply enough that even his fae magic couldn't rid him of the imprint.

"If you came to ogle me, you're not doing a very good job of it. I recommend the rotted hole between the slats to the door's left if you'd like to get a better view next time."

I bite the corner of my lip. The captain's tone isn't exactly warm and teasing. "I didn't mean to…"

"You didn't mean to barge into my room?"

"I didn't mean to catch you after… Well, I didn't think. My feet just carried me back here. I wasn't thinking…" I stop myself, then dig my feet into the ground. "No. You're the one who shackled me to your bedpost. Where else was I supposed to go when this is where I've been sleeping?"

"Anywhere, so long as it's away from me. Forgive me, I should have anticipated you'd wish to return to your chains."

I close my eyes and try to keep the tears stinging my eyes at bay. There's a light thud on the ground, then the sound of fabric sliding against skin. When I'm confident he's clothed sufficiently, I open my eyes, then turn to go.

"Wait," he says as my hand hits the doorknob. My fingers tremble around the curve of the metal, my heart thudding, warning me to get out of the captain's rooms, but my feet remain planted.

"Come here," he says, and my limbs obey.

When I turn to face him, I'm relieved (and mortifyingly disappointed) to realize he's slipped a white shirt over his chest. It's slim-fitting, hugging his musculature.

I've changed my mind. This is worse than seeing him shirtless.

I pad toward him, carefully, since I've learned that the boat is liable to sway underneath me at random moments. He waits patiently, his green eyes marking my path toward him as he leans against the bedpost. The way his arms are folded against his chest highlights the divot between the muscle and bone in his forearms. I try to avert my gaze to some part of him that's not so tantalizing, that doesn't make my head swirl, my legs tremble with the desire to come closer. But there's not exactly anywhere to look that serves that purpose unless I'm going to block my eyes again.

As I come closer, the scent of teakwood envelops me, quickening my pulse.

"You're trembling," he says, rubbing his short-cropped beard with his forefinger and thumb.

"I never know what you're going to do to me," I say, though I regret the words as soon as they come out of my mouth.

He grunts, then goes back to crossing his arms. "Vorin told me he saw you the other night."

"Who's Vorin?"

"The unfortunate sailor tasked with guarding the bunker now that we have a thief on board."

The taste of faerie dust lingers in my throat. "Oh."

"Oh, indeed."

The captain takes an exaggerated step backward, then rounds the other side of his bed, undoing the chain that once kept me secured to the bedpost. My throat starts closing up, but I remind myself that if the captain wanted to harm me, he's had plenty of opportunities.

"It was a test, you know. Earlier, when I gave you the key to this," he says, gesturing to the shackle in his hand.

"I doubt you were expecting me to pass, anyway," I say, voice flat.

He flicks his gaze up at me, staring through those long, dark eyelashes. "No. And yet, somehow, I'm still disappointed."

And how disappointed would Astor be if he knew about the pouch Peter gave me, the one that's still tucked underneath my waistband?

When he advances, I back up, but only a step. Nothing useful. He's close now, close enough that if he were to breathe a shade deeper, his chest would brush against mine. "That's all you're going to do?" he asks, running his thumb over the chain in his hand. "Back away from me?"

I swallow, then retreat again, but the captain is faster. He grabs my wrist with his left hand, the grayish Mating Mark on his forearm appearing as sickly as ever. I tug my arm away. His grip only tightens.

"What's wrong?" he barks in response to my whimper. When I turn my face away, he ticks his tongue. "Look at me."

I do.

"That hurts," I say, my voice catching as he digs his fingers in tighter around my wrist. I hate the way my voice trembles. How weak and terrified and pitiful I sound.

He holds my gaze, and I'm transfixed by his green eyes. There's a rage burning in them, and I wonder if he's about to throw the plan to fool the Carlisles overboard. Go ahead and take whatever revenge on me he's been plotting. But then he says, calmly, "If it hurts, then fight back."

A wry laugh escapes my lips. "What would be the point?" I glance at his sharp-tipped ears that mark him as fae, the muscles wrapping around his arms, his sheer size compared to mine.

"Because then at least you could say you tried. That you went down fighting."

"It's foolish to engage in a fight you know you're destined to lose," I say, to which the captain twists my wrist.

I let out a gasp as pain spikes through me, but the captain's movement was deliberate. There's no cracking of bone.

It's when I choke back a sob that he shoves me to the ground.

It's so sudden, I hardly have time to register what's happened until my back hits a basket of folded blankets. They break my fall, but they also close in over me, making it difficult to regain my balance as I struggle with the moving ship to get upright.

The captain strides toward me, green eyes vibrant and flaring, his face one of nightmares. "Get up," he says, the anger in his expression absent from his voice.

"You're the one who pushed me down," I cry, my limbs still trembling too much to support me. I struggle to rise, and when I finally succeed, the captain shoves me down again.

I let out a whimper as my back hits the floorboards this time. The captain towers over me, stalking me in circles.

"Get up."

"Why?" I ask. "What's the point if you're just going to shove me back down? Just do it."

"Do what?"

"Whatever it is you think I deserve for existing. Whatever you think will spend all that hate."

Rage flashes in his eyes. I brace myself for his boot to meet my head, but it doesn't. He just stares at me and whispers, "Get up. Fight back."

I steady myself and rise, but go limp before the captain comes at me again.

This time, my arms don't even catch my fall, and the impact has me biting through my lip. Coppery blood paints the inside of my mouth. When I laugh through bloodied teeth, the captain looks down at me. Something like regret flashes across his face, but it's quickly replaced by disgust.

He's staring at me like a child might a broken toy when he asks, "Why don't you fight back, Darling?"

CHAPTER 11

WENDY

*T*he next morning, it's Charlie who gets stuck babysitting me.

She'd made it known that she was less than thrilled about the situation, reminding Astor she was hired on to be a gunner, not to be the caretaker of a dust addict—"No offense," she'd added. Then she'd taken me above deck to the healer's quarters and taken to working on my swollen and bruised wrist.

From the window I can see the coastal city of Morella, where we've docked to replenish supplies and have repairs made. According to Charlie, Astor is rather sour about the estimate the craftsmen provided. Apparently, the repairs could take a few weeks. As I watch the dock workers bustle about, my legs ache for solid ground. Not that I'll be getting that anytime soon.

"I see your first training session didn't turn out too badly," Charlie says as she dips a cloth into the tip of a bottle of clear liquid and flips it over. "On my first day, I had a pair of bruised ribs and black eyes to match."

I blink, confused. "Training?"

She furrows her brow, revealing a tiny dimple there. "Maddox said it was your idea to join the Carlisle job. It was your idea, wasn't it?"

I blink. "Well, yes. But no one said anything about fighting."

She cocks an angled brow at me. "You didn't think you could just join a band of privateers without learning to throw a punch, did you?"

I'm about to admit that's exactly what I thought, but the more times I rehearse it in my mind, the more stupid it sounds. It dawns on me that I had technically told the captain that I was happy to train for the mission. What I'd meant as an invitation to train me in the art of stealth, he'd taken as a request for a lesson in combat. I glance down at the galley, where the sailors are bustling about the deck. "I didn't realize that's what he was doing."

Charlie's soft smile is the type that saves face, though I'm not sure if it's for me or Astor. "Not the best communicator, is he?"

"You'd think with how he always manages to find the perfect chink to lodge his insults, he could learn," I say, dryly.

"So what?" She presses the damp cloth to my bruised wrist. It hisses when it hits the wound, burning worse than the salt air around us, but already the purple blotches are fading to a sickly yellow. "Did he just attack you out of nowhere?"

I shake my head, but Charlie levels me a scolding glare—the type that's difficult to take seriously on her sweet face—since the movement messes with her ability to tend to my wound. "No, he pushed me. Well, he grabbed my wrist, and I told him it hurt, so he told me to fight back."

"And did you fight back?"

"Well, no, but…"

Charlie's staring at me like I just informed her I'd never made the connection between the rumbling in my stomach and hunger.

I sigh. Her unspoken assessment is probably accurate. "Where I come from, men don't shove women to the ground. Well, they're not supposed to, at least."

Charlie chuckles in a tone that I would classify as moderate condescension. "Yeah, well, where I'm from, women aren't supposed to be gunners, but I had to get over that one when I decided I wanted to be a privateer."

"I wouldn't say I want to be a privateer," I say, holding the rag to my wrist at Charlie's gesture. It's frigid, like it's been dipped in ice.

"Just...just hit him real good next time. In the eye. Or knee him in the groin," she says, the cognitive dissonance of hearing such a feminine voice talk about a man's groin banging against my skull as she speaks. "The men'll say that's cheating, but they don't seem to consider being naturally stronger cheating, so I wouldn't let it dissuade you."

My mother's training on what's appropriate, and more importantly, not appropriate to speak of, kicks in, so I ask, "You said where you come from, women aren't supposed to be gunners. Are you from Estelle too?"

Charlie shakes her head. "No. I'm from Xhana." She pats me on the knee. "I grew up as an aristocrat like you, believe it or not. Except my father got into money trouble. Racked up his debts with a nasty band of pirates, so they slaughtered my family when he wouldn't pay. I happened to be courting a nobleman at the time, so I wasn't at the estate when it happened. Needless to say, he ended our courtship when he discovered the pirates had burned our estate down, as well as my father's faerie dust mills."

Faerie dust mills? Interesting. If that's the case, Charlie is underselling just how wealthy her family was. "Pirates killed your family... so you became one?"

"Well, I always thought being a whore sounded unpleasant, don't you agree? All those nasty men's hands all over you." She speaks of it as if she's discussing which brew to serve during afternoon tea, but there's a subtle quiver to her tone, a tell in the way her left eyelid twitches. My mind flashes back to the parlor, and all I can do is nod gently as she continues. "Besides, we're not pirates. Not really. Captain Astor's a privateer. I know what you're thinking—but he really is picky about the assignments he takes. He doesn't kill innocents."

"Except for my parents. And the guests at my masquerade," I say.

Charlie peers at me apologetically and bites her lip.

· · ·

81

"How was that?" I ask, straightening my spine. Charlie sits cross-legged across from me on my bed. Someone moved it into her room for me now that Astor has taken his bedroom back and Charlie has been temporarily demoted to my chaperone. Parchment with Charlie's bubbly script is laid out between us across the bed, overflowing with notes on Cressida Rivers, the woman I'm planning on impersonating.

Charlie blinks, her smile somehow both genuine and forced. Apparently, my performance was awful enough that even Charlie is having difficulty coming up with something complimentary to say. "You've got it all memorized perfectly. I saw you—you didn't peek once."

"Well, yes, but how did I do?" I ask. We've just spent the past half hour role-playing a conversation between Lady Carlisle and me, Charlie playing the secret-trader as I answered her questions. Again, it takes a moment for Charlie to produce a response, her supportive smile unwavering.

I groan, slinking into the mound of pillows behind me. "I'm going to get us killed, aren't I?"

"Not necessarily," says Charlie. "Maybe the Carlisles aren't familiar with Delphian cadence and will assume it's a difference in dialect."

I cut my eyes across to her. "Assume what's a difference in dialect?"

"Wendy, you sound like you're reciting your own ransom while a knife's being held to your throat," Charlie says, then quickly adds, "but we've still got plenty of time to work on it."

It's probably not worth mentioning that we've been working on this for two weeks already, and I still can't seem to get the hang of it. Memorization isn't the problem—I had all the facts of Cressida River's life branded into my memory by the end of the first day. It's pretending to be Cressida Rivers that I can't quite seem to get a grasp on.

"You're just stiff, is all," says Charlie. "Just, you know, loosen up a little." She rolls her shoulders as if that's all it will take to unwind fifteen years of constantly anticipating impending doom.

Because my eyes are beginning to cross from sleep deprivation, I fix my attention on a knot in the beam above us. "This is useless. I'm not quick-witted enough. I can hardly get the right words out when I'm being myself. Much less when I'm trying to be someone else. I'm not going to be able to come up with answers fast enough to be convincing." I drag my palms over my face as I groan, my chest wound tight with frustration.

Charlie shifts on the creaking bed and exhales slowly before clapping her palms on her knees. "Okay, well, maybe we just need to think about this differently. Take a different approach. You said your parents trained you to charm suitors, didn't they? Just think of the Carlisles as potential suitors."

I peek through my fingertips at Charlie, who actually has the audacity to look hopeful, then roll myself upright, extending my fingertips in front of me on the bed as I stretch out my back, sore from cowering over the notes on my alias.

"That's different," I say. "When I was chasing a husband, it's not as if I was having to pretend to be anyone else."

Charlie raises a skeptical brow. "You weren't?"

I open my mouth, but the words get stuck in my throat, like a shard of chicken bone lodged at the base of my tongue.

But then an idea flutters across my mind, wistful and wild and a smidge mad. Perhaps it's just the late night and utter despair. But it feels right. More right than forcing facts out of my mouth like we've been attempting for the past several hours. "Charlie," I ask, running my fingers over the pages of notes on Cressida Rivers, "does the captain have one of these for the Carlisles?"

WHILE THE STACK of notes on the Carlisles at first appears daunting due to the weighty thud it makes when Charlie dumps it on the bed, I find these facts exceedingly easier to memorize than the notes on Cressida Rivers.

It helps that the Carlisles are actually interesting.

What's easier to remember? That Arthur Carlisle once hid in the pit of an outhouse for three days because he'd gotten a tip that rival gang lords were planning to collude there? Or that Cressida Rivers' favorite flower is a lilac?

Charlie keeps me company into the wee hours of the night, her enthusiasm for our task rekindled. Admittedly, I can't tell if it's because the Carlisles are so intriguing or because she no longer secretly considers working with me a lost cause. If I were to ask, she'd tell me it was the Carlisles, regardless.

We're about to practice another conversation between Arthur Carlisle and Cressida Rivers when there's a knock at the door. Charlie and I glance at one another, confused.

A moment later, Captain Astor enters the room.

"Everything alright?" Charlie asks.

Captain Astor wrinkles his brow. "Why do you ask?"

Charlie and I exchange a glance. "You don't often visit in the middle of the night," she says.

Captain Astor blinks, like the passing of time has taken him by surprise. Snuck up on him like an undesirable task. "I've been poring over the blueprints of the Carlisles' manor. Was about to transition to freshening up on the target when I realized my intel had gone missing." He stares pointedly at the stacks of parchment piled on the bed.

"It was Wendy's idea," says Charlie, who I at first assume is abandoning me to the captain's wrath, until she adds, "She's rather brilliant, you know."

Charlie fixes the captain with a stare that is somehow both pointed and pleasant.

"I told you to have her memorize the fact sheet on Cortland and Cressida Rivers," says Astor, not bothering to hide his annoyance given the way his boot is tapping against the floor.

Before Charlie can defend me, I spout, "I already did."

Astor flicks his hardened gaze toward me. "How Cressida and Cortland met." I might break into hives for how he doesn't even bother to raise his pitch at the end and make it a question.

"She was his tailor," I answer all the same.

"Her parents' names."

"Fredrick and Opal."

"How she broke her arm as a child."

"She fell out of a tree."

"Type of tree."

"Pear."

"Cressida's puppy's name."

I offer him a knowing look. "Cressida hates animals. She made her husband donate his Labrador to an orphanage when they wed." Pleased with myself would be an understatement for my reaction when the captain's scowl deepens. "You know, one would think you would want me to succeed, considering we're working together."

Charlie's head has been oscillating between the two of us the entire time. She yawns, then slides her hands from her hips to her knees before bouncing off the bed and whipping her shawl around her shoulders.

"Where are you going?" asks Astor.

"Somewhere that's not within clawing distance of the two of you," she says cheerily, before hurrying out the door, leaving me alone with the captain.

"Why'd you convince Charlie to steal the Carlisle files?" are the first words out of his mouth.

And just like that, I'm riled. Though I shouldn't be surprised given my company. "You don't get to do that," I say.

"What do I not get to do?"

"Tell me I'm too witless to come up with original thought, then accuse me of scheming."

For once, the captain appears speechless. He crosses his arms, tracing his thumb up the ridge of his forearm.

But I'm not done. "Empty-headed or conniving?"

"Pardon?"

"You have to pick between the two," I say.

"Fine," says the captain, his jaw clicking. "I pick conniving."

When my mouth seeks to curve, his gaze lingers there. "Why do you look so pleased?"

I purse my lips and bite down on my tongue, trying and failing to hold back my response. "Maybe that's the one I was hoping you'd pick."

Unamused, the captain sweeps me up and down with his gaze. "Are you prepared for tomorrow?"

"I already told you I have all the details memorized," I say.

"Yes, but can you play the part?"

I stare at Cressida Rivers' fact sheet and trace Charlie's handwriting with my fingertips, if only to give me somewhere to look other than the captain.

When I don't answer, the captain sighs. While his voice is twinged with impatience, it's surprisingly not unkind. "Can you play Cressida Rivers, or do I need to start prepping Charlie to do it?"

"I'll be fine," I say.

"Show me."

My heart pounds in my chest. I'd rather not put on a performance for the captain, but he's not exactly a person worth arguing with once he sets his mind to something.

"Fine," I say. "I'll let you lead."

Something flickers in his eyes. "You'll let me?"

I say nothing, simply wait.

He watches me carefully, then pulls up a stool and crosses his legs like he's a posh aristocrat. I'm almost tempted to laugh. Almost.

"Your wife is lovely, Rivers. Had I known how beautiful Delphian women were, I might have spent more time there myself."

I fight the blush rising to my cheeks and allow a sly smile to curve on my lips. "I'm Kruschian. Though I'm sure Lady Carlisle would prefer you visit neither."

Whether Astor is pleased that I didn't fall for his trap, I can't tell from his cool expression. "Ah, that's right. Yet you've lived in Delphi most of your life, correct? Tell me about Delphi then. I hear the countryside is lovely in the spring."

"I wouldn't know."

Astor raises a brow. "You're not fond of traveling?"

"This lifestyle of doing what I want when I want is new to me, I'm afraid. Cost of living might be of little consequence to the nobility, but to the working class, it's everything."

"Ah." He turns toward my pillow, our stand-in for Cortland Rivers, with a condescending smile. "Snagged yourself a working-class wife. How quaint."

My grin is calculated, plastered to my face but still controlled. A challenge. "Quaint. That's what my clients all thought as they blabbed their secrets to their friends, forgetting I was there at their feet, measuring them up."

Astor's imperceptible facade cracks, just slightly. It's barely there, in the twitch of his lip on the right. "And here I was, thinking I was the one dealing in secrets."

"Yes, and you've made yourself a reputation for that, haven't you? Me? I'm just a...what was it? Ah, *quaint* tailor."

I catch Astor in his stare, refusing to break first, even as I note his chest rising and falling underneath his white linen shirt.

"Where did you learn to do that?" His question sounds more like a demand.

I allow the unnatural air of confidence to drain from me, let my shoulders droop into a more comfortable position. "Do what?"

"You know."

My knees find my chest, and I hug them into myself, suddenly embarrassed by my display, though I can't explain why. There's something about letting Astor see how easily I can let myself be molded that makes me feel exposed. Naked except for a painted mask. Now that I'm myself again, it takes me a moment to search for the words, but when I find them, they come out easily. "I don't know how to be a specific person. But what I do know is how to be whoever the person sitting across from me wants me to be." I absentmindedly stroke the Mating Mark on my cheek. "At least for a while, that is."

Astor leans forward, his stool balancing on the front two legs. "And what if the person sitting across from you wants Wendy Darling? Could you be her?"

His green eyes pin me with such ferocity, my breath catches, fog flooding my mind. "I'm afraid I'd need more information on who's asking," is all I manage to choke out.

Satisfied with addling me, Astor pulls his coin out of his pocket and taps it against his knee. "That's why you wanted the Carlisle notes. So you can figure out how to be whatever either of them wants."

I nod.

"Clever, but it won't work."

I recoil, offended. "What makes you say that?"

"Because the only woman in the room that Carlisle wishes to be strong-minded and willful is his wife, and that's only so she can bully information out of their guests."

"I know that," I say, tapping on the notes beside me.

"Considering that brazen performance of yours, clearly, you don't," Astor says, rising from his stool and stretching out his legs.

There's a moment where I hesitate, where I almost let him leave without me defending myself. When I speak, my voice is hardly louder than a whisper, but I say it all the same. "That version of Cressida wasn't for Carlisle."

Astor pretends not to hear me, but I don't miss the way his hand flinches on the way out.

CHAPTER 12

JOHN

The fact that Tink is really quite pretty should not make it more difficult for me to torture information out of her.

If Wendy were here, she'd tell me there's no reason to torture information out of anyone.

But Wendy isn't here.

And besides, my sister trusted the creature who haunted her for her entire childhood. So I don't know why I'm bothering listening to her voice inside my head.

When I'd dragged Tink's limp body into the cave, I'd been ready to restrain her. I'm still not sure how long it takes the fae to overcome rushweed, so I'd brought ropes in my satchel just in case.

As it turned out, I didn't need them. Because inside Tink's lair was a cage.

It looks hewn from the stone of the cave wall itself. No, it's as if it's always been a part of the cave. If I didn't know better, I'd think the stalactites and stalagmites grew together perfectly to form the bars, even the door and its lock. I found a key Tink keeps hidden underneath her small cot.

I'm not sure who made this cave, or who they made it for, but that's not the pressing question at the moment.

"Did you hurt my sister?" I ask, staring at the faerie inside the cage.

I'm not sure what I was expecting. For her to snarl at me, probably. For her actions to be as untamed as her disheveled hair, cropped and golden and looking as though someone has recently run their hands through it. For her to be as unhinged as her tattered burlap garb and shredded wings would imply.

There's a wildness in Tink. That's as evident as it could be in the way she cocks her head. She might be trapped inside the cage, but there's no mistaking that she's the predator here, her stunning blue eyes calculating as she examines me.

When I was younger, I heard men label women as calculating as if it were a defect. I never understood that. But now, looking into Tink's cunning eyes, I understand. She's terrifying.

"Did you hurt my sister?" I ask again.

Tink nods. I detect little emotion in her reaction, except for the twitch of her full lips. A hint of pleasure there.

My heart raps against my hollow chest cavity. "Is she dead?"

I'm not sure what I'll do to Tink if her answer is yes.

But Tink doesn't nod this time. Instead, she blinks, her round blue eyes flashing with surprise, just for a moment. She tries to hide it from me, tries to regain her composure, but it's too late.

"You didn't know," I say, though I can't bring myself to be relieved. All this proves is that Tink didn't kill her, not that she's not dead. "You didn't know Wendy is missing."

Tink's expression shutters.

Chills prod the back of my neck.

She really is quite pretty.

Her cheekbones slice against her otherwise delicate features. Rather than detracting from her femininity, her cropped hairstyle only highlights her distinct features. Full, pink lips, casually sly in their angle. A delicate brow. Long, blond eyelashes. Wide blue eyes.

Pretty is a tad of an understatement, and that's just her face.

I know from the burlap sack that's barely long enough to reach past her buttocks that her lean tan legs are just as beautiful, but I don't let my gaze dip to examine them more thoroughly than what I can see from the periphery of my vision.

That Tink chooses to wear clothing at all is a glaring contradiction to what I've read in history books, packed with illustrations of wild fae dancing naked through the woods, unashamed of their exposed flesh.

The burlap sack might simply be a practical measure to ward off injuries common in the forest, but in case it's not, in case Tink wishes to cover herself from the view of onlookers and a burlap sack was the best she could find on this island, I'd rather not ogle. Especially considering I have her caged.

"Do you have any idea what might have happened to my sister?" I ask.

Tink gnashes her glinting teeth, and the vision of a nightstalker flashes in my mind.

"It's possible she could have been attacked on the island," I say. "But we haven't found any remains."

Tink again tilts her head at me. That's about all she can do with the rushweed in her system. Curiosity brims in her eyes. I'm familiar with the look. People offer it often when they perceive that I've been too blunt, or when I've refrained from inserting the correct dose of emotion into my words.

That's ridiculous, of course. You can't tell someone's feelings strictly by the way their voice sounds or their diction. Sure, it can be a fair measure, but most people can manipulate those variables to make others infer what they want them to.

Which reminds me that Tink could have been doing just that when she acted surprised to hear that Wendy was missing. I examine the faerie, recalling how much she hates my sister for catching Peter's attention. Had I dismissed so quickly the idea that she's to blame for Wendy's disappearance?

I'll have to be more wary of her fae glamour.

Even if Tink didn't hurt Wendy herself, she's obsessed enough with Peter that she wouldn't betray him if she knew he was the one to blame.

"If you don't tell me where Wendy is, you'll come to regret it," I say, nodding toward her shredded wings.

This time, fear flashes across Tink's face, but again, she masks it quickly enough. She closes her eyes, making as if to fall asleep.

"You're not even going to bother answering me?"

Eyes still closed, she grins—the wry sort.

"What? Are you so bored on this island that you enjoy riling others up? I'm sorry to break it to you, but I'm not one to be easily riled." Well, except when it comes to those who hurt my family. But I refrain from mentioning as much. "You won't like what happens if you don't answer me."

Tink's smile dissipates, but her cheeks and forehead are smooth, betraying no fear of me. She thinks I'm a boy talking a big game. Threatening her with cruel words, but no follow-through.

I'm not a bad person. Not a sociopath either, though there was a time when I thought perhaps I was. After I overheard Wendy's sessions with her alienist, I spent my early adolescent years reading through works of the world's most renowned alienists on the subject. They claimed that the defining characteristic of a sociopath is that they lack empathy.

I might have believed that definition applied to me, if it hadn't been for my family. In fact, I did believe it for a time. Had resigned myself to the morbid truth that I feel nothing for others.

But then Michael had gotten to be old enough that we noticed him struggling with what other children could do with ease. I would hear the comments others made about my brother. Comments that were probably meant to be well-meaning, or at least they'd convinced themselves they were well-meaning. People do that often—gossip and tear down others, then pat themselves on the back for being concerned.

He didn't understand what they were saying about him, of course. But I did. And I felt on his behalf what he did not. Absorbed every mark against him as if it were branding my own soul. And then there was what I overheard one night in the parlor, happening to Wendy.

I'd felt that too. But feeling had led to fear. Perhaps if I hadn't been capable of feeling, I would have stepped in and helped.

No, I'm no more of a sociopath than my sister is. I simply reserve that empathy for a select few.

I'm choosing not to extend that to Tink.

IT TAKES me over an hour to make the fire. Neverland is humid, so even with the flint I snuck from a closet back at the Den, it takes a while for the handful of dry spindles I could find to catch. By the time I finally set my carefully arranged tent of sticks aflame, I'm second-guessing myself. Whether I can actually go through with this.

I plunge my dagger into the fire anyway. Watch the dull blade turn the color of a molten sun.

Despite having dosed her with rushweed and caged her, I've tied Tink's hands together as well. Just in case. When I open the cage door, Tink can do nothing but offer me a challenging grin. The rest of her still can't move.

She shows no sign of fear. Not even when I brandish my still-glowing dagger.

"Talk," I say.

I'm met with a defiant smirk. She doesn't think I'll do it.

That's because she doesn't know me.

When I place the blade against her—a long line tracing her clavicle—I feel nothing but the lackluster protest of the outer layer of her skin, which sutures immediately after the blade punctures it.

She doesn't scream, choosing the clamp her jaw instead, but her eyes fling open, tears welling in them. She's a tough woman, and she's fae, so I imagine the tears are more from shock than anything.

There's a bright red mark left behind.

When I touch the blade to her again, she spits in my face.

I keep going.

The second branding is more difficult. Straight across her thigh. I know it's a relatively safe place to burn her. More fatty tissue to absorb it. No vital organs to damage. That's why I chose it. But it feels intimate, and as Tink whimpers, I don't hear Tink, but Wendy, crying softly from the parlor after a suitor readjusts his cravat on the way out the door.

The thought makes me ill, and for a fleeting moment, the panic begins to set in. The doubt.

I can't do this.

But I've failed Wendy one too many times. I won't fail her again.

I make another mark, and as Tink cries, I remind myself who I'm doing this for.

Who I'm protecting.

IT'S ONLY LATER that night as I'm lying awake in bed, considering what more I could possibly do to break her, how she could be so stubborn in spite of such pain, that the realization hits me in the gut.

As I cooked Tink's skin, she didn't refrain from telling me because she wouldn't.

It's because she can't.

CHAPTER 13

JOHN

When I visit Tink the next day, I come prepared, a journal I snuck from Freckles's now-empty room and a quill in hand. A bottle of ink tucked into my pocket.

Tink's asleep when I enter, curled up on the floor, her limbs all sharp angles and bones.

It looks terribly uncomfortable. I wonder if it's painful, sleeping on the floor when you have so little fat to guard your bony edges. Guilt taps at my conscience, so I pull the wrapped food out of my pocket before I bother with the writing utensils. Logically, I know it's not my fault that Tink is so malnourished. I wasn't the one who brought her to this island, and a night spent in a cage isn't nearly long enough to have had a long-term effect on her health.

I repeat these facts to myself. But it's just like writing a word over and over, until it no longer looks as if it's spelled correctly.

Funny how even facts can appear false when we dwell on them too long.

Of course, the fact remains that I tortured her last night.

"I brought you breakfast," I say, unwrapping the jerky I snuck from the kitchens this morning.

Tink stirs. It takes her a moment to register I'm here and pull herself out of slumber. But her ears flick, and she jumps from the floor, the rushweed clearly having worn off.

I don't miss the way she adjusts the bottom of the flimsy sack covering her body. Like she's worried about what I might have seen while she lay sprawled and asleep.

"I wouldn't have looked, even if there was something to see," I say. My intention is to comfort her, but all I manage to do is produce scarlet blotches on her face. I'm used to the reaction from Wendy, who is rather easily embarrassed, but what I'm not used to is the rage blazing in Tink's blue eyes.

I get the feeling I said something wrong. Now I'm the one with heat creeping up my neck.

Not knowing how to repair it, I toss the jerky through the bars of the cage. "I'm sorry to be impolite," I say as Tink's eyes trace the jerky bits plopping to the floor. "I just figure if I put my hand through the bars, I'm not likely to bring it back again."

She nods to my missing pinkie as if to reinforce my point.

"Exactly," I say, cleaning my throat. "I'm not keen on losing any more of my phalanges."

Tink crinkles her nose as if the way I speak has an odor to it. Again, my neck flushes. *Fingers* would have done just fine.

She wastes no time in snapping the rope restraints I secured around her wrists last night. Good thing this cage is made of stone, though it still brings gooseflesh to my arms to consider how this cage might have been formed.

When she picks up the jerky, she sniffs it. Fair, since I poisoned her last meal. I watch her turn it over in her hand, contemplating. There's a stubbornness in the set of her jaw. She doesn't have to speak to tell me she doesn't want to eat the food I offer her. It's written all over the pride in her stance, her eyes.

But her throat bobs in shallow waves as she swallows. Probably clearing the saliva pooling in her mouth at the scent of meat.

When I was a child, I read a book once about the relationship between the body and the brain. The author, a scientist, posited that most of the time, the body allows the mind free rein. But even this is only an illusion. Because as soon as the body deems the mind no longer capable of making decisions in its best interest, the body takes back the reins.

The author listed examples such as shipwrecked sailors eating their friends once starvation set in. The way, if you hold your breath too long, your body will make you pass out, then reinstate breathing.

When this phenomenon had been simply text on a printed page, I'd eaten it up, soaked it in. Wished for nothing more than to study such cases myself. But when Tink's resolve not to eat the food offered by her captor breaks, it's nothing like reading from a textbook.

The textbooks never mentioned the self-loathing in a person's eyes when they lose control of their body. Never mentioned how broken a person could look. When she consumes the jerky, she does it with such violence, one would think she was punishing herself.

I have to glance away and remind myself I didn't cause her hunger.

But I did cause the red stripes across her thighs, already healing because of the magic in her blood. That doesn't stop the faint red lines from pricking me in the side, drawing blood of their own.

For Wendy. I did it for Wendy.

Somehow that doesn't seem enough.

Through the bars, I pass the flatbread I brought for myself. She quickly snatches it up, like she's worried I'll take it back.

When she's done, I clear my throat. Her ears flick, so I know she heard me, but other than that she ignores me.

That's fair. "I'm sorry about before. I didn't realize that you couldn't answer me."

Tink's spine goes rigid. Apparently that was the wrong thing to say too, though I can't imagine why. It's only the truth.

"I brought these," I say, pulling out the writing utensils. "Are you literate? I mean, can you read and write?"

The look Tink flashes insults with more precision than words ever could.

"Right, I'm sorry," I say, keenly aware of how much apologizing I'm doing. Carefully, I push the journal through the bars, followed by the quill and ink.

For a moment, I think she'll refuse to touch them. But then she crumples up the leaf I wrapped the bread in and tosses it at my face.

I don't manage to catch it before it smacks me in the glasses.

Tink yawns, picks the journal and quill up, dips the quill in ink, and begins writing. My heart races in my chest, the adrenaline of an idea, simple as it is, fueling my body, making my limbs quake.

I feel as if I'm on the edge of discovery, my excitement for learning battling with the possibility that the information Tink holds about Wendy's fate might pick me apart from the inside, leaving me empty. Remind me of the failure I truly am. Incompetent to accomplish my one purpose—protecting my sister.

When she's done, Tink blows on the sheet to make the ink dry faster. I have to blink to make myself stop fixating on her full mouth before she notices. Then she snaps the journal closed with one hand and offers it to me through the bars. I take it, flipping it open to the first page, chest brimming with anticipation. As soon as I glimpse the contents of the page, my excitement pops like a balloon at the carnival.

Tink can write, that's for sure. But not in any language I recognize. The characters are neat and precise, but they're not any alphabet I'm familiar with.

"But you can understand me, can't you?" I say.

Tink blinks at me like this is her first time meeting an idiot. I suddenly feel a heightened awareness of my own stupidity. This woman's presence takes a flame to the folds of my brain and melts them like wax.

"Right. You understand Estellian; you just never learned the characters."

Tink purses her lips and raises her eyebrows as if to say, *And the idiot's finally got it.*

"Do you think I could teach you?" I know the question is worded the wrong way as soon as it leaves my mouth, but it's not as if I can take it back.

Tink's expression goes blank. That's fair.

I tug at my collar. "Let me reword that. Would you allow me to teach you?"

Tink cocks her brow.

I groan, then try again. "Would you allow me the honor of teaching you?" I almost add, *most fair lady*, but decide that's a bit much.

Tink shrugs, then starts picking at her jagged nails.

It's not a no.

CHAPTER 14

WENDY

The night we leave Morella, I'm woken to a crash as a cannonball goes barreling through the wall of our cabin, missing my head by a hair. It lodges itself into the opposite wall, its shiny black facade taunting me in the low faerie lamp light, reminding me just where my head might have been pinned.

Panic pounds in my chest. I jump from my bed, mirroring Charlie, who already has a saber in hand and a blade strapped to the thigh of her leathers. "Stay here," she tells me in the most commanding voice I've heard her use.

"Stay here?" I ask, exasperated. One would think almost having your head taken off in the middle of the night would deem a space unsafe, but Charlie just gives me a look that says that if I leave this room, I'll have more than a cannonball to be concerned about. She rushes out of the room, and I lock the door behind her.

From above, I hear shouting. The whirr of cannonballs. The crash of wood and the clank of swords. Screams and gurgles infiltrate the more elemental sounds, and each one of them brings me back to the night of the masquerade. To the moment the captain I thought would rescue me orchestrated a massacre.

I shouldn't be shocked that his ship is now under attack. I imagine Captain Astor has made some enemies in his day.

Even though I'm worthless when it comes to fighting and am not sure I'd want to be fighting on Astor's side anyway, I need to do something. I get dressed, shedding my sleep shirt for a tunic and a pair of trousers.

There. At least when I'm brutally murdered, my body will be clothed. Less mortifying that way.

I work my bottom lip between my teeth, pacing the room as I listen for hints of who's winning up above. Of course, the sounds are no use in uncovering the truth and only serve to perpetuate worst-case scenarios in my mind. I worry for Charlie, though this can't be the first time she's encountered an attack like this in her line of work. Still, I don't like the idea of anything happening to her.

Maybe that's why I'm relieved when I hear the click of a key against the lock of our door.

"Charlie, what's going o—"

It's not Charlie. In steps Ascor, the man they call Teeth on board because his name is too similar to the captain's. He has a master key ring he's clipping back to his belt. Even from across the room, his breath reeks, filling my nostrils and making me want to gag. Only decorum has me holding in my bile when he grins at me, thin, blistered lips giving way to a set of blackened teeth.

My instincts might be a tad dulled, but they're not completely dysfunctional. Unease settles in my stomach, dread creeping up in the waving of rising hair on my forearms, the back of my neck.

Be what he wants, then run, I tell myself, already settling onto the balls of my feet.

"Mister Ascor," I say, my tone sweet. Compliant. It's much easier to slide back into this persona than it should be. Perhaps because it's not so much false as it is natural for me. "I'm terribly frightened. What... what's going on up there? Please, I don't want to die." Ironic, given what I'd attempted the night I met my own wraith, but Teeth doesn't know about that.

"No, missus. Don't worry your pretty little head about that." Teeth offers me a wink. "You wouldn't be as pretty dead."

My stomach churns, and I instinctively take a step back. Surely this man hasn't snuck down into my rooms in the middle of a skirmish, abandoning his post just because he knew I'd be alone.

Surely.

But Teeth takes another step forward, his beady eyes full of a hungry greed I've witnessed before.

My voice might shake, but I still manage to force the words out. "The captain will kill you if you touch me," I say. "He's keeping me for himself."

Teeth laughs. "We both know the captain would rather claw his eyes out than touch you. Believe me, I don't understand it. But that's alright. The captain's a unique man. Others won't have his reservations."

My heart turns to ice. *Others.*

There's no time to process his words before he lunges for me. At least prepared enough to sidestep out of the way, I let loose a scream, but it's lost in the roar of the battle on deck. I race for the door, but as soon as my hands reach the latch, Teeth grabs me, one hand at my mouth, the other around my waist.

Once again, my body betrays me, my limbs slackening beneath his touch, my spine frozen.

Teeth spins me around to face him, securing both my wrists in one hand as he dips his other hand into the pouch at his side. No matter how hard I try to make myself writhe and struggle, I can't seem to move. My mind flashes back to my altercation with the captain. How disgusted he'd be at my inability to fight back.

Teeth jabs his finger into my mouth, coating my tongue with something bitter. Something that takes me back to a cave on a beach and the captain's resignation as I pressed a spoon to his chapped lips.

Horror overcomes me.

It starts in my torso, then spreads out to my limbs, my legs and arms going limp in Teeth's grasp. My body is paralyzed, heavy with the weight of the rushweed as it works through my system. I can't move. Can't fight.

All I can do is laugh. Laugh at the irony of the same drug I'd used on the captain now being used on me.

But that is the unfortunate thing about being a woman. They're going to do worse things to me than I ever did to him.

Teeth strokes my hair, whispering in my ear as he rips a piece off my tunic and uses it to gag me. "There, there. It's alright. They'll treat you well where I'm taking you. I've found you a good home, little pet. You'll have all the gold and jewels you could ever desire."

TEETH HAS to transport me across the deck to get to the safety boats. He keeps to the shadows, dragging my limp body over splinters in the wood that tear into my clothes and dig into my flesh as he sneaks behind crates. Rain pelts us, making the deck slick. The fighting is a bloodbath, and I can't tell who is making it out on top, or if both sides' blood runs together in dark rivulets, already being washed away by the evening storm. I tell myself to close my eyes. Remind myself that I don't want to see a throat slit, not when all I'll see is my parents gargling as they fall to the floor.

But I can't bring myself to close my eyes. Not when I keep searching for Charlie among the bodies on deck, praying she's not one of the headless corpses. For the first time, I long to see Astor's face. To glimpse his reaction when he realizes Teeth is hauling me away.

Just this once, I'd love it if someone actually saved me. Because clearly I'm not capable of it on my own.

Teeth has made it to the edge of the rocking ship by the time I spot the captain. He's at the helm, fighting off a band of three invaders on his own with his back to the wooden wheel. Even if I wanted to, I couldn't look away. There's something about the grace of his stride, the way his sword acts as an extension of himself. When he fells his opponents, he makes it look like art. Like a brush against a canvas. And I can't look away. Could never want to.

Please see me, I whisper to him in my mind. I cry into the gag, but it's no use.

It's only when Teeth hoists me over the side of the ship, pulling on the rope secured to my waist, that Astor finally sees me.

Shock flashes through his eyes, and the distraction costs him. An opponent parries Astor's attack, backs him against the helm by using his weight against him. It doesn't take long for Astor to recover, but it delays him long enough for Teeth to loosen the rope, my body dangling above the dark ocean as he lowers me until I can no longer see Astor.

Below me is a boat, beaten heartily by the waves.

Peter, surely Peter's here. Somewhere in the shadows, waiting to strike. But no, Peter said he could only come during the Sister's errands. And I have no way of knowing if he's on one right now.

Greedy hands grasp at whatever they can get their hands on to pull me into the boat. One of them whistles as his stray hand catches my breast. Blackness swarms the edges of my vision. There's a sawing sound above me. Someone hacking at the rope Teeth used to lower me down. The rope gives way, and I fall, slamming face first into the base of the boat. Saltwater lining the bottom goes up my nose, or so I assume. It takes me a moment to realize it's my own blood, gushing from my pounding nose.

"Make sure it's the right one," one of the men says. Someone flips me over, yanking my stray hair out of the way and running his hands over my Mating Mark.

"It's her alright," he says. "Imagine what Vulcan'll pay for this one. It's pretty too," he says, running his thumb all the way down the part of my Mating Mark that rounds my jawline.

His touch, his words, transport me back to the parlor. I gag into the cloth stuffed into my mouth, and the man above me has the gall to offer me a look of sympathy. "Don't worry, love," he says, his smile all teeth and, I believe, truly meant to be comforting. "You'll have it better from now on."

CHAPTER 15

WENDY

The blood has crusted on my nose by the time I wake. At least one of the men who kidnapped me finds this displeasing.

"Boris. I told you to get her cleaned up. The client will be here any minute now."

"Pardon me, Master Zane. I thought you said the appointment was at midnight."

"You know he's always early." Even in my daze, I detect a sneer in Zane's voice. "But he always underpays. Male owns half the region, yet we'll be lucky to have enough to keep our lamps fed..."

I flutter my eyes open, taking in my surroundings. I'm laid across a table, the chill of its surface seeping through my clothes and into my back. Muffled by the walls of the windowless room, the clacking of hooves against cobblestone and the bustle of footsteps hint at a city outside this room. When I try to move my fingers, they don't respond. The rushweed must still be working its way through my system.

It doesn't matter.

There's not much fight in me anyway. I'd hardly been able to summon it against Teeth. I wonder what the captain did to him. Teeth never made it onto the boat, and I'm certain the captain witnessed him casting me overboard.

It doesn't really matter what happened to the traitorous crewman. It doesn't change my circumstances one bit.

The room itself is dimly lit. There are a few faerie lamps on the wall, but everything else is cast in shadows that stretch over velvet duvets and a cedar post bed. It's the type of place where I imagine the lighting is supposed to serve a double purpose. Intensify the aura of seduction, the allure of the forbidden, while also distracting from a few key details: the leopard skin rug on the floor is fake, the gilding on the walls made of pyrite paint. If I had to bet, the table I'm laid across is finished with scagliola, made to imitate a block of marble.

Growing up with my mother's tutelage, I could sense these things with my eyes closed. She thought it was a useful skill for getting a husband. As if the men of the aristocracy cared about these sorts of things.

The second man, Boris—the one who smiles as if he believes himself to be kind—offers me a pitying look and takes a cold rag to my face. I wince when he applies pressure to my nose, a spark of pain budding there. But I don't cry out.

I'm well schooled in not crying out.

"Sorry about your nose," Boris says. "Don't think it's broken, though."

I don't answer. I don't even look at him. Just stare up at the ceiling above me, trying not to think about why he needs to clean me up before their prompt client arrives. As he wipes my face, tears well in my eyes. Partly from the stinging, partly because of what my future holds.

"Oh, don't cry, missus. You're going to the best of our clients. Say, you have the look of a lady. Am I right?" When I don't answer, he continues, undeterred. "It won't be all that different from being married off, I swear."

When again I don't acknowledge him, he sighs. As he brushes off the last of the blood from my nose, he says, "You'll want this first one to like you. My master's other clients aren't so gentle with their women."

One tear trickles down the side of my face before I blink the rest away. When I speak, my voice is cracked and dry. "Will he keep me like this? Unable to move?"

The man doesn't meet my gaze. "No. But the others would."

THE MAN who intends to purchase me strides into the room what must be only a few minutes later, shedding his coat. He doesn't have to utter a word for Boris to grab it from him and hang it on a nearby pyrite hat stand.

When the client looks at me, his eyes peel me apart. He's the sort of handsome that's off-putting. Symmetrical in a way that's almost dizzying. Unnatural, though his ears are as rounded as mine. His ash-colored hair is perfectly combed out from a straight part down one side, the hair trimmed close to his head below the part. His jaw is firm, and altogether he has the look of someone who is used to getting what he wants.

Must be nice.

"It's rather subtle, isn't it?" the potential buyer says, tracing a cold, pointed fingernail down my mark.

"True, but with the proper attire, I'm sure it could be made to stand out, Master Vulcan," says Zane, the man clearly in charge of this enterprise.

"I didn't say it was a bad thing," the buyer—Vulcan—says. "There's a place for subtle beauty. With my collection being as extravagant as it is, there's certainly a place for a piece that's more…subdued."

For some reason, I don't get the impression that this man is an artist looking for inspiration.

Zane opens his mouth, but his client cuts him off. "Leave us. I wish to speak to the girl alone."

Zane hurriedly scuttles out, leaving me alone in this man's presence. Unprotected against his cool, assessing stare. I close my eyes, readying the little corner in the back of my mind, the place I'll escape to so I don't have to witness what this man does to me.

"There is no need for that yet, my dear," says Vulcan. "I wouldn't dare take you in a place like this. You are too precious to be treated like a common whore."

"Just an uncommon whore then," I say, surprising myself with my boldness. I'm past the point of feeling. Cold and numb, and unfiltered. "How delightful."

I wait for Vulcan to slap me, but he doesn't. "I understand your reticence. You'll hate me for a time; they all do. But you'll come around."

"You sound so confident," I say.

The man offers me a noxious smile. "I can only form my opinions based on the evidence provided. My muses are happy. They live a life of luxury they never would have dreamt of on the streets."

"Those men didn't get me from the streets," I say.

He lets out a calculated laugh. "No. Just the belly of a pirate ship. I'm sure you were treated quite well there."

My chest aches. Astor hadn't touched me. Well, other than throwing me on the ground and yelling at me to get up.

"I will make life easy for you, you know," Vulcan says. There's something genuine about this man. Like he truly believes himself to be kind, generous. Benevolent. It's unsettling—he's convinced himself so entirely, it's difficult not to believe him. "You say you didn't come from the streets. You were an aristocrat then?"

"Once."

"Tell me. What would your life have consisted of had you stayed?"

I frown, not liking where this path is heading.

"You would have been married, would you not?" he asks. "Probably to a man much older than yourself? One who would use you to produce an heir who would one day control you as much as his father did?"

My mind flashes back to Lord Credence snaking his hands down my backside at the masquerade.

"He may or may not have been kind," Vulcan continues, "but likely not. Men of the aristocracy rarely are. I am offering you no less than what you would have received as the wife of a nobleman. You might lack the title, but you will have everything your heart desires. I will ensure it."

"And I'll be one of many in your collection?" I ask, unable to help how my voice wavers.

A sly smile curves his lips, revealing the perfect points of his canines. "They are all as close as sisters, I assure you. I imagine you've not had many of those."

"You claim you offer me a desirable life, yet you would treat me as a pet."

"Pets, my dear," says Vulcan, stroking the ridge of my collarbone, "often have more desirable lives than wives, do they not?"

I find that words leave me, even as his assertions cut to my soul. It shouldn't be tempting, that kind of life—and it isn't. But it gnaws at me—the way there was a time in my life when his offer would have seemed attractive. When I was at my lowest, back when I would trade every last bit of myself just to find someone who would take me, who would rescue me from my Fate.

I think there was a time when the idea of only being subjected to one man's whims and desires might have been appealing to me. Not having to worry about being shuffled from one pair of hands to the next. Assurance that his lust would be occupied elsewhere most of the time. That there were other women who would share the burden of pleasing him. Other women who understood.

But that was before Peter, before I found my Mate. Back when I'd lost hope of ever finding him. And though my hope has been rattled, though I know the chance of a future between Peter and me is slim, I can't help but grasp for that sliver of light. The future where I find a way to break his curse. Where he and John and Michael and the Lost Boys can find happiness. Somewhere, somehow.

If Peter hadn't come for me the night I plunged myself overboard, I might be tempted to go with this stranger willingly. Then again, if Peter hadn't come for me, I'd be dead.

But Peter is out there. He'll track down Astor's ship, and when he discovers I'm missing, there will be a reckoning.

This stranger's blood will mingle with shadows when Peter gets ahold of him. He might have permitted Astor to have me for a time, but I'd only felt betrayed because I'd forgotten that Peter knew Astor. The captain has done nothing to hurt me. Peter must have known that I'd be safe when he gave me up, though I hadn't seen it at the time.

But this man.

This man, Peter doesn't know.

I weigh my options. Boris warned me to be likable, desirable to this client. Said the others wouldn't be so gentle with me. Is it better to feign compliance to this man, or disgust him and place my bets on the hope that Peter will find me before I'm sold off to someone else?

As if in answer, wraiths rise from underneath the sheets of the nearby bed, forming the figures of women sold like goods and the men who got their money's worth out of them. The shadows whimper, but none of them scream. Their almost-silent cries fill my ears until I can hardly stand it.

Maybe it's just my body's panicked response, wishing to avoid the danger that's more imminent, but a little voice whispers in my head. *Be what he wants. At least he'll take you out of this place. At least he'll have to move you. Give you a chance to escape.*

"You won't hurt me, then?" I ask, allowing the trembling to suffuse my tone. It's easy, when my limbs are rattling against the table, my body's reaction to fear unaffected by the rushweed.

"Never," says the man, cupping my cheek as if to show how gentle he is. "By this time next year, you'll be glad for your decision. You'll accompany me to events and operas and see the wives who hide their bruises underneath their cuffs and collars and paint. And you'll be the one pitying them."

I let out a regretful exhale, thankful at least not to be breathing in the heady perfume of the room for a moment. It's making me dizzy.

Barely, just barely, my finger scrapes against the cold facade of the table. Of my own accord.

Hope buds between my ribs. It's not much. The ability to wriggle my fingers won't free me from Vulcan's grasp. But it's more than I had only seconds ago.

"Promise me you'll be good?" he says, lifting my chin.

The words are too familiar. As if I've uttered them before. "I'll be good."

VULCAN LEAVES me with the servant Boris, insistent that he dress me more appropriately. Apparently he's hosting an all-night revelry at his manor and I'm to be in attendance—to be presented, I imagine—and the journey is without an adequate place to stop and prepare me beforehand.

The result is that Boris and Zane have to pull a double shift just to fix me up. It's a humiliating process. My sodden clothes are ripped from my body like they're cobwebs from the doorway of a treasure trove. Though the only touching the two men do is to bathe me, there's a vulnerability about it, being unable to move, that makes me want to scream. When they're not looking, I test out different muscles, seeing which ones will move. So far, all my fingers are functional, and my left wrist, along with my ankles and toes. It's not much to work with, but it's better than nothing.

Once the two men have dressed me in a fine silk gown Vulcan brought in case their given attire didn't suit—apparently it didn't—I decide to take a gamble, figuring once they have me inside the man's carriage, the chances of escape will be minimal.

"Please. Please don't sell me to him," I whisper. "Anyone else."

I try to squeeze tears out of my eyes, but I'm either too numb or too buzzing with adrenaline to cry at the moment.

Zane scoffs, but Boris offers me a sympathetic pat on the shoulder. "It'll be alright, missus. You're one of the lucky ones. He won't hurt you."

I don't bother explaining to him how his definition of hurt is rather narrow.

"Please. Please, I don't want to go with him. The things he said he'd do to me. Just send me with someone else, please. Even if they hit me,

I don't mind. Don't make me go with someone so vile, who's going to make me..." I trail off at just the right time, then start wailing. "Please, I just wanted to be a wife."

Boris's eyes go wide, and he exchanges a look with Zane, who looks about ready to roll his eyes. "Naïve aristocrat," Zane mumbles under his breath, as if he thinks I can't hear him.

"It's not her fault her parents didn't tell her how babies were made," says Boris, but Zane appears unaffected.

"Please," I cry again.

"Sorry, little lady," says Boris. "I'm afraid payment has already been exchanged."

I let my face fall, like I've been struck. "Can't you just give it back? Surely there's someone else who would pay you more."

Zane snorts. "Your buyer's the best-paying man in the kingdom."

"I thought you said he underpays," I say, sniffling. "I thought you said it wasn't going to be enough to cover the lamps."

Zane's face goes hard. "Mind your own business, or you'll get yourself into trouble where you're going."

A lump forms in my throat, so I let myself sob. This next part is going to be tricky. I need to be what Zane wants, while also getting him to believe that my plan was his idea all along.

"I'll run away," I threaten. "I'll run away, and then he'll blame you."

Zane rolls his eyes. "That's not how this works, child. Once money has changed hands and you're in his possession, you're his responsibility, not ours."

Boris ruffles his brow. "It would only hurt you to run away, missus. I'm telling you, Vulcan's the kindest master you're going to get. In a city like this, you'll just be plucked off the streets by someone less generous. Other places won't give you to a good home, just chain you to the bed. Or sell you to a foreigner where you can't be traced. You don't want to be sold again."

I let out a shuddering sigh, but allow myself one peek at Zane. Something has kindled in his expression, his interest clearly piqued by the servant's last statement.

Sold again.

Excitement swells in my heart, making it hammer against my chest. It's a long shot that the master will take my bait, even less chance that the plan will actually work. But men drowning in debt have a tendency to put on blinders and do anything they can to get out of it, so if I'm right...

When they finish dressing me, the master dismisses his servant from the room, his beady eyes still examining me, a scheme playing out in his head.

One that I put there.

CHAPTER 16

WENDY

The buyer is stroking my cheek, planting a wet kiss on the corner of my quivering lips, when something crashes into the carriage.

My body goes flying into the roof, tumbling as the carriage rolls over. Pain pounds my limbs as the carriage rattles me, shaking me like Michael does his hands when he's excited or frightened. When the carriage finally comes to a rest, it takes me a moment to take in my surroundings.

The carriage is a wreck, Vulcan limp, his head hanging to the side as it presses against the carriage door, now resting on the ground. I can't tell if he's dead. I don't really care. There's a roar of panic outside on the street, people scrambling to not only help but leer at the tragic accident.

Outside, someone shouts for everyone to clear the way. A pause, then the door above me flings open, hinges squealing in protest. Inside stares an unfamiliar face—thin and unassuming, slightly balding. He's the type of man you'd hire to do work you want to go unnoticed. The kind of face even witnesses wouldn't recall.

I feign confusion as he reaches in and loops his arms underneath my armpits. In the hours since being poisoned, the ability to use my limbs has returned, though I'm still weak. Teeth must have given me a low dose, or a diluted one. As the man struggles to haul me from the cabin, it takes all my self-control to maintain my dead weight and keep from assisting him. I'm caught between wanting to escape the scene before Vulcan wakes and needing the henchman to believe I'm still unable to move.

When I finally surface, the balding man heaving, I let out the tiniest of sobs, shaking off the awareness that if something had gone awry, I'd be dead.

Around me, villagers gather to speculate underneath dingy faerie dust lamps. We must be a village or two over from where Zane runs his business. That would make sense, given we'd been in the carriage for almost an hour. Zane would have wanted to make sure the accident happened outside of city limits, to keep Vulcan from suspecting him.

Assuming Vulcan's still alive.

I hadn't bothered checking.

"It's alright, I've got her," says the weaselly man pulling me from the wreckage. I lean my head onto his shoulder, limping as he keeps his hand around my waist to help me walk. I'm sure that in a few hours, everything will ache, but right now I'm operating on adrenaline. I allow my head to loll around until I can see back to the carriage. The wreckage is awful. A mare slammed into it, now neighing as she kicks her feet wildly in the streets, bystanders steering clear. I can't help but notice that Vulcan's driver is pinned under the carriage, his eyes wide and empty to the dark sky.

Guilt rolls over in my stomach.

I did that. I planted this idea in Zane's mind.

As Zane's henchman drags me through the streets, drawing me away from the crowds, I wonder if anyone will notice.

No one does.

When the shadows of a dark alley obscure us, I notice another carriage parked there, waiting for us. I'll have to be quick.

Thus far, I've exaggerated my lack of control over my limbs. They're still weak, some of my control over them lost under the influence of the rushweed, but not to the extent that I've made my enslaver-turned-rescuer believe.

When the henchman forces me into the carriage, I make him work for it, tripping and fumbling, making him drag my limp, dead weight into the cabin. He's human, and certainly not in his first half of life, judging by the number of wrinkles forming on his balding head. By the time he's got me onto the floorboard of the carriage, he's huffing and doesn't have the energy to scramble over my body and drag me into my seat.

Instead of climbing over me, he slams the door, dousing the inside of the cab in shadows. The latch clicks into place behind me. Mercifully, there's no secondary click of a lock. Cheek pressed against the wooden floorboards, I wait for the sound of the henchman's huffs to round the carriage.

I'll have a very small window to make this work. My muscles protest, but I use the seat to drag myself to my feet.

As soon as I hear the man reach the anterior of the carriage and tell the driver I'm secured, I unlatch the door on my side, willing my legs not to give out on me when I open the door and jump.

The impact should be simple, but it feels as if I've fallen from the top of the nearest thatch roof. It doesn't matter though. The aching in my muscles will be nothing compared to the pain of the punishment awaiting me if I'm caught.

The henchman is still talking to the carriage driver. "Just give me a moment, why don't you? Need to stretch my legs before getting crammed back into that cab."

"Zane said—"

"Yes, well, Zane isn't who had to drag that girl through the streets or drive that horse into a carriage rounding a corner, now is he?" The henchman adds, under his breath, "I'm getting too old for this."

Relieved at the henchman's stalling, I limp down the back of the alley, following the gentle glow of light from what I hope is the opposite street. If this alley turns out to be a dead end, I'm in trouble, but I don't allow my mind down that sullen path.

Once I reach the end of the alley, I turn the corner and toward the light, my stomach clenching when I realize the light is from a faerie dust lamp hanging over a doorway at the back of a building that jams up right next to another.

There's no way out.

As of now, I'm out of sight. I rush toward the nearby door, still limping, and tug at the handle, but it's locked. Around the corner, the henchman swears loudly.

He knows I'm gone. And that I couldn't have gone far.

For a fleeting moment, I wonder if my punishment will be lessened if I stumble back, head hanging, and turn myself in. If he'll keep my almost-escape to himself, thinking it'll reflect poorly on his expertise that he let me escape to begin with.

It could work, but then I'd be in a worse position than what I began with, property to be sold to whichever male bids the highest.

No. No, I won't turn myself in. I'll fight back. Make the henchman kill me if I have to.

I fist my hands at my sides and sneak to the corner. If I can't be strong, at least I'll be unexpected. As the henchman approaches, chanting, "Come out, little girl. We know you can't have gone far," I prepare myself.

When he reaches the corner, he makes the mistake of looking the wrong way, and I lunge. I go for his neck, wrapping my arms around it as tightly as I can manage, using my body weight against him as I hang on his back, cutting off his airway. The man flails, thankfully already winded. When he backs up and slams both of us against the wall, stars sparkle across my vision. I let out a cry, partly from the blunt force to my skull, partly because the man digs his long, dirty fingernails into my forearms, drawing blood.

Still, I hold tight, running on the adrenaline of terror and the desperation not to be hauled back to that awful brothel. With each time he slams me backward up against the wall, I count. One. Two. Three, four, five. I've no idea how long it takes a man to lose consciousness from strangulation, but as he pounds my already sore body against the wall, my grip around him loosens. With every blow, I have to remind myself that the more he exerts himself, the quicker he'll pass out.

Down the alley, the driver calls out, "Aye? Found her yet?"

The henchman rasps in reply, and I have no idea if the driver can hear our struggle. It ends up not mattering, because the henchman slams me again, and this time my skull cracks against brick. Pain lances through me, and my hands slip. The harsh exterior of the brick building scrapes my back as I fall, trapped between the henchman and the wall. When he turns to face me, his eyes are storming with vengeance.

"I oughta kill you right here and now," he says, heaving in panicked breaths as he glares down at me. When he props himself on his knees, he examines me like a hawk, cocking his head as he presses his hand to my throat and squeezes.

The muscles in my chest lurch, grasping for air, but they're met with the stricture of this man's hand at my throat. I can't breathe, and my body realizes it quickly. I flail, just like the man was doing only moments ago, overexerting himself. I find I can't help the useless reflex.

"You're not worth your trouble," he says. "You know what I'll do? I'll tell them you died in the carriage crash. I'll tell them Vulcan slit your throat once he realized what had happened so you couldn't get away. Didn't want anyone else to have what was his."

Tears bloom at the corners of my eyes, trickling down my cheeks. I don't want to die like this, discarded in a dank alley for the rats to get me. An unknown corpse no one will report to John and Michael, leaving them to always wonder what happened to me.

Still, it's better than the brothel.

"Don't. Touch. Her."

The voice rings out from the alley, rage brimming inside a steel furnace. When Astor steps from the shadows, his figure is as sharp as ever. Not for the first time, I consider how it almost hurts to look at him, his green eyes blazing with menace.

The henchman doesn't move, but there's enough command in

Astor's voice that he at least releases his grip enough for me to breathe. I gasp, gulping down air as soon as I can get some.

"You're still touching her," says Astor, tapping his foot.

"This one doesn't belong to you," says the henchman, his voice more assured than his face, which is breaking out in sweat at his brow.

Astor doesn't miss a beat. "I'm aware of that."

His eyes flick toward mine, just for a moment. Just long enough to make me wonder if I imagined it. When he clucks his tongue, Charlie and Maddox step from the shadows, flanking Astor on either side.

Slowly, the man, eyes trained on Maddox's bulging arms, extracts his hand from my throat, though when he stands, it's between me and Astor.

"I can't return to my master empty-handed, you understand."

Astor's smile is oily. "I'll ensure you don't. But you won't be returning to your master with her."

The henchman's eyes flick over to Charlie. "That one, then. In exchange?"

If Charlie is fazed, she doesn't show it. Her face remains as still as a doe in the wood.

"Who do you work for?" asks Astor.

The henchman laughs. "As if I would tell the likes of you. He'd have me killed."

Astor flashes him a razored grin. "You're a town away. Good thing you have a head start."

The henchman blanches as next to Astor, Maddox starts playing with his blade. He really does look more menacing than I realized, all brawn and wicked amusement. The henchman must think so too, because he spouts out, "Give me your word you'll let me go if I give you the girl."

Astor laughs. "You're not in the position to bargain, I'm afraid. If I were you, I'd tell us who you're working for and take my chances."

The henchman chews on the inside of his cheek. He must recognize that the best he can do in this situation is to try to please Astor, so he says, "Zane. Owns the Marble House."

"That's all? There's no one else?"

The henchman shakes his head.

Maddox and Astor share a practiced glance, and Maddox steps forward, knife glinting. But then Astor puts a hand out, stopping Maddox.

"No need," he says. "Get Wendy out of here. You too, Charlie. I'll attend to this one."

Charlie and Maddox are at my side in an instant, Maddox pulling me into his arms.

When the henchman begs for his life, Captain Astor's laugh echoes through the alley. "You might have considered that the first time I asked you to stop touching her."

CHAPTER 17

WENDY

Once, after my mother had allowed a particularly grisly suitor into the parlor with me, then left us alone for the better part of an hour, I'd found her in the wine cellar and begged her to end this plan of hers to find me a husband to break my curse.

Blood was still staining the fabric of my dress from where the man had bitten my shoulder. The pain of it was nothing compared to the hollowness in my chest.

I'd squared my shoulders and summoned that last bit of courage left in my bloodstream. When I spoke, I hadn't sounded brave, nor had I sounded at all sure of myself. "I'm afraid this plan of ours"—why I'd said ours, to this day I still can't fathom—"is proving ineffective."

My mother had just stared at the dusty wine bottles, refusing to look at me. She never could bring herself to look at me immediately after the parlor. The next morning, she would be herself again, as if nothing had ever happened. But tonight I was dirty—a reminder of her failures as a mother.

"Oh, Wendy, my girl. Don't be so pessimistic. Lord Erasmus is noble. He understands his responsibility to you."

I fought back the urge to argue that noble men don't take advantage of their potential brides, and continued. "Mother, if I can't find a husband before my twentieth birthday—"

She snapped her head toward me, an ever-present smile on her face. At least she was looking at me now. "My sweet girl, we have years to find you a husband."

Years. Years of enduring the groping hands of hungry men. I wasn't sure I'd make it years.

"John's found a book," I'd explained, my voice warbling. "He says the fae are vulnerable to iron."

"The fae are vulnerable to nothing, my dear, except upholding bargains," said my mother, still searching for the perfect nightcap.

"Yes," I'd said, fighting to keep my voice level. "But if we cannot fulfill our side of the bargain, I should like to be prepared."

My mother had cocked her head at me with a thin-lipped smile. Then she'd brushed her hand against my cheek, stroking my Mating Mark. "My dear. I wish it were so. I wish I could train you to defend yourself against him. You have no idea how often I've imagined fighting him off myself. But we are not made to fight. Our bodies are at too much of a disadvantage. We must learn to resist in other ways. Our wit, our..." She bit her lip and sighed. "It would be simpler if you could fight your way out of this. But we must be wiser than that. We must be what they want us to be."

Her words had landed in my pride, pummeled as it already was. I hadn't been foolish enough to believe I could win a fistfight between myself and the fae Shadow Keeper. I'd only wanted something to give me an advantage, the element of surprise. A weakness I could exploit when it came time to run.

That conversation in the wine cellar is all I can think about as Charlie and Maddox carry me by carriage back to the ship. Being what men wanted me to be had only gotten me so far. Sure, it had provided me an opportunity to slip from Vulcan's grasp. But even then, I'd eventually been cornered in an alleyway, another man's hand at my throat. And there was nothing I could do to escape. No words I could speak to outsmart a man who couldn't be reasoned with.

My mother would have wanted me to go with Vulcan. To be what he wanted me to be, too. She would have thought I'd be safe there.

Charlie and Maddox each fuss over me in their own ways—Maddox constantly asking if I need water, like that will somehow fix anything that's happened over the past night. Charlie pulls my head into her lap and tells me to prop my feet on Maddox's legs, who doesn't protest. I try to fall asleep, but there's little use, so I ask questions.

"How'd you find me?" *And why did Peter not?*

"The captain saw Teeth passing you off to the traffickers," Charlie explains. "He tried to get to you, but by the time he cut through the attackers, you were gone."

"Teeth wasn't though," says Maddox. "He was still trying to escape in one of the safety boats, but he knew the captain was coming after him. His hands were shaking so bad he couldn't get the knot untied that secures the boat. He told the captain everything. Apparently when we made port in Morella, he contacted a band of traffickers. Told them we had a girl with a Mating Mark. Offered to get you off the ship if they could cause a distraction. So they leaked the information to a band of pirates they knew would go after you."

Charlie flits her hand. "Can no one even be bothered to hire their own mercenaries these days?"

Maddox continues. "All the while, the traffickers were at the ready to steal you away. Suppose Teeth thought telling us was his best chance at keeping his life."

Charlie lets out a wry laugh. "He did manage to extend it by several hours. We needed him to lead us to the traffickers. By the time we got there, you were gone. One of the servants must have taken a liking to you, because he told us the name of the buyer and where he'd be keeping you. Even told us of his master's plot to steal you back. So we came and got you."

She says it so simply. Effortlessly. Like coming to get me was a given.

"You make it sound like it was easy," I say.

Maddox glances at Charlie. "She might have left out some details about how Astor went about questioning the traffickers."

That's fine with me. I don't really want to know. "Did you see any other girls there?"

Charlie strokes my hair. "Evans came with us. Astor had him stay behind and get them to safety. He'll meet us back on the ship."

The muscles in my shoulders relax a bit. "And Teeth?"

"Once Teeth led us to the traffickers," Charlie says, "well, let's just say he'd outlived his usefulness."

ONCE WE'RE BACK on the *Iaso*, Charlie helps me bathe and change. I barely register the boards that someone has nailed into the wall to repair the hole where the cannonball went careening through the cabin before I crawl into bed and doze off.

I sleep the day away, though my rest is punctuated by dreams of men either stealing me from my bed or crawling into it. Maybe that's why, when I wake and discover it's nighttime again, I find myself searching for the captain.

"You won't find him out here," says Maddox when he finds me on deck. His tone is sly, though it's doing a poor job of concealing the concern in his gray eyes. "Try the map room."

The map room. The room where I first spied on the captain and learned of his plan to fool the Carlisles.

When the door creaks open, Astor is leaning over his spread of maps, palms splayed atop them. He opens his mouth to say, "I'm not to be disturbed at the m—" but stops himself mid-sentence, ears flickering.

"Darling," he says before even looking up. When he finally does, his gaze is curious rather than cold. He doesn't ask me why I'm here. Just waits expectantly.

With Peter, everything is a game. With Astor, everything is a challenge.

I shuffle over to him, knitting my fingers together in a loose fist in front of me. "I need to ask you something."

"Then you should ask it rather than waste your words and both of our time," he says, though not as cruelly as his words might otherwise suggest. It's more like he's nudging me in a more assertive direction.

I reach for where I've rehearsed the request in my mind, but where there should be a script, I find emptiness. I don't know why I'm like this—why I can assemble a sound argument when I'm alone, then find myself flummoxed once it comes time to spout the actual words. Feeling stupid, I flush.

It's a simple request, one I'm fairly sure he won't deny, yet still, I feel like I've hit an impenetrable wall in trying to ask it.

Astor cocks his brow, and it's enough to set me off.

I punch him in the face.

Well, that's a bit too generous. I attempt to punch him in the face. He catches my fist in his much larger palm before I get anywhere near him, his jaw ticking with an emotion I can't read. It's not anger though. I've seen the captain angry, and this isn't it.

"And here I was," he drawls, "thinking I've been behaving myself as of late. What have I done this time? I must admit, usually I know."

Reasons rattle between the edges of painful memories, but I can't form them into coherent words. It's the tenor of my mother's voice telling me what kind of things men might want from me that won't leave evidence behind. It's the touch of velvet against my splayed hands, underneath my painted fingernails. It's the wishing to be stolen away so that I'll no longer have to fear my fate, only know it. It's Vulcan's fingers tracing my jawline, the temptation to heed his words, just stop fighting. It's all of that, and it's too much to put into words.

So I punch at Astor again, this time with my weak hand, hoping he'll understand.

He catches it—it would be a shock if he hadn't—then cranes his neck to the side. "Is this it?" he asks. "Is this what you want?"

There's a knot forming in my throat. Because this isn't at all what I want, not really. What I want is for nothing bad to have ever happened to me. What I want is to have never known a man's greedy touch. What I want is not to be terrified all the time. What I want is for my parents to be alive—but not be them. To be alive, and to be versions of themselves that would have protected me. To have been thrown into an impossible situation and gotten it right.

I can't have any of that.

"This is the best I can do," I say. "This is the best I can settle for."

I expect a reprimand, but I don't get it. A wave of understanding washes over the captain. In a flash, it's gone, replaced by a tactical practicality. The fierce facade of someone who knows the hairline difference between succumbing to the blade and conquering it.

I brace myself to be thrown to the floor, already willing my bones to get back up, but the captain has other plans. Instead of shoving me down, he pulls me into him, so that my chin rests against his heaving chest. His grip slides on both sides so that it's firm around my wrists. The feeling of being constrained like this makes me want to gag. Makes me think of Teeth's hand on me, my inability to escape. Shadows speckle my vision, but the captain just whispers, "Look at me."

I do.

I do, and it hurts.

Astor is the rugged sort of beautiful. There's not a single soft feature on his face. His tanned skin is slightly weathered, a byproduct of years at sea. His jaw is set, its sharp angle visible even under his dark beard—he keeps it trimmed so neatly. When my gaze lifts, I feel the sting of the needle that pierced the pointed tip of his ear, where his golden earring glints.

But his beauty isn't what hurts. It's the way he's looking at me like I'm the one capable of wounding him.

"Where are my weaknesses?" he asks. I can't help but notice the way his eyes trail my cheekbone, my nose, down to my lips.

His breathing quickens.

I try to angle my knee toward his groin, but he's gripping me too close for me to get a good shot. My efforts result in a weak jab against his thigh, one he barely seems to notice.

"Look again," he says.

I jump, thinking to slam my head into his, but he's a head taller than me, so that's bound to fail. When I stomp on his boots, they're plated with steel.

"Not there," he whispers.

Before I know what I'm doing, I'm pushing myself onto my toes. Astor's craning his neck over me. The movement has his chin grazing my forehead, his mouth at the crown of my head.

When I tip my head back, his eyelids are heavy, obscuring the upper half of his beautiful green eyes. He looks drunk, and though he tightens his grip on my wrists, I know it's only to steady himself. To hide the trembling that's crept into his fingertips, his muscles.

"Where then?" I venture to ask, half breathless.

His fingers trail my wrist, up my palm, across my fingertips. But then his touch finds my ring finger, the cold metal of Peter's emerald ring.

The tension between us snaps.

Astor skates his hand back down to my wrist. "My thumbs," he says, voice now as serious as it is disinterested.

I blink. "What?"

"The weakness you're looking for," he explains, words coming out rushed. He nods toward his grip around my wrist. "It's by itself, doesn't have anything else to support it. If you shift all of your weight there, your attacker will have a difficult time holding on."

I nod, grateful the strain of trying to get out of Astor's grip must be masking the heat on my face. It's more difficult than Astor makes it out to be and takes me shifting my feet and body weight, rolling my wrists at just the correct angle.

Eventually, he lets go, but I have a feeling it's not because I overpowered him.

"Well done, D—Wendy," he says, swallowing as he returns his attention to the map stretched across the table. "Now, if you don't mind, I truly was busy when you arrived."

There's no harshness in his voice, but I'm mortified all the same.

. . .

I'M HARDLY aware of my short journey back to my and Charlie's cabin. So oblivious am I to my surroundings, so embarrassed by my encounter with the captain, that I don't notice that I'm not alone in the room until Charlie's voice rips me back to the present.

"Wendy? What are you doing?"

What am I doing? I glance down, almost surprised to find my fingers unraveling the pouch of faerie dust Peter gave to me the night I threw myself overboard. I'd hidden it under the bed, and it's been a nightly battle to keep it there.

The soft, fine powder already coats my fingertips. I can almost taste its sweetness on the back of my tongue.

Charlie, standing over me from behind, swoops in and wrenches the pouch from my hands. "Go wash your hands off," she says. When I don't move, stunned just as much by the fact I hadn't even realized what I was doing as I am by getting caught, she stuffs the pouch into her pocket. Then she drags me by the wrist over to the water basin. She doesn't move until she deems my hands sufficiently scrubbed.

"I'm sorry," I mutter, still feeling as if I'd been sleepwalking.

Charlie sighs, tugging at the end of her braid. "You've had a rather awful few days." She chews on her lip, hands on her hips, then flicks her head to the side. "Come on. Actually," she says, "meet me on deck."

Too ashamed of my lack of self-control to argue, I do as I'm told. On the way, my mind races, trying to account for the time between leaving the captain's cabin and the moment I sifted the pouch of faerie dust out from underneath the bed.

By the time I reach the deck, Charlie isn't far behind me. She comes ambling up next to me, pouch in hand, the loose hairs framing her face whipping around in the night's cool breeze. It's the type of cold that should feel invigorating. I just feel exposed.

She beckons me to follow her to a section of the deck railing out of sight from the night's crew. Then she hands me the pouch. "Go on, then."

I blink, peering over the railing down at the foaming black waves. The rocking of the ship is making me nauseous, or perhaps it's simply the compilation of the last few days' events.

The pouch grows heavy in my hand. My mind races, thumbing through my options for any possible scenario that would play out with me successfully getting the faerie dust back to our cabin. But Charlie is staring at me intently, and I'm not talented enough at sleight-of-hand to switch the pouch out with something else.

Charlie sighs, though it's more patient than not. "I'll do it for you if that's what you need. But it would be best if you did it."

Peter had wanted me to have this, but there's no way of explaining that to Charlie. No way to tell her about my attempt to take my own life because of the wraiths, not without betraying Peter visited me.

I could throw Charlie overboard.

The waves are angry tonight, crates sliding across the deck every few minutes. The wind is howling. It's unlikely anyone would hear it happen. And Charlie wouldn't be expecting it. It's doubtful I could overpower her otherwise, but aided by the element of surprise...

"Wendy?"

Shame and realization wash over me in equal measure. I shove the murderous thoughts back down, horrified they even popped into my mind.

"Right," I say, hands shaking as I hold the pouch over the railing. I will my fingers to let go. Such a simple motion, but they seem locked in place. Like the faerie dust itself holds the key and has no intention of sharing.

"It's the only thing that helps," I whisper, not really intending for Charlie to hear.

"I know," she says. "But we'll find you other things. I promise."

I let go.

THE NEXT DAY, Maddox informs me that he's been assigned to teach me to defend myself.

CHAPTER 18

WENDY

"Well, you have excellent grip strength," says Maddox, clearly stretching for something positive to say.

Our first training session started an hour ago. It hasn't gone well. In that time, he's almost cut my arm off twice with blows I didn't have the strength to parry, nor the speed to avoid.

"Maddox here is too optimistic," says Charlie, perched on the edge of the ship watching us like we're here for entertainment. "He starts everyone off like this: way in over their head."

Maddox rolls his eyes then offers me a wink. "Charlotte is just bitter because I gave her a paper cut on our first day of training."

Charlie guffaws. "A paper cut? It went down to the bone."

"That's not how I remember it."

"That's because your brain magically erases any negative memories. We had to dock for a fortnight until the healers could extract the infection. I thought for sure I was going to be left behind."

"And did we leave you behind, Charlotte?" says Maddox.

Her lip twitches up as she kicks her heels against the edge of the boat. "No."

"Then I'm not sure what you're complaining about."

I'd be laughing, except my ribs hurt from where Maddox slammed me across the chest earlier. Thankfully, he'd had the sage wisdom to switch to a blunt weapon by that point.

"This is hopeless," I say, resigned to the fact that there's little I can do to avoid my frequent kidnapping.

"Nah," says Maddox, poking me in the side with the blunt edge of his sword. "I wasn't kidding about the grip strength. You haven't dropped your weapon once. Even when I've landed a blow and knocked the breath out of you. That's more than some can say."

"Yes, I'm sure my ability to hold on to my hilt for long periods of time is going to really come in handy," I say, tugging my arms upward to keep the short sword from dragging on the ground. Even holding it in front of my chest in the stance Maddox taught me is a labor. "I'm hardly able to keep a defensive stance for more than a few minutes."

"Unless you're going into battle anytime soon, a few minutes is all you need."

"Enough time to escape. Right," I say, trying and failing to make the words seem comforting. "One would think that all that climbing I did would prepare me more for this," I say.

Charlie shrugs. "Climbing's mostly in the legs."

IT TAKES me finally dropping my short sword and almost slicing Maddox's foot off for him to end our training session for the day. Thankful for an opportunity to collapse into bed, I make my way for my and Charlie's room, but she bounces in front of me, blocking my path.

"Where do you think you're going?"

"Somewhere my muscles can sufficiently melt," I say, to which Charlie tsks.

Charlie is under the impression that I'm depressed.

Granted, staying in bed despite the location of the sun in the sky or the quality of the weather for the past few weeks, except for my brief hiatus to train with Maddox, was probably what gave her that impression. In truth, my brief flare of bravery in approaching the captain about training me had been a short-lived flicker that had soon been doused in the hopelessness of my situation.

"I don't think so," says Charlie, motioning me to follow her deeper into the hull of the ship.

I try to track our path, but the inside of the ship might as well be a labyrinth with how many "shortcuts" Charlie takes through strange spaces—she even has me climbing through a vent at one point, which is more fun than I care to admit.

Eventually, we make our way back up a ladder hanging down from the deck above, and I'm left to wonder why we went so deep into the ship in the first place.

"Surely there's a more efficient way to get around," I say. "Unless the person who engineered this ship also wrote mazes for the paper."

Charlie flashes me a grin as she slides a brass key into a lock and opens a creaky door leading into a dark, long hall. "There is a more efficient way to get here. You're just not allowed to know it. Captain's orders."

"Is he always this paranoid about the aristocrats he kidnaps?" I ask, rolling my eyes. "What does he think I'm going to do?"

"Nothing, I'm sure. It's not as if you've ever escaped him before. Or managed to keep him prisoner for weeks. Or kneaded the mind of a brothel owner in your hands like it was made of dough."

I stop, blinking. "You're making all that sound much more impressive than it actually was. John—my brother—helped me escape Astor the night of the masquerade. And Astor was already unconscious when I bound him in Neverland. Otherwise, I never would have been able to incapacitate him. And the brothel owner wasn't exactly the most clever being I've encountered."

Charlie tosses her long, silky hair behind her shoulder. "The captain says you used to free-climb the outside of your parents' clock tower. You don't think that's gutsy?"

I flush, though I don't know why. "More like irresponsible."

"I think you'll find that on vessels such as this one, we have more pleasant vocabulary for the reckless among us," she says. "I would ditch the word 'irresponsible' if I were you. Leave it back with the aristocrats."

I bite the inside of my cheek, but I smile all the same as I examine our surroundings. The hall galley is long, with small square windows cut into the hull of the ship, each with a flap that closes over it. Only a few of them are open at the moment, enough to let the day's light in so no one has to light a lamp. It might not be the deck, but the taste of the salty sea finds my lips nonetheless, the careless crash of the waves beyond us filtering in through the windows.

My spirits have lifted already.

Lining the hall is a row of cannons, planted with even spaces in between like a farmer might sow seeds. Crew members tend to the cannons, cleaning out and oiling the barrels.

Charlie cocks her head toward a cannon with no one stationed at it. "Come here and I'll show you how to clean it," she says.

"Not how to fire it?" I ask.

She offers me a closed-mouthed smirk, her head bobbing. "Maybe. If I can convince the captain it's a good idea and not one that's going to land him in trouble."

I laugh at the ridiculousness of it all. I'm pretty sure I'm the least dangerous person ever to have graced the planks of this ship. Charlie must find the concept absurd too, as she lets an amused giggle escape her lips. "What does he think I'm going to do? Blow his head off?"

Charlie opens her mouth, then shuts it quickly.

"What?" I ask.

"It's just..." She leans in conspiratorially. "I'm not sure the captain's as much afraid of what you'll do with a weapon, but what it will do to him to see you wielding one."

I clear my throat and spin Peter's ring around my finger as one of the crew members behind us snickers.

As Charlie shows me how to care for the barrel of the cannon, I find it surprisingly relaxing, even the feel of grease against my hands.

"What made you want to be a gunner?" I ask.

Charlie lifts her brow. "What makes you think I had a choice? It was the only position available on the ship. And I needed a way out."

I don't ask what she needed a way out of. Her home city, perhaps? The memory of her parents' slaughter? Instead, I ask, "And the captain hired a disgraced aristocrat girl to be a gunner on his ship?"

Charlie shrugs, then sighs, running a greased hand through her hair. The motion leaves smudge marks against her forehead. "His crew happened to be docked in Xhana a few months after it happened. I'd been living on the streets, scrounging for food and begging for the mercy of the villagers, trying to hide from the people who murdered my family and overran their estate. When I met the captain, it was sheer happenstance. He was meeting with a merchant at a tavern in town. I'd come in, begging the establishment owner for a job. I was so hungry. He overheard me and ended his meeting early. Asked me if I learned quickly and if I was willing to put on some muscle to lift heavy objects. Said he only had one position available on his crew, and I'd have to get my hands dirty if I wanted it. I met him at the docks that night. Haven't looked back since."

I crane a brow at her. Something about her story doesn't quite add up. "The captain offered you a gunner position just because he heard you were looking for a job?" Surely he couldn't have been that desperate. Charlie's strong; there's no doubting that. But her strength doesn't compare to the fae crew members. If she'd been starving at the time, I'm sure she looked feeble. There's little I know about being a gunner, but I assume it takes more than a few days of training. Astor would have had to invest heavily in Charlie to make hiring her worth his while.

Charlie sighs, placing her hand on the barrel of the cannon and stroking it. "It wasn't just any job I'd been applying for. The tavern I met Astor in doubled as a brothel. And I was fourteen."

Shock drums through me. Not that a seedy brothel would take advantage of a starving fourteen-year-old girl like that, but that Astor, the man who had slaughtered my parents in front of me, had cared. Had even noticed. Not only that, but he'd given a job that involves heavy labor to a teenage girl, a fallen aristocrat, who, up to that point, had probably never lifted anything heavier than a paintbrush.

"It wasn't charity, though. Well, it was at the time, but I assure you,

I've made up for what must have seemed like a poor investment on his part in those first few months. Took me a while to get stronger. I was slow moving the cannonballs at first. But I worked harder than anyone else here. Stayed up tending to the cannons when all the others had gone to bed. Still do," she says. "Besides," she says, patting the cannon like it's a pet, "I'm happier doing this than I ever would have imagined. There's something about working with my hands. The exertion of it all." A soft smile breaks loose on Charlie's face. "I was always jittery back at home. I didn't have anywhere to focus my energy. Now, I do. And I like to think I'm good at it."

"You like it then?" I ask. "Being a gunner?"

Charlie nods. "Yeah. I..." She bites her lip, as if being transported back in time. "We're not as strong as them, you know. It doesn't matter how hard we train, how hard we fight. I could train for years, and Sorell—you know, the scrawny fae who works in the kitchens?— could still overpower me if he wanted." She runs her hand over the cannon affectionately. "But put me behind one of these, and none of that matters."

"It evens the playing field," I say, thinking of my inability to wrench myself from Teeth's grip the night he took me. "If only we could carry one of these around with us," I say.

Charlie's eyes flicker. "Yeah, if only."

"Remind me to flee the continent if you ever find a way to make a cannon portable," says a half-bemused voice.

Charlie and I turn to find Astor standing behind us, arms crossed and expression equally as perturbed, though I can't imagine why. I suppose his face is just stuck like that.

"I assume the fact that the two of you are cleaning out the barrels of the cannons means that Darling is sufficiently prepared for our meeting with the Carlisles," says Astor, managing to sound as if he actually assumes the opposite.

"You tested me yourself," I say, remembering, somewhat smugly, the night I'd caught Astor off guard by playing the type of woman I thought he might like. "Remember?"

Astor doesn't answer my question. Instead, he offers me a smile that's only fitting for a person one wishes to fail. "Make sure you dress the part," is all he offers.

I glance at Charlie, confused.

"Did you not inform her?" asks Astor, clearly annoyed.

"Inform me of what?"

Charlie doesn't pay me any attention. Instead, she addresses her captain. "I didn't want her to have all day to build it up in her mind."

A cold sweat breaks out on the back of my neck.

Astor rubs his brow between his fingers and groans.

"Charlie?" I grind her name through my teeth.

"Right. I might have forgotten to mention. We're approaching Laraeth."

Meaning I'll be dining with the Carlisles. And impersonating Cressida Rivers. Tonight.

CHAPTER 19

JOHN

*D*isappointment jabs at my side. Like when Father used to make me run with him in the morning and I always ended up with cramps.

So, Tink doesn't like it. I shouldn't care. It's not like I've stayed up until the wee hours of the night the past several days planning the perfect communication board for her. I'd had to recruit Benjamin for help—he's excellent at whittling, and my left hand presents a dexterity problem. I'd told him it was for Michael, of course. As much as I trust Benjamin to be well-meaning, he doesn't know when to keep quiet, and I don't want him knowing I'm making this for Tink and that information getting back to Peter. I'd ended up asking Benjamin for two boards. In truth, I'd wanted one for Michael as well, as his is collecting dust in Darling Manor. I'd claimed that it's useful to have one that's portable and one that stays in our room. Benjamin had over-delivered, presenting me with two wooden boards with carved inlets in which to place communication tiles.

Still, I'd put a lot of thought into the words (and symbols to match the words) that I'd had Benjamin carve into the wood.

A faint giggle echoes from behind the bars. Tink is watching me.

Laughing at me. When she sees I'm paying attention to her now, she pushes out her bottom lip in a dramatic pout.

Great, my prisoner is mocking me.

I'm afraid your son doesn't possess the presence befitting a male heir, I hear in the back of my mind.

I shouldn't have held onto the words of my father's advisor this long. I shake the voice, grasping at me from the past, out of my mind.

I release a slow exhale and adjust my glasses, still sliding down my nose. If only I'd remember to fix the wire frame, this wouldn't happen. I've just been so busy with everything else.

As if on cue, Tink pushes at the bridge of her nose, the space between her eyes crinkling. There's cruelty in her eyes when she opens them.

"Ah. Acting like a child today, I see," I say back, impressed with my ability to keep my voice unaffected. "Well, that's good, because since you don't like my communication board, we have to resort to childish drawings."

I push the journal back through the bars, which she plucks up with her hideously long fingernails.

Hideous is a strange word when referring to Tink. It truly only applies to her fingernails, nothing else. I note as much as she tucks the journal into her lap and draws her knees into herself, I assume to keep me from seeing whatever she's sketching. Like she doesn't want to give it away before the big reveal.

There's a softness that overcomes her usually harsh features as she draws. Maybe it's the way she bites her bottom lip in focus, or the slight crinkle on the skin between her eyebrows, but when Tink's focused, she almost looks pleasant.

Almost.

She's always pretty. Always beautiful. But never in an inviting way. That's probably fair, I remember with a sting of guilt. I've tortured her, after all. There's no reason for her to want me to look at her.

When she's done, she plops the quill back into the bottle, splashing ink on her already stained fingers, then waves the journal in the air like a fan. Once the sketch is dry, she hands it back over to me.

I'm not sure what I was expecting, but it wasn't for my bowels to turn inside out at the sight of the rendering.

It's a sketch of me. More accurately, it's a sketch of my corpse. A rather accurate rendering of what I might look like dead. And it's a sketch of Tink, too, munching on my arm like it's the perfect breakfast.

I look up at her over the journal. "I see you started with my already maimed hand," I say, holding up my left hand and my stump of a finger.

The caged faerie winks.

LATER THAT EVENING, I can't help but notice that Smalls is sulking in the Den.

"What's wrong, buddy?" I use the gentlest, most brotherly voice that I can. Like I would use with Michael, who sits beside me, lining up the peas he pocketed during dinner—organized largest to smallest, of course.

Smalls shoots me a look of suspicion. "Nothing," he says, pushing past me, his face reddening.

"That's not true," says Benjamin, without looking up from the toy boat he's whittling for Michael. "Smalls is upset because he's been leaving food out for Tink, and she hasn't come to get it in a while."

My stomach turns over, and I don't miss the way Simon, who has been tossing loose roots into the fire, perks to attention.

"Why are you leaving food out for Tink?" I ask, trying to keep my pitch from hiking.

Smalls turns around and shrugs, his shoulders slumping. "I dunno."

I turn to Benjamin for another answer, but he's back to whittling, his focus homed in on the anterior mast.

"Probably has a little crush on her, don't you, Smalls?" says Simon. Though his voice is just as cheerful as when we first arrived on the island, there's no missing that he's dropped several pounds, the way his fingers tap against his thighs. Perhaps he's still dealing with the aftereffects of killing Nettle in defense of the rest of us.

"No!" Smalls's face has flushed red, his quick outburst causing his hair to flurry up on his forehead a bit. "I just thought she might get hungry, that's all. And now that she hasn't picked up the food I set out..." He trails off, unwilling to finish the sentence.

Despite myself, a bit of sympathy flares up in my heart for the boy. I understand the aching disappointment that comes from failing to protect another. "I'm sure a faerie like Tink knows how to take care of herself," I say.

Smalls looks less than convinced, but more than that, he looks like there's something he's not telling me. He darts his gaze about the room, as if checking for the other boys' permission.

"She's not emotionally stable," Simon explains, noting the younger boy's distress. Even as he says it, something I can't quite place flashes across his face. A hint of irony in the way he chuckles and supports himself on his knee while sitting. I can't get a read on Simon lately. It's like he's still himself, just on the edge and at risk of teetering off. "Before Neverland, Peter took care of her. Made sure her needs were attended to."

I frown. The Tink I know can write, though not in any language I understand, and seems rather capable of taking care of herself. Though maybe she's afflicted with an illness that causes that to fluctuate. Or maybe Peter assumed Tink couldn't take care of herself because of her inability to speak vocally. Either way, it doesn't sit quite right with me.

"And once she got here?" I ask, uncomfortable with where my curiosity is coming from. Doing this for Wendy, I remind myself.

Simon sighs. "Peter tried, but she couldn't be reasoned with. She ran off, but still wanted him. Her moods were all over the place. He was worried she'd starve, forget to eat, that sort of thing. So he always left out food for her."

"Until?" I ask.

"Until she attacked Wendy. That was it for him. After that, he cut her off," admits Simon.

I turn to Smalls. "So you started sneaking food to her?"

Smalls looks down at his feet. "She shouldn't have hurt Wendy, but..." He swallows. "I just didn't want her to be hungry."

I nod, not knowing what else to say.

Once Smalls shuffles back out of the room, and Benjamin has retired for the night, I turn back to Simon.

"What happened to her before Neverland?" I ask, too cautious to ask why Tink can't speak. I'd rather not tip Simon off regarding my close encounters with the faerie. Still, my curiosity can't help itself. I have to know if it's a congenital condition, or something that happened to her.

I worry that it's abuse she endured.

Simon just stares at me for a moment, then says, "Ask Victor."

I FIND Victor in his room, sharpening the blade of his dagger on a piece of flint.

"What happened to Tink before Neverland?" I ask.

"What happened to Tink before Neverland?" Michael repeats, in an almost exact impression of my tone.

Victor frowns at me, looking up from his blade as he shifts on his bed. "Why? Have you found her?"

"No." I tuck my hands into my pockets, shaking my head. I know better, but I look away, not able to bear lying to Victor's face.

If he notices, he doesn't bring it up. Instead, he says, "When Peter found her, she was with a traveling circus."

I frown. "Tink worked for a circus?" It's hard to imagine Tink having the patience to entertain crowds.

Victor grimaces. "She didn't work for a circus. She was one of the displays."

My stomach turns over, hollows out. "Why would anyone want to put Tink on display?"

Victor frowns in confusion, then realization dawns on his face. "Right, I've forgotten you've never seen her."

My face must turn green, because Victor shakes his head. "I'm with you. It's disgusting. But that doesn't mean I can't infer what their motives were. She has the misfortune of being both beautiful and rare." He runs his hand through his dark hair, sighing. "That's probably why Thomas and I used to chase her down and torture her, as much as that makes me sick to think about now."

"How do you know this? About the circus, I mean?" I ask.

Victor places his blade on the bed next to him, then rubs his palms over his thighs. "When Peter discovered what Thomas and I were doing to her, he took us aside and explained the horrors that had happened to Tink. How they made her who she is today. I've never felt so guilty as the moment he told us about finding her in a cage, lined up next to the circus animals."

It feels as if I've been dunked in ice water. They kept her in a cage.

"Why didn't you tell me this before?" I ask.

Victor frowns. The bed creaks as he shifts his weight, cocking his head. "I didn't know it was relevant."

I groan, rubbing my eyes. "Of course it's relevant."

"Well, now you know."

I wish I didn't.

THAT NIGHT, I sneak back to the cave.

As I undo the latch on the cave cell, Tink watches me, gaze steady.

Her hands are trembling by her sides. When she notices me glancing at them, she tucks them behind her back and offers me what I imagine is the most intimidating smile she can muster.

It's fairly effective.

"I'm not here to hurt you again," I say, fiddling with the lock. I can hardly look her in the face as I say it, so I have to avert my eyes. My mouth goes dry, and as I feel for the feedback of the pick, the lock clicks. For a moment, I wonder if I'm about to die. If she's going to come bursting from the cage and break my neck. Maybe that will be too quick of a death for her captor, and she'll want to feast on me alive instead.

I'm fairly certain she's not actually a cannibal. But technically, eating me wouldn't be cannibalism since she's fae and I'm human, so I'm beginning to rethink that one.

Tink stands, her legs shaking, though I can't tell if it's from fear or lingering weakness from the rushweed. Still, she doesn't attack. At least, she hasn't yet. She looks me up and down, as if searching for evidence of some kind of trick or treachery. She must not find any, because she strides past me, hardly offering me a second glance as she exits the cage.

It's as if I'm invisible to her. A mere blip, an inconvenience in her life's story. I think back to what Simon said about Tink being mentally unstable. Will she even remember me, or will her time in this cage be indistinguishable from her nightmares?

"I apologize," I say as she makes her way out, "for hurting you. It was morally wrong, and I can't tell you how ashamed—"

When I glance up, Tink is already gone.

CHAPTER 20

WENDY

*L*araeth is a port town, just like Jolpa, except cleaner. Whereas Jolpa stinks of fish oil and the occasional plague, Laraeth smells of fresh salt air and a host of fragrances traded from around the world. There's a headiness to the air—but that might just be the faerie wine in such abundance it scents the wind.

I have to breathe through my mouth as we dock, as we scale down the ramp and onto the pier. The captain shoots me an inquisitive look, but I shake my head. My loose lips have already shared too much with the captain. There's no need to tell him about my mother pressing faerie wine to my lips when I was young. Of the night my father found me passed out in the wine cellar.

Estelle trades in common goods, but Laraeth trades in the exquisite. It's the type of town even my wealthy parents would have aspired to own property in, though those hopes would have been futile. The only way to own property in a place like Laraeth is to inherit it. And that's if you're lucky enough not to have parents paranoid to the point of assuming you've been plotting to kill them for an early shot at your inheritance.

It's a more reasonable fear than one might think, given the rate of patricide in Laraeth is the highest in the region. Granted, the rate of the inheritance ending up in the hands of the true offspring when murder is suspected is rather low. You'd think people would question whether the risk of a hanging is worth the potentially nonexistent reward, but the actuaries can tell you otherwise.

Marble houses line the coast, tucked into the mountainside. I can't imagine what a pain they must be to keep looking as pristine as they do, but those who live here have more coin than they know what to do with. Hiring an army of workers to wash the exterior is probably a small price to pay for the beauty the coastline exhibits. It's still midday, so the sun glares off both the waves and the manors' facades, making the streets of Laraeth almost blinding to walk through.

The walk to the Carlisle manor isn't far from the coast, but it's set in the crag of one of the rolling seaside mountains, so we wait for a carriage at its base.

At his command, my arm hangs off the captain's.

"Your gown is too tight," he says, scanning the teal evening gown Charlie happened to have lying around. Considering most of Charlie's possessions were burned when her family was slaughtered, I don't want to think about who this gown belonged to originally. Whether that woman is still alive or is rotting at the bottom of the ocean.

"It's not as if I chose it for that purpose," I snap at him, conscious of how little of my bosom the clingy dress leaves to the imagination. If it weren't for its high neckline, it would remind me of something my mother would have picked out for me. Well, picked out for my suitors.

Astor shakes his head, confused. "No. I mean, you're hardly breathing."

I blink, steadying myself on his arm.

"We should have had Charlie loosen the corset." If I didn't know better, I'd think he was scolding himself.

"It's not the corset," I say. "Believe me, I was wearing them long before I had the body structure for them."

His eyebrow arches. "Then why are you struggling to breathe?"

I swallow, my fingers tightening on his forearm despite myself. My left hand dangles at my side, grazing the air rather than risk grazing my dress. I imagine the position does look rather stiff. "It's the velvet," I say, gesturing with my chin down to my gown.

When Charlie had first shown it to me, I'd come close to hyperventilating. But I'd found myself in that armchair in the parlor enough times to know how to defer my panic for later. The pocket in the back of my mind that I used to hide away in is still there, and I've been curling into it since Charlie helped me slip into this gown.

"Am I intended to take 'it's made of velvet' as a sufficient explanation?"

I divert my attention toward a crab scuttling near my feet. "The armchair in my father's smoking parlor was lined in velvet."

When I peer up at the captain, anger has suffused his harsh features, his heightened pulse ticking against his set jaw. "You should have told me."

I actually manage a laugh, which makes me feel a tad dizzy. "Why? So you could kill an innocent woman for her gown in order to replace this one?"

Annoyance ripples between the captain's furrowed brows, but his lips quirk ever so slightly. "No. I'd have lifted it from a shop like a proper gentleman."

It shouldn't work, but his subtle joke loosens a bit of the tightness in my chest.

"I'm fine, I assure you," I say, even though that's a blatant lie. Anytime my fingers graze the velvet, I feel like crawling out of my skin. "Before I entered society, my brother John and I used to draw pictures in the velvet wallpaper lining the ballroom," I say, though when I look at the captain, I add, "though I guess you've seen it."

He swallows awkwardly, and for a moment, it's almost as if he's going to look away. He doesn't, of course. The captain doesn't apologize, doesn't back down.

"For a while, he kept asking me why I'd stopped," I say. "I could never bring myself to tell him. He always took such responsibility over my well-being when we were children. I imagine if he'd known, he would have blamed himself."

"He would have," says the captain, examining me with those sharp green eyes. "And he'd never forgive himself either."

"You know," I say, biting my lip, "it wasn't his fault. There's nothing he could have done to keep it from happening."

The captain blinks. He opens his mouth, like he's about to say something, but then thinks better of it. After a moment of deliberation, he says, "We're early, you know. For the carriage." When I shoot him a questioning look, he straightens his shoulders and jerks his head toward town. "No need to stand around twiddling our thumbs."

BY THE TIME the carriage comes rattling around the bend of the mountain pass, there's another layer of fabric between my hand and the captain's arm—a pair of black satin gloves he purchased for me from the nearest tailor.

The carriage driver is a short, bulbous man with wiry gray hair and weathered skin that hangs in loose jowls around his neck. His name is Druisk, and he's got the type of humor you laugh at out of pity, but find endearing anyway.

"I hear the two of ya are newlyweds," he says as he opens the carriage door, which is the color of a robin's egg. "No luggage?"

"We won't be staying the night," explains Captain Astor.

The elderly man chuckles. "Can't blame me for asking. I never know if that's the case or if the newlyweds just prefer to sleep in the nude."

I hurry myself into the cab, avoiding Druisk's outstretched hand offering assistance as I scamper in, cheeks heated.

The captain swoops in after me, scooping his arm around my waist and pulling me into his chest playfully as he turns over his shoulder and says to the driver, "That wasn't the plan, but I'll have to purposefully forget our luggage the next time we stay overnight somewhere."

My belly instantly hollows out.

The elderly man's face lights up as he chuckles and says, "Me and me wife are the same way."

The moment Druisk slams the door shut, the captain extricates himself from my side and sidles as close as is physically possible to the door, leaving what might as well be a chasm between us.

I pretend not to notice.

CHAPTER 21

WENDY

*P*retending not to notice the way the air had thickened between me and the captain is a simpler task, given the view out my window. The mountain pass looks out over the glassy, shimmering sea to the east, then a snowcapped mountain range to the west. As we wind around the mountain, the view oscillates between the two, making the ride altogether pleasant.

Except for the captain's looming presence, of course. The man exudes the energy of the sea on an uncharacteristically warm day following a cold front—the sky might as well be red, the wind treacherous and heady with the weight of a stirring storm.

"Charlie says I should have asked you before I forced you to train with me," he says out of nowhere.

I blink, schooling my neck not to turn to face him. I'd rather not look at the captain at the moment. He's traded his usual captain's attire for a black suit and tailcoat, and he looks too much like the man I once danced with. The man who slaughtered my parents in front of me. Slick and handsome and sharp enough to cut me into pieces.

Because I'm hoping to end the conversation, I say, "Charlie also says I shouldn't have expected to assist the crew without learning to defend myself."

An aggravated huff sounds behind me, but I keep my eyes trained on the bustle of the docks below as we round the curve.

"I wasn't thinking," he says. "About how it might feel for you to be touched like that."

I can't help myself; I shift around toward the captain, though the sight of him sends pangs through my chest. "I assure you, grabbing my wrist isn't what those men had in mind when they touched me."

The captain's eyes are trained on my wrist, but he won't find my bruise. It's long healed. Besides, it's not like that fae eyesight of his can see through my satin gloves.

"But that is why you freeze up when you're in danger. Your mother taught you that if you screamed, no one would come. She taught you not to fight back."

I bite my lip. "Please stop."

But the captain's not done. "She made you train your body not to respond when it was in danger."

"I've fought back before," I protest, thinking of struggling with Tink in the ocean as she tried to shove my head below the water. But he's right; I've only ever truly fought back against a woman. I suppose I'd attacked the henchman in the alley as he rounded the corner, but that was different. I'd launched myself at him first. Once he'd gotten his hands on me, I'd given up. "Fine. I seem to be paralyzed by a man's touch," I say, then shooting daggers with my eyes at the captain, add, "Are you satisfied to hear me admit it?"

"Not at all," he says, but he remains silent the rest of the ride.

By the time the driver brings the carriage to a halt outside the Carlisle manor, even he can sense the tension in the carriage.

"Oh, how my wife and I love a little lovers' spat," he chuckles as he ushers us onto the pebbled drive. "Nothing beats the lovemaking afterward, I assure you." He winks at the captain. "But I'm sure you already know that. Probably why you picked the fight with her to begin with, isn't it?"

I don't check Astor for his reaction. Instead, I retreat, allowing the world around me to go quiet as I examine the manor stretching out before me. Beautiful doesn't seem a fair word to describe it. Massive panels of glass reflect the midday sun, making up the majority of the structure, the windows towering above us like watchmen protecting the sprawling land that cascades down the mountain. Bordering the glass are sections of ebony brick that stretch to the heavens in spiraling turrets that meld into the side of the mountain itself.

I can almost feel the brick underneath my black satin gloves, scraping against my fingertips. The rush that would spike inside my blood if I were ever to reach the top of one of those towers.

"Welcome to the Carlisle Manor," says the driver, sounding pleased with himself, as if he were the architect of such a masterpiece.

"Strange," I say, taking the captain's arm as a footman meets us and leads us toward the ornate doors. I ignore the way the captain flinches under my initiated touch. "You'd think that people who deal in secrets wouldn't have built a house with so many windows."

"But isn't that exactly what they're selling?" asks the captain. "The luxury of peeking in where you're not supposed to?"

I nod in concession, but something about the house bothers me. "Except that it's just an illusion. You can't see into the house, not really. Not with the way the sun reflects on the windows."

"You can't see in during the daytime," the captain corrects.

THE INSIDE of Carlisle Manor is just as breathtaking as its exterior. Crystal chandeliers reflect scattered lights all about the halls. Wooden paneling and battens painted a deep teal line the walls, giving the place a soothing aura, which I immediately mistrust. Displayed in ornate silver frames are paintings of famous heists, all contributing to the manor's air of intrigue.

"Is your interest piqued, Darling?" the captain whispers, though I can't help but notice the way he doesn't press his lips to my ear like he once did.

When I turn to look at him, he flicks his head ever so slightly toward the parlor we're being led into. I catch a glimpse of blonde hair inside, so I flash the captain my prettiest smile, one that comes too easily due to my years of practice. When I speak, I sound like a girl who marvels at the world instead of fearing it. "I feel as if I'm being let in on a secret, don't you?"

Astor blinks and clears his throat, stiffening under my touch. Or maybe it's the feigned delight in my voice that has him cringing.

"Ah! Lord Rivers," says a thin man with porcelain skin, blond hair, and wire-rimmed glasses. "What a pleasure it is to be graced with your acquaintance. And your wife," he says, flashing a pretty set of teeth at me. "Well, aren't you just a prize?"

He takes my hand and kisses my knuckles. I silently thank Astor for thinking to supply me with the satin gloves.

Lord Carlisle's wife soon follows him, though if I hadn't memorized Astor's notes on these two, I would have assumed she was his sister. Her fair complexion and general roundness of face are similar enough to his to be eerie. She looks to be about my age, so much so it takes me a moment to remember that she's seventeen years my senior.

"Why, Lady Rivers, I just know we're to be the best of friends," she says, an expression I've always found off-putting since it is almost always spoken upon a first meeting based on nothing other than appearance and preconceived notions. Or, in Lady Carlisle's case, wanting something from me. Thankfully, my mother gave me her smile, and I wear it dutifully.

"Congratulations on your union," says Lord Carlisle. "From what I understand about the customs of Delphi, it seems the two of you must be residing in the heavens at the moment."

"Isn't it so romantic, Arthur?" says Lady Carlisle, clapping her hands together. "Say, we should take a year, just the two of us, to never be apart."

Arthur Carlisle winks at his wife. "But then how would we divide the duties of our business to make it flourish?"

The mention of money must be an aphrodisiac for Lady Carlisle, because she bites her lip and blushes a deep scarlet.

The couple leads us into the parlor, and after half an hour of chatting about things of no importance over tea, Astor begins tapping on the cedar armrest of the loveseat they insisted the newlyweds share. "As you well know, my wife and I are not here simply for a social call."

I fight the urge to roll my eyes. Astor might mock me for being an heiress, but at least I learned tact. "What my husband means is that we've spent our entire journey hoping, desperately really, that you might be able to help us. We're quite in love, you see," I say, taking Astor's hand from where it's resting on his knee next to me. I imagine it's taking every morsel of self-control in him not to flinch underneath my touch, but slowly, he sinks into the role of adoring husband and begins stroking my fingers, as if lost in thought.

I ignore the way my skin heats under his touch, even with the satin of my gloves separating us.

"Yes," says Lord Carlisle, crossing his foot over his knee as he leans backward in his chair. "We have to admit, we were a tad surprised to hear a couple so acclaimed for their ardent love needed our help. Usually, people come to us a few years into marriage."

"You mean when the love dwindles and one spouse is looking to undo the other with a secret?" Astor asks, his fingers tensing in my hand.

Lady Carlisle purses her lips through her smile. "That is typically the case, but we expect it will not be for the two of you. Especially considering you've come here together."

"I assure you I'm not the type of husband to betray my wife," says Astor, and though I wait for him to feign adoration for me, he keeps his stare level with Lord Carlisle's. I wonder how often Astor has to repeat those words to himself as he's planning to rid himself of his Mating Mark, the last strand of magic that binds him to his dead wife.

I wonder how much unnecessary guilt plagues him.

"Our problem, you see," I interject, pinching Astor lightly in an attempt to get him to behave, "is that my husband and I are both Mated."

"So we can see," says Lady Carlisle, her blue eyes dangling on my Mating Mark ravenously. "I must say, I'm a tad envious. Not only has the idea of a Mated Pair always stolen my heart, but those golden freckles of yours are quite fashionable. I imagine, now that you've gained a Lady's status, girls from all over will be painting their faces to look like yours."

I try not to wriggle uncomfortably. It's easier than it should be.

"The problem is—"

"We're not each other's Mates," the captain says, finishing my sentence hastily. Like he's been waiting this entire visit to clear the air on this matter. I wonder how much it's been killing him to masquerade as if his Mark belongs to me, not to the woman he so obviously adores, even in death.

Lord Carlisle glances between my freckles and Astor's Mark. The captain has kept his sleeves covering his forearm, so the only part of the Mark visible is the portion that still glows gold. From here, his Mark appears as alive as ever.

"I had been wondering why they don't match," Lord Carlisle says. "Though now you've assuaged my curiosity."

"We want them gone," I say.

The lady quirks her head, but she purses her lips and says nothing. I try to avoid her assessing gaze.

"Yes, I see how those could complicate matters should you ever come across your true..." He stops, reconsidering his word choice. "Those with Mating Marks to match," says Lord Carlisle, folding his hands together.

"So you'll help us?" I say.

Lord Carlisle strokes the ebony vase resting on the side table next to his seat. "That depends. Exactly what is it that you want to know? The process to remove a Mating Mark?"

"That is unnecessary," says Astor, freeing his hand of mine to prop his elbows on his knees in front of him. "We're informed of the process. It's someone to perform the ritual that we've yet to uncover."

I quirk a brow at Astor. Already, he's kept me in the dark. Other than the fact that a shadow soother is necessary to the process, I was under the impression he didn't know how to remove the Mating Mark. Unfortunately, I don't manage to school my expression before the lady of the house cocks her head at me. Her eyes shift greedily between me and Astor, digging for the reason behind why he's kept back information from the object of his affection.

"You're aware it's an unpleasant ordeal, then," says Lord Carlisle.

"Shouldn't be a problem."

"Hm," Carlisle says. "Well, I'm afraid I don't possess the information you need. But my wife and I are hosting a dinner party tonight, and I have a feeling that one of our guests might be able to enlighten us on this subject."

"Which guest?" I ask.

He flashes me a grin as practiced as mine. "If I told you, that would take the fun out of it, wouldn't it?"

Astor stands to leave, shrugging at his coat. "We're unable to stay. As it is, we've already lingered too long. If I'd known this was going to be a waste of time—"

The lord stands to meet him, a head shorter with his chin jutted upward to meet the captain's gaze. "I assure you, Rivers. Stay the night with us, and we'll have the information you need by the morning."

I crane my head, feigning confusion. "I thought you said you could have the information by the end of the dinner party."

"I said the guest would be attending the dinner party. I didn't say that's when we'd procure the information," says Lord Carlisle, glancing at his wife, who grins mischievously at him from her seat.

Unease twists in my belly, but I can't quite pinpoint its source. Lady Carlisle turns her attention to me, examining my every move.

A test.

I jump from my seat and grab onto Astor's arm. "Cortland, please," I say, with all the desperation I can muster. "Don't be stubborn. They're offering us a way out. I can't...I can't bear the thought of my heart being stolen away from you. Please, it's just an evening."

Astor flicks his green eyes down to where my fingers are clutching his arm. For a moment, I think he's actually going to shrug me off. But then the tension in his shoulders loosens, and he cups my cheek in his hand. "You know I'd do anything to keep you, Darling."

Without my permission, my mind flashes back to the first night we met, the captain's thumb on my jaw. *You missed a spot*, is what he'd said as he'd stroked my Mating Mark where my maids had forgotten to apply paint.

I douse that moment in the sticky scent of my parents' blood, the thud of their bodies hitting the floor.

"Of course, as awkward as it might be, we must discuss payment," says Lord Carlisle, attempting to break the stare Astor and I share.

"I was under the impression you traded in secrets," says Astor, without taking his eyes off of me.

The lady of the house giggles. "Well, we have to make our money somehow. Most of our guests pay, but for those who can't afford it— which is not the case with a wealthy couple like yourselves—occasionally a secret will do. So long as it's worth our while."

"You mean so long as it's the type of thing someone else would pay good money for," says Astor, ignoring her aside about the Rivers' wealth.

I turn toward the Carlisles. "Isn't the knowledge that the Rivers' marriage is on a treacherous path due to our Mating Marks valuable enough? You don't think someone would pay good coin for the lead that there's a woman out there somewhere who's capable of stealing my husband's heart...and his inheritance?"

Astor shoots me a warning look that I don't need words to read. *You're not exactly being the weak-minded girl the Carlisles want you to be at the moment*, he seems to say.

Still, there's a glint of amusement shining in his eyes.

"You assume the worst of people, Lady Rivers," says Lord Carlisle, lips strained at the edges.

"Surely you can see why I fear the information spreading," I say, allowing my eyes to cut across to Lady Carlisle, who is tapping her sharp, blood-red fingernails against the side table. "The scheme would be simple to organize. All an enemy would have to do is find my husband's Mate, then trap the girl in a contract to split the inheritance in exchange for the information about her Mate's whereabouts."

Lord Carlisle leans forward, matching Astor's posture, then rests his thumb against his bottom lip. "And if your husband's Mate is already spoken for? She might not agree to the scheme."

My heart pounds against my chest, my Mating Mark searing against my cheek and neck. My answer comes out stilted, but resolute all the same. "Trust me. She would agree. She wouldn't be able to resist."

Astor doesn't move, except for the slightest twitch of his Mated hand. Lord Carlisle's grin is cruel, slithering up his cheeks. "You two are in a precarious position, aren't you?"

"Lady Rivers makes a decent argument," says Lady Carlisle. "Your secret would fetch a high price among several of our patrons. Except the secret becomes worthless once the two of you break your Mating Bonds."

I flash her a grin, pleasant enough that my mother would have been proud. "Then you'd best sell the secret with haste instead of trying to benefit from it yourself. While it's still worth something, I mean."

At that, I think I catch Astor smile, though it's in the periphery of my vision, and by the time I turn to him to check, all evidence has vanished.

"You found yourself a clever wife, Corbin—Cortland," says Carlisle, correcting himself effortlessly. "I'd tell you those are more valuable than beautiful ones, but it seems the both of us have been fortunate in both arenas."

Astor plays his part well, turning to admire me as he places his hand at the crook of my neck and grazes his thumb across my jaw. If I didn't already know it's channeled loathing simmering underneath the surface, I'd likely mistake it for something else. "Fortunate, indeed."

CHAPTER 22

WENDY

The Carlisles are more clever than either of us have given them credit for.

When the servant rings the bell that the first of the dinner guests have arrived, Lord Carlisle absconds to meet them at the door, while Lady Carlisle escorts us to the dining room.

It's as extravagant as the rest of the manor. The western wall is made entirely of glass paneling, except for the golden rims that separate the individual panes. The result is a fiery sunset of pinks and oranges that works as a grander mural than any esteemed artist could ever hope to paint. In the distance, the sea shimmers, reflecting the sky as the sun descends on our dinner. The opposite wall is also made of glass and looks into a music parlor, where three blindfolded women in lavish gowns pluck at the strings of emerald-encrusted harps.

The table itself is carved of oak, with lace runners and crystal vases as centerpieces.

The only other guest to have arrived is a withered old man whose eyes rake over Lady Carlisle's form in a way that reminds me of my dance with Lord Credence at the masquerade. Instead of wilting underneath his greedy stare, Lady Carlisle greets him by trailing her long fingernails down his arm with a practiced grin.

Lord Carlisle returns with the remainder of the guests, and a servant shakes his hand with both palms. Odd behavior, for a servant. I can't help but notice how Lord Carlisle glances at whatever is in his hand, then tucks it into his inner coat pocket when the servant pulls away.

Not long after, Lady Carlisle has the servants show us to our seats. The usher leads us to the far end of the table, but when Astor goes to take the seat beside me, the usher clears his throat hesitantly.

"My apologies, sir," says the usher. "But it's the household custom for couples to sit at opposite ends of the table."

Astor swivels his head toward Lady Carlisle in question, but our hostess just giggles. "My husband and I find dinner parties so much more interesting that way. I hope the two of you don't mind. It won't break your Delphian customs, will it?"

There's a subtle challenge in her eyes, but Astor meets her stare. "No. As long as you don't escort one of us out of the room, our customs will remain intact. Though I will miss dining with my wife."

Lady Carlisle doesn't appear to hear him as she takes the seat next to me at the head of the table opposite her husband. The usher herds Astor to the seat at Lord Carlisle's right hand.

"What's wrong, dear?" asks Lady Carlisle in a singsong voice. "I thought I'd be earning you a break. Don't misunderstand me, Delphian customs are romantic, but woman to woman, surely you'd like a chance to get a breath away from your husband every once in a while," she says conspiratorially behind the napkin she's using to dab her lips, despite the fact we've yet to eat.

I choose my words carefully as I take my seat, trying to judge what exactly the lady of the house is looking for in my response. There's mischief in her eyes, a hunger for gossip. I wonder if that's her personality, or if profiting off others' secrets has trained her to crave it.

"I do love Cortland's company above all others," I say, hesitantly.

Lady Carlisle leans in closer. "But I must admit, it is a bit of a relief to get away. Just for a moment."

"You're not fond of your people's customs?" asks Lady Carlisle, as a servant fills our silver chalices with faerie wine.

Charlie's voice rings in my head, her interrogations coming in handy at the moment. She was smart to drill the facts into my mind, especially with the heady scent of wine threatening to distract me.

"Actually, I'm not Delphian," I say. I can't help but notice Lady Carlisle's face fall when I evade her trap. I suppose it would be more thrilling if she caught me trying to impersonate Lady Rivers. Though perhaps she and her husband set these safeguards for all of their guests. Astor and I can't be the first people trying to obscure our identities. "My family moved us to Delphi when I was nine. I'm Kruschian."

"Are you?" Lady Carlisle says, her smile still painted on.

"Surely you knew that. After all, I thought you knew everything," I say, more pleasantly than I mean.

Lady Carlisle laughs, more pleasantly than she means.

"Anyway," I say. "Kruschians are much more stoic with our emotions. It's unheard of for a man and his wife to sleep in the same room, much less never leave the other's presence for a year. It's taking...well, I'm adjusting," I say, glancing down at Astor admirably for heightened effect.

I'm not prepared for him already to be looking at me.

We both avert our eyes. Quickly.

The servants bring the soup, setting it piping before us.

"Early on, being in love still feels a bit scandalous, doesn't it?" says Lady Carlisle, watching our exchange intently. "The passion is so intense, it sometimes feels as if everyone around you can scent it. But I assure you, darling, we can't."

My spoon stops halfway to my mouth, until I realize she's not identifying my name. Just using a common word. I let my shoulders sag with overt pleasure as the hot broth hits my tongue.

"You like it?"

"It's marvelous," I say, grateful for something truthful to be coming out of my mouth tonight. The broth tastes of lemon and rosemary. There's a freshness about it that feels clean. Pristine, even.

"Let me ask you, Lady Rivers," says Lady Carlisle. "If, by chance, my husband and I are unable to procure the information you seek, is there some other secret I might search out for you in its place?"

I swallow too quickly, the soup scalding my throat. My pulse hammers at my jaw, but I try to contain my excitement by waiting to respond until after I've dabbed my mouth with my napkin and set my spoon down. "Perhaps there is a predicament you might help solve. Though I wonder if the answer would be the same for both questions. You see, I have a friend afflicted with a Fated curse."

The lady's eyes sparkle. "What's the nature of this curse?"

I bring the chalice of wine to my lips and pretend to drink, potently aware of the sparkle of the wine swirling in the cup. Down the table, Astor glances at me, a flicker of concern rippling across his jaw. My getting myself drunk isn't exactly in the best interests of our scheme.

"I'm afraid my friend's secret is not mine to tell," I say, ripping my gaze away from Astor's and back to Lady Carlisle's. "But if I by any means could find a way to free her of it, that information would be of great value to me."

The lady sits back in her seat, contemplating. "I could look into it for you. Assuming we're unable to get the information your husband desires." I don't miss the blade in her words, seeking to sever my will from Astor's. If only she knew how unnecessary such an attempt is. "Though I worry that, too, will be difficult to come by. I'm afraid the Sisters haven't been known to give up their secrets easily, nor do they make a habit of gracing us with their presence."

"That's too bad," I say.

"Perhaps you might have another question."

I don't know why I say it, why I let it slip out. But I spent weeks trying to get information from Astor in the cave on Neverland, to no avail, and the question has haunted me since that fateful night of the masquerade.

"What do you know of…" I almost say the Darlings, but then again,

I don't know how far news of my Mating Mark has traveled, so I pivot mid-sentence. "Of Captain Nolan Astor?"

I don't know if it's my imagination, but it's as if I can feel Astor's pointed ears tilt across the room.

"I know he's a vicious pirate who fancies himself a privateer," scoffs Lady Carlisle. "I know he's left bodiless heads up and down the coast of the Shifting Sea." She takes a sip of wine and, over the edge of the chalice, says, "Repeat customers, too. But he's as elusive as trying to hold back a waterfall with your bare hands. No childhood to speak of. No parents. No anything tying him to the rest of the world. If you have information on him, I assure you, my husband and I will go to the ends of the earth to get you whatever secrets you want."

I shake my head, mouth going dry, then pretend to nurse my wine. "No, nothing about him."

Lady Carlisle raises a brow at my choice of drink. "You can cease pretending. I know you haven't taken a sip of your wine."

I chuckle nervously. "It's not for lack of being tempted."

My hostess doesn't bother being subtle about the way her gaze worms its way to my belly. "That's bound to happen if you never leave the room without one another."

I flush, but make myself smile all the same. If only so I don't have to explain why I'm not touching the faerie wine.

"What's your interest in Captain Astor, darling?" says Lady Carlisle. Again, I'm taken aback by the pet name.

"It's not really a question about him," I say as the servant places a plate of blackened salmon and braised asparagus in front of me. Normally, food like this would make my mouth water, but for some reason, I've lost my appetite. "It's about his wife. Do you know what happened to her?"

The lady's shrewd gaze rakes me over. "You can't have known her. She died fifteen years ago."

"She was my nanny," I say, having no idea whether this information will match up with what Lady Carlisle knows about Iaso, but she seems appeased as she nods her head, looking off into the distance like she's numbering years.

"Yes, I suppose that makes sense."

"She disappeared. My parents wouldn't tell me where she went. But then, years later, they told me she'd married a pirate and died shortly after. But they wouldn't tell me what she died of."

"That's because they didn't know." A pleased smirk overtakes the lady's lips. "I'm afraid that kind of secret is going to take additional payment."

I open my mouth, unsure of what my soul is about to spill to find out what happened to her, why it makes Captain Astor hate my parents so. Perhaps that's why I'm so surprised when I lean over to her and whisper the most awful secret I know in her ear.

"Well, darling. That's quite a secret indeed," she says, her gaze skating over me.

Down the table, Lord Carlisle clinks his fork to his crystal, readying to make an announcement. I can hardly hear him over the buzzing in my ears as Lady Carlisle leans over and whispers the story of how Iaso Astor met her end.

CHAPTER 23

WENDY

I hear nothing that happens during the rest of the dinner. When the guest on my right attempts to talk to me, my mouth reverts to my mother's training. Judging by the man's pleased smile when our conversation is over, I've answered his questions just to his liking.

When a servant escorts Astor and me to our rooms, I don't mark the path down the hallways. My feet simply follow, and I don't stop them.

It's only when the servant shuts the bedroom door behind us that Astor says, "Something's wrong."

I offer him a smile, and he sneers.

"I don't want your mother's fake smiles, Wendy." My heart thuds at his use of my given name.

"Right. Of course." I wander over to the desk in the corner of the room and pull out the chair before collapsing into it.

Astor goes still, his shoulders tensed in his suit coat as he stares at me from across the room. "If you're worried over the bed, I won't force you to share it with me."

I let out a shrill laugh, staring at the ornate bed draped in silken sheets. The bed itself is too small for two to sleep comfortably, not without holding one another. Like the Carlisles are playing a private joke on us. "I don't know how you can stand to touch me at all."

Astor traces his fingers over the bedsheets. "What did you and Lady Carlisle discuss during dinner?"

My mouth goes dry as I stare into the windowed wall, made entirely of golden-ribbed glass. A taunting reminder that they're always watching. That nothing we do is private.

"We'll have to sleep in the same bed. They'll know if we don't," I say, nodding to the looming glass panes.

Astor curls his nose in disgust, but he doesn't argue with me.

"I'm sorry," I say. "You shouldn't have to do that."

He's fisting the bedsheets now, steadying himself on the frame of the bed as he squeezes his eyes shut. "How much do you know?"

I open my mouth, but I can't find the right word. *Everything* doesn't seem true.

"Enough," is what I end up settling on.

"That's not particularly specific, Darling."

"I didn't think you'd want me to recount it."

He cuts his eyes to me. "I'm accustomed to having to do things I don't want to do."

My heart pounds, bruises, breaks, then repeats the cycle over again. When I speak, my voice trembles. My limbs are as feeble as a wilted daisy petal, as brittle as dried bone. "She said your wife—Iaso—was special. Said she was a healer, but not the traditional sort. Whereas most healers' powers are transferred through touch, Iaso's worked differently. She had to use her own blood."

Astor isn't looking at me anymore. He's staring out the window, his grip rattling the bed frame.

"Lady Carlisle said the rumors are that Iaso was called to Jolpa during the plague. That she visited as many households as she could manage, but she could only work so many at a time, because she had to mix her blood into the medication. She didn't want anyone to know how her healing worked. Was afraid the truth would put her in danger. Make her blood valuable. Besides, she had to rest often in between healing sessions.

"According to Lady Carlisle, Iaso received word that an aristocrat's daughter had fallen ill. That she was close enough to taste death. Iaso was supposed to be resting, allowing her blood to replenish. She told the messenger she couldn't come, but her compassion won out in the end.

"What she didn't know was that the aristocrat knew her secret." My throat closes up, because this is the part of the story Lady Carlisle didn't know the details of—who told the aristocrat that Iaso's blood would heal the child. That it was the Sister's voice that whispered from the shadows. The Sister who had betrayed Iaso's secret. I'd always been told that when my parents made their bargain with the Sister, it had been the Sister's power that healed me. But they'd lied. The Sister had fulfilled her end of the bargain through Iaso. "When Iaso visited the girl, she wept over her and told the girl's mother it was too late. She'd never succeeded in healing someone so close to death."

Astor is heaving now, supporting his weight on the bed with his fists digging into the sheets.

The next part comes out hollow. Stiff. Like I'm reciting the script of Cressida Rivers' fact sheet. "Lady Carlisle didn't know which one of the parents slit Iaso's throat. Which one of them bled every drop of blood from her body and bathed the child in it, making her drink of it too. All she knew was that Iaso died, and the little Darling girl lived."

When I'm done, the silence is the worst part. I would have thought letting the story out, expressing it like an infected wound, would relieve some of the guilt bearing down on my chest, but it only allows it to infiltrate the surrounding air, threatening to suffocate me.

I know it's foolishness, but it's as if I can taste Iaso Astor's tangy blood in my mouth, as if I can hear her gurgling cries, feel her sticky blood against my bare skin as my mother bathed me in it.

Astor clenches his teeth. There's no life in his eyes. The flicker has gone out. "You weren't supposed to know that."

"Why not?" I don't know why there's so much accusation in my tone, but it's there all the same. "I'm the one who got to live, didn't I? You don't think I deserve to know the price that was paid so I could...

So I could…" I frown, unsure of what I've done with the life that should have been Iaso's.

Surely I've done something, but all I can remember is dancing with her husband at the masquerade, hoping his Mating Mark was the match to mine. All I can feel is the heat of his touch against my cheek as he stroked my Mark, the burning in my chest every time he looks at me. In my heart, I know I love Peter, that my soul belongs to him. But as the guilt weighs down on me, all I can see is every time I've looked upon Nolan Astor, and the wicked girl within has craved the man whose wife died for me.

I tell myself never again. Never again will I betray Peter like that. Never again will I betray Iaso Astor like that.

"It wasn't your fault." The way he says it is like he's trying to convince himself as much as he is me.

"But you hate me all the same," I whisper, loathing myself for how that of all things is what's bothering me right now.

I wait for him to confirm it. It wouldn't be the first time he's told me he abhors me. But it stings all the same when he swallows and admits, "Despite all logic, yes."

"I wouldn't say it's despite all logic for you to hate the girl who got to live because your wife was forced to take her place." I sink my face into my hands, but I can't bring myself to cry. It doesn't feel fair to the captain's pain to have to watch me suffer over something that ripped him to shreds.

"I don't know how you even stand to look at me," I whisper.

Slowly, I hear the captain's weight shift. The subtle scuff of boots against the floorboards as he approaches me.

When he leans over the desk, placing his palms flat over the wood, I make myself examine his rotting Mating Mark. The ghostly tendrils that snake to hide underneath his sleeve. His wedding ring glints underneath the lantern light. The sight of it makes me nauseous. Tonight I've been playing the part of his wife, the ring she placed on his finger assisting me in getting what I want.

When he finds me staring at it, he grimaces. As if he too senses the betrayal of how we've used that ring tonight, he pulls it off his finger and tucks it into his pocket with the solemnity of an apology.

"Would you really like to know?" he whispers, taking his finger and knotting it underneath my chin, craning my head up to look at him.

His expression is gentler than it should be. His eyes softened, his posture tender, almost adoring. It takes me a moment to realize he's putting on for whoever's watching us from outside the window.

The realization doesn't serve to blunt the sharp barbs of his words. "When I look at you, do you know what I picture?" he asks, trailing a finger across the furrows and bends of my Mating Mark. I hate the way my chest fills with flames, despite my begging it not to. "I picture you sinking your teeth into my wife's bleeding throat." He dips his thumb to my lip, exposing my canine and running his fingerprint over its tip. "When I hear your voice, I make myself imagine what it sounded like when she cried out and I wasn't there to save her. When we touch, I feel her cold skin against my flesh the night Maddox and I found her body washed up on the shore of Jolpa. If you move, if you breathe, if you laugh in my presence, I mark it as a reminder of how still, how lifeless her body was when we took her back home to bury her. Every moment with you I use to commemorate all the ways I failed her when I let her leave the ship that night. That, if you must know, Darling, is how I stand it."

When he withdraws, I let out a pained gasp, but he's already turned back to the bed, so I can't measure his reaction. He only dims the lantern light beside the bed and turns down the sheets.

Then he gestures with an open palm and says, as if we've been discussing the quality of tonight's soup, "You first, Darling."

CHAPTER 24

WENDY

I can't sleep in Astor's arms.

There would have been a time when I'd have worried he'd close his hands around my throat and choke the breath out of my lungs with a laugh.

But the captain's hatred of me is more sinister than that. He doesn't want me dead. He wants me alive, an enduring reminder of his wife's death, a punishment uniquely suited for him, forcing him to relive the agony of losing her every moment he spends in my presence.

The sad part is that I understand it—the desire to mask your pain with a different sort. What doesn't make sense to me is why the captain is so insistent on getting rid of his Mating Mark, if he's so intent on castigating himself for his wife's death. One would think keeping the Mating Mark would be the masochist's choice. Then again, a person can only suffer so long before it becomes too much to bear.

The captain's pain might fuel him, but what of the moments he's seemed weary, worn down? He might act as though he takes the pain like a beating he knows he deserves, but is that behavior driven by his broken Mark? Or is the rational part of Astor intact enough to free itself from his self-destructive bond?

Through the night, I feel him. Every exhale. Every roll of his head against the pillow. Every time his body, tense with grief, nudges against mine.

He doesn't wrap his arms around me. He must figure there's not enough visibility through the window to make a difference since we're under the blankets, but his proximity is enough to suffocate me. Enough to drown me in the truth.

I shouldn't exist.

I shouldn't have existed for a long while now. Every breath I take is one that's been stolen from the lungs of a more worthy woman. A woman more useful.

More loved.

And for a painstaking moment I'll never admit to myself after this night, I envy Iaso. I imagine what it would be like to be loved that fiercely. For love to be the rudder of my husband's every thought, every action, every instinct, over a decade after I'd taken my last breath. I let my imagination crawl to dark places, to the shadows of my deathbed. Except I'm the one with the healing magic, the one whose throat is valuable enough to slit. The one with the blood worth spilling.

In this dream of mine—someone else's nightmare—I'm the one loved enough for two men to scour the shoreline for me, just to recover my swollen corpse.

I fall asleep like that, but when I wake to the moon peeping in through the glass paneling, I'm still just the girl who was bargained away. The girl no one ever loved enough to keep. Again and again and again.

I'm blinking tears away, abhorring myself for allowing my body the relief of tears at a loss that's not mine to mourn, when a shadow flickers across the vast windowpane. At first, I'm convinced I'm imagining things, but then the shadows warp into wings that stretch across the eerily gaping moon.

Peter.

My breath catches, and I'm a child again. Too frightened to move. Convinced that if only I remain under the warm safety of the covers, they'll protect me. But that's a youthful notion. The only thing underneath these covers is the man who blames me for the death of his wife. The man who uses my visage as a stake to pin him closer to an ever fading memory, lest the pain begin to drift and leave him alone in his misery.

So I extricate myself from the side of Nolan Astor. My bare feet hit the cold wooden slats of the floor, my toes curling in anticipation.

He's come for me. Peter's come for me. The realization rushes into my lungs until I can't breathe.

Regret twinges at my chest, and at first, I don't understand it. Why I'm not soaring over Peter's visit. But then I remember that I failed to learn how to rid Peter of his curse. That I failed to find a way to make him love me, truly love me. Because if there's anything I've learned from the captain, it's that love and pain are inextricable.

Besides, as much as my heart goes out to Peter, like a moth drawn to the flame or a fish to the shadows, I'd rather the captain not know he was here. Rage simmers in the captain's soul, and if the two fight, I'm not sure who will come out on top. Who will come out at all.

So I flick my neck to the side and tiptoe across the room before slipping out the door.

As I PAD down the long hall, the shadows follow me from outside the windows, mimicking my every step. A way for Peter to tease me, I'm sure. But I'm not in the mood for games.

I just want to go home.

Not that I know where that is.

There's a door at the end of the hallway that's unlocked. When I enter, I click the door shut behind me. It's a reading room of some sort. Not large enough to be a full-on library, but a quiet annex. The type you might offer to your more reclusive guests to enjoy when the party becomes too overwhelming. Orange coals glow in the hearth, leftover from whoever used this room last.

Outside the window, the shadows swell, expanding until massive wings drape from corner to corner of the windows.

There's a latch hidden carefully above one of the panes. I find it when I run my hand over the golden-leafed ribs. A jittering click, and the window cracks. Shadows leak through the small slit and coagulate on the floor, producing a tower of smoke that soon takes the shape of a man.

"Peter," I say, his name wistful on my tongue. He reaches for me, still in his shadowed form, his mouth hungrily finding mine as he wraps me in the dark swell of his embrace.

Underneath my roaming hands, shadows knit into flesh, into sinew and bone, until the lips exploring mine are no longer cold and ethereal but warm. Warm and here with me.

"Wendy Darling," he says, my name in the tone of his drunken voice setting sparks across my skin.

"It's been so long since you last came. I thought...I thought you had lost me." Relief washes over me with every graze of his touch. It feels so nice to be touched. For him to want to touch me. Especially spending the evening with the captain's body taut with disgust at each point of contact with my skin.

"You're mine, Wendy Darling," Peter whispers between kisses. "There's nowhere in the realms you could go that I wouldn't find you."

My mind is dizzy with desire, but reason taps its skeletal fingers against my skin. "You have to go. Before they wake up."

Peter trails his mouth to the bone behind my right ear. "Not yet."

His words spark a tingle down my spine, but I can't let it get the best of me. "Peter, visiting me on the captain's ship is one thing, but the Carlisles have reach, the dangerous sort. If they discover I'm a fraud, there's no telling what they'll do to me." And Astor, I don't add.

"I thought..." Peter pulls away, eyes still dark as coals. In a flash, I'm reminded of the danger of Peter in his shadow form. The silken voice who told the Sister he'd have taken my body ages ago, if his gentler self hadn't made him wait.

I'm wondering now which has the reins.

But then Peter grabs me by the waist and shoves me onto the

couch, his fingers grasping at the laces on the back of my gown, which I'd been too embarrassed to take off in the presence of the captain, and I have my answer.

"Peter, stop," I say, fear lancing through me as the gown comes undone at my back. My skin grazes the velvet of the couch, and the muscles around my spine seize up.

"Where did he touch you?" he whispers, undeterred by my protests. I push against his chest, but there's no getting him off of me.

"Nowhere. Nowhere, I swear," I say.

"You wouldn't let me touch you, but you'd let him." Peter's arms and hands shift into shadows again, splitting into several limbs, all the more to snake up my skirts and twist around my undergarments.

"Nothing happened," I insist, but to no avail. "Peter, Peter this isn't you. Please, I know this isn't you. You have to get control of him. Please, for me."

I squeeze my eyes shut, as if not watching it happen will make it go away. That little corner of my mind is still prepared like a readied guest room, its iron walls ready to keep me safe and hidden until it's over. My limbs go limp as I escape into that place.

My little room has always been empty. A safe place, just for me.

It's not empty any longer.

There's a voice that's infiltrated its walls, crept in unnoticed. A monster under the bed that's taken up residence.

Fight back, it commands.

I'm not strong enough, I cry.

This time, it's not the captain's voice, but Charlie's. *The men'll say that's cheating, but they don't seem to consider being naturally stronger cheating, so I wouldn't let it dissuade you.*

It's no use. He can't even feel pain, I whisper back.

The captain's voice again. *Your mother taught you that if you screamed, no one would come. She taught you not to fight back.*

I scream.

It's shrill and sounds like a cat dying, like someone's picking my fingernails off one by one. It's a noise that's never come from my mouth, one I wasn't aware I was capable of making.

I scream, and he comes for me.

Astor barrels through the door, green eyes glowing with panic, black hair disheveled across his forehead. His gaze dips to the scene in front of him, and I witness it unfolding through his eyes. Peter above me, pinning me to the couch, my legs and undergarments exposed from where he's tossed my skirts aside, the tops of my breasts on display from where Peter—not Peter, his shadow self—became frustrated and ripped my bodice.

I'm not sure what I'm expecting. For Astor to slam into Peter's side, perhaps. But he stands there, hands flexing at his sides for a moment, mouth agape in horror as he takes in what's happening.

Something snaps the captain back to reality, and his eyes focus in on mine. It's the briefest glimpse, but it's drenched in sorrow.

I think it's the first time he sees me and doesn't imagine his wife's blood staining my lips.

When the captain speaks, his voice is hard. Eerily calm. "Touch her again, and mark my words, I'll pick apart those wings of yours and use the bones as toothpicks."

Shadows swathe Peter's face again, so when he smiles, his teeth are blindingly white.

My stomach turns over. Not him, it's not him.

"Peter, please don't do this. I know you're in there," I whisper. "This isn't you."

When I reach up to touch Peter's cheek, the captain flinches, but so does Peter. When he turns back to face me, the shadows melt away. The ink drains from the whites of his eyes, until it's Peter—just Peter, staring down at me.

He blinks, then flexes his hands, like he can't remember how they got tangled up in my skirts. His eyes go wide at the sight of the tops of my breasts, and he gapes for a moment before swallowing and turning his gaze away. In a blink, he's off of me, then throwing the nearest blanket over my body to cover me.

"Wendy Darling, I'm so—"

"Don't speak her name," says Astor, his voice as sharp as the dagger glinting in his hand.

174

Peter opens his mouth, but the captain cuts him off again. "You will not look at her again. You will not address her again. You will not *think* of her again. Not unless she asks you to, and only then after our six months are up. Which," he says with a cruel grin, "I don't believe is anytime soon."

I bite my lip, wanting to reach out to Peter, to tell him I forgive him. That I know it wasn't him. That I know there's a curse eating away at his soul, stealing away his control. But the captain's face is painted with murder, like he's eager for an excuse.

Which he now has.

"Peter, *run*," I yell, just as a dagger comes flying. A dagger Astor is allowed to throw according to the terms of their bargain, since Peter has left Neverland.

My warning is just timely enough, because Peter dodges, but the knife grazes the leather of his wing all the same. He doesn't flinch, doesn't cry out, but of course he doesn't.

Still, he shifts into shadows, and in the blink of an eye, he's gone. Out the window, swirling in a shapeless mass as he disappears into the stars.

"Leave it to you to warn the man who was about to rape you," says Astor, crossing the room and grabbing his dagger from where it lodged itself between the wooden slats of a side table.

The words sting, sharp as the glinting dagger he wipes off on his pants and sheathes.

"Get up," he says. "We're leaving."

"But we haven't learned what the Carlisles know about removing Marks yet," I say, hugging the knit blanket around me.

Astor keeps his eyes averted, probably because the blanket is knit with a loose stitch that doesn't completely cover me. "And whose fault is that?"

I jerk my chin back as I sit up. "Now I'm really curious how you intend to pin this on me."

Astor grits his cheek. "Last I checked, I wasn't the one doing the pinning."

My cheeks drain of blood, and Astor bites the inside of his cheek.

When he speaks again, he's emptied his voice of malice. "How did Peter know you were here?"

"How am I to know?"

"You gave it away somehow, didn't you? During your conversation with Lady Carlisle at dinner?"

My cheeks flush at the same moment my blood drains. "Oh."

From the hall, someone claps. Lord Carlisle steps from the shadows, a smug grin on his face. "I have to say, I'm a tad offended you assumed my wife to be so dull. But people have a tendency to make such assumptions, don't they? All they see is a petty gossip with a pretty face. But, then again, that's always served its purpose. My wife has made me rich, you see. Can one really put a value on others underestimating your intelligence?" He cuts his gaze to me. "Though I seem to have overestimated yours, Wendy Darling. That is your name, isn't it?"

CHAPTER 25

WENDY

I flinch under Lord Carlisle's creeping gaze, which isn't quite so reserved as Captain Astor's. Even though it's my secret he's after, not my flesh, it makes my skin crawl. Like he has his hands all over me.

"You didn't think my wife would make the connection when you inquired regarding the circumstances surrounding the death of Captain Astor's wife?" Lord Carlisle asks.

The captain flinches. I can't bear to look at him.

"We deal in secrets and shame, Miss Darling," says Lord Carlisle. "You really thought we wouldn't know about your Mark? We knew who you were as soon as you entered the room. But as for who you were Mated to if not Captain Astor here—now that was a mystery. One that became clear enough when you told my wife of the realm of the Shadow Keeper, of the illness that wreaks havoc in the minds of the murderers he shelters."

My stomach twists. I'd been so desperate to discover what happened to Iaso, I'd given Lady Carlisle the first secret to come to mind. As I hadn't told her how to get to Neverland, I assumed the secret would do Peter and the Lost Boys no harm.

"To get the Shadow Keeper himself in our debt, now that was a prize," Carlisle says. "Thankfully, we have a contact that keeps up with him when he runs his little errands for the Sister. He was all too eager to learn where you were when we informed him you were playing someone else's wife. Though I'm surprised he didn't steal you back for himself. What was it he so desperately wanted, Miss Darling?" He poses the question as if my tattered dress doesn't betray the answer.

Red blotches crop all over my body, which is all the more mortifying given how much skin is exposed. My reaction seems to only encourage Lord Carlisle's taunts. "I have to say, even my wife didn't see that coming—your Mate's, shall we say, insistence? It seems you put up a fight. Tell me, have your allegiances shifted so quickly?"

"Speaking of your lovely wife," says Captain Astor in a tone that suggests otherwise, "why isn't she here gloating? The opportunity seems like something she wouldn't pass up without good reason."

Carlisle flashes his teeth, the lantern light streaking across his golden, slicked back hair. "My wife is occupied with..." He rolls his tongue like he's tasting for the right word, searching for a specific note in a fine wine. "Entertaining, at the moment."

A reedy old man with wandering eyes. Lady Carlisle's fingers trailing a tad too long on his arm.

I swallow, and I can't decide whether the bile in my stomach directed toward Lady Carlisle is disgust or pity.

"Well, I'd hate to remain here and distract you from that lovely mental image," says Astor through his teeth. He strides to the couch and grabs my hand, pulling me to my feet. "Wendy and I will be off now."

Carlisle offers us a feline smile, then steps into the doorway. "Oh, you know better than that, Captain Astor. With a bounty of six thousand silvers on your head?" He clucks his tongue as he cranes his neck to the side. "You, of all people, can't blame me for snagging a fly that's already wandered its way into my web."

Astor stares the lord down and slides his dagger from its sheath. "You have to the count of three to get out of my way, Carlisle. Before I cut that clever tongue of yours from your mouth."

"You'll be doing no such thing." Carlisle whistles, and the bookcases in the reading room swivel open. Out march a band of guards, six of them. Human, from the looks of their rounded ears, but even with Astor's fae agility and strength...

"There's too many of them," I whisper.

I expect anger from the captain, a biting retort, but he just turns to me, flashes me a conspiratorial grin, and says, "Do try not to challenge me like that, Darling. Unless, that is, you intend to close your eyes."

The closest guard launches himself at Astor's back. At first, I think he'll land his blow, but Astor's ready for him and snatches his wrist, careening him over his back and slamming him into the coffee table in front of me.

There's a crack, though I can't tell if it's the wood splintering or the man's skull.

The others aren't stupid enough to come at Astor one by one. Instead, they congregate around him. Unfortunately for the guards, Astor managed to swipe the sword from the first man's sheath and is now parrying the attacks of the five men who surround him.

One slashes forward, but Astor is ready. He shoves his sword into his opponent's weapon before the man lands his step, using the man's shift in balance to cast him backward into two more guards. The three of them go barreling to the ground in a tangle of flailing limbs.

The next man to take a step toward Astor loses his head.

I'm too slow to look away, and the head lands with a squelch at my bare feet, spattering blood onto my toes as the man's loose hair tangles around my ankles. Shock sutures me in place, my stomach turning over, but a firm grip lands on my shoulder, leading me out of the room.

I'm still staring at the lifeless head. The brunette man.

I recognize him as the servant who offered me my soup. A guard in disguise or a servant trained in combat, it makes no difference.

He's just as dead, either way.

By the time I regain my wits and realize it's Carlisle shoving me into the hallway, Astor is out of sight, still grappling with the last two guards.

I dig my heels into the ground, but Carlisle is surprisingly strong for his lean frame. And I'm so tired. It's not the same tired as when I struggled against Astor when he kidnapped me from Neverland, when I wilted in his arms, so fatigued of struggling and failing.

I'm tired of being pushed around. Taken places I don't want to go. Tired of hands where I don't want them. Tired of my feet moving without me telling them to.

I've no weapon to fight back with, but according to Charlie, I'm less in need of a weapon than I am a weakness.

"Wait!" I scream, rounding in Carlisle's arms to face him, clinging to his coat in desperation. "You don't know what he's planning. Please. Please, you have to help me."

Of course, Carlisle has no intention of the sort. But I'm a kidnapped girl—one Carlisle probably assumes has been forced under threat of knifepoint to go along with Astor's plans. I'm convincing enough for his ears to perk at the idea of some master scheme.

Encouraged by Carlisle's slowed pace, I grope at his coat like I'm grasping for purchase at the side of a cliff. Muttering incoherently helps, because although Carlisle growls at me, "Spit it out, girl," he's focused on my warbling lips, which he's convinced are the only obstacles between him and tradable information.

I'm clinging to him with such force it keeps him from noticing my fingers easing into his inner coat pocket. That is, until I attempt to hide the folded piece of parchment I lifted in the pocket of my torn gown. Carlisle glimpses it, his face flashing with anger as he plucks it from my hand, then grabs my wrists and squeezes.

The press of his fingers against my wrists aches, but for the first time, I know what to do.

I throw all my weight into bearing down on his thumbs and rolling my wrists out of his grasp. At the same time, I bring my knee to his groin.

The lord keels over, gasping for breath. His grip abandons both my wrists and the parchment, granting me sufficient time to pluck the parchment from the ground and race down the hallway. I shove it into my dress pocket, praying it's what I think it is.

I barely make it halfway down the hall before Carlisle catches up to me. He digs his fingers into the hair at the nape of my neck and yanks me to the ground. The back of my head slams against the floor-boards, sending my vision swimming.

Carlisle steps over me, straddling me with his legs. There's a sick longing in his gaze, a high he gets from anticipating violence. My stomach turns over as he speaks. "You shouldn't have touched me there if you didn't want me to show you what—"

Carlisle doesn't get to finish his sentence.

This time, I close my eyes just in time to miss witnessing the carnage. Something wet and sticky spatters across my face. Coppery blood and gore twinge at my throat, and something heavy falls on my chest.

"Don't look," says a voice as familiar as the sunrise. "Unless you want to, of course."

I don't, so I keep my eyes sutured shut as Astor grabs the mass that's toppled onto my chest and flings it off of me. Then he grasps me by the shoulder and lifts me with one hand to my feet, leading me away.

"You can open your eyes now."

I do, and it's to Astor's face close to mine, his hands on either side of my jawline. I go to turn my head, but his grip won't let me. "Don't look that way," he says. "Just look at me."

I nod, swallowing back sobs as he turns, then takes my hand and leads me through the dark halls. Footsteps sound around the corner, and faster than I can react, Astor wraps one hand around my mouth, the other around my waist, and pulls me into an alcove.

The press of his hand against my mouth feels like having a cloth soaked in Carlisle's blood shoved into my throat. I gag, which makes Astor draw me even closer. "You're okay," he whispers, "but you won't be for much longer if you don't stay quiet. Do you understand?"

When I don't answer, he breathes into my ear, "Wendy, I need you to confirm that you understand."

I nod frantically, and feel his reaction—the easing of his chest against my back.

Just then, a host of guards rush by, as well as men dressed in uniforms of crimson and black—the colors of Laraeth. Lady Carlisle must have sent a messenger to the authorities. I count thirty of them and suddenly understand the importance of remaining quiet. Astor might have been able to take six of them at once, but even he couldn't fend off that many.

It hits me then, that I could make a noise. Call out to the authorities. Astor might snap my neck if I did that, but there's a part of me that bets he wouldn't. He needs me alive if he wants a shadow soother to help him remove his Mark. Besides, he likes having me around so he can keep punishing himself for his wife's death.

I could cry out, and the guards would save me.

But then what? It's not as if I have a home, a family for the authorities to return me to. All I have are my brothers and Peter, and I'll never be more equipped with resources to seek out a cure for Peter's curse than I am with Astor.

So I keep quiet until the guards' footsteps fade into the night.

And into the shadows, Astor and I fade away.

CHAPTER 26

WENDY

This poor carriage driver. Druisk, I think his name is. Astor has him at knifepoint, angled up against the side of the carriage so that his aged back is cracking.

"You don't have to be rough with him," I hiss through my teeth.

"Forgive me if I don't consider you the authority on who does and doesn't have the right to be rough with whom," Astor hisses back.

The lump in my throat is enough to silence me momentarily. Sweat drips down the carriage driver's wiry sideburns. He's trembling, though whether from fear or difficulty holding his balance in the obtuse angle Astor's gotten him in, I'm not sure.

"I told ya, sir. Already took the last guest down the mountain an hour ago. Stopped by the local pub for a pint on my way back, then—"

"Tell us where the man lived," says Astor. "Or else I'll have to go back in and cut the information out of your employer." He digs the edge of his blade into the man's throat for emphasis.

"Don't care much for the lady of the house to be honest," says Druisk. "Never had the kindest things to say about me wife."

Astor looks as if he's about ready to give up on this world, when the carriage driver says, "Besides, I don't know where he lived. Asked me to drop him off at the docks."

Astor glances at me, but we're both having the same thought. If the guest who knows how to get a Mating Mark removed went to the sprawling docks, which take up half the coastline in a city like Laraeth, there's slim chance we'll find him. For all we know, he boarded a ship and is out at sea by now.

Astor tosses Druisk aside, then commandeers the horse at the head of his carriage.

"I thought you said you were gonna get the information out of the lady of the house," says the carriage driver, sounding a tad disappointed that Lady Carlisle's throat will remain intact tonight.

"The authorities already took her in," I explain. We watched them from the bushes as they hurried her away for questioning after they'd searched the house and failed to find us. Judging from their chatter, they'd assumed we'd run off to the docks. Which they're most likely swarming as we speak.

Panic surges in my heart for Charlie. I'd rather she not get caught because of my folly. Before I have much time to consider her fate, Astor grabs me by the waist and tosses me onto the horse.

I land with a thud, bewilderment knocking the wind out of me more than the landing.

Astor turns back to the carriage driver, still shivering on the ground as he props himself up on his elbows.

"You won't believe me if I swear not to tell a soul, will ya?" Druisk says.

"I'm afraid not," says Astor, though there's genuine regret twinging his voice.

"You don't have to kill him," I say, hastily. "They already know who we are, and he doesn't know where we're headed."

Astor blinks, then sheathes his sword and hops up on the horse behind me without another word.

We ride halfway down the mountain in silence before I've hoarded up enough courage to ask, "The crew..."

"We'll rendezvous with them in Naverough," he says. "I told them to meet us there if we didn't return by midnight."

"So you knew there was a possibility that the Carlisles might force us to stay."

"Everything's a possibility. I just make it my aim to account for as many outcomes as I can."

I bite my lip, trying not to feel the warmth of the captain's chest pressed against my back as the horse takes us down the treacherous mountain path. Eventually, the quiet gets to me, and I can no longer rein in my thoughts. "And did you account for not getting the answer to your question?"

The captain doesn't deign to answer.

It feels foolish, but I shove my hand into my pocket and pull out the folded piece of parchment.

Immediately, I sense his attention swivel to my hand.

"What is that?"

"At dinner, I noticed Lord Carlisle glancing at it. I couldn't help but remember that he'd misspoken your—well, Cortland Rivers' name. He called you Corbin. It made me think that surely he had to have a system to keep up with his many guests. And then I saw a servant hand him something before dinner—"

Just then, the wind picks up, snatching the parchment from my hands. I gasp, but Astor snatches it out of the air, muttering in annoyance as he tucks it back into my palm.

"Read it. My hands are busy," he says, tugging on the reins. "But try not to drop it this time."

I roll my eyes. "No, 'Thank you, you're a genius, Wendy'? 'You saved the mission, Wendy'?"

"I might be more amenable to offering you praise had you not also ruined the mission."

That's fair. When I open the parchment, it's exactly what I hoped— a guest list, full of descriptions as well as addresses. I scan the document until I find the description I'm looking for.

"Tertius Vale. Wiry gray hair. Dabbles in sailing. Tarot Lane. Red house. Likes blondes."

Astor grunts, which is altogether unsatisfying, but I can't help the smile that curves on my lips when he says, "Well done, Darling."

We spend the next few minutes in silence, and I try to focus on how pleased I am with myself. Retrieving Lord Carlisle's cheat sheet is the first thing I've done right in a long, long while.

Perhaps that's why we both feel the need to ruin the moment. Return to the familiar embrace of our unpalatable equilibrium.

Astor speaks first. "Are you...alright?"

My throat stings as I think of the panicked moment back in the library annex. Of Peter tearing my dress apart as I tried to push him off of me, to no avail.

"I'm fine," I lie.

Astor grunts.

"Thank you, by the way," I whisper as the locusts sing in the trees on the mountain pass. "That wasn't how I wanted it to happen for us."

Astor's fingers clench around the reins, his fingernails scraping at the bare skin of my waist where there's a hole in the blanket I've wrapped around myself.

"It wasn't how you wanted it to happen," he repeats back, flatly. Like he's reexamining the entirety of our language for any alternative interpretation. "Please tell me you're referring to something other than what I walked in on between you and the winged boy. Please tell me you're not entertaining the idea of ever letting him near you again."

My heart pounds against my chest. "He's not himself when he's in his shadow form," I say, though I can't describe why I so desperately feel the need to explain. "It's not Peter who's in control; it's someone else."

"Please stop talking before I go and hurt your tender little feelings."

A sob lodges in my throat. "I'm trying to thank you."

"No, you're trying to find an excuse for him. An explanation that would justify what he did. Does Peter know what he's like in his shadow form? Does he know what his shadow form would like to do to you?"

I inhale a sharp burst of salt air. It burns in my throat. "He knows his shadow self is ill-mannered. If Peter, the real Peter, wanted to hurt me, he could have." *He could make me do anything he wanted,* I don't say.

The mark on the inside of my elbow burns, reminding me of the bargain I made with Peter the night in the clock tower—a blank check for Peter to cash at his will.

Astor actually snorts. "And tell me this: can Peter control shifting in and out of his shadow form?"

I open my mouth, ready to tell him of course not, but that's not entirely true. "He can control it within Neverland, but the Sister requires him to be in shadow form when he visits the other realms. He's not responsible for what he does when it takes over."

Hoping to end the conversation there, I retreat into myself. Astor's not done, though. "Would you excuse a man for beating his wife if he only did it when he was drunk?"

I wince, glad at least Astor is behind me and can't witness my reaction. I know the correct answer, that I wouldn't. I'd say if the man truly loved his wife, he wouldn't touch the bottle that led to his loss of control, that led to her pain.

I can't admit to that. Astor knows why. But it hurts too much to acknowledge, so I pull out the only weapon I have.

"And am I to forgive what you did to my family on the grounds that it was revenge that drove you to it? That you had a good reason to lose control?"

Astor's voice is soft, low, when it tickles my ear. "I don't lose control, Wendy Darling. And lest my memory fails me, I don't recall asking for your forgiveness."

CHAPTER 27

WENDY

*T*ertius Vale has returned from the docks and is already asleep by the time we sneak through his manor windows and into his room. We have to tiptoe over weeks-old meals left to mildew and clothes strewn about. The manor itself is large enough to demand servants, though Vale seems to be the only one inhabiting the house.

Explains why he felt the need to visit the Carlisles and sell them a secret. Though in the end, it wasn't coin he asked for, but a night with Lady Carlisle. Perhaps that's why he no longer has the capital to pay servants. Too much wealth squandered on prostitutes and opium down by the docks.

I'm not sure why my blood froths in the presence of this man. I don't know him, and he's certainly done nothing to me. But as I stare down at his wrinkled face, I witness a dozen others, all eager to get their hands on me, none of them deterred by my youth. There's something that tells me that if Vale had lived in Estelle, he would have loved being one of my parents' dinner guests.

Bet he wouldn't have married me, either.

I can't tell if it's that hunch or the sickly scent of days-old milk left in a half-full bottle by his bed that's rattling my senses.

I'm not at all sorry when Astor wakes Vale by nicking his throat with his blade.

The man jolts in bed, which only serves to dig the cut deeper, though Astor is prepared for such a reaction and angles the knife so that he won't spill too much blood. No need to risk slicing an artery that might keep us from getting the information we need.

"You," hisses the wiry old man as he blinks up at Captain Astor. They hadn't been seated near one another at the table, but he must recognize him all the same.

"Me," says Captain Astor with a feral grin.

I'm not sure whether he despises Vale for the same reasons I do, or if he just enjoys the thrill of threatening someone he perceives as weak.

My guess would be the latter.

"What do you want? I don't have any money, as you can probably surmise," Vale says, licking his chapped lips as he glances about his disheveled room. Almost like he's embarrassed. It's so sad, it's a tad disgusting.

"Your poverty shouldn't be an issue," says Astor, snaking the blade of the knife around the man's throat and lifting his jowls like he's peering underneath a curtain. I have to hold back a cruel laugh.

"We want someone who can perform a Mating Bond removal ritual," I say. Astor glances at me, crinkling his forehead like he's surprised I spoke up, but he gestures for me to continue all the same. "Tell us, and tomorrow morning when you wake, you can tell yourself we were only a nightmare you're glad to be rid of."

Astor appears amused as he watches me. "A tad dramatic, Darling, but not untrue."

Vale snorts. "I very much doubt I'll think I dreamed this up, given the scar I'll have from this blade."

I dig my heels in. "You can pretend you cut yourself shaving."

"Are you really planning on dying on this hill?" asks Astor, flicking his eyes over to me through his heavy black eyelashes.

My heart flutters at the laughter simmering underneath his expression. "We must die somewhere," I volley back.

Astor sighs, then leans over the man, digging the knife in deeper. "Very well. You heard my companion. Tell her you'll believe she was a nightmare when you wake up in the morning."

The man rolls his eyes. "Surely—"

Astor knicks a chunk off Vale's skin. He yelps. "Fine, fine. It shouldn't be too much of a stretch of the imagination," he grumbles.

It's probably not the professional pirate—excuse me, privateer—thing to do, but I beam.

"Would you like to hold the knife, too?" Astor asks, his tone rendering his subsequent eye roll redundant.

"I'm tempted," I say, which is a lie, but a fun one. "But I'm happy to be the one to do the interrogating this time. I'll spare you having to clean up the mess. I know you hated it last time."

Vale's eyes widen, like he can't tell whether I'm bluffing but isn't willing to find out. Astor turns his face away like he's bored, but I know he's biting back a smile. He wouldn't aim one of those in my direction if that knife was held to his throat instead.

"I hate to inform you, but you're hours too late," says Vale. "I sold that particular secret tonight. To Lady Carlisle. Though I imagine you know that."

"Yes," I say, trailing my finger along the bedside. "I also know that secrets aren't exactly limited resources. They don't burn after you use them like coal or oil."

"Though they do become less valuable the more you tell," says Astor, "so don't be trying to weasel payment out of us."

"Yes, sparing Vale's pitiful life should be plenty payment," I say. It's rather easy to curl up my nose at the man.

"It seems I'm a dead man either way," Vale says. "And no offense, little lady, but I fear the Carlisles more than I do you. They don't take well to people double dipping with the secrets that are supposed to be exclusive to them. Last man who did ended up bird food after being skewered at the top of the lighthouse."

"Well, if it's Lady Carlisle you're worried about," I say, picking my nails, "then I suggest you'd better run when we're done with you. I can't imagine you'll miss this place much, seeing how you don't seem to bother to take care of it. As for Lord Carlisle, I wouldn't worry about him."

"And why not?"

Vale's looking a bit too apathetic for my liking, so I bat my eyes coyly. "Why, because I killed him, of course."

This time, Astor slides his eyes over to me with such annoyance, I almost laugh. I'm not sure what's come over me. Maybe it's my body's strange reaction to the fear that jolted through me when I thought Peter was going to force himself on me, maybe it's because Carlisle's blood still coats my tattered gown from where his head rolled onto my chest. Maybe it's more than that. Maybe it's just that I'm tired of being timid.

Maybe I've snapped.

"And you?" asks the old man to Astor.

I answer before the captain can respond. "He does what I tell him to."

Astor tenses, but the corner of his lip twitches upward.

This, the old man seems to believe well enough. He's probably had plenty of secrets coaxed from his lips by shrewd women.

"And you're sure Lord Carlisle is dead?" he asks. Like he thinks he has some rapport with Lady Carlisle now that they've shared a bed.

"Positive," says Astor.

The man sighs, slinking into his pillow as he closes his eyes. "I can't tell you where, but I know the name of the man who does."

I pick at my nails. It's something I saw the leading lady do at a production my parents took me to when I was young. That was before I fell ill of the plague, of course. Before everything changed and they feared letting me out of the manor.

"Dear," I say, running my finger along Astor's shoulder. He tenses underneath my touch but doesn't pull away. I don't know why I'm doing this, but it's as if I've stepped into a persona that's swallowed me whole. "Explain to Mister Vale here why that's not going to be good enough."

"Of course, Darling," Astor says as he allows the tip of his blade to hover at the curve of the man's eye.

Vale pants, blinking furiously. "Please, it's good information. You're looking for the Nomad. He's got what you're looking for."

Astor stills, cocking his brow.

"You've heard of him?" I ask.

Astor doesn't answer. He just stares down at Vale, desperation written all over the man's face.

"You're sure?" Astor asks.

Vale looks like he's about to nod, then thinks better of it as Astor lowers his dagger and Vale's drooping skin scrapes across the blade.

"Yes. He knows the secrets of the dead, you know."

"What does that have to do with removing a Mating Bond?" I ask.

Astor chooses his words carefully. "The dead possess a different sort of magic than the living."

I snap my head toward Vale. "You're saying the Nomad can talk to the dead? Get them to perform the ritual for us?"

"Not talk to them," says the man. "The Nomad's been there, to the realm of the dead itself. Made friends...and enemies...of those past."

The hairs on my arms stand on end, but my shrill laugh sounds convincing enough. "And we're supposed to take your word for it?"

"Lady Carlisle did."

I bite my lip.

"And who else have you told?" asks Astor.

The man peers up at him with glittering eyes. "Now, you know I can't tell you that. But don't get to thinking I'm the only one other than Lady Carlisle who knows."

"Perhaps you're bluffing so I won't kill you to keep it a secret," says Astor. "As it is, you're no good to me, dead or alive."

My breath catches. "Astor—"

"Close your eyes, Darling. Unless you'd like to do it yourself."

In the end, I leave the room. I tell myself it's because I hold all life sacred and that it bothers me that Astor's taking one.

But really, I just don't want to witness another throat slit by Astor's hand.

It reminds me of what he is, who he's killed, and why. And for reasons I don't care to admit to myself, I don't want to associate any of that with Astor anymore.

When he's done, he climbs out the window, following me, wiping the blood off his blade and onto his pants before he sheathes it.

Then he sneaks a glance at me. I'm expecting him to scold me. Or mock me for being unable to watch him kill that man. Or perhaps ask me what came over me. Why, for a moment, I became someone else.

Instead, he says, his green eyes glittering, "Well done, Darling."

Then he offers his arm and escorts me away.

CHAPTER 28

WENDY

Since Astor gave the crew commands to meet us in Naverough if we hadn't returned to the ship by midnight, we have to cut inland. While the ship will have traversed easily around the bay and into the harbor of the next city, there's a mountain range separating the two. Astor assures me that the trek is manageable, especially by horse. There's a mountain pass that cuts through the range. As it is, it will take us hours to arrive.

The idea of spending so many traveling hours with Astor at first has me wriggling in the saddle, unable to still myself. Once the adrenaline of interrogating Vale dies down, the reality of the night's events crashes to the forefront of my mind, one grisly scene after another competing for attention.

We killed Arthur Carlisle. Well, Astor killed Arthur Carlisle, but I might as well be an accomplice. We'll have made enemies—anyone who might have had unfinished business with Carlisle and paid up front. Not to mention his wife, who likely still maintains enough connections to hunt us down.

She knows who I am. And she knew enough about Peter's whereabouts to contact him, though I'm still unsure how she managed that. I'm still convinced she doesn't know how to journey to Neverland;

she said she used a contact in this realm, probably someone Peter knows from the errands he runs for the Sister. But still.

If I was going to predict anyone to have the tenacity and resources to figure out how to reach Neverland, it would be her.

Wendy Darling had taken her husband.

The only question is, how far will Lady Carlisle go to exact her revenge?

I consider the lords and ladies I met growing up, those who were friends, or at least ran in the same social circles as my parents. Few of them seemed happy together. Even those who pretended, batting each other on the shoulder and holding hands in public. Those were the couples often found slinking away from each other's grips once they thought they were out of sight.

Lord and Lady Carlisle had put on a pretense of being infatuated with one another, but surely most of it was for show. The pair might have operated as incredible business partners, but there can't have been love between them. Surely not. Not when Lord Carlisle seemed so calm, so pleased, knowing exactly what his wife was doing with one of his dinner guests in his own home.

Business partners. Business partners with wedding bands.

That's all they had been. Surely.

I comfort myself knowing that in a place like Laraeth, Lady Carlisle will be the sole inheritor of her husband's estate. Perhaps she'll see Arthur's death as an opportunity, rather than a reason to seek vengeance.

For John and Michael's sake, I pray so.

For a while, as we ride, I'm able to keep my mind busy with the eternal loop of pondering Lady Carlisle's next move. But in the corners lurk what happened in the library annex tonight. What Peter —rather, his shadow self—almost did to me.

I hadn't wanted to approach the subject with Astor, not when he refuses to look at things from any but one, very accusatory angle. But I know Peter. And the shadow in the parlor—that wasn't him. At least, not who he would be if he hadn't been altered by the Sister, if he hadn't been warped outside of his control.

Except for the confusion when he realized what he'd done—that Peter I had recognized, even if it was for the briefest moment. It hadn't been sadness, hadn't been pain, really. But a numb resignation. That wall that Peter hits when any normal person would feel hurt. A callus too tough to cut through.

Still, I can't forget the fear that lanced through my heart when I realized he wasn't going to stop. That I had no power other than to beg, and that my pleas meant nothing. I can't forget the feel of velvet at my fingertips and hands touching skin I had wished to remain covered. Shame still tingles on the patches of skin that, while now hidden, feel as bare as they did when Peter tore my gown.

I can't. I can't go back to being the weak girl in the parlor. I can't be touched like that again.

I can feel myself begin to shake, and because I fear Astor will bring up the events of the night again, I breathe deeply, trying to calm myself.

For the first time, I'm confronted with doubt. A question I hadn't considered.

I've wanted nothing more than to free Peter of his curse. Made it my utmost goal, my purpose.

I've been so fixated on healing Peter, I haven't considered what I will do if I fail. It's never been a question of whether I will return to Peter, just when—before the six months are up because I've helped Astor finish the task, or at the end of it.

But tonight I got a harrowing glimpse into what my future might hold if I don't manage to free Peter from his curse.

And because I can't abide the thought of losing the part of Peter I love—the kind man who dances with me in the stars, who always catches me when I fall, who's shown my sad spirit heights I'd never hoped to graze on my own, my spirit too short to reach; because I can't imagine a life apart from my Mate, I refuse. I refuse to answer the question, though it beats at my mind.

I have to break Peter's curse. I can't. I can't...

"You've had a...difficult night," Astor says. "Why don't you try to get some sleep?"

196

"I doubt very much I'll get any sleep on a horse," I say.

"Let me guess. The debutante can't sleep without a pillow and a set of silk sheets?" says the captain, though there's no venom in his tone.

"The silk is unnecessary, but the pillow is paramount," I say, grateful he's attributing my trembling to exhaustion, when we both know that's only half of it.

Astor clicks his tongue and kicks at the horse's side. It comes to a stop. In a fluid motion I'm not expecting, nor that I fully understand the physics behind, Astor takes me by the waist and flings me around and behind him, switching our spots in the saddle. I hardly have time for an alarmed exhale.

"There," he says. "Now you have a pillow."

I stare awkwardly at his back, arms fidgeting at my sides. Impatiently, Astor lets out a groan and takes hold of my hands, wrapping them around his waist. When I don't budge, Astor says, softly, "You'll feel better if you sleep."

"You don't know what awaits me in my dreams," I whisper quietly.

"How about this? If I detect any sign that you're having a nightmare, I'll wake you up."

My lips twitch into a soft smile. "They always say you're not supposed to do that."

"Then it's a good thing that I don't know who 'they' are or why they think I care what they say."

I let a careless chuckle leave my throat. "You promise?"

Astor opens his mouth, then quickly shuts it. Over his shoulder he offers me a smirk. "Nice try. You know I don't make promises."

"Worth a shot," I say, the teasing between us making it easier for me to nestle my cheek into his back, at the muscle just between his shoulder blades. His back is firm. Warm. Not at all like a pillow. But it's somewhere steady to rest my head.

I close my eyes and let myself feel the gentle ebb of his ribcage as he exhales, his breaths shallow. A moment later, warm skin closes over the back of my hand at his waist. A spark sizzles from where he rests the pad of his thumb at my knuckles, coursing up my arm and burning my cheeks. He must feel my whole body tense, because quietly he explains, "So I can keep you steady once you fall asleep."

His thumb grazes over the back of my hand so subtly, I wonder if I'm imagining it. If I'm imagining how he avoids scraping it against my ring accidentally.

I fall asleep like that, Astor's heart pounding gently against my ear.

When I dream, it's not of Peter's hands all over me in the parlor as I feared, but of Astor, easing his fingers into the spaces between mine as we dance, for a blissful moment unaware of the bloodstained rug below our feet.

THE COASTAL TOWN of Naverough is the illegitimate daughter of whatever royalty birthed the thriving city of Laraeth. While both cities sit enthroned in a cliffside bordering the coast, the similarities end there. Instead of the marble facades of Laraeth, the buildings in Naverough are made of poorly hewn stone, the roofs hardly weather-resistant enough to make up a port city.

Though *port* is a bit too strong of a word for what's in the bay. It's more like two shabby docks, one of which looks about ready to make its hasty escape into the sea any day now. That's, of course, where the *Iaso* is docked.

The shadows that usually encapsulate the ship have retreated, presumably into the magic-infused black box that Evans keeps watch over. I'd asked Charlie about it once. She'd explained that while the shadows are excellent when warding off attention in the seas, or frightening other voyagers, they're a coveted black market item and best kept secret among a city of people who could fetch a high price for one if stolen. She'd had a similar explanation when I'd asked her why our escape from Neverland was the only time I've experienced the *Iaso*'s ability to fly. Apparently it requires quite a bit of faerie dust to sustain and isn't a feature that Astor wants advertised.

Rain pelts Astor and me as he guides the horse to the dock. I'm soaked and shivering, and I give in to the urge to cling more tightly to

Astor's firm torso. He tenses, and for a moment, I wonder if he's stopped breathing.

"What happens to the horse?" I ask as we trot through the uneven streets and approach the docks.

Astor nods his head over to a seaside inn, a shabby but clean-looking place compared to the rest of the town. "I'll leave him tied up here. The innkeeper will notice soon enough that it's not one of the animals of the guests and will peddle him off, I'm sure."

He slides off the horse and offers a hand to me. I take it, unsure I'll be able to get down myself. Not with how my thighs and torso are aching with fatigue from riding through the night. Sure enough, when I whip my leg over the horse, it cramps and I fall, sliding down the beast's hide.

Astor's there to catch me, one hand around my waist, pulling me into him to steady me, while the other remains unwavering around my own hand. Rain pelts us from above, dripping off his forehead and onto my nose, rolling down to my lips where his gaze lingers, just for a moment, before he sets me down, my feet squishing in the mud.

I clear my throat and tear my gaze from his to peer down at my feet, only inches away from a pile of what looks to be horse manure.

"That could have been tragic," I say, chuckling at the absurdity of possibly being any more filthy than I already am, covered in grime and gore.

"I wouldn't have dropped you," the captain says, his tone less playful than mine. I glance back up at him in surprise, but he's no longer paying me any attention, just tying the horse up at the post.

By the time we slog through the muddied streets and onto the docks, Charlie and Maddox have already slid a rope ladder down the side of the boat and are waving to greet us.

When we scale onto the deck, Charlie looks me up and down, her gaze asking a single question. *What happened to my dress?*

The answer is, shredded to bits and dumped on the floor of Carlisle Manor, but explaining what happened to it is going to involve bringing up Peter, and...

"I'll buy you a new one in the next city we dock in," says Captain

Astor, heading off Charlie's question before she can ask it. But he soon amends his statement. "The next city that doesn't stink of refuse."

"I will hold you to that," Charlie says, to which Maddox chuckles. "Though the last one had ruffles at the bottom of the skirts, and I have to say, if you're already having a new one made…"

"No ruffles. Got it," says Astor, his closed-lip smile genuine if not a bit weary.

CHAPTER 29

WENDY

*C*harlie and Maddox have a million questions for us upon our return, but Astor dismisses them, claiming he'll debrief them after he's had time to rest. When Charlie's and Maddox's eyes swivel to me, Astor glares at them and rephrases his initial condition to "after *we* have had time to rest." The result is a less than subtle look between Charlie and Maddox, which the captain pretends not to notice. Begrudgingly, they both shoo us off toward the cabins.

As I shuffle down the hallway toward my and Charlie's room, Astor's voice follows me, stopping me in my tracks. "Dine with me."

I let out a shaky laugh as I turn around. "Why?"

"Because we succeeded in our mission, and success merits celebration."

I bite my lip. It's not really as though I succeeded. I'd gone to the manor intending to learn how to break Peter's curse. Instead, I'd almost fallen victim to it. Still, that we're on our way to consult a man who's traversed the realm of the dead fills me with hope, strange as it may sound. If he knows an individual who broke a Mating Bond, perhaps he knows how to break Peter's curse.

Even if he doesn't, even if I'm not a single step closer to my goal, I can't help but bask in the thrill of what we've accomplished. The goal isn't mine, but I've witnessed enough of Astor's tenderness to know I don't wish for him to hurt. I don't wish for him to be shackled by his withered Mating Mark.

Strange, my two missions: bring the man I love pain, and remove the pain of the man I don't.

"It's almost morning," I say.

"Does that negate your need for sustenance?"

"My clothes are soaked from the rain," I say, fully aware it's a weak excuse.

"Then you had better hurry to get changed then," Astor says. "I don't like to be kept waiting. Especially when it comes to a hot meal."

I nod, biting back a smile, and scurry off.

I HAVE to take a steadying breath before I knock on the captain's door. Part of me wonders if he'll have changed his mind in the time it took me to ready myself for dinner. My tattered gown was sodden, making it difficult to wrangle off. I had to recruit Charlie, who seemed suspicious as soon as I asked to borrow another one of her gowns rather than slide into more comfortable attire.

When I'd told her I was dining with the captain, she'd treated me to a sharply arched eyebrow. Explaining it was just to celebrate our success hadn't done much to temper her suspicion.

Although I'd feigned indifference, I hadn't resisted much when she insisted on fixing my hair into a slightly more intricate braid than usual.

For a while, no one comes to the door. The seconds stretch out for minutes before I get up the courage to knock again, though this time the knocks are more timid.

Shuffling feet, and a shadow appears underneath the doorstep.

My heart twists into knots, but I don't have time to flee before the door opens, and before me towers Astor. He's running a towel through his still-wet hair, black strands dripping over his forehead.

It occurs to me he's bathed, and I haven't.

It also occurs to me that I definitely should have bathed. There's no telling how I stink after our excursion. Granted, I've changed, but I probably still reek of gore.

I'm about to mumble an excuse to flee the premises when the captain gestures me inside. "Took you long enough. I was about to retire to bed."

There's no accusation in his voice. Just amused teasing. Indeed, he's not dressed for dinner, in his captain's coat like I might have expected. Instead, he sports a pair of loose trousers and a white shirt, carelessly askew at the neckline. He must have just thrown it on. Even the bed is already partially unmade.

My eyes glance over to the table, where two plates sit prepared but untouched.

"I thought you weren't going to let your food get cold," I say.

The captain ignores me as he shuts the door behind us. The cabin feels cozier than the last time I was here. Maybe it's a by-product of the lack of shackles at my wrists.

When I sit at the table, small enough that it only fits the two of us, he takes the seat across from me. A plate of blackened trout, grits flavored with cheese, and broccoli florets the crew must have obtained in Laraeth sits before me, though it's not steaming.

My stomach twists when I notice the goblet sitting in front of me, but when I bring it to my lips, I'm relieved to find it's just water. There's not even a bottle of wine on the table.

The silence between us is painful as we scarf down our meals. The trout has gone cold, but my stomach isn't complaining. I hadn't realized how hungry I'd become.

Finally, when I'm beginning to think the silence will break me, the captain asks, "Did you have a theater tutor?"

Unfortunately, I'm halfway into a bite of trout, so the captain will have to wait. Once I've gulped it down rather forcefully, I say, "An odd question, don't you think?"

He picks at his grits. "I don't think so. In fact, I think it's quite relevant given your performance at Vale's."

"Oh. That." My cheeks burn and I take a gulp of water as if it were a swig of soothing wine, burning on the way down. "I suppose I did make it seem as if I were the boss behind the operation."

"You were rather convincing. Though perhaps I was simply eager to be convinced."

My tongue goes dry, despite the water. "And why is that?"

"I've always told you I'd like to see you assert yourself."

My tone goes chilled. "Funny. I don't remember you saying as much. What I do remember is you insulting my timidity and weak-mindedness."

The captain returns to his meal, looking slightly abashed.

"No," I say when I can't bear the silence any longer.

He quirks a brow, swirling his fork around the edge of his plate.

"No," I go on. "I didn't have a theater tutor. I wanted one, but my parents felt it unwise. They thought it would lead to me wanting to join productions."

"I was under the impression that such activities were finding their way into high society."

"Well, yes," I say, glancing away as I rub my palms against the tops of my knees. "For children whose parents let them leave the manor."

Captain Astor leans back in his seat. "Ah."

"But John and I used to put on shows for Michael. For the longest time, my youngest brother only spoke when he was repeating something dramatic. For a while, we thought his jargon didn't mean anything, but when we realized he was using the dramatic quotes and songs in contexts that fit, we started exposing him to more of those things. We wanted to give him more to say, more ways to express himself. So John and I used to write and perform plays for him. Up until...well, up until I entered society, I guess. When it became obvious that my time should be devoted to...well, other things."

The captain clenches his fingers against the edge of the table but says nothing except, "You love your brothers dearly, then."

I nod, trying to quell the burning in my eyes. I'd rather not cry in front of the captain.

"Are they..." He looks as if he's choosing his words carefully. "Should I have taken them too?"

The words needle through me with shock, the implication infuriating. "You act as if you stole me for my own benefit rather than your own."

The captain stares at me. "Can it not have been both?"

My cheeks heat with anger, but there's no use tantrumming. "Peter saved Michael the night before you took me. Michael fell from the cliffs. Peter caught him. He won't let anything happen to him. To either of them."

The captain's gaze darts to my hands, where my fork is trembling. When he speaks, he sounds as if he's attempting to approach a fawn in the woods. "The other boys on the island…"

I slam the fork against the table. "They're good boys. At heart. Nettle was misguided, eaten up by his own anger at what he perceived to be Peter's betrayal and Thomas's evil nature. Simon happened to get roped in. None of them would lay a hand on either of my brothers unless it was for one of their silly wrestling matches."

I expect the captain to argue, but he says, "I'm glad to hear your brothers are safe."

For some reason, this offends me most of all, but as I'm incapable of ascribing reason to my offense, I instead offer him a question. "Do you have any siblings?"

Astor blinks, like no one's ever asked him that question. "Maddox," he says with a lingering tone, "might as well be a brother. And a better one than most could boast of, blood ties or not."

"Have you been friends for a long while, then?" I already know the answer to this from the first time I spoke with Maddox, but I'd like to hear as much as I can of the captain's side of the story. I've found that when it comes to getting information, sometimes it's best to remain quiet.

"Since before I was captain," Astor says. "Maddox and I served under a cruel master. When the crew attempted to overthrow the captain, Maddox got me—and Iaso—out. Together we amassed our own crew. Though we've lost a few along the way." Astor's eyes dip to the corner of the table.

My mouth goes dry. "Would you tell me about her? About your wife?"

Astor's thumb finds his wedding ring. He's wearing it again. "Why would you need to know?"

I don't know how to explain it, my unfaltering curiosity—almost obsession—with the woman who stole Astor's heart, never to give it back, not even after a decade and a half in the grave. "I suppose I don't *need* to know. But...don't you ever just want to know other people? What they love? What they hate? The aches they can't seem to bury?"

The corners of his lips twitch. "I wouldn't have thought you'd want to know a scoundrel like me, Darling."

"And I wouldn't have thought you'd want to know a spoiled heiress who looks as if she's barely been weaned, but I'm not the one who invited you to dine with me, now am I?"

Astor brings his chalice to his lips, hiding his reaction. "You know, you can be insolent. When you want to be."

"I'm not being insolent, I—"

"I didn't say I disliked it." He sets down his chalice, then pushes his plate meticulously to the side. "What is it that you want to know about her?"

"How did the two of you meet?"

A hazy look muddies his green eyes. "I don't remember."

I crane my neck at him.

"What?" he asks.

I shake my head. "You're just the type of man who seems like you'd remember the moment you met the love of your life, that's all."

"What makes you say that?"

"You're rather intense."

The captain chuckles, though he does so without smiling. "Iaso and I grew up together. Knew each other since we were children. That's why I don't remember meeting her. I don't remember falling in love with her either. Just the certainty that I would marry her one day. That certainty...it was like walking. I knew I'd learned it somewhere, but couldn't remember when. Just that it was ingrained within me."

"What did you love about her?" I can't help but ask.

The captain stares, not at the wall, but into the distant past. "She was a riot." His lips quirk into an almost-smile. "Always getting into trouble and dragging me into it. She could make me laugh...Well, she was clever with her words. Witty. Sharp. Quick."

I try to ignore the way my heart twists in my chest as the captain describes the perfect woman—so unlike myself.

"She knew what she wanted from life. At least, she thought she did. She wanted to be a cartographer—she was a savant with ink and a quill. But then, one day, she cut herself on a splinter jutting out from an abandoned storehouse we liked to play in. Her blood dripped onto my knuckles. They'd dried and cracked from the salt air. And it healed my skin right up. Something changed about her after that. She was still just as boisterous, loved to laugh. But she'd found her purpose, and she gave it to others. Her blood, her smile, her laughter. Her life."

My back goes rigid, but there's no anger in the captain's tone. Just tragic awe for an enchanting girl now dead.

"Why do you really want to know?" he asks.

The words come out before I know I've let them. "I wanted to know what kind of woman took my place." *One who's better than me*, is what I don't say. "It sounds like the world is a worse place without her." *And with me*, I neglect to add.

The captain's gaze flickers over me, and I can't stand to dwell on the inkling he's thinking the same thing, so I say, "Did she always love you back?"

His face softens, breaking the tension. "Hardly. She took quite a bit of convincing. For a long while, though I was her closest friend, she thought me too brash to be fit to be a husband."

"You?" I feign shock. "But you're so gentle."

"Yes, if only you could have been around to tell her as much. Lobby on my behalf."

Judging by the look on his face, it seems the words just slipped out. Like he wishes he could take them back. A shadow falls over his expression, and I expect him to make me leave, but instead he says, "What about you, Darling?"

I wriggle in my chair. "What about me?"

"What did you want from life?"

I blink. "I'm unsure what you mean."

He shrugs. "I wanted a ship. A name for myself. For others to fear me. Iaso wanted to heal the world of pain and disease. Maddox wants enough gold to retire the crew to his own private island. Charlie wants Maddox, but more than that, to find her place in a world that burned hers down. What I can't seem to figure out is what Wendy Darling wants."

I pick at the shoulder sleeves of my dress. "For a long time, all I wanted was not to be taken by the Shadow Keeper."

Astor cocks his head to the side, like he's a predator who can sense my fear, my lie.

I sigh. "But that's not altogether true. Part of me wanted to go with him. Years before it happened."

"Why?"

I find myself tracing my Mating Mark, the gentle ridges that brand my cheek. "I think the answer to that question is obvious, don't you?"

"I wouldn't say that."

I raise an eyebrow. "You don't think the fact that he's my Mate had anything to do with me being drawn to him? Is that truly an argument you want to make?"

"I'm better than you at arguing, Darling. I promise you, I'll win."

I can't help myself. I find myself leaning over the table, elbows digging into the slats in the wood, spine stiff to the challenge. "I thought you didn't make promises. And besides, I don't know how you intend to make a stronger argument than the Mating Mark that quite literally binds Peter and me together."

The captain doesn't avert his gaze. "Watch me."

For some reason, the challenge feels like it's about more than winning an argument. It smells of parchment and melted wax sealing an invitation—one to search his sharp features without shirking back, without the social parameters telling me to avert my eyes lest I stare too long. *Watch me.* It's permission to examine the scythe-like line of his jaw. The ruggedness of his sun-weathered skin. The poison in his green eyes.

"I think," he says, and when he locks his stare onto me, I let it land. Soak in his unerring attention rather than shrinking from it. "That you'd been holed up in that manor so long, with nothing to feed that marvelous imagination of yours except your books... I think you wanted out. And I think Peter was the first to offer you his hand. The first to present you with an escape."

Something like regret creases the corners of the captain's piercing eyes.

"Well," I say, cheeks heating, "I don't see how that's a more compelling argument than the Mating Bond."

"Whatever you say, Darling. You didn't answer my question, though."

"Which question?"

"What," he says, his lips careful with the words, "do you want?"

His voice chases a chill down my spine. I play with the ring on my finger, still just a hair too loose. Peter was going to get it altered, but he never got that chance. "Peter and I are going to get married with the Lost Boys as witnesses. Michael's going to be the ring-bearer, though I imagine that'll mean one of the other boys will have to make sure he doesn't go running off to collect seashells. John can't be the one to do it, because he's going to give me away. And then we're going to live where time and society can't touch us. No more rules, nothing weighing us down. We're going to fly every night under the stars."

"Yes, yes, I know that's what going to happen. But what do you want to happen?"

I blink. "I just told you."

I expect the captain to cluck his tongue condescendingly, but he doesn't. He just stares at me, a challenge in his eyes, but his voice is softer than his expression. "What do you want, Darling?"

Stolen glances. Casual brushes. A trail of fire on my jaw. *You missed a spot.* For a man to speak about me the way the captain speaks about his long-dead wife.

"I'm growing tired," I say, standing from the table and pushing my chair back into place. The captain rises, but I shake my head and wave him away. "I can see myself out."

"Wendy."

I'm fidgeting with my ring, not daring to look at him, when thunder cracks across the sky outside. At the same time, a wave jostles the boat. The jolt is quick, and I'm not prepared. I go careening across the floor, scraping my knees against the floorboards. A splinter lodges itself in my skin. I hardly notice it.

Not when my ring is gone.

I search the cabin frantically, praying it didn't fall in between the floorboards, down into whatever lies below the captain's quarters.

Tears spill from my eyes, and I have to catch my sobs in my hand. My ring—the one piece of Peter that hasn't yet been shattered.

The captain's face appears before mine. "Sit down. Just for a moment. I'll find it for you," he says, and I'm too embarrassed by my outburst to argue. I return to my seat, tapping my shoe against the floorboards as the captain searches the cabin.

Moments later, he plucks something silver and gleaming out of a crack between the floorboards. Relief washes over me as I catch sight of the glimmering object between his fingertips. He's running his thumb over its ridges, staring down at it contemplatively.

"Give it back," I say without thinking.

He turns to me, and where I expect anger, hurt sparks in his face. "I am," he says, striding over to me.

When he reaches me, I stretch out my hand to grab the ring, but the captain catches my hand in his, gently running his thumb over my knuckles, leaving trails of fire in his wake. I'm not sure what he's about to do.

Then Captain Nolan Astor kneels.

I should be looking at my trembling hand, watching Peter's ring with the attention of a hawk. Making sure it makes it onto my finger. But all I can see is Astor, kneeling before me, not daring to break eye contact, boring into me with the most beautiful imploring green eyes, burrowing into my soul.

My chest burns. My soul aches.

Cold metal contrasts with warm, calloused skin as the captain slips the ring back onto my finger, never once releasing my gaze.

"There," he says with a whisper, twisting my ring around my finger one last time, though he remains on his knee before me. "Just like you wanted."

CHAPTER 30

JOHN

I'm perched on a lone log, long ago carried away by the waves only for the sea to spit it back out, leaving it to petrify on the beach and be used as a bench, when Peter, just returned from his most recent excursion, approaches me.

"Can we talk?"

It's the most genuine request I've heard from Peter. Usually he's commanding, if not cavalier. Not as if he's giving you an order, but like he can't fathom anyone denying him anyway, so why bother posing it as a request?

"About what?"

"About your sister."

My chest bottoms out for a split second.

"Why? Did you find her?"

Peter shakes his head, looking off into the distance as he places his hands on his hips. We might as well be discussing whether he found a stray cat.

"Any news, then?"

"No," he says. "It's not that."

"Then what is there to talk about?"

If I ever thought Peter was capable of feeling discomfort, it would be right now. His jaw works, like he's been planning a speech and has forgotten all the right words. Peter isn't used to others being skeptical of him. It throws off his innate charm.

"I love her too, you know," he says.

"Something tells me it's not quite the same," I say, placing my deadpan reaction between the two of us. Beyond us, eerie waves lap against the onyx shore.

The beginnings of a smile appear on the edges of his mouth. "You're implying that the love of a sibling is greater than that of a lover."

Tink's face flashes before my eyes. "It's more unique, at least."

He cocks his head. "How do you suppose?"

"It's not replicable. Sure, you can have multiple siblings, but if you lose one, the other could never hope to replace the hole in your heart where the other once was. Loving one sibling doesn't make the love for the other fade over time."

Peter flashes me his teeth. "What are you implying?"

"I'm saying if something happens to my sister—if we find her dead—you'll move on. And the next girl you pluck from her bed will wash away the pain as well as faerie wine would."

"You think that the widowed don't still miss their deceased once they remarry?"

"Sure," I say, my voice crueler than I'm used to hearing it, "but Wendy never married you, did she?"

Peter's face goes cold, like I used to see it do with Wendy when she pushed him too far. I'm still not confident that my comment pierced him like I was intending, but I think it at least landed.

"Why do you insist on being enemies, John?" Peter asks, advancing. "I swear to you, we want the same thing. We want Wendy back here, safe with us."

I snort. "I want Wendy safe. Not back here. Not in Neverland."

"Don't you want for Wendy what she wants for herself?"

I stop for a moment, contemplating. "I think Wendy is twenty years old. I think that it's rare to find a twenty-year-old who knows what they want. I'd be even more surprised if Wendy did, knowing her. She spent her entire life striving to wriggle out from underneath the clutches of a curse. There was no thought given to what she wanted or didn't want. Just what was going to keep her safe."

"That's not really an answer."

I stare at my sister's captor. "Yes, well you should know about non-answers."

"And if I get Wendy back?" he asks. "And I give her time to make her decision about whether she wants to stay? What then? Do you trust her to be able to decide what she wants?"

"I don't trust anyone to decide what they want."

Peter's eyes narrow. Less in anger, more in curiosity. "And why is that?"

"Because that which we desire the most is rarely the thing that would bring us the most happiness in the end. The two simply aren't compatible."

"And you're better suited to decide what would make her the happiest?"

I consider this a moment before answering. "I wouldn't have feelings of being in love muddying my reasoning. So, logically, yes. I do think I'd be better suited than her at figuring out what would make her the happiest. But it goes both ways. She'd be better than me at making decisions for me, too."

Again, Tink's face flashes across my mind. Somehow, I doubt Tink is who Wendy would pick for me to be spending so much time with.

"It must be difficult living in your head," says Peter.

"Remind me: is difficulty inherently bad?"

Peter actually smirks, conceding the point.

Before he leaves, he turns back around.

"Yes?" I say.

"Could you..." Peter pauses. "Would you mind telling me what she was like? Before Neverland, I mean."

"Didn't you visit her nightly when she was a child?" I practically spit.

Peter frowns. "My shadow form...it's not quite me. It is, but I have

difficulty retaining my memories from it. Even the memories I have…
they're not…from the lens of how I might have seen her."

A shiver walks up my spine, but it might be the most honest thing
I've ever heard Peter say.

"Do you want to hear about before you or after you?" I ask.

"I think both would do."

"I don't have many memories of her before she fell ill. She was only
five, I was four. But I remember her being especially protective of me.
I remember that our manor might as well have been an entire realm
for the two of us to explore. People always thought she was quiet. Still
do, I guess."

"Wendy's not quiet?" Peter asks, cocking his head to the side.

I can't help the chuckle that escapes me. "Not when she's comfortable. She'll talk your ear off if you manage to get close enough."

Peter slides his hands into his pockets. "Did she keep secrets from
you?"

The question catches me off guard. "Everyone keeps secrets."

"Mmm," says Peter. For a moment, I think we're done, but then he
stares out into the crashing white waves and says, "Something's
wrong. With you, I mean. You're more sullen than normal."

"I can't see why you care," I say, not particularly eager to share my
disappointment in myself for letting Tink go.

Peter levels me with his icy blue stare. "I care about Wendy's
happiness. And you and Michael are intricately intertwined with that."

I stare at him. "But you wish we weren't."

Peter offers me a sly smile. "Don't group your brother in the same
category as yourself."

I huff. "At least you're honest."

"And you're hiding something."

My back goes rigid.

Peter nods toward my hands. "They've been shaking."

"My sister is missing."

"She's been missing for three months. The shaking is new."

"Maybe I've just now come to terms with her not coming back."

Peter watches me, eyes observant. "I'll get her back, John. You and I are united in that."

I watch my sister's fiancé, her predator, her monster, and wonder where the truth is hidden behind his cool facade. If he cares for Wendy at all. Or if he's angry to have had his favorite toy stolen.

If she was stolen at all, or if he stuffed her away.

I don't know who to trust.

I used to be able to trust Wendy, before he came along and changed her. But it's not as if I haven't changed too. I have pain on my hands. Tink's pain.

"You can talk to me, you know," says Peter. "Whatever it is, I likely understand it more than you would think."

"I was supposed to protect her," I say, more to myself than to Peter. "That's all I've ever wanted, ever since the night she came to my room and cried and told me about the bargain our parents had struck when she was sick. She was still so young when she found out. And I swore to myself I wouldn't let you take her. That I'd exhaust all resources to make sure nothing bad ever happened to her. But it wasn't enough. In the end, you took her anyway. Worse, I'd devoted so much energy into being suspicious of you..."

Peter gives me a knowing but patient look.

"That I never saw Captain Astor coming," I say, suddenly aware of the possibility that Peter could very well be telling the truth. Have I been so blinded by my hatred for him that I've neglected to acknowledge the other enemy?

"You're not the only one who failed her, I'm afraid," says Peter, though he's not looking at me anymore. Instead, he stares out at the frothy sea.

I can't help but wonder if he's talking about losing her to the captain, or something else entirely.

"It's cruel, you know," says Peter after a long stretch of silence.

"What is?"

His face is as unaffected as ever, his tone even apathetic, but I recognize the ability to separate oneself from one's emotions. "That sometimes, the price for protecting those you love is losing that bit of yourself that was good enough to want to protect them in the first place."

My chest rattles, my mind flashing back to branding Tink's flesh. How her whimpers—silent as they were—had reminded me of Wendy's from that night I hid outside the parlor. I'd had to close my heart off to my love for my sister in order to torture the information out of Tink to save her. At least, I'd thought I'd had to do it. To protect Wendy, I'd sacrificed not only Tink, but the part of myself that still cared.

I'm not entirely willing to accept that, though. I'm not willing to accept that the part of me that would die for my sister is gone with my innocence.

"Did you hurt her?" I ask.

Peter doesn't look at me. "Not in the way you're asking."

I think of Wendy whimpering from inside the parlor. How I was too stunned to run and ask my parents for help.

My throat stings. Peter might be laden with guilt for getting Wendy addicted to faerie dust, but he only gave it to her to protect her from the shadows, from herself. I've done worse to my sister.

"Do you think she'll forgive us?" I ask, though I don't specify for what. For not calling for help when she was being abused. For not seeing the captain coming. For letting my obsession with protecting her go so far that I tortured an innocent person, someone who had likely been abused just like my sister.

Peter doesn't answer.

I'M on my way back to the Den when, in the dark, something bumps into me, nearly knocking me over. Panicked, I search the nearby forest for any signs of an assailant, but no one is to be found.

When I slip my shivering hands back into my pocket, my right hand curls around a set of wooden tiles.

I pull them out and examine them in the moonlight.

Three tiles. A sun. A downward-facing arrow. And a cave.

CHAPTER 31

WENDY

I start leaving my ring in my room.

I figure it's safer tucked in a box underneath my bed than it is on my finger, too loose to stay put. I don't want it going overboard because I stumble on the slick deck or because the waves rattle my balance.

If Astor notices, he says nothing, though I get the sense that he peers at my hand when I'm not looking. I can't tell if that's an eerie intuition or if there's a wretched part of me that simply hopes it's the case and is misinterpreting the direction of his attention.

He keeps showing up—the captain. Places I'm not expecting him. Places Charlie isn't expecting him either. In the mess hall, on nights we have after-dinner cleaning duty. On deck at night when I'm questioning Evans about how he reads the stars.

Charlie likes to make vague comments about Astor's tendency to find himself in the same room as me, though none of them are too terribly indicting.

At night, I can't sleep. Not without waking to Peter's phantom hands on my chest, my back, the hem of my undergarments. I keep thinking someone's crawled into bed with me, but when I wake, Charlie's snoring dutifully across the room.

There's a worry tingling in the back of my mind. That I'll wake up, fingers digging into Charlie's throat like they once dug into Michael's. But that was partially due to the shadows that creep all over Neverland, and I haven't encountered a wraith since the night I threw myself overboard. Perhaps they don't like boats. Perhaps there's something about being in the middle of the sea that frightens them. Like they'll get caught on deck in the sun and have nowhere to hide. Exposure like that used to frighten me, too.

Still, I'm not sure how inextricably linked Peter's inability to feel pain is to his shadow self. If I free him from the former, it's quite possible he'll still suffer from the latter. As much as Astor seems to think Peter has a choice in shifting into his shadow form, I know the Sister has a chokehold on him that Astor doesn't quite understand.

I love Peter. Adore him. Desire nothing more than to spend the rest of my life with him.

But if he ever shifts into his shadow form around me again, I intend to be prepared.

Maybe that's why I start throwing myself wholly into my training with Maddox.

THE NEXT TIME WE DOCK, Astor purchases a dozen pig carcasses.

By the time the afternoon rolls around and it's time for my and Maddox's session on deck, I realize exactly what the carcasses are for.

I curl my nose at them. They stink of salt, somehow more concentrated and gritty than the familiar scent of the sea. But that's not the worst part.

"I can't," I say, my short sword that Maddox gifted me from their leftover stock in the weapons galley trembling in my hand. We've been training with it for the past several weeks, and practicing with a real sword has yet to bother me. It's longer, heavier in my hand than the dagger I drove into the back of Victor's father. And besides, I've been sparring with the wind. The densest thing I've cut into has been the spongy fog that descended the day before we docked.

Maddox usually grins at me no matter what we're doing, but today his expression is grim. The crew has gotten used to us training on deck, so they pay us no mind as he strides over to me and places a gentle hand on my shoulder. "Astor warned me this wouldn't be the first time you've cut through flesh."

My knuckles go white on the hilt of my short sword. "Warned you? I'm surprised he didn't make the fact that I'm a murderer sound like a triumph."

Maddox examines me carefully before saying, "Most everything Astor says about you is praise."

When I furrow my brow in disbelief, Maddox laughs. "Well, as close as Nolan gets to offering praise."

"That sounds more believable," I half-grumble, ignoring the way my chest almost swells at the idea of Captain Astor almost-complimenting me.

"Yeah, I don't know if I've heard him pay someone a true compliment since Iaso—" Maddox stops himself, and I pray it's because he misses her too and not because he catches the brief twinge of envy that flickers across my face. "But, then again, Iaso would have never picked up a sword, much less been willing to slice through someone's—"

He stops as I level him with a bland stare. Color tinges his ruddy cheeks and he shifts awkwardly toward the carcasses. He looks like he'd boil his own foot and eat it if it meant keeping any more words from spouting out of his mouth.

The good news is, when it's finally time to hack into the first pig carcass, I find it's not so bad. Turns out, the feel of slicing flesh humming through a blade is more cathartic than I would have thought.

"WELL, I wouldn't call you an artist," says Maddox, looking grimly at the hanging carcass I've hacked into rather obtuse bits. Chunks of pig flesh litter the deck, and most of the crew gives us an even wider berth than normal.

"Funny," I say. "I would have thought they'd be used to messes."

Maddox's smile stretches outward instead of upward. "Messes? Yes. Unassuming women who look like they're getting high off of hacking flesh to bits piece by piece? Even Charlie doesn't do that."

I offer Maddox a bashful grimace. He just pats me on the back and hides that he doesn't know what else to say with a nervous cough.

I'm examining my not-so-handiwork, readying to clean the mess up so no one will get the wrong impression about me, when footsteps approach from behind. I swing around to find the captain peering at the butchered pig with equal parts amusement and disgust. "Kill a man like that," he says, picking the carcass apart even more than it already is with his sharp eyes, "and the authorities will hang you."

"Even if the other person hurt me first," I say.

Neither Astor nor Maddox answers. It wasn't exactly a question anyway.

"You're supposed to be training her to defend herself," drawls the captain to Maddox. "Not how to turn an entire population of people against her."

Maddox shrugs. "Maybe she just wanted to make sure her opponent was dead."

"Which. To be fair. He definitely is," I say, gesturing toward my workmanship.

The captain rolls his eyes. "And if there's more than one opponent? You think you're going to be able to administer death by a thousand cuts if you're surrounded? Better for their deaths to be swift, even if it's more mercy than they deserve. The point is to survive."

"Really?" I say. "I thought the point was to make sure no one ever touches me again."

The captain shakes his head. "You won't get to land that many blows on an opponent that's not already dead."

He whisks out his sword. A sickening slash, and the bottom half of the second pig's corpse lands with a thud on the deck below.

"Yes, well, not all of us are strong enough to do that," I say, annoyed.

The captain tosses me the blade, hilt first. I barely have time to catch it.

"Well, then. Maddox, you know where to take the lessons next."

CHAPTER 32

WENDY

This time, when the officers of the ship assemble in the map room, I'm actually invited. As the meeting convenes, I sidle in to stand next to Charlie, who is propped on a stool cross-legged. Across the table is Astor, Maddox at his side, everyone else filling up the outer rim of the table.

I fight the urge to brush my fingers over the vellum map spread across the table.

"As some of you know, the tip Miss Darling over here" —Astor nods in my general direction without actually looking at me, and my heart skips at the mention of my name—"procured for us in Laraeth leads us in the direction of the Nomad."

A series of murmurs bounce between crew members. Most of them sound like grumbles, suspicion abounding.

"I take it the Nomad isn't going to be easy to find," I whisper to Charlie, who purses her lips.

I also take it that when the captain said "some of you" he really just meant me, Charlie, and Maddox, given we're the only ones who don't seem surprised by the news.

"Not to sound pessimistic—" says Evans.

"Oh, are we trying out a new personality, then?" interrupts Maddox.

Evans just rolls his eyes and continues. "How likely is it that the Nomad even exists?"

Charlie shrugs. "I've heard of him."

"Yes, well, we've all heard of embodied magic broken off from the Fabric of the realms, too, but I don't hear the captain asking us to trek across the sea in search of them."

"Next time," Astor says with a sly smile and half of a wink. "And I have every reason to believe the Nomad is as real as anyone in this room. Vale would have known better than to sell the Carlisles information that was faulty. People don't do that and live to see the light of day."

"Except for us."

Heads swivel in my direction. My face flushes. "I…I didn't mean to say that out loud."

"Wendy Darling," says Astor, "are you trying to support my point or disprove it?" His green eyes are shimmering in the dim light, and though there's nothing but command in his voice, his usual cruelty is absent.

"Neither," I say, abashed. Astor's jaw tightens almost imperceptibly before he looks away.

The captain continues. "The Nomad has been charged with over three hundred crimes across three continents. The rumors about him might be rumors, but they're consistent. His crimes are consistent, too. Assassination. Forgery. Trafficking." Astor's finger taps against the table at the mention of that last one.

"Yes, well, rumors also say that he never tells a lie, so we know not everything about him is true," says Charlie.

"Why's he called the Nomad?" I whisper to Charlie.

When she opens her mouth, Astor answers instead. "We direct our questions to the entire table." I blush more than his tone calls for. He's not scolding me, just informing me of the rules. Still, it's as if everyone's eyes are on me, considering me unworthy of being here.

"She wants to know—" says Charlie, but Astor cuts her off.

"Wendy can speak for herself."

Charlie sighs, then nudges me in the side, and I swallow my anxiety, speaking louder than before. "Why do they call him the Nomad?"

Astor's eyes flicker and take hold of mine. I quickly glance away.

Evans is the one who answers me. "Would you like the realistic answer, or the mystical one?"

"Both," I say, then quickly add, "But save the best for last."

Maddox grins. "He's going to think you mean the realistic one."

Even Astor's mouth twitches.

Evans continues on as if everyone at the table isn't making fun of him. "Those prone to wild fancies believe the Nomad traveled through other realms before settling in this one, though they don't anticipate he'll stay long. Thus, the name. Those of us with our heads attached to this realm of existence call him that because he has no home. Unless you count his fleet of ships."

"How is that different from all of you?" I ask. A few people chuckle, though not at me. Astor's lip twitches upward.

"If what's said about him is true," says Astor, bracing his hands on the map before him, "the Nomad brings his city with him."

"A fleet of ships?" I ask.

"Something like that," says Astor.

"That's beside the point," says Evans. "Even if we manage to find him, there's still the problem of being allowed into his...community. Apparently, they're quite strict about letting people in."

"Yeah, you have to have a passcode," says Maddox, looking like a child who's just been given a baby dragon for Solstice. "That doesn't sound too complicated. Just tell me who I need to charm."

Everyone at the table laughs except for Charlie, who takes a drink.

"If only it were that simple," says Astor. "Unfortunately for us, the password changes every forty-eight hours. Except for those who receive a personal invitation from the Nomad himself, only the inhabitants of the Nomad's community know it."

"So we find a way to get invited," says Maddox, who I imagine has never suffered the experience of being left out.

Evans rubs his temples. "There's slim chance of that."

"You said the inhabitants know the passcode," says Siv, the bald man who was in charge of securing Michael the night of the masquerade. He hasn't exactly been polite to me since my arrival. Then again, I did distract him so that John could strike him over the head. "Meaning they leave the bounds of the community at some point. We could convince one of them to give up the password." He strokes the edge of his dagger in emphasis.

Astor shakes his head. "Torture proves rather ineffective on those loyal to a cause. The Nomad isn't simply a leader, he's their purpose. By the time he's done recruiting his followers, he has their loyalty for life."

"Well, even that has an expiration date," I say. Again, every head turns to me, and I realize I've mumbled under my breath again. I expect Astor to remind me of the table rules, but Siv answers first.

"How insightful. Really, Captain, I can't believe you didn't invite her to our meetings before now," he says.

The words land at my chest, striking a blow in an already tender place. I stand on my tiptoes, waiting for Astor's reaction. I can't decide if I'm waiting for him to join in on scolding me or if I expect him to rip into Siv for openly disrespecting him.

He does neither.

Instead, he just looks at me, a challenge in his fiery green eyes. *Go on*, they seem to taunt. Or maybe taunt isn't the right word. Prod. Stoke.

I search for my voice, and I find it somehow. "His followers might be loyal to him while they're alive, but that doesn't mean we can't get the information out of them."

"Do you speak to ghosts then?" says Siv.

Astor holds his hand up, silencing Siv, and smiles at me, the realization of what I'm thinking dawning on his face.

"Not quite," I say, though *not yet* is what I should say. "But wraiths have a fondness for me. And they're not always loyal to the people who created them."

I would know, I don't add, thinking of the wraith who succeeded in talking me off the side of this ship.

"Are you suggesting, Darling," says Astor, "that we torture and kill one of the Nomad's followers, then use the wraith that's formed from their pain to obtain the passcode?"

The words get hung up in my throat. Astor's staring at me. His question wasn't a taunt. It's genuine. *Do you really want to become this?* is the question dancing in his eyes.

I think back to Zane's brothel. How many patrons Vulcan said frequented their business daily.

"I'm sure we can find someone who deserves it," is all I say.

As the rest of the crew files out of the map room, I stay close to Charlie. It's pitiful, but I'm still shaking from having spoken up in front of the entire crew.

"Charlie," Astor calls out from behind us as we reach the door. "Do me a favor and leave Darling behind."

For a moment, I consider whether my heart has actually ceased to exist. Charlie tosses Astor a conniving look over her shoulder, winks at me, then leaves me stranded.

"How'd you enjoy being a part of the scheming?" asks Astor, still rolling up maps on the table, clearing the space.

"Better this time," I say, interlocking my fingers behind me so Astor won't see me wringing them. "The sound quality is much better in here than it is in the hall."

The captain presses his lips together in a half-smile. "Plus, you get a better view this way."

I refuse to let myself blush. The captain isn't referencing his own appearance anyway. "Much better than peering through the crack in the door," I say. "You should really consider getting that fixed."

"Noted," he says.

I find myself swaying, bouncing on my toes impatiently as I pick at my fingernails behind my back, but the captain doesn't seem to be in a hurry to address whatever it was he kept me back for. Finally, when I can't stand it anymore, I clear my throat.

"Yes, Darling?" he asks, peering up from his papers, his green eyes lined evenly with his dark eyelashes.

"I..." I shake my head. "Was there something in particular you wished to discuss with me?"

The captain's eyes flicker with amusement. "Nothing in particular."

WHEN I REACH MY ROOMS, I'm still buzzing from the excitement of having spoken up at the meeting. While I return to my usual habit of analyzing my words—annotating them and revising my points to sound more fluent, infusing my voice with more confidence than I'd had in the moment—I'm not as embarrassed of my imperfections as usual. It ends up being for the best that I can't seem to calm my mind, because Charlie clearly has no intention of me getting any sleep.

She bursts into the room, then promptly drags me two floors below deck, explaining on the way that she has something to show me.

We arrive in a large storage closet where the maintenance supplies for the cannons are kept. In the corner is a table, across which dozens of metallic parts are strewn. Framed in greasy gadgets like the suckling pig at a Solstice dinner party is a long black barrel with a handle. It sits atop a black velvet piece of cloth, like Charlie couldn't stand for something so beautiful to simply lie upon the desk.

"You know when you were talking about portable cannons?" asks Charlie, bouncing on her toes, her energy filling the cramped storage room with an infectious buzz.

"You invented one?" I ask, wonder striking me as I run my fingers over the smooth barrel.

Charlie looks abashed. "Well, sort of. It still needs some tweaking. And the design didn't come entirely from me. You see, it's been attempted before." She rushes over to a pile of books on the table and flips through one, showing me countless pictures of similar prototypes. "The problem is that the faerie dust burns too hot for such a small barrel. The wrought can't take the ignition inside, not like the thicker cannon barrels can. Several researchers have tried, but they always end up with damaged barrels."

"But this one works?" I ask, tempted but somewhat frightened to pick up the small but intimidating object.

Charlie nods, though she bites her lip. "Snuck off yesterday and tested it while the rest of the gunners were firing routine test shots with the cannons." She takes the weapon, her grip gentle enough to coax a wild creature, then pops open a compartment. She produces a metal ball from her pocket and clicks it in place before pressing the compartment closed. As quickly as she loaded it, she whips open the compartment again, emptying it. "It fired alright," she says, peering down at the invention like she's vacillating between pride and regret. "But the aim was off."

She places the invention back on the table, wraps the handle in the velvet wrap—I assume so I don't get my oily fingerprints on it—then hands it to me. When I hesitate, she gasps. "Oh, I forgot you hate the feel of velvet," she says, quickly removing the velvet wrap and flinging it to the side, as if fingerprints no longer matter.

"How did you know that?" I ask.

"The captain told me to make sure that if you needed to borrow a gown again, to make sure that it didn't have any velvet on it."

A lump forms in my throat, but it's not the painful sort. Charlie misinterprets my shocked gratitude for embarrassment and flits her hand. "Don't worry about it. We all have our quirks. I can't wear necklaces. Makes me feel like I'm choking."

"How'd you keep the faerie dust from melting the barrel?" I ask, eager to stop talking about the captain.

Charlie glances up at me, looking somewhat guilty. "The faerie dust that's used to power the ship or lanterns or whatever else—it's been altered in the factories. I used to watch them do it—take raw faerie dust and concentrate it—back when my family's business thrived. I got to thinking, what if the faerie dust wasn't so concentrated? What if it was raw?"

When I offer her a confused look, she pulls a pouch from her pocket. My eyes widen in recognition. It's Peter's pouch, the same Charlie had convinced me to throw overboard.

"I switched out the pouches," she says, chewing on the inside of her cheek. "What you threw overboard was just a pouch of sand. I'm sorry —I shouldn't have lied to you. I just thought that if you felt like you had some agency in getting rid of it—"

She sputters to a stop as I wrap her in a quick and somewhat awkward embrace. I'm not one to touch others often, and the gesture feels like it's all bones and limbs, but when I quickly retreat, Charlie offers me a relieved smile.

"Feeling like it was my choice to get rid of the faerie dust was the best thing that's happened to me in a long time," I say, trying to keep my gaze from wandering to the pouch in her hand. To be quite honest, I'd rather she not have even admitted it was still on board. My mouth tingles just knowing it's near.

"Oh. Right. Sorry," Charlie says, returning the pouch to her pocket.

"It's alright," I say. "I've got to learn to ignore the urges at some point."

"Is that what you tell yourself about Astor?" asks Charlie, not looking up from her new weapon.

My stomach jumps into my throat. "What do you mean?"

Charlie gives me a knowing look. Suddenly the skin between my shoulder blades itches, and I scratch at it absentmindedly.

"I'm betrothed to Peter," I say.

"Right. That's why you're not wearing your ring."

"It's too big. It fell off my finger the other night. The last thing I want is for it to slip through the crack in a plank or fall overboard."

"Mhm."

I can feel the blotches appearing on my neck, my chest. "Charlie, please. It's not going to happen. Between Astor and me, I mean."

She looks up at me through her pretty, thick lashes. "Because you love Peter."

A twitch breaks out in my eyelid, but I nod all the same. Charlie looks less than convinced, but as she wipes her grease-laden hands on her apron, she sighs placatingly. "Tell me about Peter, then. What is it about him that has you so smitten?" She smiles, but for the first time, it looks forced.

Still, I'm grateful for the opportunity to turn the conversation away from Astor.

"Peter…" I bite my lip, searching for the words. How does one explain why they love someone, when the feelings come without thought or intention? "It's like all my life, my feet have been stuck on the ground, but Peter takes me to the heavens."

Charlie bites the inside of her cheek but says nothing.

"What?" I ask.

"Nothing."

"Charlie."

She taps her finger on the table and sighs. "It's just…you talk about having your feet on the ground like that's not where feet are supposed to go. It's kind of their purpose, don't you think?"

"It's just a metaphor," I say.

She shrugs as if to say, *but not a very good one.*

"He's my Mate," I say.

Charlie's gaze flicks across my cheek. "It's the Reaper's sickle, right?"

"How'd you know?"

"I'm a pirate, Wendy. I know my constellations."

I let out a resigned laugh. "You know, it's sort of embarrassing when you make it sound like it's so obvious."

Charlie grins at me. "It is kind of obvious." She stares at my Mark more intently. "Does Peter have the rest of it, then?"

I nod. "He has the oak on his back."

Charlie bites her lip.

"What?"

"It's just—isn't it kind of a tragic story? Doesn't the Reaper kill his lover so that he can be with her in the spirit world? But then he ends up trapping her soul inside of a tree or something?"

"I thought you said you knew your constellations."

"I do," she says. "I was just making sure you knew them."

"It's just a story," I say, bristling.

Charlie frowns. "Do you trust him—Peter?"

"Of course," I say, but then the memory of his hands ripping apart my bodice assaults me, making my faith stumble. "Well, I trust that underneath his curse, there's a Peter I can trust waiting for me. I trust that the good part of him is still there."

"That you can save him," she says.

"That I will save him," I correct.

She nods, looking back down at her workstation. "Does he tell you everything?"

"Neverland is timeless. We have forever to get to all that," I say.

"Is that your idea or his?" Charlie asks.

I frown, thinking back to the conversation I had with Peter in the vegetable garden after Joel died. I'd told Peter how much it bothered me that we were betrothed, yet I hardly knew him. He'd asked me to be patient with him.

"We both have things we need time before we share. We understand that about each other."

Charlie glances up at me. "Things you've never told anyone else?"

My face flushes hot at the memory of telling Astor about what happened to me in my parents' parlor. How he'd told me afterward that he didn't regret killing them after what they'd made me do. "Things that have never gone well when I've told anyone else," I say.

"Mm."

"I should have trusted Peter," I say, staring at the wall. "Had I told him that I had Astor on the island, trapped in that cave, none of this" —it occurs to me that I don't know what I'm referring to, but I won't admit that—"would have ever happened. I don't know why I'm like that. Why I have to solve everything myself."

Charlie's brow knits together. "I think you're being too critical of yourself."

"You're saying it didn't land me in trouble not telling Peter about Astor?"

"I'm saying that maybe you're not giving your gut enough credit," is all she says. "Have you ever considered that there was a reason your instincts told you not to trust him completely?"

My stomach chills, Peter's hands on me in the Carlisles' library annex making my skin go clammy. "Maybe there was part of me that, even then, knew he was cursed."

"And what if you can't break the curse?"

I shake my head. "I have to break it. For him. Charlie, you weren't there when he told me he couldn't be what I needed. He doesn't think he's worthy of my love as long as he's like this."

"He told you that he couldn't be what you needed?"

I think back to the night I overheard Peter speaking with the Sister. "Well, sort of. He told me he couldn't be the Mate I wanted."

Charlie offers me a sidelong glance. "Always believe a man when he tells you he can't be what you need. If you don't, then you can only blame yourself when he proves you right."

CHAPTER 33

JOHN

*T*ink has rearranged my communication board.

That's my first thought when I enter the cave where I first trapped Tink. I'd snuck out of the Den after dinner, hoping Tink's combination of the SUN and DOWN tiles meant to meet in the evening. I make a mental note to make her a NIGHT tile for ease of communication. Apparently I was correct, because she's perched, thighs resting against her heels on the cave floor, looking rather pleased with herself as she glances between me and the mangled communication board.

"Oh no. No, no, no," I say, grasping for the wooden pieces. "All of this was arranged alphabetically. I guess you'd have no reason to know that, but I organized it that way for a reason."

Tink swats my hand away from the board, causing me to drop "GO." It clatters against the wooden board as I choke in pain. When I withdraw my hand, I notice a faint line of blood tracing my skin from where her long nails sliced me.

My mind starts rattling off the plethora of types of bacteria that live underneath the fingernails. I can only hope that not quite so many have had time to develop in a place like Neverland.

"Ouch. Thanks for that," I mumble, wiping my blooded hand against my pants.

Tink plucks a tile from the board and tucks it in my palm, which I open.

It's the tile for "YOU'RE WELCOME." I roll my eyes, which earns a twitch of her lips, the effect of which is a warm sensation in my chest.

I decide I might have to roll my eyes more often.

"Really, it's best if we have an organization system," I say. "That way it's easier for us to remember which words are where on the board. At least until muscle memory takes over."

Tink points to the set of eyes. "LOOK." Then she encircles a set of tiles with her outstretched finger: a stick figure running, another walking, the last swimming.

Realization slaps me over the back of the head. "You grouped the verbs together."

Tink beams and points to "YES." The sight of her genuine smile almost knocks me over. Another thing I'll have to make a habit of— pointing out what a genius she apparently is.

As I scan the board, I notice a set of meticulous patterns. Not only has she grouped all the verbs together, she's also rearranged the board so that the pronouns are in the upper right-hand corner, anything that could be used as a direct object on the bottom few rows. "That certainly mimics the way we speak more fluidly. I should have considered that we don't choose which word we say next based on what letter of the alphabet it begins with."

Tink points to a new tile. One she must have carved herself. It doesn't have any written script underneath it. It's just a turkey, its bulging black eyes empty.

Incredulous because I'm uncertain turkeys even inhabit this island, so I can't see the point in wasting a tile, I ask, "What does a turkey have to do with anything?"

Tink jabs me in the chest, then points to the button again.

"Ah. I assume stupid is what this means?"

Tink nods smugly.

I press my lips together to keep from smiling, then grab the tile and scrawl "STUPID" underneath her depiction.

As I examine the rest of the board, I notice several new tiles, none of them bearing a word underneath their icon. I'd planned on teaching Tink the tiles that are slightly more abstract today. The tiles that I couldn't think of pictures to represent. The ones that aren't as intuitive, like "BE" or "BUT." However, it appears Tink has already devised other plans for our session.

She hands me a quill and a tile of a frowning woman with a slanted brow, baring her teeth, then points.

"Angry?" I confirm, before marking it on the tile.

As it turns out, she has tiles prepared for every emotion under the sun, and as we work filling them out, I find myself bobbing in impatience. "You know, this really isn't—"

She points again at the tile of a woman with cropped hair resting her chin between her thumb and the knuckle of her forefinger, staring up at the sky.

"Think?" I ask, less than confident that's what she means.

Tink shakes her head.

"Ponder?" I try again.

Tink places her hand over her chest.

I have to hold back the urge to groan. What we need is a tile for "VEX." "Feeling like you want to think?" I ask.

Tink glares at me, then points to "STUPID."

"Fine. Pensive, wistful, reflective, ruminative?"

Tink points to the number "ONE" at the top of the board.

"I don't see how 'PENSIVE' is all that functional—"

Tink taps "WANT."

"Fine." I scribble PENSIVE onto the tile.

I expect Tink to tire of our task before she does, but she works diligently, scribbling on the blank tiles as I try to figure out what she means. This goes on for hours, and I wear out before she does.

That makes sense. I'm not the one who's been unable to communicate for who knows how long. Still, I can't see why, after years of silence, she'd want to communicate "PENSIVE." It's not as if it's a high-frequency word.

Once she's finished the last tile, I show her the articles and the more abstract prepositions, thinking those will prove more difficult to memorize. There aren't exactly intuitive images for the words "a," "the," and "of." She'll just have to memorize what the words look like.

When we're done, Tink having memorized the articles in a span of seconds, I rest on my heels across from her and scratch the back of my neck.

"I'd like to start over, I think," I say, extending my hand. "I'm John." It's meant to be the offering of a handshake, but Tink either misinterprets the gesture or doesn't care for the formality, because she tucks a tile into my palm.

It's the tile for TINK.

When I glance up at her, she's smiling. But there's something else too, tears welling at her eyelids. I don't entirely understand. It's not as if she's finally figured out a way to communicate information I didn't know. But I figure it best not to acknowledge the soft tears.

Besides, they tug at my ribcage, and that's not exactly productive. Empathy gets you hurt, John.

"Have you always been unable to speak?" I ask. "Verbally, I mean."

Tink shakes her head.

"Was it illness? A surgery? Apoplexy?" I'm not sure if Tink knows what apoplexy is, but I've learned to assume that she knows more than I think she does unless I want to get called stupid. Or asked if I think she's stupid. I have yet to figure out a way to differentiate between the two.

Tink bites her lip, and again shakes her head.

"How did it happen?" I ask.

Tink looks at the board. For a moment, I think she'll reach for one of the tiles, but she doesn't. She just shrugs.

"We don't have the words for it?" I ask.

She doesn't look at me this time. I can't decide if I believe that, or if she just doesn't want to tell me how she lost her voice. It shouldn't matter. Doesn't matter. What matters is finding out what happened to Wendy.

"Did you see what happened to my sister?"

"YES."

My heart pounds against my chest.

"Would you tell me? Please?"

Tink cocks her head and traces the tile that says please with her finger. A soft, sad smile tugs at her lips.

"What?" I ask.

She shrugs. "JOHN SAY PLEASE." She frowns, blinking tears away. "JOHN ASK."

Something swells in my throat. I swallow it away. I want to prod her forward, but something in my instincts tells me it's better to wait.

Eventually, she points to the "PIRATE" tile, the one I made so she'd have the vocabulary to talk about what happened to Wendy, if that really was the case.

"Peter was telling the truth, then."

Tink flicks her eyes up to me. There's something in them that I get the sense can't be expressed with the tiles.

"WHAT PETER SAY."

This is the first time I've realized I haven't actually told her.

"He says Captain Astor, the pirate who killed my parents, tracked her down to the island and kidnapped her."

Tink nods, looking...pensive, I regret to admit...then scans the tiles. "PETER NO SAY ALL."

"He lied?"

Tink just shrugs, as if I'm asking a philosophical question.

"He at least omitted part of the story, then?"

Tink nods, a bit too eagerly.

"What did he omit?"

Tink stares at the tiles for a long while. After what feels like several minutes pass, she sighs. I watch her, the thoughts racing behind her vibrant blue eyes as she scans the tiles. It kills me not knowing what's happening inside her mind. That my access to her thoughts is reduced to a set of wooden tiles and slight gestures, subtle changes in her facial expression.

If it tempts me to scream in frustration, I can't fathom what it's doing to her. How starved of communication she must be to feel so excited about having a few dozen words to use. When the rest of us have thousands.

Tink crinkles her forehead, rubbing at her temples. When she doesn't find what she's looking for in the combination of words, she wilts. But a moment later, the despair is gone, and her back is straight again, fortified with a determination I can't grasp.

She takes one of the blank tiles and sketches a box wrapped in a bow. "Reminds me of a Solstice gift," I say, then add, "Do you celebrate Solstice where you're from?"

She gives me a look that makes it clear that what I'm saying is irrelevant, so I go to scribble the word on the tile. "Gift?" I ask to make sure.

She shakes her head.

I think for a moment. "Give?"

"YES."

When I'm done, she snatches the tile away, her hand grazing mine as she does. Were we not discussing the fate of my sister, I might linger longer on the way her skin brushed against mine.

Tink takes a handful of tiles, then arranges them on the floor of the cave. When she takes her hands away, the words imprint themselves in my mind.

"PETER GIVE PIRATE WENDY."

CHAPTER 34

WENDY

I don't sleep that night.

Usually, when I can't sleep, I can pinpoint the exact place and time that my body is reliving. I know the exact reason it refuses to let me bury myself in the solace of slumber.

This is different.

I'm restless, my limbs jittery. When I wander my way down to the bunker where they keep the faerie dust, I'm relieved to find the guard standing on duty. He waves at me with a toothy grin.

"Miss Darling," he says cheerfully. "Little late for ya to be wandering down here, ain't it?"

He's right. I usually pad down here first thing in the morning, as well as in the afternoon, when my brain has a difficult time focusing on tasks. My timing used to be because that's when the cravings were the strongest. Now, as the stretches between intense cravings grow longer, it's more habit than anything. I've come to look forward to seeing the guard. There's a certain comfort to knowing I'd never make it inside the bunker. That the guard is always here to stop me. Always here to offer me a friendly smile.

"Couldn't sleep," I say, to which his smile twitches. "I would have thought someone else would have relieved you tonight."

He shrugs. "Rainer was supposed to have scrub duty tonight but has a case of the trots, so Charlie had to fill in for him, meaning Schruin had to fill in for her, meaning I had to fill in for Schruin."

"Right," I say.

He offers me a wink before I leave.

THE DECK ISN'T QUITE empty. It still has to be manned at night. The waves don't exactly stop just because the rest of us do. But it's empty compared to this morning, and the crew working the night shift isn't the type to snitch. So I slink toward the nearest mast, my fingers curling into fists.

It's been ages since I climbed anything, so I hardly make it a few feet off the rungs before the weightless sensation makes me dizzy, sending shivers of needles throughout my body.

That's fine. I actually prefer it this way.

Halfway up, I realize the mast isn't quite so stable-feeling as my parents' clock tower or the cliffs back in Neverland. It's sturdy, but that doesn't stop it from being rocked by the waves. On the way up, I often find myself moving with the rhythm of the sea.

Still, I cling tight, refusing to look down.

There's a nest at the top of the mast, one that I have to maneuver my body to climb into. When I glance down at my feet to figure out where to place them, I end up getting a glimpse of the boat far below. I'm not exactly unaccustomed to heights, but usually the ground doesn't move so much. Thankfully, there's a gentle breeze tonight, so I'm able to gulp in several breaths of salt air to steady myself.

There's little to see now that I'm situated in the wooden nest, not with how the moon is barely a sliver behind the clouds. But that's no matter. I didn't come up here to see anyway.

"I did give you a room, did I not?"

The familiar voice has me jolting, which is problematic given the way I've perched myself on the rim of the nest. Firm hands steady me before I can launch myself off the edge and end up nothing more than spatter on the deck beneath.

I look to my side to find Astor standing next to me, having removed his hands from my shoulders and back to his sides.

"I didn't hear you climbing," I say.

"Well, it is quite windy."

"It's not that windy."

"Yes, Darling, but I thought it more polite to blame your lack of awareness on your surroundings rather than on you."

I huff, pulling my coat taut and my scarf tight around my neck to protect me from the evening chill, but the corner of my lip twitches all the same.

The captain takes up the perch across from me. His legs are significantly longer, so they can't help but tangle with mine. I try not to flinch at the feel of his legs wrapped around my ankles. Mostly because if the captain notices that we're touching, he isn't letting it show.

Astor keeps his hands in his pockets, staring at me like I'm a fleeting eclipse and not a girl he kidnapped then proceeded to befriend.

Befriend.

Friends.

Is that what we are?

"Vor says you visited him tonight?"

I shift uncomfortably. "He told?"

"He always tells."

"Oh."

"Oh, indeed."

If the captain means to rebuke me, he must relent, because he quickly bounces to another topic. "Did you have trouble sleeping before?"

I raise a brow. "There are a few events that might demand the use of a *before*. You're going to have to be a tad more specific."

For a moment, he says nothing, and I can't help but wonder which event is playing through his mind. If he's imagining the bloody death of his wife, or perhaps the murder of my parents, or the night he kidnapped me from the beach in Neverland. Perhaps Peter assaulting me in the Carlisles' home.

"No, you're right," he says, sighing. "I think I'd rather not."

I can't describe why, but my heart deflates a bit.

"Wendy," he says.

"Captain."

Something akin to hurt flashes in his eyes. "Are we not on a first-name basis?"

"Perhaps if I knew your first name." The lie just slips out, but I watch his face and posture for tells. A twitch of the brow. A flick of his ears. A bulging in his jaw.

Anything to know I can affect him a fraction of how much he's capable of hurting me.

I'd been on a high after he backed my plan to use my shadow soothing to our advantage. Over and over I'd replayed his reaction to my boldness in my mind—the subtle pride as he'd stared at me. I'd felt so connected to him, for once rowing in the same direction.

My recollections had been innocent in nature, starting with his look of pride tonight and progressing to mentally compiling every subtle compliment he's ever paid me, but going no further. Innocent, I'd repeated to myself as I'd wrapped his praise around my heart like a child wrapping the twine of a kite around her finger.

The thoughts themselves were pure, wholesome.

It was the frequency of them, the saturation of them that had soon soiled my daydreaming with guilt. And now that he's in front of me, all beautiful arrogance, I can't help but let him needle his way underneath my skin.

Astor narrows his eyes, his gaze unfocused. Like he's sifting through a box of memories, sure he'll find the evidence he needs. "I introduced myself the night of the masquerade. And Maddox is known to call me by my given name on occasion."

I shrug, hiding my hands inside my pockets lest their twitching give away my deceit. I'm not sure why I'm lying. Captain Nolan Astor was how he'd introduced himself at the ball to Lord Credence. I'd remember his voice anywhere, the way it fit his name perfectly.

And yet.

"Well, what is it then?"

Astor stares me down, like he's trying to find some evidence of a lie. A joke. He must not find what he's looking for in my face because he says, "You're right. Captain's my preferred, anyway."

I let out a quiet huff. It's more scorn than I meant. "You are so stubborn."

He quirks a brow. "Am I?"

I place my hands on my hips, trying to keep my balance on the side. "You're not going to tell me your name, all because I hurt your feelings by not hanging on your every word."

"I assure you that you have no such ability, Darling."

I flit my hand in the air. "Yes, yes." I don't know what's gotten into me tonight, but I do my best impression of the captain, dipping my voice as low as I can get it until it sounds gravelly enough to leave a scratch. "Hurting my feelings is a right reserved for one person alone." The captain tenses, but I'm sleep-deprived and annoyed and tasting the bitter lack of faerie dust on my tongue. "Oh, and I almost forgot, 'And you, Darling, will never be that person.'" I offer him a smile that feels unfamiliar and cruel on my lips. "Did I get it right, Captain?"

I wait for Astor to burst. To send me careening off the side of this mast. My fists ball at the ready. It's not as if Maddox's training would be of much use against Astor, but there's a tension crawling underneath my skin that's begging for him to take a step toward me.

I think I could land a punch before he sent me overboard. Part of me thinks it would be worth it.

Instead, he just offers me an amused smirk. "Can it be? Has the pup finally learned to bite?"

I don't know how I went from feeling so calm, so peaceful up here, to my skin itching with the need to dig my fingernails into his flesh until I draw blood, but the craving for violence is swelling up within me. It's like I'm a child taken to the fair on a hot day, dehydrated and worn out and lashing out to go home.

Except I never got to be that child—not after I fell ill.

I want the captain to come at me, but he doesn't. He just leans back against the rim of the nest. "What's got you so riled?"

From his tone, I'd think he was being sincere. If the words were coming from anyone else's mouth.

I open my mouth to explain, but there are too many things, too many thoughts swarming together, competing for my attention. And I can't pinpoint any one of them. They flit around me, evading my grasp as I lose focus and try to curl my fingers around another at the last minute.

"It's…it's nothing," I say.

"Oh, I doubt that."

"I'm fine," I say, taking a breath that's supposed to be steeling and instead feels more like an accident as I turn to climb down the mast.

"You're angry," he says.

"I'm not an angry person."

"And do you actually believe yourself when you say that?"

I whirl around to face him, keeping my palms behind me, pressed to the mast. "I'm not an angry person," I repeat. "I don't have outbursts. I don't scream or yell or hurt people. That's you, in case you've forgotten. I assure you I haven't."

He cocks his head at me. "I'm not the one you're angry with, Darling."

My heart races. "I already told you; I don't get angry."

He shakes his head, looking pensive. "No. No, you don't. You don't get angry. You *are* angry. It's so much a part of you, you can no longer recognize it in yourself."

I stare at him, not bothering to hide the mockery on my face. "You think you know everything. But really, you're just a bitter man who thinks himself unaccountable because of something that happened over a decade ago. Do you think you're the only one who hurts? Do you have any idea what it's like to wake devastated because it's morning again, and you have to spend another day trapped in your own body? Shackled in your own mind, prisoner to your own thoughts? Do you know what it's like for your own mind to hate you, spend every moment of the day torturing you—and for no apparent reason? At least you had a reason."

The captain's eyes have gone wide, his breathing ragged, but he stays plastered to the rim of the nest, unmoving.

"You don't have a monopoly on missing a piece of yourself, you know. I'm sorry, alright?" I say, and I realize I'm screaming now. Hopefully my voice gets lost in the howl of the wind before it can reach the ears of any on the deck. "I'm sorry that she was supposed to be here, and I wasn't. I'm sorry that instead of Iaso, the world got stuck with me. You think I haven't felt it?" I say, grasping the fabric of my shirt above my heart. "You think I haven't known all this time that I wasn't supposed to be here? That I've outlived my welcome in this world? Sure, maybe I didn't know exactly why I'm not worthy, but that didn't close up the hole in my chest. So go ahead," I say, holding my arms wide in front of me, a mockery of invitation. "Tell me you hate me. Tell me you can't stand to look at me. It's nothing I don't hear every day of my life, ringing in the back of my skull. Say it, and then you can join the chorus in my head. Just know your voice isn't nearly as original as you believe it to be."

"Wendy."

"No. No." I hiss through my teeth. "You might think you're stuck with me, but you chose that. You stole me from Neverland. That was your choice. And before that, you came after my family. Your choice. And when all of this is said and done..." I clutch my stomach, unable to breathe. "When it's done, and you get what you want from me—for me to talk to the shadows or the dead or whatever it is that you need from my shadow soothing, guess what?"

When he doesn't answer, I scream. "*Guess!*"

The captain blinks, pushing himself up and stepping toward me slowly.

"You get to be rid of me. You get to..." I clutch my stomach, pain writhing in my belly as I search for the words to make him understand. "You don't have to be in my head. I can't get away from me. I can't..." My fingers find my hair, knuckles bulging, but the words remain holed up inside me all the same, no matter how hard I try to pry them out.

"Darling," the captain whispers, taking my fingers and unraveling them from my hair. Some of the sting at my scalp goes away, but he doesn't let go of my hand. Instead, he slides it downward until my hand is a barrier between his and my cheek. "There is nowhere I could go, no corner of the world I could hide, where that would be the case. Where I could get away from you."

I listen for the taunting, for the vile loathing, but it's absent.

My breathing takes up the space between us. He's so close now, with so little room in this nest. Close as the day I hit him and he determined not to train me anymore.

"You're wrong, you know," he says. "I don't think I'm the only one who feels it."

My heart gives a lurch, wondering if he can see the desire written all over my face. Wondering if he's caught the glances I've stolen when I thought he wasn't looking.

"If you'll let me," he says, staring me down, "I think I could help."

I can't breathe. Can't…

"Stop me if I'm wrong," he whispers, though the words are useless as I'm paralyzed under his touch. He brings his thumb to my temple, rubbing it in circles at a patch of my hair. "This is a cage, isn't it?" He tucks my hair behind my ear, taking care to graze the bone behind my ear before slipping his touch to the base of my skull. "A prison you can't escape. Do you think I don't know what it is to wake every morning disappointed? Clinging to my nightmares, because the alternative is that I have to live yet another day chained to myself? Do you think I don't know about the whispers?"

I open my mouth to retort, but he brushes a finger over my lips to stop me. My head spins at his touch as he shakes his head. "Just a few more moments, Darling, please. I want you to know. I know your whispers are different, that they come from the shadows. They lodge in the deepest corners of your mind, waiting to catch you alone. Waiting to ensnare you. Except that's the worst part. Because even when you're in a crowd of people, you're always alone. They're always standing between you and everyone else, drowning you silently while all the others see is a beautiful smile."

He's so close now, cupping my jawline in his sturdy, warm hands.

His ragged breath warms my nose. Any closer and our lips would touch, and I would know what it feels like to let my enemy kiss away the pain.

Tears run down my cheeks, and he lets them. Doesn't try to wipe them away. Doesn't try to erase them.

I nod my head, letting out a nervous laugh in between choking sobs.

"You don't have to do that," he says, his thumb caressing my jaw as his gaze dips to my mouth.

"Do what?"

"Smile while you weep."

Inside me, something cracks. And I can't tell if it's a bone in my chest, or my soul, or if my heart is just ripping in two—one part remaining loyal to my parents, the other taking sides with the captain. Either way, it's a fracture I can't ignore.

I can't ignore that this is wrong.

He killed them. Killed my parents. Letting him touch me—it's a betrayal. Not just to my parents, but to John, who idolized our father. To Michael, who doesn't understand why his mother no longer sings him to sleep.

To…

I sense the absence of Peter's ring on my shaking hand. A phantom weight bearing down on my soul. Peter, who is trapped by the Sister's curse. Peter, who I forgot about.

When I pull away, Astor lets me go. I'm not sure if I imagine it, but I think I catch a glimpse of relief in his expression when I'm the one to stop things from escalating.

"I think I'm going to retire for the night," I say, shrugging my coat up my neck where his touch still burns. Can he see it redden in the moonlight?

"Sleep easy," he says, a softness tinging his voice. His hands fidget at his sides, like he doesn't know what to do with them.

When I turn to go, his voice halts me at the mast, the wet wood slick under my fingertips. "Wendy," he says, grabbing the crook of my elbow, though not roughly.

"Yes?" I say, my heart pounding, my mind praying he doesn't ask me to turn around. Doesn't ask me to stay. Because I don't know that I have the strength to resist him a second time.

The captain squeezes me, just barely. Does he remember where he's touching? That underneath the fabric of my shirt, his fingers rest just above the mark that signifies the bargain I made with Peter that night in the clock tower?

When he speaks again, I think I know the answer to that question. "The shadows can't have you."

CHAPTER 35

WENDY

*I*t takes weeks, but Evans's sources eventually pan out, and we get a lead that the Nomad's community of ships is situated off the coast of a town called Zereth. Over the next few days, I throw myself into my training sessions with Maddox. Not that swordplay will be of much use against the wraiths I'll be up against. But something about slicing through the ropes Maddox procured after I ruined the last pig carcass makes me feel as if I'm preparing.

When we finally dock in Zereth, Maddox informs me that Astor and I will be performing this mission alone. My heart falters. Astor has been avoiding me since the night in the crow's nest. Well, I can't know that for certain, considering I've also been avoiding him. Before I can inquire why Astor isn't bringing anyone else on the mission, Maddox comes at me with his broadsword, and I'm forced to utilize my breath elsewhere.

THE MAN we stalk from the silky black water of the outskirts of Zereth has no face in the shadows. Just a blurry, bulky torso, silhouetted by the moonlight, and a pair of substantial arms that he uses to row out into the bay and toward the nearby coastal town.

Astor and I huddle in another rowboat, trailing him in the mist. I'd worked myself up earlier today wondering if Astor planned to address what happened—or rather, didn't happen—in the crow's nest. As it turns out, stalking someone doesn't exactly lend itself to conversation. Astor's been quiet most of the night, a behavior I've been more than eager to mimic. As it is, I doubt we've been spotted. So far, the man has yet to check over his shoulder. He has no reason to expect anyone is following him. Perhaps that means...

"You're hoping he won't be worthy of being killed," says Astor, rowing steadily behind me. I'm rowing too, but I'd be lying if I said he wasn't doing most of the work. Water sloshes against the sides of the boat, lapping inside and wetting my shoes.

"Is it so wrong that I don't want to kill someone?" I say.

"Not wrong. But not exactly productive either, given our plan."

"You won't kill him if he's innocent," I say. "Will you?"

Astor doesn't answer. My stomach twists over. I shouldn't have said anything. Should have kept my idea to myself. I feel as if I'm going to be sick and reach for the side of the rowboat in preparation to lose the contents of my stomach.

When Astor sees me lean for support against the siding, his hand lands on the back of mine. "He's guilty, Darling."

When I turn back to look at Astor, I imagine my face has drained entirely of color. "How do you know?"

"Because," he says, "aren't we all?"

"I'm not sure that's comforting," I say, though I don't throw up over the side of the boat. My stomach oddly settled, I lower myself back into the damp wooden seat and row.

WHEN WE REACH THE SHORE, we tie our boat to a dock and creep across the pier, trailing the man from a distance. We follow him until we reach a shabby brothel on the far side of town. It's called the Caged Swan.

Astor looks at me knowingly, perching his hand right above my shoulder, resting it against the corner of the building as he leans over me to peer around the corner. He's close enough I can feel the heat of his chest against my back, but not its weight.

"At your command, Darling," he says.

My throat tightens up, anger and regret and guilt mingling to make a sour mixture. Like pickle juice mixed into coffee. "Just be quick about it," I say, knowing full well that what Astor will have to do to this man to produce a wraith will be nothing of the sort.

THE MAN IS NO LONGER a blurry silhouette by the time Astor drags him limp into the alley where I'm hiding. It took only a few moments for Astor to approach our prey from behind and incapacitate him, landing a carefully aimed blow to his temple. The man's body had crumpled like a dying spider.

Astor lays him at my feet, and I can't help but trace his every feature. The soft curve of his nose, the slackness of his jaw. Even in the dim moonlight, I can glimpse stubble. He must have shaved just this morning.

He didn't know it would be the last time he ever did that.

"Darling? Where's that mind of yours headed?"

I work my jaw, staring down at the unconscious man. "Why is it difficult this time?"

Astor sighs, then kneels beside the body, looking up at me. He almost looks innocent from this angle. I'd laugh at the idea if I weren't about to commit murder. "Taking a life—it's different when you've planned it. Carves at a different part of your soul. Deeper down."

"I thought taking the first life carved out everything I had," I say numbly. "I'm surprised there's anything left."

Astor's face softens. "You have more left to you than most, I fear." After a moment, he says, "There's a barred window around the back of the brothel if you'd like to peek in. What you'll see inside will make you feel better about this."

I shake my head. "I don't want to use someone else's misery to make me feel better about my own choices. Whatever's happening in there," I say, nodding toward the Caged Swan, "they didn't choose that. I'm choosing this."

"Darling," Astor says, as the man begins to stir in front of us, "I won't think less of you if you close your eyes."

For a moment, I desire nothing more than to turn away, bury my ears in my hands, and wring my eyes shut. But then I think of the Sister, what she did to Peter when she took away his pain. She stole away his ability for his actions to affect him. By removing the emotional consequences, she transformed him into something wicked.

Something that would hurt the ones he loved to get what he wants.

"Thank you, but no," I whisper. "I want to remember what my choices cost."

Astor blinks, and for the first time, I glimpse something like doubt encroach upon his haunted features.

If his expression means anything, he doesn't tarry to explain it. He just nods, swallows, then turns back to the man.

Dagger in hand, he holds it over the man's leg. I imagine him sawing away at it, but he hesitates just as his blade rests on the man's knee.

"Darling," he says without looking at me, "I'd really rather you not stay to watch this."

Steeling myself, I wrap my arms around my waist. "I can handle it," I force myself to say, even though I might pass out the moment this man's screams are muffled by the gag Astor stuffed into his throat.

When Astor finally looks at me, there's no plea in his eyes. No begging. Only resignation in his dry throat. "I'm afraid I'm not asking on your behalf."

I blink, confused, but Astor holds my stare until realization washes over me.

"Oh. You don't want me to watch you."

Something flashes in his eyes—guilt's splinter lingering underneath the flesh's outermost layer, forgotten for a time until it's pushed deeper and the pain resurfaces. It's only there for a moment, gone so quickly I might have missed it if I'd blinked.

253

But I hadn't blinked.

A moment later and it's gone, replaced by a haughty smirk. "Would you protest if a painter asked you not to watch them from over their shoulder?"

I pause, not at all fooled by his arrogance. There was a time when I would have believed that swaggering veneer.

"No. No, I wouldn't," I say.

I don't turn around until I glimpse the relief on Astor's face. When I turn the corner, I stay close enough to hear the man's muffled cries.

Astor doesn't make a sound.

* * *

THE CORPSE that is left after Astor's done is less gory than I expected. Like Astor knew just where to draw the lines to expedite agony without making a mess.

Blood coats the man's shirt, ripped open at the chest, but there's none on Astor's hands. I'm not sure whether he wiped them before he called me to come out from behind the corner or if he really managed to do this sort of damage without spilling a drop of blood on himself.

The only sign that Astor just tortured a man to death is on his brow, where a thin sheen of sweat has collected. I imagine cutting a man open is an arduous business, but I expect there's more to Astor's bodily reaction than just that.

Slivers of red ink stain the man's chest, his neck. Like he's been marked for quartering.

I did that. Perhaps not with my own hands, my own blade, but it was my idea all the same.

I wonder if this man ever stood over the women chained to the beds in the brothel just around the corner. If the girls cried afterward. If he ever thought to himself, I did that.

I find I don't really care.

"Well, Darling," says the captain. "Do we have company?"

I bite my lip, scanning the shadows. We picked an alley heavy with them, backlit by the faerie dust lamps on the street. The shadows sneak from underneath garbage bins like stray cats in the night, some of them warbling with the flicker of the lamp light. But none of the movements resemble anything living.

"Nothing so far," I say.

Astor raises a brow. "What exactly is the success rate of creating a wraith, Miss Darling?"

I swallow. "How am I supposed to know? I've only known I'm a shadow soother for a few months."

"Excellent," he says, staring at the brick wall on the other side of the alley.

I can't help but glance down at his hand. It's trembling, still clutching onto his dagger, blackened with sticky blood.

My heart stops. "Was that...was that your first time...?"

Astor's eyes snap up to me. "If you're asking if that's the first time I've ever tortured another being, I'd think back to the fate of your parents, Darling."

Anger and grief threaten to flare up within me, but I'm too focused on Astor's shaking hand to notice. "Psychologically, it was torture. But you've never done this before—tortured someone physically."

"Don't try to play detective into my past, Darling. You're much too good at making false assumptions to inform your decisions."

Hurt coils in my belly. Both at his insult and my own stupidity. Of course he's tortured before. He'd even stayed behind after I was kidnapped to punish the henchman who almost killed me. "I wasn't trying to—"

Just then, a shadow curls up in a plume from the corpse's chest, filling in the air with the shape of the man Astor just killed. He's not shaking like the man was. He's just a shadow, just a memory of pain brought to life. If pain is a being, can it feel itself?

"Astor," I whisper, staring at the shadow.

He traces the line of my vision, narrowing his eyes. As if he thinks if only he focuses hard enough, he'll be able to glimpse the wraith.

"Hello," I say, voice shaking. I realize I've never intentionally addressed a wraith before.

The shadow turns its blurred head, searching the alley until its attention lands on me.

"You're a pretty little thing," it says. "Why, it's a wonder they allow you to be out here." He nods toward the brothel. "Perhaps they don't know about you. Perhaps I should tell them."

I fight the blood threatening to drain from my face, remembering this shadow can't lay a hand on me. The worst it can do is frighten me, and only if I allow it.

"Why would you do that?" I ask, gooseflesh forming on my arms as I wrap them around my stomach. I'm rocking back and forth despite myself.

"People pay good money for a pretty girl like you. I could use good money."

Be what he wants you to be, I tell myself.

I let myself shake, don't try to hide my trembling hands. "Please," I say. "I can't go back there. Please don't make me go back. I'll do anything."

The shadow glides toward me, sizing me up. "Anything?"

Careful who you give your anythings to, I remember Astor telling me one night when I had him trapped in the cave off of Neverland's shoreline. I wonder if he's thinking about that now as he listens to only one side of the conversation.

"Anything," I say, taking care to be breathy. I try not to glance at Astor, who's examining me with hard eyes.

"You know, I'm in need of a maid," he says. "A private one."

A chill wraps up my arms. I know exactly what this man, this memory of a man, intends, but I play naïve. "I know how to cook. And I can clean while staying quiet, out of the way."

The wraith nods, a smile breaking over his face. "I can't bring you back with me. The No—our leader doesn't like us bringing in our own women. If you want to get past the guards, you'll have to have come yourself. And with a passcode."

I nod, pouring desperation into my reaction.

When the shadowed man leans over and whispers it into my ear, I tremble. I can't decide whether it's fear of this terrible creature I made, or the unease at how little regret I have over making it.

CHAPTER 36

JOHN

"TALK."

I stare down at the tile Tink just pushed across the floor of the cave toward me and blink, wondering if my glasses really are getting so warped that it's changing the meaning of letters now. It's silly, I know, but I can't bring myself to take them off in front of Tink. Can't help but want her to take me seriously.

"We've been talking for hours," I say, confused. I've been questioning her about Peter for at least an hour, to no avail, and was helping her create new tiles for at least two hours before that.

When Tink first confirmed Peter's story about Wendy being taken by Astor—adding the part that Peter gave her away—I'd been skeptical.

Well, I'm still skeptical. That's why I've been questioning her. She came to Neverland in love with Peter, after all. Attacked my sister out of jealousy. If she's still in love with Peter, it stands to reason that she would perceive whatever happened to Wendy as Peter giving her away. Our minds have a nasty habit of warping reality into a more palatable version of itself. And as little as I trust Peter, it's difficult for me to imagine someone so possessive handing Wendy over to another man.

Still. I can't make sense of someone like Tink, someone so bold and independent, letting Peter have that kind of control over her.

Wendy letting him control her—that makes sense. She's been letting others guide her path for years, as much as it grieves me to see it. But there's something about Peter having such a hold over Tink that doesn't line up. The last puzzle piece that won't quite fit into place, no matter how hard you try to jam it.

Tink taps her long fingernails against two tiles, whisking me out of my thoughts. "JOHN TALK." When I open my hands in a questioning gesture, she rolls her eyes. "TINK BORED. JOHN TALK."

"About what?"

"JOHN."

"You really must be bored if you think me talking about myself is going to help."

Tink just stares at me, taking a sip of water from the cup I snuck her from the Den, and waits.

I run my hand through my hair. It's getting much too long, falling in my face and scratching at my eyes half the time, my glasses too loose to protect them as they slide down the bridge of my nose.

"Okay, then. I'm the second child of a nobleman. I prefer people in books to most of the people I've met in the real world." My gaze lingers on Tink's face. "Only excepting a select few," I say, clearing my throat. "I don't think my father ever loved my affinity for the library. Not that he opposed it. I just think he hoped to have someone to spar with in the courtyard, but...well, look at me," I say, gesturing to my narrow frame. "Still, he didn't mind so long as I kept watch over Wendy and Michael. Kept them safe. I know you're thinking that a more brawny son would have been better equipped for that. You'd be right."

I glance back at Tink. I'm not sure what I'm hoping for from her. She just blinks.

"I tried," I say. "I really did. It was my responsibility. Wendy had her curse, Michael his condition. I was the only one of the three of us who didn't need safeguarding. That left the protecting up to me. But I wasn't built for it, I guess. I tried to make up for it by learning as much as I could about Wendy's curse, by reading all the books I could about Michael's language and learning patterns. A whole lot of good all the knowledge did for them. Wendy's lost, and Michael..." I shake my head, squinting my eyes like that will somehow expel the headache that's coming on. "He keeps asking for our mother. I can't even explain what happened to her. He's just stuck in a nightmare where his mother and sister are gone, and I can't convince him that he's awake. Don't know that I'd be brave enough to, even if I thought he'd understand. You know, I spent all those years educating myself about the Shadow Keeper, when I should have been digging through my father's books, taking note of who his enemies might be. If I'd been looking at the appropriate data, I would have seen Captain Astor coming."

Tink scoots closer. My heart races.

"I told Wendy I wanted to kill him—the captain. I was so angry with him. Thought I'd accounted for every last variable, and there he went, stealing in through a blind spot and ripping my life apart. And now he has Wendy, and I can't keep my mind from traveling down the logical path of what he must have been doing to her all this time she's been gone."

I shake my head, feeling sick as the truth of the matter spills out. Why I've been so hesitant to believe Tink's and Peter's accounts of what happened to Wendy. It hits me in the gut—the realization that it's easier for me to believe my sister dead, murdered for witnessing something she shouldn't have, than alive and tortured, abused by the ruthless captain.

I'm not sure what that makes me.

"I love my sister," I say, though I'm not sure who I'm trying to convince. "She's smart, intelligent, but that's not always enough. She sees the best in people, and she lets that seep into her evaluation of them, warping her perception. It's like her mind erases the evidence against them. So the conclusions she draws make sense, but only because she's omitted much of the truth. I walked in on her and Peter one time. It was after she'd freaked out and attacked Michael—some stress response to killing that man on the beach. Peter had drugged her to calm her down. I thought he was just sedating her so she wouldn't hurt herself or anyone else. But when I came to check on her..."

My mouth goes dry, and I glance at Tink. She's no longer looking at me. I'd forgotten for a moment why she ended up on this island. Because she loved, possibly still loves, Peter.

"He said she was alert. That the drugs had already worked their way out of her system." The question lingers on my tongue. It's harder than it should be to push it out. The truth just *is*. It's not something we should fear; it remains immovable regardless of our knowledge of it. Our knowing it doesn't change it. "You know him better than I do. Should I believe him?" I ask.

Tink watches me carefully, then pushes tiles forward. "YOU FRIEND HOME?"

I grimace. "Not really. I had friends when I was young, before Wendy got sick. Before her curse. After that, my parents didn't let many people near us. Even when they did, it was for Wendy to snatch herself a husband. I tried to befriend some of the suitors. But it's hard to make friends when you don't share similar interests. Besides. I don't really need friends."

Tink cocks a brow. "MY FRIEND?"

My heart stops in my chest. "Well, if you're looking at the strict definition of friend..."

Tink smiles and shoves me, quite hard, on the shoulder.

"I don't think you want to be my friend," I say, though this must warrant further explanation, because she presses on the question mark tile. "I'm not very likable."

Tink makes a conceding expression and shrugs, which isn't exactly comforting. "YOU SAY..." She bites her lip, searching for the correct word. Eventually, she puts "RIGHT" forward but appears less than pleased with it.

"I say...correct?" I squint, trying to interpret her meaning. "I say... the truth? Oh, I tell the truth."

She nods.

I laugh, and it's the dry sort. "Yeah, well, people don't like the truth all that much."

Instead of responding, Tink looks into the distance, outside the cave where the overhanging pines jitter in the wind.

"What?" I ask.

She picks up a tile. "PENSIVE."

I let out a surprised laugh. This one's not so dry.

The smile she offers me would knock me off my feet if I weren't already on the ground. She's beautiful. When I first met Tink, I'd thought her feral, crazed. But maybe she'd meant for me to think that. Staring at her now, her soft cheeks and intelligent eyes, it's wild to think I ever thought her duller than me.

I thought she was insane. But maybe she was simply choosing to be exactly what everyone already expected of her. Perhaps it's simpler that way.

A question forms on my tongue, but as I'm a rotten coward, I mold it into something else. "Do you like the truth, Tink?"

Her pretty eyelashes flitter in surprise. When she presses her tile into my palm, she lets her hand linger there.

I open my palm to find the word "NO" glaring back at me.

The laugh I let out this time is somewhat strained.

Tink holds up a finger, indicating for me to wait. Then she fishes another set of tiles from the board. "BUT I NEED."

For reasons I can't explain, something feels like it's lodged itself in my throat. "You need the truth."

She nods, her expression earnest. "WENDY NEED TRUTH TOO."

I squint, the island salt air burning my eyes. "I think I hurt her without meaning to. Said some cruel things. About her and Peter."

She shakes her head, then points emphatically at the tiles. "WENDY NEED TRUTH TOO." She searches the rest of the tiles until she finds what she's looking for. "IF HURT?" Tink shrugs, then flits her hand as if to say, "So what?" "JOHN LOVE WENDY."

"I wish I could talk to her again," I say, the bulge in my throat expanding. I imagine it pressing against the base of my tongue. "Be gentler this time. I think my message got a little lost in my bluntness."

"YOU FIND WENDY."

I raise my brow. "You think I can? Now I think maybe you're not being honest with me. You know lies don't make me feel any better."

She shrugs as if to say, *"Worth a try."*

"You know, I wish I could hear your voice." The words are out before I even realize I've said them, my tone deeper, more gravelly than usual.

Tink offers me a sly smile. "IT UGLY."

"I don't believe that for a second."

"HOW YOU THINK?"

When I offer her a confused look, she slaps a rather regretful finger on "HEAR."

How you think hear? I run over it in my mind. "Oh, how do I think your voice sounds?"

She nods, and then tosses me a tile for me to carve "SOUND" onto.

I let out a nervous chuckle as I'm working. "I dunno. I guess I imagine it deeper than most women's."

As Tink looks as if she's once again contemplating eating me alive, I wave my hands. "No, I mean in the sultry sort of way. Like a stage singer. The kind of voice that sounds like you smoke pipe tobacco, but somehow still young sounding."

Tink stares at me.

"Tell me I'm wrong," I say, my heart racing. Her stunning blue eyes glint with challenge, but she doesn't pluck the "WRONG" tile from the board.

I offer her the smuggest attempt at a smirk I can manage with my heart pounding out of my chest. Man, I bet she can hear my reaction to her with those pointed ears of hers.

"That's what I thought," I say. "I'm not often wrong." Then, something oddly bold comes over me. "Besides. I've had too much time to think about it to be wrong."

Tink cocks her head to the side. "THAT ALL?"

My throat goes dry. I could pretend I don't understand her meaning. Avoid the question altogether. But that doesn't seem fair to her. Not when she's been deprived of communication for so long. "You're asking if your voice is all I've thought about when it comes to you?"

She nods.

My breath quickens. "You did say you like the truth, didn't you?"

She shakes her head, and as my stomach drops, she pushes a tile into my hand. I don't have to look at it to know which one it is. "NEED."

If this were one of the adventure novels in my parents' library, if I were the hero and she the heroine, I'd tell her all the things I love about her body. Maybe that is what Tink wants from me, but I'm not exactly one of the macho men in those romance books either, so I figure I have to work with what I've got.

"Sometimes I think about what it would sound like listening to you read poetry. The gentle cadence of it, the lilt of your tone. I think about your mouth forming the words. But even then, sometimes I wonder if I shouldn't be dreaming about that. Maybe I should think about you as you are now. So then I let my mind wander to learning this beautiful language," I say, pointing to the notebook I brought her last week. She's already filled it with a graceful script that it kills me not to be able to read. "I dream about you teaching me this language. Then I could finally have the key to what's inside your mind." My hands are shaking, but I take a chance and reach for her, run my fingers through her cropped hair, at the nape of her neck. At my touch, she goes utterly still, except for her eyelashes fluttering. Emboldened, I add, "I mostly wonder...I wonder about where you came from and what your favorite sound is, which food you miss the most from your home. What your phrase is, the one that everyone else associates with you even though you hardly notice how often you use it. Last night, I couldn't sleep because I was imagining being able to ask you the most frightening bedtime story you could remember from your childhood. Whether you like your eggs fried or scrambled. Stupid, meaningless things like that. I think about introducing you to Michael and how I won't have to explain to you how just because he communicates differently doesn't make it any less valid. I...ummm..."

Tink is much too close now. Well, too close depends on one's reasoning. Too close for me to maintain my thought process? Yes. Objectively too close? For all possible purposes?

I wouldn't say that.

It hits me then with the way her pretty blue eyes flick up to mine that she expects me to kiss her. That's what all the signs would point to, at least. But I am a man, and my sex has been known to misinterpret such signs for our own benefit, allowing the truth to be warped by our own desires.

My mind rifles through all the possible scenarios of why Tink might have gotten this close to me. So close I can see the tiny flecks of black in her blue irises, little onyx crystals I think I could make a pastime out of counting. I could have a smudge of dirt on my cheek, one she's just about to wipe away. Perhaps she's noticed the way my glasses have slipped down my nose.

Even if Tink does want me to kiss her, it would be foolish to do so. Wrong, even. Wendy is missing, and I shouldn't be dallying with a woman, neglecting my responsibility.

My mind goes back to how I felt the night Michael scratched my arms up as I tried to keep him from clawing at himself, then found Wendy kissing Peter in his room. I'd been livid. And now, with Wendy kidnapped by Captain Astor...

"Excuse me," I say, guilt making my voice constrict as I scramble away from Tink.

Hurt—obvious enough even I can detect it—flashes across her expression. It stings at my conscience, knowing I've made her feel that way. Rejected.

It's an injustice that a woman like her should ever feel that.

"It's not..." I go to explain.

But Tink is already gone.

CHAPTER 37

WENDY

The Gathers—we learned from the wraith what the Nomad calls his fleet—isn't so much a town as a community of ships strung together with rope bridges. Its backdrop is a barren cliffside made up of sleek onyx rock. There's a dock floating on the outskirts of the community, though what it's anchored with I can't see. When Astor and I arrive, servants jump onto the dock from an adjacent boat.

"You can't be here, strangers," says a man whose weathered wrinkles seem at odds with the firmness of his physique.

"Ah, but we have the passcode," says Astor, voice betraying no hint of deception.

A woman dressed in sailing attire follows the man out onto the deck. "Highly doubt that. The Nomad hasn't granted any newcomers passage in months."

"Darling," Astor says, leaning in from behind, close enough that his warm breath fogs at my ear.

"Wanderer," I mumble. When the two sailors squint at me, Astor prods me in the spine. "The passcode's 'wanderer,'" I say, this time infusing my voice with enough force to overcome the lapping of the water against the dock.

The man shrugs, then gets to work tossing Astor a rope so he can reel us in and secure us to the dock. The woman, on the other hand, seems less eager to assist us, suspicion deepening the crow's feet framing her eyes.

THE MALE SAILOR leads us across the Gathers, the three of us ambling across an assortment of rowboats, ferries, and ships, all of which are tied together with braided rope ladders. Black waters lap against the sides, causing the train of boats to bob up and down at the whims of the calculating sea. The dance of the lantern lights on board might be soothing to watch if it weren't so eerie.

Finally, we reach the center of the network—a grand ship that looks as if it's meant to sail oceans, not in caravans. There are no ladders connecting this one to the others, just ropes slanting between decks. Scalable, but not with ease, given the movement of the water below.

"You two first," says the servant.

When I hesitate, Astor leans over and whispers, "You'd better go, Darling," then adds, "Unless you'd prefer to grab onto my back."

I flush and quickly turn away so Astor won't see. Still, I'd seen how torturing that man to death had rocked him earlier. I shouldn't—but there's a part of me that feels a responsibility to take his mind off of it, relieve his pain a bit. Especially since it was my idea. "You know, I've never heard a man sound so torn between desire and disgust."

Unable to help myself, I glance back to gauge his reaction. The corners of his mouth twitch in a manner I find unreasonably satisfactory. "Thank you," he says.

"For what?" I snort.

"For putting that sensation into words for me."

Now I'm the one embarrassed. By the time I get to the rope, my hands are shaking badly enough that I can barely hold on. I can no longer tell if it's from the aftermath of my interaction with the wraith earlier tonight, or if it's the competing excitement and guilt over Astor and I using each other as distractions.

"Absolutely not!" yells the sailor behind us, noticing my trembling hands. "You'll have to carry that one, mister, or she's not coming!"

Anger rises in my throat. "I can climb just fine," I bite back, though my warbling voice hardly sounds convincing, especially as it's no match for even the sound of the gentle waves.

The sailor rolls his eyes. "The rope's shaking like a sailor who ran out of brandy three days ago, and you're not even on it yet. Captain, carry your plaything or leave her here, but I'm not risking one of the Nomad's guests falling. He doesn't like it when his visitors make for alligator food. At least, not before he meets with them."

Tears sting at my eyes, making me feel petulant. It shouldn't matter whether I can prove that I can climb a stupid rope or not, but...

"You feel good at this—climbing," says the captain, staring at me intently.

A lump forms in my throat as I nod.

"Is it enough for you that you and I both know that you're perfectly capable of doing this on your own?" he asks.

I glance back at the sailor, holding his hands at his hips impatiently. "I suppose you can't just throttle him, can you?"

The corner of his mouth twitches. "If that's what you ask of me, Darling. Though, I'll warn you, I imagine it would make for a most unpleasant remainder of our trip."

Already feeling my spirits lifted by the reassurance the captain believes in me, I nod. "Alright. You can carry me then. But just know that I'm always going to assume you paid that man to be ornery just to get the chance to hold me."

The captain stares at me awhile, a softness glinting in his eyes. "Consider me caught."

I let out a surprised chuckle, but before I can respond, he lifts me into his arms. Without thinking, I find my legs wrapping around his torso as he stares up at me, his gaze dancing across my face, his hands secure at my waist.

"I'm pretty sure this is the wrong way," I say.

"I didn't notice," he says, quickly shifting me to his back. We scale the rope like that, me clinging to him for life itself.

. . .

WHEN THE UNPLEASANT servant leads us through the winding corridors in the hull of the massive ship to a back room filled with a dazzling array of collectibles, I have to school my expression at the man who stands from the desk and introduces himself.

The Nomad is young. At least, he looks young, about my age. He has sandy hair, a sturdy yet sleek build, pointed ears, and cunning sapphire eyes that scan over me and the captain quickly, his gaze lingering on the captain's hand and my cheek. I watch him try to fit the two Marks together, the brief glimpse of confusion when he realizes they don't match.

"What's this?" he asks. "Did the Fates bring me fates-crossed lovers? Those three do possess a cruel sense of humor."

A shiver prances across the bulges of my spine as I search his boyish face for any signs of a lie.

"You're wondering if the stories about me are true," the Nomad says, folding his hands together as he props his elbows on the scattered pieces of parchment that lie strewn across his desk.

"Are they?" I ask, remembering what Vale told us. That the Nomad once crossed into the realm of the dead.

The Nomad examines me, then offers me a casual smirk as he leans back in his chair. "You can never count on all of the stories being true." He cranes his neck back and forth between the captain and me. "I assume you want those Mating Marks removed."

My heart gives a little lurch. It feels suspiciously like hope, but the captain beats me to answering. "Just the one," he says, offering his hand. "I'm afraid my companion here is partial to hers."

A pebble lodges itself in my chest.

"Interesting," says the Nomad, flicking his head in a gesture for us to move closer. We do, and when we reach the desk, Astor splays his hand across the desk for the Nomad to examine. The blond fae pulls a magnifying glass out of his desk and peers through it at the golden tendrils spread across the back of Astor's hand. When he reaches the dead flesh and purple scars that stain Astor's forearm, he clucks and whispers, "Sloppy."

When I turn to Astor with a questioning brow, he doesn't look at me, so I prop my hands on the desk, fingers tented. I'm so nervous, I'm shaking, and leaning on the desk helps support my weight.

"What makes you think I can help with this?" the Nomad asks, dropping Astor's hand and leaning back in his chair once again, arms folded over his chest. When Astor's hand falls back on the desk, his pinkie brushes mine, sending a wave of heat up my arm, piercing my heart.

I suck in a quiet breath. It's the slightest touch. So slight, I can't help but wonder if I'm the only one to notice. Astor doesn't move. And I don't pull away.

"You're friends with the Fates, aren't you?" I say, impatience creeping up my throat and into my voice.

Astor must interpret my shaking voice as a symptom of fear, because he hooks his pinkie around mine. My body stops breathing on its own.

Amusement flashes across the Nomad's face. "The Fates? Friends? I wouldn't call them that. Is that what you two would call one another?"

Immediately, I shift my hand away, breaking contact between me and Astor. His hand doesn't move.

"Let's just say we look out for one another," says Astor, the firmness in his voice surprising me.

"The point is that you maintain contact with the Fates, don't you?" I ask, hating the lack of assurance I betray by how high my voice spikes at the end of the question.

The Nomad taps his fingers against his biceps, arms still folded. "Communing with a Fate is a rather complicated process. And even if it weren't, the Eldest Sister doesn't like her decisions challenged. If she Marked the two of you, it's because she's scoured through all the possible matches and made a decision that's in your best interest. Even I have to admit, she's hardly ever wrong. You'd do well to heed her advice."

"We don't have complaints about who she's Mated us to," I say, at which point I think I glimpse Astor cringe out of the corner of my eye. The Nomad must see it too, because his blue eyes dart toward Astor ever so slightly before focusing back on me. "Captain Astor's Mate is dead. He just wants to be rid of his suffering."

The Nomad actually laughs. His smile would be beautiful if he weren't so eerie. If he weren't mocking Astor's pain. "You're even more naïve than you look, Miss Darling."

I go rigid. "How do you know my name?"

He smiles. "I know plenty of things. But no need to worry, it's not so sinister as you believe. I have my scouts collect information on anyone who ports near the Gathers. I understand that the two of you dispatched one of my own earlier this evening."

Astor goes stiff next to me, his hand still tented on the table, flexed and ready to unsheathe his blade, when the Nomad leans across the table. "No need for alarm. He was outside the borders of my protection, rendering retaliation unnecessary. Besides," he says, homing in on me, "the two of you are intriguing enough to live. What are you trying to do, Miss Darling? Take away his pain?"

I can take away your pain.

Unease slithers through me. He's right. I'm not here for Astor. Astor can take care of himself. I'm here for Peter, to find a way to rid him of the curse.

I should know better than to try to take away anyone's pain. Let Astor do what he wants. It's none of my business, anyway.

The Nomad must be bored of taunting me, because he turns toward Astor. "I can't help you remove the Mark. Unless you'd like me to take a blade to that wrist of yours, of course. I do enjoy the sensation of slicing through bone."

Astor withdraws his hand, tucking it into his pocket casually. "That won't be necessary."

"Pity," pouts the Nomad.

I barely hear him, shocked that such a simple solution would work. For the barest sliver of a moment, my mind takes me away with it, and I'm imagining clawing my Mark from my face. Scraping away at my skin until there's nothing left to bind me to Peter.

For a fleeting moment, I let myself glimpse through the peephole of a door I previously thought locked to me, into a world where neither Astor nor I are Marked. A world where he is free to let go of his wife, and I am free from the Mark that ties me to Peter.

But of course, that wouldn't work. Tink already clawed at my Mark on the island of Neverland, and when my wounds healed, the Mark healed with it.

"If you don't let me do it, it seems your Darling girl might just do it anyway," the Nomad says smirking at me. "You've been looking contemplative over there."

Shame washes over me as I return to the present. When I glance at Astor, he's staring at me intently. Unreadable.

But I get the eerie sensation he can read me. Stare directly into my soul and glimpse what I was thinking—the slightest betrayal of Peter. Of my Mate.

My Mate. I repeat the term in my head like my brothers' lives depend on me searing it into my memory.

"You thinking of ridding the captain here of his Mark?" asks the Nomad. "Or yourself of yours?"

My face goes scarlet, and I scramble for my defense. "I was just thinking of how that would never work."

Astor and the Nomad both look at me questioningly, but I refuse to look at the Nomad at the moment, so I focus on the captain. "Tink." When he raises an eyebrow, I go on to explain. "She's a faerie that inhabits Neverland. She had a fling with Peter in the past. He brought her to Neverland, but when it didn't work out, she refused to leave. She didn't much like having me around." I caress my face, where the scars have healed over from her attacks. "Tried to claw my Mark off. Clearly, it healed back over."

"Well, perhaps if you ever get desperate, you can ask the captain here to cut that pretty head of yours off," says the Nomad through pearly teeth.

Astor actually flinches, and the Nomad holds his palms up. "I meant no offense. The two of you truly are a serious lot, aren't you?" When neither of us answers, the Nomad sighs. "Tell you what. I'll see what information I can gather. I no longer commune with the Fates, but I might know a way."

"What's the price?" asks Astor.

"What? You don't think me a generous spirit?" Again, when the Nomad is met by unamused silence, he swivels his attention to me. "This Tink character? What kind of faerie is she?"

Confused, I shrug. "Unseelie. She had wings."

"What type?"

I scramble for the words. "Similar to a butterfly's, but the texture and color was more like a dragonfly's."

"Did they glow?"

I nod. "A little. Why?"

A sly grin overtakes the Nomad's face. "Faerie dust is a rare commodity, Miss Darling."

I blink. I've never considered how faerie dust is harvested. The memory of the dust goes sour on my tongue. Not that I hold much sympathy for Tink when she's tried to kill me twice.

"Hm," says the Nomad, who then turns to Astor to work out the arrangements.

Sensing I've been dismissed, I wander away from the desk, worn out from the Nomad's taunting. I'm pretty sure he's just stringing us along, waiting for his opportunity to wheedle something out of us. Besides, I'm drained from my brief lapse, from where I let my mind go just now.

* * *

I'M TRYING to find something for my hands to do to make sense of my conflicting feelings when I come across a sketchbook laid out on the nearby mahogany counter.

I'm not sure whether I'm allowed to rifle through this or not, but as the Nomad is still talking to Astor and doesn't seem inclined to stop me, curiosity gets the better of me. Inside the sketchbook are drawings of the ancient ones, the fae who took to the stars in death, the ones who still look down upon us.

There's not a tale depicted in this sketchbook I haven't read to John and Michael at some point or another. The first I find is a dreadful tale about a man who hunts down and brutally murders his Mate after discovering she's rejected him in favor of his brother. Michael always loved that one for some reason. Then there's the story behind a winter constellation called Ranger's Tears. In that one, a man sacrifices his wife to bring back his mistress, trading the lifeblood of the murderer for that of the victim after his wife slaughtered her in a fit of passion.

I flip through the pages until, finally, I find what I'm looking for. The Reaper and his lover, a miserable oak reaching into the heavens to grasp for him. I'm not sure how old this sketchbook is, whether it's the work of the Nomad or if he's simply collected it from someone else, but I let my fingers trace the charcoal grooves of the drawing. The dots that make up the Reaper in the sky—the ones that match my Mark—down to the rest of the drawing. The Reaper's body and the oak that make up the Mating Mark on Peter's back.

Guilt pinches my chest at the thought of my Mate. I've been off gallivanting with the captain, losing my focus on freeing Peter from his curse. The lies I tell myself aren't all that convincing—I know how close I was to letting Astor sweep me into his arms the other night, allowing myself to melt into his kiss. Denying it doesn't change the frequency with which I've returned to that moment in my mind, letting myself play out what might have happened had I leaned in rather than away. I'm betrothed—yet I turn my head for whoever is nearby. Whoever is willing to offer me a breadcrumb of attention. Even if that person ruined my life, destroyed my family.

No. I belong with Peter.

It's written in the stars. Written on my skin. Stitched to my heart. A bond as eternal as the story of the Reaper and the Oak. I trace my fingers down, finding the tombstone through which the oak burst, sure that even the grave couldn't keep her from her lover.

In the end, the expanse between the earth and the heavens was always going to be too far.

The fox digs at the base, searching to find a soul in the roots. As my fingers caress them, searching for the oak's soul, too, something strikes me as odd, but I can't quite place it. There's something about the drawing that feels both unfamiliar and familiar.

"Come on, Darling," says Astor, placing his hand on my shoulder. When I turn to look at him, my gaze lands on his hand instead, lying gently but protectively on my shoulder. His sleeve slips down, revealing his wrist.

Across the back of his hand swirl golden tendrils, coming to a point at his wrist before being cut off from any circulation, lifeless bruises extending the length of his forearm.

Except they aren't tendrils, like I've always thought.

They're roots.

CHAPTER 38

WENDY

$\mathcal{M}$y gaze snaps back to the book, sure that I'm reading a pattern into Astor's Mating Mark that isn't there. Because his Mark matched his wife's. And my Mark finishes Peter's. Because Peter is my Mate, and I can't...

But when I scour the roots on the sketch, a wave of nausea froths in my stomach as my mind overlays its tendrils on top of Astor's Mark. And then he's reaching from behind me, his arm grazing mine as he runs his fingers over the sketch, the trunk and leaves of the tree.

It confirms my every fear. My every fleeting hope.

His Mark is a mirror image of the roots, and then I see it—where the trunk and branches of the oak would have once stretched, now blanketed in dead skin and bruises.

I think I'm going to be sick.

Chest grazing my back, Astor pauses, practically holding his breath, until slowly, softly, he closes the book. When I turn to face him, he's not looking at the book.

He's looking at me.

Our gazes meet. Spar. What must be a thousand accusations in my eyes collide with his ivy irises, betraying nothing except a challenge.

Ask me, he commands with his silence.

"So she didn't know," says the Nomad, folding his hands in front of him as he props his elbows on his desk. "Well, isn't that intriguing?"

"WHAT'S GOING on in that head of yours?" asks Astor.

"I don't know."

"What do you mean you don't know? You know the truth now. You must have thoughts."

"Yes, and I might consider allowing you to be privy to them *after* you explain what is going on," I say, voice trembling.

Astor stares at me from across the tiny cabin the Nomad had one of his servants show us to while we await his answer. I suppose he thought it amusing to place us in such an intimate space, unable to escape one another after my recent revelation.

I wouldn't be shocked to find out the Nomad possesses some way of listening in on this conversation. But I'm beyond caring about such things.

I am numb. Mind whirling. Never landing.

The world spins around me, but I am unmoving, unsure of which direction to tread. Where I might land if I take a step.

So I wait. "Explain," I say, unblinking.

Astor remains at the other side of the room, leaning against a dresser. Like he can't get far enough away from me. "You're eerily calm," he says.

I stare at him, waiting.

The captain doesn't shy from my gaze, but he releases a measured exhale, his shoulders sagging. "Are you sure? This isn't the sort of story one can unknow."

"I think we're beyond that," I whisper.

He nods, one hand on the dresser as he rubs his forehead with the other. "Very well." He says it like it's the first time he's ever uttered a concession.

"Peter and I met after he was brought to the orphanage that was situated in the town I'd grown up in. It was a sort of sanctuary town for the fae. A remote fishing village away from human settlements. We used to climb trees together in the orchard behind the orphanage property. Play pirates, of all things," he says, his chuckle more like a rocky whisper. "Peter and I became fast friends. Peter had watched his mother die of the plague. They found him wrapped up in her arms days later. Had to pry him from her corpse."

I blanch, and the captain does too. "I had...other things I was working through at the time. My father had died recently, and I didn't know how to operate in a world without him. For a while, we got each other through the misery of our lives. Made plans for what we'd do when we came of age." My mind hitches on that detail. "At least, for a while," he says. "But then something changed between me and Iaso. I remember she was picking dandelions in the field outside of the orphanage one day. We'd grown up in the village together. Knowing her, she was probably avoiding her mother's chores. We were ten, but I remember seeing her picking flowers and being stunned. Even as a boy, I knew I'd marry her one day. Never considered the future could turn out any other way. But that was the moment I decided I had to do something about it."

"What did you do?" I say.

He chuckles, using his fist to cover his smile. "I yanked the dandelions from her hand and made her chase me for them."

I picture a young Astor, hiding a bouquet of stolen dandelions behind his back. "Sounds like you," I say, throat dry, to which he scratches his jaw almost shyly. "Did she catch you?"

"Oh yes. So naturally, I cast the dandelions to the ground and stomped on them with my bare feet."

"Charming."

"Yes, I always have possessed that quality."

"And how did she respond to that?"

Astor pauses, a pained smile staining his lips. "She stomped on my toes with her boots. We'd been friends before, but from that moment, we were inseparable."

I can't help but grin, though something about the gumption of this girl makes me feel inadequate.

"From then on, my dreams bent themselves around Iaso."

"And you forgot about Peter," I say.

He shakes his head. "No, not at all. I adored Iaso. Loved her with all my heart. But Peter was my closest friend, and I had no intention of abandoning him. Eventually, I introduced him to my peculiar female friend, and they took to each other immediately. We spent years plotting our futures. Since Peter wasn't allowed to leave the orphanage, and my…family situation made getting a job difficult, Iaso started taking odd jobs in the village, saving up for the ship fare we'd need to leave that wretched town. Looking back, I'm not sure Peter believed that we truly meant to take him with us when we escaped, but we did.

"By the time we were fifteen, Iaso had almost saved enough for us to escape town on a trading vessel. We planned to marry as soon as we reached port in Caraway. Buy a house and let Peter room upstairs.

"But dreams never seem to work out perfectly, no matter how well-planned. It was the first day of spring—I remember because there was a festival in the village Iaso was working. Anyway, I woke to this on my wrist."

A shudder snakes through me as I stare at his Mark. Because I was born on the first day of spring.

"Obviously it didn't look quite like this then. At first, I was over-joyed. It never crossed my mind that I'd be Mated to anyone other than Iaso. But when I showed it to her that night, she went pale, started trembling. I'd thought hers would have appeared too, but she explained to me that for females, Marks appear when they reach maturity. That if she were going to have a Mark, it would have already appeared."

I think of my Mark, appearing with my first bleeding. My mother had fainted.

"And for males?" I ask.

"For males," the captain says, choosing his words carefully, "Marks appear when their Mate is born."

I can feel the blood draining from my face, but Astor continues. "I was horrified at the idea of being bound to another woman. Of my heart being stolen away without my consent. Tried everything I could to scrub it off. I even took a brand to it, but it kept reappearing, my skin healing, the Mark growing brighter with each attempt to remove it.

"Iaso knew a Seer from the village. One who dabbled in rune magic. The Seer didn't believe a Mark could be removed—only trans-ferred. She said if we could find a host, she could give the Mark to someone else."

"That's not possible," I breathe. "My parents tried…any Seer they went to said it couldn't be done."

"Not well, no," he says. "But we were too young to know any better."

My heart snags. "So you thrust me on Peter?"

Shadows from the fireplace darken his cheeks. "No, Darling. Peter volunteered."

"Why?" I ask, tears stinging at my eyes. "Why would he do that?" I can't figure out where my anger is coming from. If it's from having my Mark traded like a commodity or if it's from the unfairness of Peter having to take me on.

Or if I'm mad because…because Astor traded me away.

"Peter loved us. Both of us. Iaso and me. Or so we thought," Astor says, staring into the fire like through its flames he can glimpse portions of the past. "He could see how much it pained us—the idea of being ripped apart. I think part of him thought he was saving our little trio. That by taking my Mark, he'd have someone, too. Everyone would win.

"But the Seer tricked us. It cost us every last copper Iaso had saved up to perform the ritual. It was agonizing," he says, pulling up his sleeves to show me. As if I haven't already seen the bruises, as fresh as if they'd been made yesterday, not twenty years ago. "She didn't tell us her magic wasn't strong enough. While she was able to transfer part of the Mark, giving the majority of it to Peter, well…you see."

I nod, gaze going blurry as I take it all in. I can't tell if the room is getting smoky from the fire, or if my eyes are just losing the will to focus.

"Peter wasn't the same after that," he says. "He grew distant. Jealous. He'd wanted a Mate of his own, but I think he blamed me for keeping part of the Mark. He felt it so strongly once it was a part of him, he couldn't imagine me ever purposefully letting you go. He didn't understand what Iaso and I had."

My chest hurts.

"As he pulled away, Iaso and I continued to make plans. When her grandfather died and left her part of his inheritance, she and I took off. By that point, Peter hadn't spoken to me in months. We thought he wanted nothing to do with us. I thought that would be the end of it. I missed my friend, but I was drunk on happiness for the first and only time in my life. Iaso and I married when we reached Caraway. We'd just turned sixteen. And everything was perfect. Four and a half years of absolute bliss. Iaso and me against the world, jumping from one adventure to the next.

"We'd always hidden her powers, afraid of others' greed. Afraid they'd take her away from me. But as the years passed and Iaso witnessed more and more suffering, she could no longer stand by when others fell ill. I tried to stop her. Warned her of what traffickers would do to her if they found out her blood contained healing properties. But she told me she couldn't let anyone keep her from doing what was right—not even me. And well, you know what happened after that."

I nod. "A girl in Estelle fell ill. And Iaso came to the rescue," I say, throat dry, a tangy taste on my tongue, as if I can remember the taste of her blood. My throat hurts. "I was your Mate first." Astor's gaze lands on my mouth. "I was your Mate. And you gave me away."

He squeezes his eyes shut. "Darling, you have to understand…"

"Oh, I understand," I say, throat bobbing.

His face goes sharp, all cutting lines and angles. "I loved Iaso. She was my best friend. You can't blame me for what I did."

"Can't blame you for what you did?" I ask, exasperated. "You still can't see it, can you? I'm not a fool. I can forgive you for falling in love with the perfect woman, your match in every way. I can forgive you for doing what you could to never let anything come between you. But the two of you, the three of you," I say, remembering Peter, "you're forgetting there was someone else in this story. You're forgetting that you ripped me *in half.*"

"Darling—"

"No, don't *Darling* me. There is something broken inside me. Something fragmented. I'm not…I'm not right," I say, squeezing my eyes shut, just for a moment. "I am torn. Always have been. And now I know why."

He squeezes the space between his brows. "I know. I never meant to hurt you."

"That's not exactly an apology," I say.

He glances up at me, gritting his teeth, and I know we're both remembering the cave, him telling me that he only ever apologized to one person.

That I'm not her.

"You didn't take me because of my shadow soothing," I say, the realization washing over me. Astor had never specified my shadow soothing was what he needed me for. He just hadn't bothered to correct my assumption. "You took me because you need me to get rid of your Mark. You don't want to feel for me anymore." When the captain opens his mouth to protest, I shake my head. "Don't bother denying it. You don't have to tell me you hate me. That you feel nothing for me. We both know anything you feel is only because of this," I say, taking his hand and rubbing my fingers over the roots on his knuckles. He tenses underneath my touch, and it hurts to feel his reaction. To know it's not him, but the magic coursing through him.

"Darling…" he says, then stops himself.

"Don't worry," I say, offering him a well-practiced smile. "I'll help you, when the time comes. I think I'd like to be rid of you, too. Maybe then we can finally be rid of each other."

His jaw ticks, the sorrow unmistakable on his expression. "If that's what you want."

There's something cruel shaping my lips as I repeat his words back to him. "Tell me what *you* want."

The captain's throat bobs. He swallows, searching for the words as he looks away.

Just tell me you want me, I cry with all my heart. *Three words, and I'm yours. I've always been yours. Since the moment I took my first breath.*

The captain takes my chin in his hand and lifts it, so that I have no choice but to look at him. His ivy eyes sweep my face, brushing over my nose, my cheekbones, my mouth, like he's searching for his answer there. Like he'll find it somewhere within me. When he presses his forehead to mine and his eyes shut, I don't blink. Refuse to look away.

But when he opens his eyes again, I realize what he was trying to do. That he thought, just maybe, if he could close his eyes, he could erase what he sees when he looks at me.

That's what I should see when I look at him. I should see my parents' murderer in the creases at the corners of his eyes, in the slant of his lip, the shadows of his dark beard, the length of his long eyelashes.

But I don't.

Because the moment he opens his eyes, all I see is him.

And all he sees is her.

"I'm sorry, Darling."

"It's okay," I say, slipping back and away from his grasp. Not daring to watch as his hand falls away from my face. I let my mother's smile play on my pretty lips. "I'm not," I lie.

CHAPTER 39

JOHN

I'm on the way back from the cave, mind still fixating on Tink and what an idiot I was for not kissing her, when voices—well, a voice, really—has me wandering from my path to the Den.

It's Simon. I recognize his voice—the suppressed quality that's painted its edges recently—but I can't make out who he's talking to. In fact, as I draw closer, pushing brush out of the way as it attempts to scratch my glasses, I realize I can't hear another speaker at all.

"He's dying," says Simon, somewhere off in the distance, still obscured by the bushes. "Why can't you tell that he's dying?"

My pulse accelerates, but I still my breathing. There's a slim chance Simon won't notice me sneaking up on him. Not with that fae hearing of his. I'd rather not alert him of my presence if I can help it.

"Please. Please, just let go. He's still alive. If you let go now, he'll recover. He's been poisoned. Please, I'm begging you to look. He can't breathe. You're killing him. Stop, please!"

Abandoning all attempts at concealing my presence, I rush through the brush. I know it's illogical, but the irrational anxiety that it's Michael being hurt races through my mind. Thoughts of how I'll never forgive myself if…

I come to a clearing, expecting to find a murder in progress.

But it's just Simon, speaking to the trees. His silky black hair is matted with sweat, his voice husky. Red lines streak the whites of his eyes, and his tanned skin has gone sallow. His gaze is fixated on the thin air, like he's listening to a judge hand down his death sentence.

"Please. I didn't know. Just tell me what to do to fix it. I'll do anything to fix it, Thomas."

Invisible spiders skitter up my spine. I should call his name. Should throw him a lifeline back to reality. If you can even call Neverland that.

But I don't. There's some sick self-preservation instinct in me that reminds me that Simon isn't in his right mind at the moment. I'm not certain that telling him his visions aren't real will help. They might very well agitate him more.

"I didn't mean to hurt you. Just tell me how to fix it."

A pause, then Simon lurches backward. As if he's been slapped. "I... I didn't..." Even without hearing the other side of the conversation happening inside Simon's mind, I can tell he's trying and failing to come up with a lie. "No. No, that's not why I came here. I came here to apologize. I came here to punish myself. Not to relive..."

Another long pause. I step forward, careful with my steps lest I spook him. I really shouldn't be coming any closer. I need to keep myself alive if I want Michael to have anyone to protect him. Call me a coward, but I'll bear the shame as long as it serves to protect my brother.

"That's really what you want?" Simon says, voice trembling. "You'll forgive me then?"

He looks unsure. Afraid. But the version of himself that's speaking to himself must be convincing, because Simon nods.

I watch in horror as Simon brandishes a blade and slits his own throat.

It's not Simon I see falling.

It's my father first, too much of a coward at the end to bear watching my mother's death. Making her witness his instead.

Then it's my mother, the slit of red at her throat the same curve of her all too familiar smile. The one she always donned like she did her pearls or her cosmetics.

Perhaps that's why I don't think.

Perhaps that's why I make a mistake.

I rush to him, to Simon's crumpled body. Because it's exactly what I've done every time I've replayed my parents' deaths in my mind. It's muscle memory now, with how many times I've visualized what I would have done had I been brave that night.

Had I been the protector my father wished me to be.

By the time I get to Simon, blood is gushing from the open wound at his throat. His eyes have rolled back in his head, his body collapsed against the green grass of the clearing.

My hands are on his throat before I can stop them. A pitiful attempt to stop the flow of blood. He's gargling now, and the sound sends me back to the masquerade, grates against my ears, makes me want to gag.

When I touch him, his eyes come into focus, just for a moment. Fixating on me. My fingers are drenched in blood. I let go for just long enough to rip off my shirt and use it to stifle the bleeding, but it's dyed scarlet in only a few seconds. Simon's fae, so his body is equipped to heal faster than a human's, but it's not instantaneous.

Not fast enough to keep him from bleeding out.

I should say something. If Wendy were here, she'd tell him he's going to be okay.

She would lie.

Since I can't bring myself to do that, I instead ask a question. "Do you know what happened to Wendy? Why Peter gave her away?"

Simon looks confused, bewildered, but he shakes his head. Wrong question, then.

"You can see the shadows. How?"

Simon opens his mouth, but only a gargle comes out.

I furrow my brow, trying to steel the panic, keep it from ridding me of my senses. If only I can find the right question to ask.

In the end, all I can think to ask is,

"Can I trust Peter?"

But by the time the question leaves my mouth, Simon is already dead.

CHAPTER 40

WENDY

The Nomad demands to meet with us separately before we leave.

"To ensure your stories match. The Nomad doesn't like to be double-crossed," the servant says in explanation as he comes to retrieve me. Astor protests the idea initially, but when I remind him he isn't responsible for my well-being, he backs off, just as shocked by my forwardness as I am.

When I arrive, the Nomad peers up from his desk, tucking his magnifying glass away as he gestures for the servant to shut the door on his way out. I can't help but notice that he's been examining the sketch of the Reaper and the Oak.

"What details do you want to know?" I ask, but the Nomad waves my words away.

"That's not what I called you in here for," he says. My chest tightens as he gestures to the seat across from him. "Don't worry, Miss Darling. I'm sure you'll find this meeting to your benefit."

I stand with my back still pressed to the door, though I'm fairly sure the servant locked it behind him. My mind flashes back to evenings in my parents' parlor, to men so certain that I was enjoying myself. So confident that I was lucky to have their hands all over me.

"Forgive me if I don't trust your assumption of what will be to my benefit."

For a moment, the Nomad almost looks serious. "I'll let you determine that for yourself, then. But please. Sit."

I nod, ambling toward the chair and taking it. The Nomad doesn't sit. Instead, he navigates to the front of his desk, leaning his back against it as he crosses his feet. "You're not here to rid the captain of his Mark."

I shake my head. "How did you know?"

"Because I fail to see how that benefits you. Though if I've missed something, please enlighten me."

I bite the inside of my cheek. At least the Nomad hasn't seemed to catch on to the feelings I'm attempting to quash for the captain, though I'm surprised he's that oblivious. Perhaps my face doesn't show as much as I fear it does.

"I'm here for my Mate," I say, folding my hands in my lap and stretching them out as I interlock them. When the Nomad glances at the sketch, I amend my statement. "Not...not that one. Peter. He was cursed by a Fate. He can't feel pain."

The Nomad brow quirks at that. "Are you a lover scorned, then? Distraught that you can't inflict the same pain he caused you by having relations with the faerie who carved your face to pieces?"

I let out a nervous chuckle, rubbing my palms against my thighs. "No, nothing like that. I don't want to hurt my Mate. I just...well, he can't love me, can he? Not truly. Not without the ability to feel pain."

The Nomad taps his finger against the desk. "Is that what love is to you, Miss Darling? Pain?"

My throat goes dry. "No. But one cannot love without experiencing pain of some sort. He bargained me away because he couldn't feel the pain of losing me. Not like I felt for him," I say, clutching my chest, reaching within for how it felt like it was being rent in two when we left Neverland. Strange, but I can't seem to remember the sensation that once felt so agonizing. Even so, my connection to Peter is still there, a strand of magic, half of what a normal Mating Mark might be, but tethering all the same.

"Hm," says the Nomad, staring down at the sketch next to him. "And you're sure your Mate wishes to be set free of his curse?"

"It's a curse, isn't it? They're meant to be broken."

"You'd be surprised, Miss Darling, how many mortals prefer to make pets of their curses."

I shake my head. "Not Peter. Peter would choose to be free if he could."

The Nomad's mouth curves at the edges. "He would choose pain? To love you more fully?"

"Just because you can't comprehend that kind of love doesn't mean it doesn't exist," I snap.

The Nomad's laugh chills my bones. "You have no idea the pain I've subjected myself to—time and time again—just for a taste of that sort of high. But you know about highs, don't you?"

Again, the taste of faerie dust blooms on my tongue. When I don't answer, he says, "So you choose this Peter, then? How unfortunate for Captain Astor."

I snort. "The captain prefers to cage himself in the past."

The Nomad's blue eyes widen, and even I am surprised by the bitterness in my voice. Unsettled, I find myself softening. "If the captain wishes to be rid of me, who am I to stop him? Why would I choose someone who refuses to choose me?"

"Oh, I don't know," says the Nomad. "Surely you can admit there's fun in the chase."

"I don't want to chase," I say. "My feet are too tired for that."

"Very well, then," he says. "I believe you and I could be mutually beneficial to one another. You see, I'd quite like to have a faerie dust supplier of my own. When you break your Mate's curse and return to Neverland to secure your happy ending, I want you to turn the faerie over to me. I'll even be generous and give you an entire year to do it."

"I doubt I'll be able to catch her," I say.

The Nomad shrugs. "Then convince your Mate to do it. Surely with his curse broken, he'll be so pleased with you, he'll do whatever you ask."

I can't tell if he's taunting me or not. "Fine, but I want two years," I say, to which the Nomad grimaces but doesn't object. "Now how do I break the curse?"

"I myself am ignorant of such matters, but in a few moments, I'm going to call your captain in here and tell him that there's a dead Seer in the Cave of Endor who knows the spell to remove his Mark."

"And is that true?" I ask.

The Nomad's eyes twinkle. "What is it to you?"

I sit back in my chair, listening as the Nomad continues, "What's relevant to you is that this Seer has the magic to break your Mate's curse."

"And how am I supposed to talk to a dead Seer?"

"There's a spell," he says, leaning in and whispering it in my ear. I shiver at the sound of the ancient words in my ear, but commit them to memory all the same.

"Now," he says, holding out his hand. "Do we have a bargain?"

When I take the Nomad's hand, something stings at the back of my neck. At the same time, he presses a cold object to my hand. "You'll be needing this," he says. "A calling stone. You can use it to bind the Seer to this world. Just don't drop it." He flashes me a smile that I'm unable to interpret as either sincere or teasing.

Then, as if the Nomad had merely been speaking to himself and not another person inhabiting the room, he returns to the sketches at his desk.

Considering myself dismissed, I make to abscond from the room, but as I rise from my seat, the Nomad addresses me, though without looking up from his papers. "Oh, and do be careful, Miss Darling. Spirits only have a limited amount of magic to offer after they die. What you and the captain want—there won't be enough magic for both. If I were you, I wouldn't use the Seer's magic lightly."

The contents of my stomach harden to concrete, the pressure of what's at stake threatening to make me sluggish. A servant soon comes to fetch me, then leads me to a parlor where Astor is waiting, foot perched on his opposite knee, which he's bouncing erratically. If he greets me with his expression, I'm intentionally ignorant of it, because I turn my attention to a painting on the wall, fixing my gaze on its ghastly depiction of a vast wasteland.

The servant leads Astor out of the room for his meeting with the Nomad. My foot taps against the floorboards. Uneasy as I am being complicit in deceiving Astor, I'm weary of sacrificing for people who aren't willing to sacrifice for me. Still, when he returns to get me from the parlor, I open my mouth, then quickly shut it, realizing I'd rather my deception be silent than spoken.

On the way out, a servant bumps into me, knocking me into Astor's arms. His arms grip around my shoulders as he stares into my eyes. I can't tell if it's an apology written there, or just resignation.

CHAPTER 41

JOHN

Simon has been dead for all of five seconds before I realize how bad this looks.

My hands are covered in blood. Worse, in my panic, I'd moved the fallen blade out of the way. I don't even recall touching it, but my handprints stick to the hilt in sticky scarlet blood all the same.

Blood pumps against my forehead, pounding nails into my skull. Simon's corpse is pale in front of me, but I can't seem to scrub the image of my parents' lifeless bodies from my mind.

Caring gets you killed.

Think, John.

I close my eyes, breathe, and banish my parents from my mind. Banish Simon from my mind. Then I walk myself through my next few steps.

One at a time.

First, I have to decide what the chances are that Peter will believe me if I tell him I didn't kill Simon. Simon's been acting strange since the night he killed Nettle. It's not illogical that he killed himself. Especially when he could see shadows, and the shadows had made Wendy violent.

But had Peter known about Simon's ability to convene with the shadows? Surely if he had, he would have had Simon on a faerie dust regimen like he'd had Wendy.

A cog turns in my brain, but doesn't quite fall into place. I'll consider that later.

Task at hand. Will Peter believe me? I work through how this would look to him.

We'd just had a conversation about losing ourselves, our morals, for the ones we loved. He knows I've been hesitant to believe him about Astor taking Wendy from the island. He doesn't know Tink confirmed he was telling the truth—in part, omitting the part about handing Wendy over. It's possible he thinks I'm still searching for the person behind Wendy's disappearance.

And it's reasonable to think I'd be suspicious of Simon. I have been suspicious of Simon. He's been acting odd since the night Nettle tried to kill me. I'm still convinced Wendy learned something that night she wasn't supposed to. Something that's had Simon spiraling.

I've been suspicious enough that whether Simon was involved in Wendy's disappearance had been my first question when he was dying. If Peter follows a similar train of thought, it's not a stretch to think I might have killed him.

Honestly, I don't know that I'd put it past myself if I truly had been convinced by the evidence.

No. I can't tell Peter.

Next problem: what to do with the body.

It's still best if the others can assume it was a suicide. Had I not rushed in to help, I could have easily left Simon's body as is, but now that his blood is all over me, some of it soaking my shirt, and my handprint is on the blade, I have to figure out how to make it look as if no one intervened.

The blade.

Once I clean my hands on my pants, I wipe the hilt off with the little of my shirt that's not already drenched in blood. When Simon dropped the dagger, the hilt was still clean. I leave the blood staining the blade and position the hilt under Simon's already hardening fingers.

Now his wound.

Much of his blood is absorbed into my shirt, but some of it had already pooled on the ground next to him before I got to him. It's not much, but I spread some of it across his wound, trying not to focus on the clammy feel of the open skin against my wet fingertip as I trace a line from his wound to the ground and spread it over the indentions made by the textile.

I'm not pleased with my work and can only hope that the blood will have dried by the time someone finds him.

When I'm done, I dispose of my shirt in the thicket, then make my way back to camp.

REGRETTABLY, it's Smalls who discovers Simon's body. I'd just been back at the Den long enough to throw a shirt on by the time the panicked shouting echoed down the rooted hallways from the center of the Den.

Peter hadn't been home, so the Lost Boys made the trek to the body together. I'd stayed behind to watch Michael, my stomach still twisting with anxiety over what I'd witnessed. Victor had returned crestfallen, weary, claiming that in Smalls's panic, he'd tried to stifle Simon's wound, not realizing he was already dead.

Waves of relief and guilt had taken me with them at that news. Frenzied elation that Smalls had inadvertently covered up the evidence that I'd been around for Simon's death. Hatred of myself for being grateful for the youth's trauma.

* * *

DINNER IS QUIET THAT NIGHT, and every night after. No one had been shocked to discover that Simon had taken his own life. Even now, days later, no one questions it, even after all the murders that have taken place on this island.

Upon his return, Peter said it was suicide, and so it is.

The only one who seems at all suspicious is Victor, who keeps glancing at me, signaling me to talk to him privately.

I keep pretending not to notice. Eventually, I'm going to have to decide how to respond to his questions. I imagine he'll believe my story, but the consequences are rather dire on the slim chance he doesn't. So for now, I'm working out how to present the truth so that it's unquestionable.

Since Simon's death, Peter's been eating every meal with us. Every meal that he's not away on one of the Sister's quests, at least. A strange habit for him to start now, as he didn't bother after the deaths of Freckles, Joel, or Nettle. Or Thomas, I assume, though I wasn't at Neverland directly after that.

He sits at the head of the table, jabbing at the Lost Boys as he normally does. As if nothing's happened. As if one of us didn't slit his own throat. He tries to keep conversation going, plugs any silence that leaks into the room with a joke or an outlandish story about something he encountered in the other realms.

It's a clear attempt to take the Lost Boys' minds off of Simon's suicide.

I wonder if he knows how ineffective it is. How the boys laugh and play along as long as Peter is in the room, then dwindle to a reserved hush as soon as he's out of earshot. Not that there are many boys left.

Since Smalls discovered the body, Benjamin has stopped whittling, claiming his fingers ache. Victor is even more sullen than usual. Though he didn't particularly care for Simon, something about the other boy's death seems to have rocked him. The normally reclusive Twins have even stopped whispering to one another.

Across from me, Smalls pokes his onions with his fork. A memory of Simon passing him his untouched onions underneath the table berates my memory. As he plays with them, Smalls's face turns a bit green. Probably running over the same memory. The ghost of the dead boy haunting him from even his dinner plate.

Peter must notice too, because he says to Smalls, "Watch out. If you don't clean your plate, you won't grow anymore."

Smalls stares at the onions in front of him, looking like he's about to gag. "I'm not very hungry," he says.

Peter's grin remains steady. "You will be later if you don't eat."

The rest of Smalls's plate is wiped clean. It's not as if the onions on his plate are going to provide him with much sustenance. Not enough that would make a difference between now and breakfast.

"Benjamin hasn't finished his roast," says Smalls, pointing.

Peter stiffens, almost imperceptibly. "Then Benjamin can finish his, too."

With a huff, Smalls does as Peter says, putting the onions to his mouth and swallowing them with a grimace.

I don't miss the way Peter's gaze bounces across all the other boys' plates, then lands on mine. I frown, then place the onions in my mouth.

They're sweet, but strong. Overpowering, almost. Wasn't that why I'd picked them to hide the taste of rushweed when I'd sought to paralyze Tink? They're tangy, but with an aftertaste of something sweet. I've always thought the onions here tasted different from the ones back home, but I'd assumed they were a different variety.

My mind begins to whirl.

When we first arrived, Simon loved onions. In fact, he'd take Nettle's. When Simon stopped eating them, I assumed it was because they reminded him of the boy he'd had to kill to save Wendy, Michael, and me.

But Nettle had gone crazy. Something had set him off, started him on this delusion of killing the other Lost Boys. And then Simon had stopped eating the onions. Then he'd gone crazy too.

Or had he?

At first, I'd thought Simon had been talking to himself. Hallucinating. But as I'd tried to stifle his wound, something about it had dawned on me as familiar.

I'd seen Wendy do that. Not talk to the shadows, but look out at the world like there was something else there. Something else the rest of us couldn't see.

Until Peter had dosed her with the faerie dust. Faerie dust, which tasted of the nectar of honeysuckles.

The onions slide down my throat, and it's possible I'm imagining the taste of nectar as they do. Possible my mind is playing tricks on me, desperate for a solution and conjuring the taste itself.

But now that I've tasted it, I can't untaste it.

Only when I've cleaned them off my plate does Peter push himself from the table.

THE NEXT TIME Peter leaves on a mission from the Sister, I stop eating my onions.

CHAPTER 42

WENDY

The day following our meeting with the Nomad, I slice clean through a pig carcass for the first time.

I'd barely paid attention to Maddox's instructions. He'd been chattering, asking me to resolve a friendly dispute between him and Charlie. Something about the Nomad's age. Or perhaps Charlie had wagered the Nomad was an elderly female. I hadn't really been listening.

I'd just picked my short sword off the rack and pivoted the hilt in my hand, its weight grounding somehow. Then I'd grasped it with my other hand and struck.

The catharsis of hacking the last pig to bits was nothing compared to that of slicing through the carcass in a single clean line. The whir of my sword cleaving through air. The resistance of the pig's spine unprotected against the quiet rage that's been aching for release since the moment my mind overlaid Astor's Mating Mark onto what was supposed to be mine and Peter's alone.

Maddox whistles behind me, staring at the dangling bits of flesh from the pig's torso, the severed spine jutting from its center. The bottom half of the pig now rolls across the rocky deck as we traverse the waves.

"Remind me not to mess with you," Maddox says, arms crossed, glancing at the short sword we've been practicing with ever since I graduated from the dagger.

"I didn't mean to do that," I say, staring down at the severed carcass with mingled disdain and disappointment.

He quirks a brow at me, his tanned forehead crinkling. "What do you mean you didn't mean to do that? That was a perfect hit. You couldn't have been more perfect."

"Yeah, but now it's over. That was the last one," I say, examining the bottom half of the carcass with a quiet numbness that snuck into the space my rage once inhabited, too quick for me to ward myself against. "Maybe we can hang that half up?" I ask, looking at Maddox hopefully.

His eyes go wide, and he swallows. Instead of reaching for the carcass, he reaches for my blade. My fingers grip protectively over the hilt, but he pries it from my hand. "Why don't we take a break?" he asks.

"Sure," I say, shrugging off my gear. As I wipe down my blade, I sense footsteps on the deck. I glance over my shoulder to find Astor staring at the remainder of the carcass.

"Nice," he says, nudging me in the shoulder with a playful uptick of his lips. "Though I think you made poor Maddox over there wet his pants."

"It's just a pig. It's not like he hasn't done that to humans. To fae," I say, expression flat.

The captain actually bristles. "No. But he never enjoyed it. Never wanted more once he was done. What were you planning to do, Darling? Hack the body to pieces like you used to before you learned to handle a blade?"

When I don't answer, he grabs my shoulder, though gently. "If you're upset, take it out on me."

When I spin back around, I flash him my most dazzling smile. "What would I have to be upset about? Just a little longer, and I never have to see your face again."

He cocks his head to the side. His lips are still curled in amusement, but I don't miss the anger simmering in his eyes. "Come now, Darling. Looking at me can't be so much of a burden."

I shrug. "I wouldn't know. When I look at you, it's not really you I see. Just my parents' blood."

My jab must land, because his hand falters, falling off my shoulder, leaving behind an emptiness I should be used to by now.

I RETURN to cleaning my sword, refusing to count the captain's steps as he walks away.

"I take it you're not thrilled about being Cap's Mate," says Maddox as I transition to helping him clean the remainder of the pig carcass.

I freeze, hands still on the clammy surface of the cadaver. "He told you?"

Maddox leans against the nearby mast, his arms crossed. "Didn't have to. The tension between the two of you is thicker than this thing," he says, tapping the carcass with his boot.

I glance away, hardly able to look Maddox in the eye. "So you knew the Mark was for me, not for Iaso." When Maddox doesn't answer, I snap at him, "I guarantee you that nothing you say is going to make me feel more naïve than I already do."

The humor in Maddox's expression falters, just slightly. "The crew encouraged him to tell you earlier."

The crew. So everyone knew. Everyone but me. "Excellent."

Maddox sighs, then squats across from me, propping his elbows on his outspread knees. "The thing you have to understand about Nolan is he hates nothing more than being controlled."

My mind goes back to my conversation with Astor back when I was recovering from my faerie dust withdrawals. *The thing you have to understand about Peter is...*

What exactly had I said about Peter?

"Yes," I say. "How horrible it must be for someone to have their Fate determined for them without their consent. Sounds dreadful. I can't imagine."

Maddox rests his cheek on his fist, his calloused knuckles pressed into his skin, making even his chiseled jawline appear boyish. "I think the two of you might understand one another better than you think you do."

Frustration simmers within me, but Maddox bats his pretty eyelashes at me, his big gray eyes making him difficult to be angry at, reminding me he's not the one who's hurt me.

I sigh, wiping the sweat from my brow with my sleeve, even as I sneak the fabric across my eyes to hide the fact I'm wiping away tears. "I understand why he did what he did. Believe me, I know. But the moment he took hold of his freedom by severing his Mating Mark, he stole something from me. He bought his freedom at the cost of mine. When he transferred the Mark to Peter, he was controlling me. Can't you see that? Astor might have hated the Sister for choosing his Mate for him, but then he went and did the same thing to me. Except he didn't even have the decency to do it correctly, and now I'm...I'm..."

"Torn," says Maddox, nodding pensively.

Shame washes over me, but relief too, that Maddox understands.

"Peter always had more influence over me than I wanted him to. I thought it was his fae glamour at first, but I later came to realize that our Mating Marks made me malleable in his hands." And he in mine, I don't say, remembering how I tricked him the night I thought he was the one killing the Lost Boys. "That was Astor's doing. And now I don't know what's real and what's a poorly done piece of magic gone awry."

Maddox examines me. "Did you feel the same way about the Mating Mark when you thought you were only matched to Peter's?"

I pause, my words getting hung in my throat. When I don't answer, Maddox continues. "At the risk of sounding like I'm not on your side, Wendy, it sounds to me like you were perfectly fine with your Fate being out of your hands up until recently."

The offense rattles me, but I can't find any evidence to argue otherwise. Once I'd realized Peter wasn't murdering the Lost Boys, I'd been relieved to know we were Mates. I'd been content to rest in the confidence that we were meant to be together, enough that I hadn't abided any doubts that had crossed my mind. Every time Peter had acted in a way that wasn't befitting or honorable, I'd rested on the confidence that he was my Mate. I just hadn't realized that particular foothold was less of a rock and more of a root.

After several seconds go by without a response, Maddox pokes me. "What's really bothering you?"

Tears sting at my eyes, my ribs cracking. When I look up at Maddox, his gray eyes are so soft, so kind, I can't help but confide in him. "He doesn't want me."

Maddox's jaw tenses, his eyes gleaming over with moisture. "Have you considered he might be under the impression that you're the one who doesn't want him?"

The laugh I let out is wry. "Of the two of us, which one of us do you think can make sure they get what they want? If Astor wanted me, he'd have me."

The words are out before I've realized I let them escape my lips. My stomach churns over, but there's no taking them back.

Maddox stands, then stretches, but as he turns away, he looks over his shoulder and says, "For the record, I do believe that you're the type of person who can get what she wants."

"Do you think people can learn to be brave?"

Charlie shifts in her bed. I waited to ask the question until I was fairly sure she'd gone to sleep. I guess I was hoping that I would be able to pat myself on the back and convince myself that I'd done everything I could do. That at least I'd tried.

I must have misjudged Charlie's breathing patterns, because she shoots up in bed, suspicion written all across her brow. "Of whom are we speaking?" she asks conspiratorially.

I groan, propping myself up in bed as well to look at her, though my inclination is to hide myself under the covers. "A hypothetical character I plan to write into a play when all this is over."

Charlie glares at me, then grabs a pillow and hugs it against her chest. "Obviously."

I sigh, giving up the farce. "I'm not brave naturally. And even if I was, I have such difficulty finding the right words in the moment, speaking my mind. They always come out wrong, and—"

"Tell me the story of how you escaped Astor the first time."

I frown, confused. "I'm not sure what that has to do with anything."

Charlie just stares at me, unblinking.

I press my lips together, then scramble for the words. "After...well, after my parents died, John pressed his pocket watch into my hand. He'd loaded it with faerie dust and set it to explode at midnight. I guess he hoped it would give me time to escape the Shadow Keeper. But after Astor attacked, John adjusted the time, so it exploded early. Siv had already taken Michael, so John and I had to find him. Once we got him..."

"Stop," she says. "How did you get Michael away from Siv?"

I blink. "John snuck up behind him and knocked him over the head with a brick. Or maybe it was a horseshoe. I can't really remember."

"And you were just standing around doing nothing?" Charlie asks.

I frown. "No, I was talking to Siv. Trying to keep him distracted so he wouldn't notice John approaching."

Charlie, appeased, gestures for me to continue.

"We ended up hiding in the clock tower, but Astor's men were closing in, so we climbed the ladder to the top."

"Why'd you choose the clock tower?" she asks.

"Because we needed somewhere to hide. I already told you..." When I trail off, Charlie cocks her head to the side, and I sigh. "I chose the clock tower because I figured hiding at the top would give me enough time to strike a deal with the Shadow Keeper."

"Now why would you purposefully run into the arms of the very being who had been haunting you for over half your life?" Charlie asks.

I bite my lip. "I needed to convince him to save my brothers. But I was going to have to go with him anyway. It wasn't as if I had any chance of escaping him."

"In my experience, there are plenty of people who'd never think of running toward their own tragic Fate, no matter how inescapable it was," says Charlie.

I hug my knees to my chest, anxiety quelling. Charlie's expression changes, pity and concern overwhelming her features. "You don't have to be fearless to be brave, you know. You don't even have to look brave or sound brave. Your voice can tremble and your hands can shake. But those things can't take your courage away from you. I'm sorry you were ever made to feel otherwise."

Discomfort swirls in my stomach. "I just don't know that I could even get the words out. And even if I could...what if he hates me for it?"

Charlie grimaces. "If I had to bet, if the captain hates anyone for what's going on between the two of you, it's himself."

I let out a wry laugh and bury my face in my hands. "I think you've managed to make me feel worse. Iaso deserves better than this."

Charlie sighs. "Iaso is gone. Has been for a long time. But you've got to decide what you're more afraid of: the captain rejecting you, or living the rest of your life wondering what might have been different had you been brave enough to start the conversation."

I peer at her through my hands. "You're not saying what I want to hear, you know."

Charlie winks at me. "That's because I'm your friend."

CHAPTER 43

WENDY

*M*y hands are shaking so violently I have to tuck them into my pants pockets and squeeze at the fabric by the time I find Astor.

He's been avoiding me; that I'm sure of. I've been searching the vessel all morning for an opportunity to speak with him, but every time I've approached him, he's found a reason to scold a crew member for their unbecoming posture, praise another for completing a menial task, or otherwise claim he's hearing someone summoning him from above deck.

When I finally find him on deck discussing the behavior of the wind with Maddox, I'm unsurprised when, at my request to speak with him, he immediately attempts to rid himself of my presence. "Ah, Darling. I'm afraid the wind has decided to be a fickle mistress today. Maddox and I—"

"Were just finishing up," says Maddox brightly, offering me a wink and Astor a toothy grin as he salutes, then ambles toward Charlie, who informed me earlier that she'd be "nearby for emotional support."

"You're avoiding me," I say, trying to ignore the way Maddox's fae ears are twitching and Charlie is looking at him expectantly. Clearly, she's expecting him to offer her updates. I wrench my attention back to Astor. "But if you could grace me with a moment of your time, I have something I'd like to say."

Astor flinches, blinking, but he goes quiet.

I find I can't bear to look at him, so I focus instead on the crate behind him, at the crack in it.

"I know you're going to hate me for saying this. And that's okay. I don't think I mind all that much. But I'm so tired. So tired of never... never finding the right words. I don't think I'm ever going to find them at this rate. I'm not sure they exist, and if they do, I'm not confident I'm capable of discovering them. So excuse me as I ramble on a bit. But I..." I make the mistake of glancing up at the captain. His face is impassive, but there's a twitch in his left eyelid. The words snag in my throat, my heart hammering out of my chest, but I force myself to fish them out. "I want you."

Astor looks as if I've slapped him in the face, causing my panic to rise. So I fist my hands at my sides and close my eyes. "I know I'm not supposed to. I know I'm supposed to hate you. I'm supposed to love Peter, but I don't. I thought I did. But I think I just liked being wanted. I think I liked how it felt to feel nothing, to leave my pain behind. But you...you hurt me, sometimes. It hurts to love you, because I have to turn inward. Examine myself. Make choices. You know how much I hate to choose. But if I got to choose, I'd choose you. So I suppose I'm asking you to choose me back. To love me. I know you loved Iaso, that you still do. And I know I'll never replace her. I don't want to. You have to know that. But just...want me back. Please. Because I keep dreaming that you tell me you want me, and when I wake up, I keep chasing the dream, trying to go back to sleep so it can be true just a little while longer."

"Wendy, I—"

"Please. Just let me finish," I say. I spent all night working myself up to say this, but my boldness has a finite limit, and I'm afraid if I stop now, I'll be too depleted to try again. "I know I'm not her. But I'm me, and that can't be so awful, can it? I see the way you want me." My face flushes with heat, the forwardness of what I'm about to say stoking coals in my chest. "I've noticed, you know. You tease me for never speaking my mind, but it's not entirely an impairment. It allows me to watch, observe. And I've noticed. You find ways to touch me when you don't have to. Astor, you remember the little details—you remembered how much I hate the feel of velvet. No one remembers that about me. And that night in the crow's nest—"

"Darling, I don't—"

"No." I hold up my palm, then crinkle my fingers because even that motion feels unnaturally forceful. I end up with a fist full of salty air. "You can deny it all you want. It hurts you; do you think I don't know that? Wanting me, of all people—I'm sure it feels like you're betraying her. But I'm begging you, Astor. Please. Let it go." I stop, taking in a sharp inhale. Make myself look him in those piercing green eyes. Prepare myself for what might be the most selfish thing I'll ever say. No, not selfish—true. "It wasn't my fault." Astor blinks, and I'm shocked by my relief at that one little phrase. "Hate my parents if you want, for what they did to her. But I'm done excusing you for holding that against me. I did nothing wrong. And forgive me if this is unpleasantly forward, but you're torturing yourself. For no reason at all. You'd rather deprive yourself of joy than release the chokehold you keep on your hatred. But don't you see? You don't have to stop loving her to love me. You don't have to betray her to love me. I'm not the one who took her from you. So please. Let it go. Let it go, if not for me, then for yourself."

Astor swallows. It feels like minutes pass before he responds, his jaw working like he keeps tasting the words, and they all come back bitter. Finally, he settles on, "You love Peter."

I exhale. "We both know that I don't."

"Darling," he says, his voice betraying no emotion. Not that I can detect, at least. "Don't I remember us having a similar conversation back in the cave? One in which you informed me that you and Peter were a thing of the past? It was the night you tried to escape Neverland and requested my assistance. You were so sure Peter was your villain. Remember what I told you then?"

I do. He told me Peter would get his claws in me again, then Astor and I could return to our normal banter. But I refuse to play this game. "This isn't the same. This isn't a case of Peter disappointing me and me running to you. This is me choosing you."

"Well, don't."

His words sting, burrowing in my ear. When he glimpses the tears in my eyes, his expression softens. "I'm sorry, Darling," he says. "But I know what love feels like, and this isn't it."

I reach for the fabric of my pants, wishing I had something else for my hands to do. Something to distract me from the pain gnawing my chest wide open. "I know it's going to be different than what you and Iaso had, but..." I tug at the strands of hair at the nape of my neck, realizing how presumptuous that sounds.

"Wendy," he says, and the regret in his expression breaks me more than his use of my given name. "This," he says, brushing his finger over my cheek, over my Mark. "This plays tricks on us. It's not real."

I slap his hand away, the sting of my blow leaving a flaming imprint across his hand. "Then don't *touch* me."

He blinks, shocked at my outburst.

"You heard me," I say. "If you don't love me, don't touch me. If you don't love me, then don't find ways to brush your hand up against mine." I wipe my hands on my trousers, like I can cleanse myself of his phantom touch. "If you don't love me, then when we're in a crowd, don't address me like I'm the only one you're talking to. If you don't love me... Well, then go back to acting like it."

Shame washes over his face, and he tucks his hands back into his pockets. He opens his mouth, shuts it, then opens it again. When he speaks, he sounds like an adult scolding a child he's quite fond of. "You'll see. When we get to the cave and perform the ceremony. You'll be glad it isn't real."

I shouldn't—it strips me of the last bit of dignity I have left, but I offer him a small smile. I can't seem to help myself; I want so badly to smile for Nolan Astor. "No, Nolan," I correct. "It isn't real for you."

CHARLIE COMES to check on me later that evening. If I were a stronger woman, I'd be making better use of my time. As it is, I've spent the afternoon curled up in bed. Had my hands not been trembling after my humiliating conversation with Astor, I might have climbed into the nearest crow's nest, but the energy it would have taken to do that safely has left me.

I hear the door creak open. Sense the light from the hallway spread in a widening ray across the floor. It cuts through the cabin and across the half of my face that's not hidden underneath the sheets. The hearty scent of shepherd's pie fills the air, alerting my stomach to its presence and causing it to roar in agitation.

Charlie crosses the room. Runs her fingers through my hair and tucks it behind my ear. "Oh, Winds," is all she says.

If I hadn't wept away every last drop of hydration in my body, I might shed a tear at her tender touch. Given my current state, I doubt my body thinks we have any liquid to spare. Still, it feels nice to be touched. I only wish it didn't remind me of my mother.

"Remind me never to be brave again," I say, my words muffled by my blanket.

Charlie purses her lips thoughtfully and scratches the top of my head. "I'd recommend you strike the attempt from the record and forget it ever happened, except...well, you were impressive. If you could have seen yourself like Maddox and I saw you, like the rest of the crew saw you, you'd be proud of yourself. I'm certain of it."

It's difficult to imagine that I came across as anything other than a muttering, delusional fool. A child unaware of her own youth. But I'm grateful to Charlie all the same. At least her opinion of me is unchanged.

"I really thought he wanted me back," I whisper.

Charlie knits her brow. "I know." I watch as she bites at the inside of her cheek. I know that look well enough to realize she's trying to decide whether what she wants to say would actually be helpful. "I think he's just afraid."

I snort. "He doesn't seem like he's afraid of anything."

Finally, she says, "Everyone's afraid of something. Astor...he doesn't like being controlled. Can you blame him for that? What if he just wants to be the one to decide that he loves you?" When I give her a look of confusion, she explains. "You find comfort in your Mark, don't you? I mean, before you discovered it was split between Peter and Astor. You're comfortable with not having to be the one to make a decision. But the captain isn't like you. Have you ever considered that perhaps the concept of having a Mate at all bothers him?"

I shake my head. "He would have been thrilled had it turned out that Iaso was his Mate. He'll never let her go," I say, wincing because that's not even what I mean. Not truly. "It's not that I want him to have to. Of course, there's room for him to love her. That doesn't take anything away from me. Except that it's my fault she's dead. And it doesn't matter what he feels for me, he can't—no, he won't—he refuses to let go of that. He believes choosing me is betraying her."

"And who would you choose?" she asks. "If you had your pick?"

My heart sinks, and I blink my tears away, though it's no use. When I bury my hands in my face, my ring scrapes against my cheek, its metallic brush stinging. I put it back on when I returned to my cabin. I hadn't meant to still be wearing it. I'd only wanted to feel the weight of someone wanting me against my flesh. Now I can't bring myself to take it off. Even now, I can feel his pull—Peter's portion of the Mating Mark calling to mine.

"When I go back to Peter, it will be as easy as sliding into an old pair of slippers," I say. "The power he has over me...I can't explain it. When I'm in his presence, it doesn't matter what I feel for the captain. Peter is always going to take precedence."

"Because he possesses the majority of the Mark," says Charlie.

I shrug. "Maybe. Maybe I just love him more."

It's a blatant lie, and Charlie knows that as well as I do, but she doesn't treat it as one. "And you're okay with that? Not knowing whether it's real?"

I wince, and when I look at Charlie, my eyes are pleading for her to understand. "I don't know that I really care whether it's real, Charlie. As long as it feels like it is. As long as I don't have to hurt like this anymore. When I'm with Peter, I don't have to be..."

"You," she says, and she sounds like a disappointed parent. "You don't have to be you."

I squeeze my eyes shut. "I was going to say that I don't have to be miserable."

"But the captain—"

"He *doesn't want me*," I practically scream. "Why can't I make you understand that?"

"Did he tell you that?" she asks.

I dig my fingernails into the bedsheets. "You heard him up there. And when I first found out that he was my Mate, I begged him to tell me what he wanted. If that's what he wanted—to remove our Mark. You know what he said?"

Charlie shakes her head.

"He said, 'I'm sorry, Darling,'" I almost choke, laughing at the irony that this is the first and only apology I'm ever going to get from Captain Nolan Astor. "And then I was idiotic enough not to take the hint."

When Charlie doesn't answer, I wave my hands. "Please, go on. Spin that in a way that means something other than the truth. That he doesn't want anything tying him to me. I'm begging you, find a way to make that somehow mean that he wants me."

Charlie perches on the side of my bed. "I don't think he knows what he wants."

"I'm too tired to wait on him to figure it out," I say. "I just want to go home."

"And home is Peter?"

"Peter wants me."

Charlie doesn't try to argue with me anymore.

CHAPTER 44

JOHN

I haven't been able to find Tink since the night I almost kissed her and panicked like an idiot. She's been avoiding the cave where we usually meet, though I've been leaving fresh tiles there every day. I wish we'd come up with a symbol for an apology, but as we haven't, the best I can do is leave her empty tiles and hope she understands that my not knowing what to say isn't a lack of desire to speak with her.

Still, the weight of what Simon saw that day bears down on me. Bothering me is the combination of three facts: Wendy could see the visions too, she and Simon are both gone, and most concerning of all —Peter seems desperate to keep the rest of us from seeing those same visions.

Which gives credence to Tink's story about Peter selling Wendy to the captain.

Peter's been gone on a mission for the Sister for the past three days. I have little knowledge regarding how long it takes for faerie dust to work itself out of the blood, but given the pounding headache I woke with today, I'm assuming it's out now. The problem is that if Peter's been gone for three days, it's likely he'll be back soon. Meaning I'll have to return to eating the onions under his watch.

Meaning I'm only guaranteed tonight to figure out what it was that Wendy and Simon saw.

I've been mulling it over, and the more I do, the more I'm convinced that Simon killed himself in the same place Thomas was murdered. That would explain why he was yelling for someone not to hurt someone else. I considered trekking there tonight, but I have limited time. And I need to find out what happened to Wendy. And why.

Which means I need to scout two places.

The only problem is that I don't know if I'll have time for both.

According to Peter and Tink's story, Wendy was taken from the beach. But there are several beaches on this island, and I don't know which one it was. I could search all night and not find the correct location—and that's assuming that story is true to begin with.

Then there's the storehouse, where Nettle died while I was unconscious. Everything seems to track back to that night. Whatever it was that Wendy witnessed. Whatever made Simon stop eating the onions. If my hunch that Peter's willingness to give Wendy away had something to do with Nettle's death, I have more of a chance of actually finding evidence there.

I've been debating all day which to choose.

In the end, I land on the storehouse. If I start with the beaches, there's a good chance I won't make it around to whichever one Wendy was taken from. At least with the storehouse, I know exactly where it is. If my hunch is wrong, I can always leave quickly and search the beaches.

THE PATH to the storehouse is as arduous as usual. If only my left hand weren't useless, then I could climb instead of going the long way around. By the time I reach the top of the cliffs, I'm antsy, already abundantly aware of how much time I've killed. Second-guessing my decision. I should have scoured the beaches.

Irritated with myself, I scan the area. If I'm right about the land having imprints of what happened on it, ones Wendy and Simon could see when they weren't being dosed, there should be imprints of Nettle's death lingering.

I'll give myself three minutes to find it. If I'm unsuccessful, I'll turn around and head toward the beaches.

As I near the empty storehouse, voices fall off the slope and through the leaves, piquing my interest. The closer I get, the more confident I am that the first voice is Peter's. Strange. He's supposed to be off on an errand. The other is a woman's that I don't recognize.

What's happening on the cliffside, I have no idea. The trees obscure my view, and I'm hesitant to get any closer, lest I be heard. Part of me—the part that has any sense of self-preservation, says I should turn around. But if Peter is talking to the Sister like I think he is, there's a chance I'll find out what's going on around here that I've been missing. Assuming I can get close enough to make out the words without either of them detecting me.

Remaining undetected is arduous in the dark. Twigs have a tendency to want to be stepped on, thorns walked into. But the matter is made worse with my smudged glasses, even with the moon shining in full force—strange that Peter's back already. He's usually off running errands for the Sister, especially the night of the full moon.

"This place is incredible, Peter," says the female. Now that I'm closer, her voice sounds like honey and brass. There's an edge to it, but the excited sort. Like she's bouncing about, buzzing with an energy nothing can quite help her shed. "I've never seen anything like it."

"You mean you've never seen trees and water?" says Peter, in a light and lilting voice.

"Oh, you know what I mean," the woman says. "It's a paradise. Well, the sullen sort. But it's beautiful. And it's ours."

My mind catches on that last word. Ours. Has Peter brought some poor, unsuspecting girl back to Neverland? A replacement for Wendy now that she's nowhere to be found? My stomach hardens.

"Ours. And the boys'," says Peter.

I wait for the woman's confused reaction, but Peter must have told her ahead of time about the Lost Boys, because she says, "I can't wait to meet them. Especially Simon and Thomas. You've told me so many stories. I'm eager to put faces to their names."

My stomach turns over at the sound of the dead boys' names. Peter clearly didn't inform her sufficiently.

Peter chuckles in a fond sort of way. An odd reaction given this woman just brought up that she'd love to meet two dead boys. "You might not be so eager once you get to know them," he says.

"You'd be surprised at how good I am with kids," says the woman.

"I thought you said you didn't have any siblings."

The girl pauses, but without seeing her face, I can't surmise why. "Growing up in the...circles that I did," she says, "well, there were other children who needed looking after. It takes time to adjust to the idea that you've been snatched out of your perfectly good life. Even for the kids who were plucked from the streets. You would think they would have liked being fed, but it came at a cost. They no longer had any agency about where they would go, who they'd see and serve. No way out."

This time, it's Peter who pauses. "I see what you're trying to do."

"Whatever do you mean?" says the woman, playing coy. I can almost see her batting her eyelashes in my mind's eye.

"You think the boys will have a difficult time adjusting to their new home."

New home? I frown. The Lost Boys have been in Neverland for... well, I can't even figure out how long. None of them seem to have any sense of time about them, and I figured it was just this place. But the way they talk about it, you would have thought the Lost Boys had been here for years.

"The possibility hasn't crossed your mind?" she asks.

Peter launches into an explanation that sounds rather rehearsed. "They didn't have any dreams back at the orphanage. Not ones that could ever hope to be fulfilled. Their dreams were to get through the night without an unwelcome visit from the warden. So no, I'm not too concerned that they'll have a dreadful time now that they're here. All they had to look forward to was being thrown out into the street, then hanging from a noose. That's where they were headed."

315

"Still. It's the idea that they can never leave…"

"Is this about the boys never being able to leave," Peter asks, "or you never being able to leave?"

The girl snorts. "Peter, don't be childish. You know I'd follow you to the ends of the earth. You're my home. But yes, if you must know, the part about being secluded from the rest of the world wasn't a feature I would have selected if it were up to me."

"Then why'd you bother coming?" The familiar apathy in Peter's voice is back.

"Because I love you. You know that." There's hurt in the girl's response. Something desperate that I haven't yet been able to detect underneath the general strength of her disposition. "Because I love you, and you love these boys."

"You're sure it has nothing to do with me getting you out from underneath the hand of your master?" Peter says, infusing his question with a carefree lilt. Like he thinks teasing her will negate his defensive response. "And now you're thinking maybe you should have run off when you got the chance?"

The girl must sense the truth behind his question, because she softens. "Peter. All I've wanted my entire life was to run. To see the world. And then you waltzed into my life, looking like the world was yours for the taking. And then I realized the world was there in front of me. You held it in your pockets. I just hoped perhaps you would share. No, if I had everything my way, we wouldn't be secluded on this island from the rest of the world. But it's not as if anyone else ever treated me like I was worth any more than the dirt underneath their feet."

"There's no use in thinking of them ever again. I don't want you thinking of anyone else, Tink."

TINK?

My mind sputters to a halt on her name. Strange, it should sound familiar, for how often it wriggles itself into my mind, how often I turn it over and examine it.

But on Peter's lips it sounds foreign. Tainted.

I hate myself for the venom that excretes into my stomach, the jealousy that climbs my throat. I should be angry on behalf of my sister, and of course I am.

But I'm upset for myself. Almost to the point of petulance.

I can't help but think of Tink's flirtations in the cave—more than that, her insistence that she couldn't speak. Anger rages within me when I consider how I thought she'd better understand Michael than most people. How I'd used my and his language to connect with her, invited her into my world and his.

And it had just been a game to her.

No, that isn't logical. I'm sure she's working an angle of some sort, probably for Peter. I'm not sure what she could possibly want from me. Perhaps she's simply tasked with throwing me off of Peter's trail.

Something sours in my gut. If Peter and Tink have been working together this entire time, what did they do to Wendy?

My sister has always been strange. Not in personality, but in her affinity for darkness, despite her sweet demeanor. Something about that has always gnawed at me. The Sister had wanted her, back when she made the bargain with my parents. But she must have had her reasons, and I can't help but believe it has something to do with Wendy's infatuation with the shadows.

What have they done with her?

No. I shake my head, reminding myself that my feelings are lying to me, distracting me so that I miss important details, wander off on side roads and forgo the logical path.

There's something strange about what I heard. The way Tink seems so confident that they've only just gotten to Neverland.

Think, John.

I tamp down the jealousy threatening to rip me away from logic, and pad closer to the tree line, careful not to make a sound. I've almost made it near enough to peek through the brush when another voice stops me.

While Tink's voice—I'm still rattled by the beauty of it, despite myself—is full of warmth, this female voice is different. Cold. Sinister. Proud.

"Look at what my Shadow Keeper has brought me," the newcomer says. "Quite the catch, isn't she? I can see why you wanted to keep her."

A chill rattles my bones. The voice is too cemented in time not to belong to an immortal. Too bored. Too full of ease and cruelty. Even knowing what I know now about Tink and Peter's relationship, that she's been lying to me, playing me for the fool that I am, the urge grasps me to run after her, throw myself between her and the owner of this voice.

But I can't.

Not when I still need to find out what happened to Wendy.

"Peter?" Tink sounds shaken, her voice warbling for the first time. There's a snapping of a twig. At first I think I've shifted and given away my position, but then I realize it's Tink backing away.

"Don't fret, dear," says Peter. "The Sister is who made this little world for us. She's the one who gave me the coin to pay off your master's fee."

"Thank you," says Tink, though even her gratitude is infused with wariness.

"You're more welcome than you know, child," says the Sister, and I find myself analyzing her voice, her every word, trying to figure out which of the three from the story she is. Assuming the story isn't fiction, meant to lead mortals astray with our own assumptions.

"I was enslaved to that circus master for years," says Tink. "With all due respect, I think I do know."

Though I can't see the Sister, I feel her smile curl the air. "Very well. Then you'll understand that I require payment."

There's a hesitation there. It's killing me not to look out past the trees. "We have nothing," says Tink.

I wonder if she's looking at Peter for confirmation. When he says nothing, her voice goes soft. "Peter? Tell her we have nothing."

Peter clears his throat. "Surely there's another currency you'll take than the price we previously discussed."

"You know it is not I who set the price. Trust me, if it were up to me, I would choose something less crude. Something I myself could enjoy. But one does not simply create an entire realm with the snap of a finger. Not unless one is the Creator, which I am not. I already informed you that my power is limited. That I must—utilize other devices."

"Peter." His name on Tink's voice, the subtle desperation with which she says it, wrenches a blade in my gut. "What is she talking about?"

"Oh, did he not tell you, young one?" asks the Sister, tsking. "A realm like this one cannot be held together with Fabric and thread alone. Sure, my Sisters and I can manipulate worlds that already exist, but creating one—well, it can't be done. Not really. Not in a way that is sustainable. Without a tether to the other realms, this world will unravel."

My heart pounds against my chest thinking of Michael being inside a world that might unravel at any moment. It seems even Tink stops breathing for a moment. "You know, then."

I'm not sure if she's talking to Peter or the Sister.

Know what?

The Sister speaks next. "Did you think you could keep it hidden?"

"It's hardly clear to me," says Tink. "I'm unsure why you thought I'd think it was obvious to anyone else. Perhaps if you explained my condition—"

Peter interrupts her. "Tink." I can see him shaking his head in my mind's eye.

"It's alright, Peter," says the Sister. "Don't you think your pet should understand? Don't you think it will be easier for her if she knows it was necessary?"

"If I know what is necessary?" says Tink. "You need a tether. I assume that's me. What are you going to do? Spill my blood on an altar? Burn me and bury my ashes in the black sand? What is she going to do to me, Peter?"

There's such accusation in her voice, I can almost see it blazing in her eyes. I have to do something. I'm not sure what they're going to do to her, but I can't let it happen.

"Nothing quite so cruel as that," says the Sister. Something clicks. It sounds like long nails clacking together.

Peter's voice is placating. "Tink—"

"Funny," Tink scoffs. "You didn't mention how pivotal I was in this process. When you said you needed me, I thought you were being romantic. My mistake."

A moment passes, then sounds of a struggle. I can't help but inch closer, trying to get a look through the trees. My heart shouldn't go out to protect her. Not when in some way she's been colluding with Peter this entire time. Not when she probably made up the story about Captain Astor taking Wendy to throw me off the truth—whatever that may be.

Was Tink's attack on Wendy part of a ruse too? One to give Wendy a reason to be patched up by Peter? To grow to trust him? But why would Tink push Wendy toward her lover? And why can't I help but want to save her from whatever horror is about to befall her?

"Let go of me!" she screams, and it's like her voice is clawing against my chest.

"Tink. Tink, just calm down. I promise it'll be over soon."

I hear her spit on him. "Don't ever promise me anything again."

The Sister laughs. "I wouldn't waste my breath trying to repair your relationship, Peter. But don't fret. You don't have to lose her. I've crafted this island with a special place you can keep her if she gets to be too much of a problem."

"Please, you have to understand," Peter begs Tink, ignoring the Sister's council. "I had to save them. The boys…"

"Were your initial motivation, yes," says the Sister. "Despite my warnings that they are not the best place to place your affections. But Tink, may I tell you the truth? Between us girls?"

The Sister must lean in to whisper it in Tink's ear, because I don't hear what she says next.

After several moments, Tink's ragged breaths devolve into sobs. "No, please. Please, Peter. You can't. How could you?"

My heart breaks. I scramble through my pockets, trying to find anything to attack Peter with. But I'm human, and he's fae, and he has a Fate behind him. There's nothing I can do to fight against him. No strength I can muster. And just like with Wendy, there's no amount of knowledge in the world that I can use in place of strength to protect her.

Yet again, I've failed someone I care for by not being strong enough.

But maybe I can distract them. Just long enough for Tink to get away.

It's stupid and foolish and rather short-sighted, but I'm about to lunge from the brush, readying my lungs to yell.

I don't get the chance. Because Tink screams, and it rattles me to my very core. It's the scream of nightmares. The scream of shadows. The kind that haunts you in the middle of the night when you've locked yourself in your room, sure that no one can get to you.

Tink screams, and then the sound is cut off. There's nothing but silence left behind.

I make myself look, dread convincing me that she's dead, but when I peer around the corner, sure Peter and the Sister will see me, there's nothing there.

Well, that's not entirely true. There's nothing of substance there.

Where I thought Tink, Peter, and the Sister were gathered congregate three shadows, and not like the one Peter takes in his shadow form. Wraiths, I realize. Shadows that have taken on the pain of their environment, soaked it up and come alive. Telling a story of pain that lanced the past with such precision, it can still be seen, heard in the present.

That's what Wendy and Simon had been seeing.

Wraiths.

When Wendy had visited the storehouse to try to steal faerie dust to get us out of Neverland that first time, she'd almost collapsed after hearing the shadows screaming.

After hearing a woman screaming.

She'd been hearing Tink.

The wraith in the shape of Tink is on the ground, clutching her own throat, convulsing soundlessly.

"They took your voice," I say, my own croaking. "To bind Neverland." My mind whirls, searching for an explanation for how this could possibly work, but my parents' library never contained as much information as I would have liked on magic. It was mostly science, and what wasn't science was mostly human speculation. We didn't have many texts written by the fae.

I don't understand the process behind it, why Tink's voice is special to them. All I know is that they took it. And that makes me want to scream.

Her wraith weeps silently, knees in the dirt. When Peter kneels to stroke her face, to comfort her, she swats him away. I don't have to see the missing color in her eyes to know the blaze in them, the accusation in the stare she offers her lover.

"He lured her here and took her voice," I whisper again, startled by my own realization.

"Tink, it'll be okay, I promise," Peter says. "I'll make it better. You have to understand. I had to do it. For the boys."

I want to rush to her, to comfort her. But of course I can't. Because although this Tink is very much real, she's simply a figment of the past. A memory. Still existing somewhere underneath the calluses of the woman I've come to know and care for.

When the Sister's shadow turns to look at me, a shiver races down my spine. My feet urge me to flee, but I remind myself my fear is lying to me. It's not actually her. Just a memory. Just a shadow.

A shadow trying to tell me something.

Tink had been in so much pain up on the cliffs when the Sister took her voice, it had made an imprint by the storehouse. Hadn't Peter come to save Wendy from a nightstalker that evening? According to Wendy's account, she'd frozen up, the shadows enveloping her.

She'd heard a woman's scream—Tink's scream, reaching out to her from the past.

"Do the other wraiths know?" I ask, trembling as I approach the gathering of shadows. "Do you know what happened to Wendy? What happened to my sister?"

The wraith in the shape of Tink peers up at me. She shakes her head, somewhat sadly, and the hope billows out of me.

But then the shadows turn into wisps, then reshape, drifting unnaturally. The shadow version of Tink stands up, though it looks less like her pushing herself up with her legs and more like falling backward.

Like they're rewinding time.

Tink's talking again, and the Sister leans in to whisper in her ear. I'm still not close enough to hear, and by the time I draw near, the Sister has already backed away. Tink and the Sister look at me again. I'd assume they were blinking if I could see any semblance of eyes.

This time when the Sister leans in to whisper in Tink's ear, I'm prepared.

At least, I'm prepared to listen. What I'm not prepared for is the revelation that changes everything.

As the Sister speaks, telling Tink of what's to come, my legs begin to quake. Tink is breathing hard, but it's nothing compared to my body's reaction.

Some get physically ill when they hear dreadful news.

I wish I had that luxury.

My body won't allow me to let it out. The truth just stays inside me, pressing outward against the inside of my skull, the flesh of my stomach, making me feel as if my skin is going to burst.

When the memory is done recounting itself, it must not think I heard because of my blank expression, my lack of reaction.

So when the Sister leans in again, I have to listen to every horrid detail again. It's for the best, I have to remind myself. It's for the best. That way I can memorize it. Recount it all perfectly to Wendy when I finally find her.

If she'll believe me. That's the worst part. I don't think she will. I'm not sure even I believe what I'm hearing.

Until something shifts behind me, tethering me to reality. If you can even call Neverland that.

Whatever is there, I can't see it. Likely a night creature. Hopefully not a nightstalker, but it reminds me that my mission is not over for the night.

If I'm going to discover the rest of the truth, I need to discover what happened to Wendy on the beach. Given the placement of the moon in the sky, I have less than two hours.

CHAPTER 45

WENDY

*A*s the town of Endor grows ever closer, I make the mistake of wandering one night. My destination is the deck—all I want is some fresh air, to feel the sting of salt against my face—but hushed voices stop me from rounding the corner in the hall.

"Is there a reason you're questioning my decisions?" says the first, unmistakably Astor.

"Oh, I don't know. Possibly because your decisions lately have been idiotic," says Maddox.

When Astor says nothing, Maddox sighs, his voice softening. "Listen. I'll be right behind you, backing whatever decision you make. You know that. I just wish you would give yourself some time to consider what you're throwing away."

"Would you question me if I found a way to cast away shackles?"

"If those shackles were the only thing securing you to the best thing that's happened to you in over a decade?" asks Maddox. "Yeah. Yeah, I would."

My heart patters against my chest, appreciation for the ship's first mate welling in my heart. He might be Astor's friend first, but that only makes it more meaningful that he considers me so highly. I'm unsure what I did to deserve it.

"Claiming Wendy is the best thing to happen to me in over a decade is a bit of a stretch, don't you think?" says Astor. "For one, it ignores that she was the worst thing to ever happen to me prior to that."

"She was a child, Nolan. And unconscious, if I understand correctly. You know as well as I do that Wendy had no more to do with Iaso's death than Iaso did. They were both victims. Just in different ways. So what is this really about?"

At this, Astor seems to snap, his tone chilled. "I don't want Wendy. Why would I want to be Mated to someone I don't want?"

"If you don't want her," challenges Maddox, "why does it matter if you're Mated to her or not? Why go through the trouble of removing your Mark if it has no effect on you?"

"Is it so difficult to believe that I wish to set Darling free from her infatuation with me? It's unnatural for a woman to feel such things toward the man who murdered her parents."

For a moment, my heart lifts, but it's a stupid moment. I let myself hope that Astor's hesitation lies in believing my feelings for him aren't real, but then Maddox scoffs. "Nice. Did you come up with that excuse before or after she confessed her love for you?"

Astor lets out an aggrieved breath. "You don't believe me?"

"Nolan. You don't believe Wendy's parents were worthy of love. In fact, I consider it proof that Wendy's presence has softened you. Otherwise, I think you'd derive some sick pleasure from making her love you."

"I didn't make her do anything."

Maddox ignores him, plowing onward. "And I don't believe you when you claim not to want Wendy, either."

"Well, if you're looking for proof of my lack of feelings, I'm afraid I have nothing to show you."

"She was right, you know," Maddox insists. "You really do look to her in a crowd. And you touch her more than is actually functionally necessary. Besides, you talk about her constantly."

"Darling has made herself vital to my mission. Of course she comes up in conversation."

"Yes, well, I guess I'm too dense to grasp how it's vital to our mission that Charlie rid the wardrobe in her room of any trace of velvet. Or how reminding us how Darling used to climb the outer facade of her parents' clock tower at the age of twelve has anything to do with the mission. Yet it somehow comes up in conversation unprovoked anyway."

Even though I can't see him around the corner, I feel the air around Astor stiffen. "I never claimed not to enjoy Darling's company."

I fight back a groan, knowing how my stupid heart is going to twist this statement into a foothold for which to support my foolish hope.

"Hah!" Maddox says. I peek around the corner just in time to witness him jamming Astor in the shoulder with his finger.

Astor shrugs him off. "That doesn't mean I want her."

"Oh yeah? What was Wendy referring to when she mentioned 'that night in the crow's nest'?"

"A mistake that thankfully did not get the chance to occur."

My heart aches at the surety in the captain's voice.

"A mistake, huh?"

"Yes, Maddox. What do you want to hear?" Astor flicks his hands, opening his palms to the ceiling in exasperation. "Would you like me to admit that I'm attracted to the girl? You've seen her yourself. You could have figured that out on your own. And yes, I'll admit that I enjoy her company, our conversations. When she actually speaks her mind instead of repeating whatever it is she thinks you want to hear, that is. But overstepping boundaries with her—it would have been a mistake. You overheard her on deck. She's gotten it into her head that our relationship is more than it is. She's...." Astor sighs, rubbing his forehead with his fingers. "Kind. She's kind and humorous and clever —I expect even more so in that head of hers than she reveals. But she's so very lost, Maddox. You wouldn't need a storm to toss her about. It's not as though I blame her for that. Her parents keeping her cooped up, Peter whispering to her from the shadows all those years, her entire upbringing hanging on one value: that she be desirable...they did her a great disservice. But she's sensed my attraction—granted, it's my fault entirely that I let it show—and my desire for her conversation, and she's warped it in her mind into something it's not. Into her salvation. And I'm certainly not that."

Maddox goes quiet for a moment. "Have you ever considered that you could be happy with her? That perhaps good conversation and a bit of attraction might be enough?"

"Have you? When it comes to Charlie?"

Maddox suddenly finds a spot on his shoe quite interesting, but Astor returns to Maddox's original question. "There might have been a time when I would have considered what we share to be more than enough. But if I could have Iaso back...well, it's not Darling I'd choose." There's a bit of shame in the dip of his voice. "She would choose me over Peter. I believed her today, when she said as much. Darling deserves better than to be first by means of elimination. She deserves better than what I have to offer. Of that, I'm certain."

Maddox frowns. "So you'll let her go back to Peter? After everything he's done to her?"

Astor doesn't answer that.

OVER THE NEXT FEW WEEKS, the pang of Astor's rejection deepens into a steady ache. Like a wasp sting that's become infected. The pain is no longer as sharp, but it infiltrates layers of skin, threatening to corrode everything around it.

I can't decide what's worse: that Astor doesn't want me, or *why* he doesn't want me.

In a way, it was easier when I believed it was due entirely to his devotion to Iaso. Convinced as I am that this remains the primary reason, it's not what I hear repeated in my mind as I lie awake in the night.

Because it's less that he still loves her. What I heard is that I don't measure up. That there was the potential for Astor to love me, but I'm simply not worthy of it.

His criticisms of me are valid. I think that's what makes them so agonizing. There wasn't a single claim he asserted to Maddox that night that hadn't been true.

I am easily tossed, more easily swayed. In a world of captains, I am a rudder. Surrounded by those infused with the spirit of the wind, I am a sail, made for catching the wind, just not keeping it, the only sign that the wind and I ever brushed hands the fact that I'm no longer where I started. That I've been pushed along, stranded somewhere I can only hope is close to the shore. Trusting that the wind cared enough to deposit me within drifting distance of a safe harbor.

I was molded to be desirable. Told I'd never find my Mate, the only person guaranteed to want me, then forced to bend to the whims of greedy hands who always found me wanting.

Wanting. Never wanted.

The more I consider it, the more I recognize why Astor cannot love me.

He asked me once if someone wanted me to be Wendy Darling, could I be her?

But I don't know who Wendy Darling is. All I know is who she is supposed to be to everyone around her.

I can't bring myself to hate Astor for stating the truth. He hadn't known I'd been listening, after all.

But I think I've been tricking myself into believing that somehow, Astor has been barreling through the facade of murky mirrors I've placed around myself. That with his harsh exterior, his constant insistence that I tell him what I want, that I speak my mind, he was picking through the not-Wendys. I suppose we both assumed that one day, he was going to find, underneath it all, me.

It hits me that he tried. Astor pulled out all the stops. Took a battering ram to the facade made of bricks I'd let others place.

But when the walls came down, there'd been nothing inside.

I think, if Captain Nolan Astor couldn't manage to find the true Wendy Darling underneath the rubble, that perhaps she was never there. Or if she was, she died a long time ago. Perhaps with Iaso Astor.

It's probably for the best that Astor discovered the truth before things progressed further between us. I think he's right. That if he'd kissed me that night in the crow's nest, I might not recover. I'd convinced myself that I liked the way Astor challenged me. That I need to be prodded to grow.

I thought Astor was the furnace to my iron, that with his intensity he'd fashion me into steel.

But I was a fool to ever believe I was iron in the first place. Must have been disappointing for him too, to believe he'd placed iron into the furnace, only to return to a melted puddle and realize that I was only ever made of tin.

Peter hadn't seemed to mind that I was made of tin. Perhaps he liked that my substance made me malleable. That's how Astor would see it.

Astor would find a way to be disgusted at Peter for seeing me for what I am, and liking what he sees. But I have grown weary of trying to fortify what was always intended to bend. I am Peter's. I have been since Astor traded me away.

Why would I bother to fight what's already been decided? That's how I think most of the time. On days when I'm stronger, when the sunshine on the deck feels comforting rather than condemning, my thoughts turn outward. Toward my brothers.

They'll never truly be safe in Neverland. Not as long as Peter is without his ability to feel pain. Not as long as he has no true reason to fight against the Sister's wishes. As much as I want to believe that Peter would never hurt them, that hope seems akin to a child hoping a street dog won't bite them as they poke it in the eye.

I can't see a way forward for myself, but I can see one for my brothers.

I only have so much strength inside for myself. So much fight. But for John and Michael, I can push a few steps further.

MAYBE THAT'S WHY, the night Maddox tells me we've almost reached the coast of Endor and that Astor and I will infiltrate the cave the following morning, I sneak out of my rooms, and lower a rowboat into the water.

CHAPTER 46

WENDY

*T*he town of Endor is quieter than I anticipated, though I'm not sure what I was expecting from a town situated near a cave rumored to be a place where the dead can reach this world. Where their whispers can reach out and speak to the rest of us.

The village is simple. Thatch roofs on cottages only large enough to house small families, though it's the type of place I expect most families have far more children than their walls should allow. Perhaps my perception is only the way it is because of my upbringing—me, John, and Michael with a manor to ourselves. Herb gardens sprout from wooden beds tucked into the windowsills. Altogether, it's a simple, quaint place. Relatively peaceful.

Except for the building looming from the top of the hill. A massive edifice built of stone. Unlike the quaint cottages, the building is boxy. Sharp lines and edges. Utilitarian.

It reminds me of the hospital back in Jolpa.

I don't know why that gives me the shivers. Perhaps because during the Plague, hospitals were where people went to die. There's something wrong with the building—my intuition tells me as much—but it doesn't matter. I need to get in and out of this cave before Charlie wakes up and realizes that I'm gone.

I'll have to climb to get to the cave. My hands are already finding purchase on the cliffside when a shadow curls around them.

I whirl around, fists raised, thinking it's Peter come for me in his shadow form. Instead, what I find is a boy obscured by shadows. No, a boy who is the shadows. He's shorter than me, and though I can't make out any of his facial features, there's something familiar about him. He beckons me, his newsboy cap bobbing on his head as he shuffles away and toward the building at the top of the hill.

I hesitate. I really should be getting to the cave. Finding the Seer and breaking Peter's curse before Astor comes after me and forces me to do the opposite.

When I don't move, the boy turns back around and beckons again.

As nonsensical as it is, my heart goes out to him. He's just a shadow. Just a memory. But he's a wraith, meaning he was formed out of someone's pain—a child's pain. This boy could be grown now for all I know. He could be centuries dead, and whatever horrible thing happened to him would still live on in this wraith.

Perhaps that's why I pity him. Because while the boy is gone, the pain is still here, and the wraith is trapped within it. This version of the boy will never be able to escape whatever tragedy befell him.

"After," I say, nodding my chin up toward the cave. "I'll follow you after I finish what I came here to do. Then you can tell me your story."

The shadow boy shakes his head. When he speaks, his voice is muffled, like it's underwater. It still causes me to jolt, my back scraping the cliffside wall. "You must come now. They brought a new boy. He doesn't know what they'll do to him. You have to get him out. You can talk to his mother."

I wrinkle my brow, confused, though I don't know why. I want to tell the boy that it's too late, that whatever he's hoping to prevent already happened ages ago. But as I open my mouth to protest, he grabs at my sleeves.

It's not as though he has any weight with which to pull me, but the gesture is desperate, and so is the "please" that escapes his lips.

It kills me to tell him no, but I can't help the boy. I can't reach into the past and rescue him from whatever hurt is about to befall him.

"Please, missus," says the boy, and though I can't see tears, the shadows go blurry at his cheeks, highlighted by the moonlight.

"I can't," I say, tugging my hand back. "It's not real." Or, it is, but not anymore. This is a memory, and whatever happened to the boy happened to him a long time ago. It's not real. Not anymore.

The boy is distraught now, and he snaps. "It is real. He is real. They brought him to the orphanage this morning. And his name is Nolan, and he doesn't know... He thinks they're going to fix him, but they're just going to make him worse. Please, his mother is still here. You can reason with her. She won't believe me, but she'll believe you."

My heart stops in my chest. "You said the boy's name is Nolan? And that building is an orphanage?"

The shadow boy nods his head eagerly, like he's relieved that I finally understand. Reinvigorated, he tugs at my sleeve. "Come on, let's go."

My legs follow, my mind in a whir as the shadow boy gently tugs me up the cliffs. Weight-wise, I could break out of his grip with ease. But I don't. Rather, I can't. My feet seem to follow whether I want them to or not.

"What's your name?" I finally ask the boy on the way.

"Peter," he says without looking at me. My heart might have tumbled to the ground if part of me hadn't already known the answer to my question. My belly writhes. I scan his back, but find no wings. That makes sense. He wouldn't have had them before the Sister.

"Peter," I whisper, watching the boy before me, wishing I could make out his features.

He leads me into the orphanage by the front door. At first, I'm fearful the shadow boy will have me arrested by accident by whatever guards work at the orphanage now, but it quickly becomes clear that the place is abandoned. Moss has crept in through broken windows and played itself across the interior stone walls, which are otherwise completely bare. Lifeless.

Prison-like.

When he leads me down the hallway, my vision begins to black in and out. But I soon realize that's not what's happening at all.

I'm seeing shadows. Everywhere.

They're all shaped like little boys, walking up and down the dark hallways, their heads hanging like they want for nothing more in the world than not to be noticed.

I think I might be sick.

Voices echo in the hall—adult ones, and young Peter takes me in through a door to the right. Inside are three shadows, one of which sits behind a desk, looking formidable, the other two opposite the desk in chairs. One is in the shape of a woman. She's trembling, though she keeps her hands in her lap and her back straight. Beside her is a boy. He's not cowering like the boys in the hall. Instead, he sits back in his chair, his legs splayed. Like he, not the warden, owns this place.

"How long will it take you to…help him?" the woman asks, her voice trembling as much as her folded hands.

"You must understand this is a process," says the warden. "This isn't an institute for petty magic. If you want that, I suggest you contact the Seer down the street. I'm sure she could provide you with a few baubles to hang around the child's neck to make him behave."

"Of course not," says the woman. "It's just that I'll miss my boy, and I'd like to have a date to look forward to."

Something tells me the shadow of the warden is grinning. "Trust me, Ms. Astor. When you get your boy back, once we've fixed him, you'll realize there was nothing to miss about the boy he was before."

I watch young Nolan, my heart cracking for him, but if he's bothered by the warden, all he does to show it is run a coin up and down his pant leg.

"Please, you have to talk to his mother," says Peter, tugging on my coat. I find myself wondering where the real Peter was this day. If he hid somewhere and listened for the new recruits whenever they brought one in. If he really did go out to the city to beg an adult to save the new boy. I wonder how much of this is true, and how much the shadows have altered the story, not unlike a memory, warping its shape over time to suit the current needs of the holder.

I watch, numb, as the mother hands over a pouch full of coin.

Astor said she was a widow. Without his father around to support them, I can't imagine a pile of coin that large wouldn't be felt at the supper table. Not in a small fishing village like this one.

When Mrs. Astor goes to leave, I can't help myself. I grab her by the shoulders. "This is a trap. The work the warden's doing here—it's not for your child's benefit," I say.

Astor's mother shifts slowly, peering at me over her shoulder. Her body has a bent quality about it. I can't tell if that's the nature of the wraith or a reflection of the truth. "I cannot keep him," she says. "As much as I love him. The warden helped me see—he's a danger to my other children." She says it wistfully. As if she's spent every night since the warden visited her home trying to convince herself otherwise. Trying to talk herself out of it. I watch her lower her hand to her belly, a belly I just now realized is swollen underneath the shadows, and realize Nolan's father can't have been gone long. "Take care of my boy, won't you?" she says before disappearing.

Numbly, I turn back to the scene unfolding before me. The warden taps on his desk, he and young Astor sizing each other up. Judging by Nolan's size, he can't be older than eight.

"You like power. That's why you hurt your siblings."

Young Nolan just shrugs, otherwise unresponsive. Still, I can't help but notice how he rolls the coin up and down his pant leg faster. In my mind, I can feel its curve in the grooves between my fingers as if they're my own.

"You're not going to speak to me, then?" asks the warden. "You're not going to defend yourself?"

"I don't do it because I like it," says young Nolan. There's no defensiveness in his tone. Just a bold obstinance.

"Hmmm," says the warden, pushing himself from his desk. "You know what I think? I think you like the feeling of power. I think that's why you hurt other children."

As he approaches Nolan, the child doesn't react, but then the warden comes up to Nolan's chair from behind and slips both hands onto the boy's shoulders, rubbing them in almost tender circles.

I wait for the Nolan I know to rip his head off for touching him. But, of course, this isn't the Nolan I know. This Nolan is a child.

He freezes underneath the warden's touch, just for a moment, but it's enough for the warden to identify just how afraid the child underneath his hands is.

Slowly, as if he's won, the warden pulls away and paces over to the fire, clasping his hands behind his back. "Come here, boy," he says. "There's a lesson I would have you learn."

Nolan stands, but it's more as if to prepare for a fight than it is to approach the warden.

The warden looks over his shoulder, though I can't see his expression through the shadows. Even the fire by the hearth is just a lick of black shadows.

"You're not afraid of fire, are you?" asks the warden.

Nolan's jaw stiffens, and he puffs his chest, striding over toward the warden with a sway to his feet that exudes all confidence, nothing of the terror that was emanating from him just moments ago.

When he reaches the fire, the warden grabs at a poker and begins irritating the coals until the flames swell, hot and aggravated. "Here's something you need to learn early. And that is, no matter how big you are, there's always someone bigger than you. Always someone with more power. No matter how firm your will is, there's always someone who can break it. Always someone who can break you," says the warden.

"If you're trying to frighten me into thinking that bigger person's you, you're doing a poor job of it," says Nolan.

The warden doesn't show any signs of anger that I can see. In fact, his tone is almost amused as he says, "You will be a delight to break, Nolan Astor. By the time we get you back to your mother, she won't recognize you."

"You don't plan to give me back to my mother," says Nolan, not a hint of fear in his voice. He has his hands clasped behind his back, mirroring the warden—probably because he sees him as powerful and wants to measure up.

"Now, where did you get that idea?"

"The other boys here," says Nolan. "They're much too old not to have been sent back yet."

"Some refuse to bend."

Nolan glances out the warden's office window and into the hall. Even now, I know what he's thinking. That every single boy walking the halls appears to have already been bent. I watch as little Nolan straightens his shoulders, unclasps his hands, and fists his fingers at his side.

The warden turns around and looks at Nolan, whose posture practically screams defiance, and even though I can't see the warden's smile writhe, I can see the way the shadow version of Nolan flinches underneath his stare.

The warden is still for a moment, then crosses the room and, with a creak, opens the door. He peeks his head out into the hall. "You, boy. Come here," he says.

A moment later, Peter's wraith enters. He's bouncing back and forth between his heels and his toes.

"Shut the door behind you. And the blinds while you're at it," says the warden.

Something slimy slinks down my spine. Peter does as he's told, then interlocks his fingers behind his back, still fidgeting, waiting.

"Well, what are you waiting for?" snaps the warden. He's picked a pipe off his desk and set to lighting it. "Don't make me order you around when you know what you're to do."

"Yes, Warden," says Peter. He brings his hands to his shirt. It's difficult to tell what he's doing because of the lack of detail in the shadows, but when he pulls his shirt open, I realize he's been unbuttoning it.

Peter's shirt falls to the floor in a crumpled heap. He glides across the room, then places his hands upon the edge of the warden's desk.

No, no, no.

"You there," the warden says, puffing smoke from his pipe as he nods toward Nolan. "There's a poker in the fire. Take it."

Even Nolan's wraith, wisps of ethereal darkness as it is, goes very,

very still. "Why?" His voice is more defensive than inquisitory. "What did he do?"

"That's irrelevant," says the warden. "Now do as I say."

"No."

"No?" There's amusement in the warden's voice. "Alright. I noticed your mother was with child. But I knew that before she came to see me. I'm rather fond of her midwife, you see. Am over at her place often. You know, I've always wondered how she tells the difference between the skullcap and the wormwort. You know, one is given to laboring women to aid in the birth pangs. Are you aware what the other does?"

Nolan doesn't answer.

"Thins the blood out. Would be disastrous if given to a laboring woman."

Nolan is breathing hard now, his chest heaving.

"Would be a shame—if the two herbs were ever mixed up," says the warden.

Young Astor doesn't beg for mercy. He doesn't even address the warden's threat. He just turns to the hearth, slowly, methodically, and takes the poker, shuffling a few of the logs in the fire with it until they crackle.

When he approaches Peter, the poker in hand, the only evidence of his trepidation is the way the tip of the poker rattles. Peter doesn't look at him. He just taps his fingers against the desk in the cadence of triplets. Like he's playing himself a song in his head to distract himself.

"Now," says the warden. "Do you know how to write?"

Nolan holds his chin up high. "Never saw much use for it." It sounds like the sort of thing a father might say, something Nolan picked up from him before he passed away.

The warden tsks. "That won't do. Our establishment prides itself in not only rehabilitation, but education. Now, it's time for your first writing lesson."

. . .

By the time the lesson is over, my ears are wringing with young Peter's whimpers. To his credit, he hadn't screamed. Not even as the poker seared his skin. Not even as the warden forced Astor to rewrite the first letter of the alphabet over and over, claiming each attempt wasn't good enough.

Only when Peter passed out, his little wraith of a body slumping headlong across the desk, had the warden declared their lesson over for the day.

Peter had revived soon enough. He hadn't said a word to either of them. Just picked up his shirt, buttoned it back on over what must have been still open burn wounds, and left.

As soon as the door shuts behind Peter, Nolan drops the poker, which rattles as it hits the floor.

"What did he do?" Nolan demands, his voice high and shrill—he's just a child after all. There's the slightest whimper in Nolan's voice. Like he's longing for Peter to have done something awful enough to warrant such torture.

"Nothing," says the warden, still smoking on his pipe.

"Then why..." Nolan's hands are shaking at his sides now. He fists them. It's clear he's trying to keep his composure, conceal how terrified he is, but his mask is fracturing. *"Why did you make me do that?"* he yells, throwing the desk chair out of his way.

"This punishment wasn't for him," says the warden, unfazed by Nolan's outburst. "You like to hurt other children, boy? Well, here you'll learn that the punishment is more effective when it fits the crime. Now bend."

When Nolan doesn't move, the warden sighs. "Bend, or I'll call little Peter back in here."

Trembling, little Nolan does.

When the warden takes the poker to Nolan's shoulder blade, he doesn't cry. When he tells Nolan to spin around to face him and places another upon Nolan's chest, the child doesn't flinch.

"You're mine now," the warden whispers to Nolan. "You belong to me. Do you understand that? No matter where you go, I'll always be here with you. You think your will cannot be broken. You think this"

—he lets his fingers trail Nolan's bare chest, then traces the curve of Nolan's arm—"is yours. You could not be more wrong."

The warden sends Nolan away, shirt still fisted in his tiny hand. I follow him out. Once in the hall, Nolan wipes his nose and buttons his shirt. I watch his fingers twitch at his sides, like he isn't sure what to do next. Like he isn't sure if there will be a next.

Then I watch him flee to the nearest alcove, fall on his knees, and weep.

I sit with him there, waiting with him as he cries, wishing I could reach out to him, touch him, comfort him. But for some reason, I can't seem to reach this particular wraith.

He's still shaking when another wraith approaches. Peter, I realize, by the way he's bouncing.

"You don't have to cry," says Peter.

Nolan's back goes rigid, and he shoots straight up. "I'm not crying," he says, wiping his cheeks with his hands, as if he can banish the evidence.

"Yes, you are," says Peter, though not unkindly. "But you don't have to worry about that. I'll teach you how not to."

"Why would you do that?" asks Nolan. "I just tortured you."

Peter flicks his hand to the side. "Oh, that? That was nothing. I've forgotten about it already."

"You can't just forget something like that," says Nolan.

"Sure you can. Just don't think about the bad things, and they can't hurt you. I can teach you, if you want. You'll need it if you're going to stick around."

Nolan clears his throat, like he's imitating what a grown man could do. He stands, wiping his hands on his pants. "Thanks, but if that's the worst of it, I can handle it."

"Did he mark you?" Peter asks. "Tell you that you belonged to him?"

Nolan flinches.

"Like I said, you're going to want my help," says Peter, holding out his hand.

Nolan takes it.

CHAPTER 47

JOHN

*T*here are echoes of my sister everywhere.

Wraiths are supposed to be made by acute events. Ones where the pain is so substantial, it's potent enough for the shadows to lick them up, drink the pain until it fills them with life.

But as I wind down the trail on the back end of the cliffside and toward the beaches, I hear Wendy everywhere.

It's as if she created wraiths wherever she went.

I had no idea my sister hurt so badly. To that extent.

Then again, the onions didn't seem to work on her, so maybe it's just that the shadows are more sensitive to my sister than they are to others.

When I reach the beach, I've no idea where to start, so I walk down by where the tide is coming in, the onyx sand glittering softly in the moonlight. It reminds me of glass, the way it glistens. Like it would cut my feet were I barefoot.

I've made it halfway down the southernmost beach when I hear voices.

One belongs to Wendy and makes my heart skip in my chest. It's foolishness, but for a moment, I let myself believe it's her. That she's back.

I approach carefully. After all, the other voice is Captain Astor's.

"You haven't slept with him, have you?" says the captain.

Something clanks against the ground. "Must you always be this crass?" Wendy asks.

"I'm afraid I must, given your love life—or lack thereof, as the case may be—is all I have to keep me entertained during my solitary confinement."

As I peek in, I hardly see anything. The moonlight skates across the cave floor, revealing the familiar shape of Wendy, hugging her knees to her chest as she so often does. On the cave floor across from her is a massive shadow in the shape of a male. The captain.

He doesn't move, other than to speak, which strikes me as odd.

Peter said the captain stole Wendy from the island, but they're sitting together, conversing, the captain hurling insults at my sister. Asking questions.

"Tell me—what about the winged boy revolts you so much?" he asks.

"It's not for lack of desire, I assure you," Wendy responds, sounding, for once, smug.

Heat stains the back of my neck. This conversation feels private, but as it's with the captain, it's not as if I can afford not to eavesdrop.

Wendy begins explaining why she and Peter haven't yet slept together. Why she's waiting until they marry. Again, the brother in me wants nothing more than to flee the scene, but knowing now what I discovered on the cliffside, what the Sister whispered to Tink... I need to know what really happened between Wendy and the captain. Why he waited to take her until after this conversation.

But then Wendy's story takes a turn. She tells of a scheme our mother conceived. A plan for blackmailing a nobleman into marrying my sister.

My heart stops in my chest. Fills with cement. No. No, no, no, no, no. My mind races ahead of Wendy's words, toward the only natural conclusion of this story. It pairs up with my memories outside of the smoking parlor that night, multiplying the memory as I realize it hadn't been a one-time occurrence.

The words deaden the beating piece of muscle in my chest. There's anger there, ready to brew, but simmering underneath the surface, not yet boiling.

It can't yet, though I want nothing more than to feel outraged for my sister.

It's your responsibility to protect her, son.

Wendy, your sister, she needs protecting.

My parents' words ring in my ears. Flashes of memories, fragments of them, plague my mind, now warped by the truth.

I want to believe it was just my mother, only she who knew. That my father knew nothing of it, but then I remember my father's billiard games. How he took me to the parlor across the manor. The less nice one. And always during Wendy's meetings with the suitors.

How he'd play with me until my mother came to signal to him at the door.

She always looked so hopeful, that beautiful smile strewn across her face.

They knew.

No, they didn't simply know. They planned. Plotted. Schemed. Blackmailed.

All in the name of saving my sister.

Instead, they'd thrown her to the monsters early.

The truth paints itself in sticky, tar-like streaks over the memories of those moments between my father and me. Those special activities that he told me were just for me. Just him and John time.

He was trying to keep me out of the way. Ensuring I never discovered what was happening to my sister on the other side of the manor.

My entire world shifts with one story. One memory. The words of one wraith to another.

My father, my idol, torn down.

And then the captain speaks. "You shouldn't have told me that."

Wendy's confused. Hurt. But then the captain explains. "I mean you shouldn't have told me that. Not if you ever wanted me to feel a twinge of guilt about spilling your sorry parents' blood."

And for a moment, the flicker of time, the ticking of the second hand on a pocket watch, I agree. I'm back in the ballroom, corpses of guests strewn about me, and there are blades to my parents' throats.

But it's not their own hands holding them.

It's mine.

Anger sluices over me as I'm the one who cuts into their flesh, spills their blood. I'm the one standing over them as their bodies crumple.

My father reaches for me, hand over his throat as he tries to hold the blood in. I don't reach for him back, though even now, I want to. Want nothing more than to erase the truth from my mind, place my father back up on his pedestal, forget what happened.

It's as if I'm a navigator who's just been told that North never existed.

I fragment. Every value I stand upon crumbles from underneath me.

"You have no right to be angry with them," says a voice. I snap my head up, toward the wraith of the captain, still as death on the floor. "You knew. You overheard what happened that night, and you never told a soul. Think of all the times you could have saved your sister from her fate had you not been such a coward."

No. It's just a wraith. Not even the captain. But his words ring true, nevertheless.

"I should have killed you that night, too. Your sister would be better off. You tell yourself your mission is to protect her, but so did your father. You're the same, just like you've always wanted. You thought you didn't measure up to him, but you do. You allow harm to befall the ones you love. And then you retreat into books and tell yourself you're doing it for their good. Finding a way to save them. But really, you're just as much of a coward as your father. He trained you well. Better than you ever realized."

I fumble for words, for a response. It's irrational to argue with a wraith at all, but I can't seem to find a valid counterargument.

"I'll find her," I say. "I'll protect her from now on."

The captain only laughs. "Protect her? How? You're not capable. Not because you don't have the knowledge, but because you don't have the courage. How many times could you have saved her, but you didn't? Do you even realize how many times she was assaulted in that parlor after you knew it was going on? How many encounters you could have prevented?"

"No," I say. "I didn't know it was happening routinely. I thought...I thought..."

Even though I can't see the face of the captain's wraith, the air tilts upward with his cruel smile. "I hope you rot like your father, John Darling. I hope you meet his same Fate."

THE SAND IS heavy underneath my feet, weighing me down as I trudge back toward the Den. Every step, it's as if lead has filled my legs. It's filling me up, almost to my lungs, ready to snatch the breath out of me, suture my airway so I can't steal any more of it.

My mind is flitting about, landing every which way. The whimpering Wendy made that night I overheard her in the parlor. The constant backtrack to every memory of my father and me.

I'd spent years poring over books in the library, trying to save Wendy from the monster in the window.

When all along, the monsters were in the house.

And I was one of them. Complicit.

All at once, the grief I never let near me becomes too strong, washing over me in waves, drowning me. And I know I'm not strong enough to bear it. Too much of a coward.

But then the grief rinses away, leaving nothing but a plan in place.

One last thing I can do to protect my sister. To protect Michael.

Better off, is what I remind myself.

And I know what I have to do.

My sister is surrounded by monsters who claim to love her. The best I can do for her is rid her life of one of them.

I only wish I could speak with Tink one last time.

In the end, the best I can do is leave her a series of tiles in the cave where we used to meet. Then I head to the reaping tree.

CHAPTER 48

WENDY

I never make it to the cave. Even if I had it left in me to betray Astor, by the time I leave the orphanage, my hands are trembling too badly to make the climb.

What the wraiths showed me back in the orphanage—it might have happened decades ago, but I know from experience that these sorts of things don't die in the past. Hadn't I seen the evidence of how it still affects Astor the night he'd asked me not to watch as he tortured the man in the alley? He'd been trembling after, and I'd made the foolish assumption that it was because he'd never tortured anyone before.

He'd informed me that I didn't know what I was talking about.

How many times had he been forced to torture Peter? The other boys at the orphanage?

As I make my way across the sleeping town of Endor and back to the murky waters, there's something else about the vision that bothers me.

You belong to me now, the warden had said.

I already knew from Nettle what the warden used to do to the boys at night. He'd abused Thomas to the point of sending him over the edge. When Peter and the Sister had rescued the Lost Boys from that filthy place, Thomas's mind had turned to plotting murder, not just of the warden, but of any family member complicit in sending the boys to the orphanage.

There's a part of me that can't bring myself to believe that the same fate had awaited Astor at night. It's a stupid thought, but I almost feel as if Astor walks with his chin too high, his shoulders too set, to be carrying that around with him.

Memories like that—they cling to dusty surfaces and hide behind the facial structure of strangers who happen to resemble an abuser. It's the kind of touch that sticks to your soul like tar and only makes your fingers unusable and sore the more you try to rip it off.

It breaks you.

And it's difficult to imagine that underneath all of Astor's confidence and poise...

It doesn't seem possible.

He doesn't like being controlled. Wasn't that what Charlie had said when she'd tried to explain why he detests being Mated to me?

Somehow, I find myself back at the *Iaso*. I have to wait an hour for my hands to stop trembling, but once they do, I scale the ladder and drop myself onto the ship's deck.

When I sneak back into my and Charlie's room, she's still fast asleep. Crawling into bed, I lie awake, unable to erase what occurred from my mind. Though I didn't really see it happen, the images have branded themselves into my soul. Nothing can scrub them away. I want to scream into my pillow, to tear something to shreds. I want to hack at a pig carcass, but I'd ruined the last one.

More than anything else, I fixate on the brand that remains across Astor's chest. The brand that marks him as the warden's. The words that passed from the warden's lips to his ears. *You're mine now. I'll always be with you.*

And then I see it, for the first time. In my mind's eye, I see Astor fall in love with Iaso. I see him have hope in the future through her. Hope to leave the warden behind.

And then I was born, and the Mark appeared on his hand.

You're mine now. I'll always be with you.

And I understand.

When Astor spent his and Iaso's entire life savings to rid himself of his Mark, it wasn't simply that he didn't want to fall in love with another woman. It's that, consciously or not, I had claimed him. I had Marked his skin and reminded him that never again could he truly be free of me. That he belonged to someone else.

He doesn't seem like he's afraid of anything.

Everyone's afraid of something. Astor...he doesn't like being controlled.

It hits me then, why I'd ventured out to the cave tonight. I'd told myself it was about freeing Peter from his curse. Told myself it was more important than Astor's wishes, because it would ensure I could keep John and Michael safe.

But deep down, I know it hadn't been about that at all.

I hadn't wanted to let Astor go. I'd wanted him to be mine, whether he wanted to be mine or not.

Guilt punctures my lungs as the realization washes over me. As in my mind, it's me branding him with a poker, my lips leaning into his ear, whispering that he'll never be rid of me.

ASTOR, Maddox, and Charlie are arguing when I find them on deck the next morning. I can hear their bickering from down the stairs into the lower level, but the wind is howling with enough force that I can't make out what they're saying.

Or maybe it's just the buzzing in my ears blocking it all out.

It's not until I draw close that their voices come into focus.

"Just so we're clear, I'm not at all on board with this decision," says Maddox, crossing his hefty arms across his chest.

"Then it's a good thing you're not the one in charge," says Astor, mirroring Maddox's posture.

Charlie throws her hands up in the air. "Why you insist on doing everything on your own, I'll never understand. If this is about W—" She clamps her mouth as soon as she sees me.

Slowly, Astor and Maddox both swivel toward me.

I can't help myself. When I see Astor's hardened face, I search, just for the span in between blinks, for the boy who was left at the orphanage in the hands of a monster.

"Yes, Darling?" he says, more patiently than I'm expecting.

Maddox grinds his teeth, tapping his foot against the deck.

"I was going to ask..." I glance in between the three pirates standing before me, sensing I'm interrupting something important. Heat flushes my cheeks, discomfort swarming in my belly at the realization that they've been discussing me. Even if it was nothing particularly negative about me, it feels as if I've poked my head in where I'm not wanted. Clearing my throat, I start again. "I was going to ask if it's alright if the two of us went to visit the Seer alone."

Maddox looks down. Rubs the back of his neck with his palm. Charlie stares at me, her wide, beautiful eyes full of pity.

When Astor doesn't answer, I feel the need to explain. Find myself hugging my waist with my arms as the wind swirls around the deck. "It's just that you and I won't be Mated after the Seer casts the spell. It just feels...I don't know. Private?"

Maddox grimaces, but he doesn't object. Neither does Charlie, who places a gentle hand on my shoulder and offers Astor a venomous look as she walks away.

"Yes, Darling," the captain says. "I think we can grant that."

THE CAVE REMINDS me of black opal, shiny in spots where the condensation has coated the rock in a glistening layer of moisture. Down below, waves crash against the cliffs, and I'm taken back to the night I tried to escape Neverland with John and Michael. The night I'd discovered the truth behind the Lost Boys' origins.

I'd thought I'd known everything then. I'd been wrong.

The climb to the cave had been demanding, but I'd refused Astor's assistance. The hostility in my heart toward him is gone; I just can't stand for him to help me. Not after what I tried to do to him last night.

Not after I tried to keep him.

We haven't spoken much since we left the ship. Just a few words here and there. All logistical.

It's killing me. He's killing me. His silky black hair, wet from the spray of the ocean, the glisten of sweat across his brow where his hair falls across his forehead in jagged points. His eyes, like the foliage just after it rains. Cool and glowing and eerie.

The first time I met Captain Nolan Astor, I remember thinking that touching him would draw blood.

Now I know who made him sharp.

When we enter the cave, our footsteps echo across the hard ground.

"You didn't tell me you were one of the children at the orphanage," I say quietly, my voice rebounding off the walls, so that my statement repeats itself until it sounds more like an accusation.

Astor's ears twitch. "How did you come across that information?"

I let the corner of my mouth drag upward, like I'm trying to be sly or playful, but I'm just so tired I'm not sure it has the same effect. "I didn't, but you just confirmed it for me."

Astor examines me. I'm not sure he believes me, but I'd rather him not question my activities last night.

"If you were enrolled at that orphanage... Nolan, Peter told me about what kind of man the warden was. How he treated the boys at the orphanage."

Astor stops, his boots halting against the stone. Before I can continue, he says, "If that's the case, you can understand why I omitted that part of the story."

A lump swells in my throat. I search Astor for the boy I saw last night, but then again, I'd only glimpsed a shadow of him. Besides, while that boy is somewhere within Astor, he's had years to thicken the armor surrounding him. "You could have told me," I say, immediately frustrated with how that sounds. "Not because I deserve to know that about you. Just because—well—I would have understood. To some degree, at least."

Astor shifts uncomfortably. With each moment that passes, I sense him slipping. It's in his face, the way his cheeks empty of color and his brow tenses. And it kills me. Maybe because apathy is as familiar to me as my own reflection—at least, the reflection of the Wendy Darling who left her family's manor. I'm not sure I've looked in a mirror since then. It's as familiar to me as Peter's expression when he's confronted.

And I hate seeing it on Astor. Astor, who's passionate. Astor who, instead of being ruled by a simmering rage, has learned to steer it.

Astor shakes his head slightly, his face softening. "I'm afraid it's not the same, Darling—what happened to either of us."

A lump swells in my throat, my heart hammering against my chest because I'm not sure where he's going with this. My throat goes dry as I scramble for a way to understand. "I know I was older. That I at least understood what was happening..."

Astor swallows, then blinks. "No, Darling. I mean that you've never done anything to deserve what happened to you."

Pain ripples through my ribs. "You were just a child."

Agony warps his beautiful face. The way he stares at me is like I'm a child and there's a concept I'm not yet capable of grasping. I still hate that he sees me that way. "Does the timing of my punishment make a difference? When evil was written into my story from the beginning?"

I frown, hardly able to believe what I'm hearing. "Surely not," I say. "What?"

I'd laugh, if it weren't such a painful topic. "You're the most obstinate man I've ever met. Surely you don't believe someone else wrote your story."

He actually lets out a quiet laugh at that.

It's hard to believe that our story is coming to a close. In some ways, it feels as if it's yet to begin. But even if Astor decided not to remove his Mating Mark, I'd still belong to Peter in twelve days. I have a calendar Charlie gifted me back in the cabin to prove it.

"Astor," I say as we descend into the cave.

"Darling."

"When this is over, we won't be bound. But I'd like for you, when all of this is said and done and you're sailing across the sea a free man... It would mean a lot to me if you remembered me fondly."

Astor stares at me for a moment, sea spray still wetting his dark eyelashes. "I can keep that promise," he says.

My heart aches, ripping from the inside out, but as I reach for his hand, a rumble rips through the cave.

And the cave ceiling falls in.

CHAPTER 49

❦

WENDY

The first thing I do when I come to is call for Astor.

"Nolan," I choke through heaving breaths, expelling dust and rubble from my airway. The weight of several rocks bears down on me, but Astor threw me out of the way of the falling rocks as soon as he felt the ground shake. My head is pounding. I must have hit it on the wall when the ceiling caved in.

"Nolan," I call out again, blinking furiously and trying to get my eyes to focus so I can assess my surroundings. Fear races through me, and for a moment I worry he might have been crushed, and I'll have to go through this life knowing he's not here with me in the world, but then his voice calls out from the other side of the rock formation.

"Darling, Darling, are you okay?"

Relieved, I tug at the hair at the crown of my head, and then, wiping the grime off my cheeks and placing my hands at my hips, catching my breath, I say, "I'm fine. Just a little dizzy, that's all."

There's a pause on the other side, and my heart skips when I realize it's Astor sighing in relief. "Well, that was exciting, now wasn't it? Just wait for me to clear the rubble and I'll come get you."

"You could go back to the ship and get the crew to help," I say.

No answer.

"Astor." I tap my foot against the rocks.

"I'm not leaving you."

My heart shoots into my throat, but I shoo it back into a more reasonable place. "Technically, I'm alone in here with that wall separating us. You could get me out faster if you had help."

Another pause. "Are you afraid?"

I bite my lip, checking my surroundings. "I don't particularly love the idea of being back here with a creepy dead Seer, but no, I wouldn't say I'm afraid. Just a little shaken up from the fall."

"Then wait there until I can dig you out."

I roll my eyes, listening as rocks scrape against each other as Astor removes them. I'm reaching for one on my side, intent on helping and about to ask what he thinks made the ceiling cave in, when he calls my name.

"Wendy Darling."

"Yes?" I ask.

"I didn't say anything," says a muffled Astor from the other side.

"Wendy Darling," I hear from behind.

My stomach twists, and I turn with it. The tunnel is dark, except for the glowing lichen that line its walls, casting a blueish hue across the space.

"Astor," I whisper. "I think the Seer knows I'm here."

The scraping of rock against rock grows faster. "Then you'd best help me move these rocks," he says.

"Hurry, Wendy," whispers the voice. "We don't have much time."

Slowly, I hoist myself from the wall of fallen rocks. I chew on the inside of my cheek and squint, knowing I'm going to regret this. But still, I take a quiet step. When Astor's movements don't change pace on the other side, I take another step.

This one is louder.

"Darling? *Wendy*," Astor says, almost as if scolding me. "Please don't tell me you're wandering down the tunnel after a strange voice."

"I've been told before that I am fairly slow-witted." I say it teasingly, even though my heart is about to explode out of my chest from apprehension.

"Don't you dare go down that tunnel without me." There's a hint of panic in his voice, infusing his otherwise commanding presence. I want nothing more than to obey him—that's my first impulse.

But down the hall, someone calls my name. "Wendy, if you want to save him, you have to come now."

Save him? My heart pounds wildly at the thought that Astor might be in danger. "How do I know I can trust you?" I ask.

"Because, Darling, I—" Astor must realize I'm not speaking to him, because he snaps his teeth together.

The wistful voice doesn't answer my question, but there's something about it that's as familiar as a childhood dream. Something about it that feels safe.

"Wendy, I'm begging you to wait," says Astor.

I bite my lip and follow the voice down the hall.

The voice leads me down the tunnel. It has no body that I can see, but I might have expected that from a ghost. It's not until we reach a wide-mouthed cave that the voice swells louder, reverberating all around me. Only, in the cave I can no longer make out the words the spirit speaks to me. It's as if the sound has expanded to fit the space of the cave, rendering it no longer intelligible.

My mouth is dry, but I take the calling stone from my pocket and utter the spell given to me by the Nomad all the same. For a moment, it seems as though nothing has happened. But soon after, a rush of wind fills the cave, coming from nowhere and all directions. It brings with it grayish lights that melt together until before me stands the imprint of a woman.

I'm not sure what I was expecting from the Seer. Probably someone decrepit, wrinkled. She is dead, after all.

But the ghoulish woman standing before me is none of those things.

Well, except for dead.

Though the faint light of the lichen on the cave wall shines through her body, I can still make out her curvy figure, her vibrant red hair, her pale skin and smattering of freckles. The way she carries herself would indicate that she's older than me, though her cheeks are round and youthful.

"Wendy Darling, you must run," are the first words from her mouth, startling me even more than her conjuration.

"It's okay," I say, reaching out to her, like I think I'm going to be able to calm her. Instead, my hand slips through her shoulder. She doesn't seem to notice.

"You're not safe here," she says, her gaze flitting frantically around the empty cave.

I shake my head, trying to gather the words to explain. "I know you can see the others, but they can't touch me. The spell—it only brought you close enough to communicate with me. Whoever else is here with you—they can't get to me."

Even so, a chill snakes down my spine. When her blue eyes meet mine, I expect to find confusion in them. Instead, I find pity.

"Death has not taken my mind," she says. "It's you who does not understand."

Deciding it's useless to argue with a paranoid ghoul, I do my best to explain. "There was a fae. People call him the Nomad. We were told that you had the magic to break a curse." I hesitate there, realizing this is my last chance. The last moment I get to decide.

I could keep Astor.

Just a few words, and I could rid Peter of his curse and keep Astor bound to me.

But then what? Live the rest of my life pursuing a man who doesn't want me? Catching him, then having to wonder for years if his love is true, or simply the byproduct of magic? After what I witnessed in the orphanage, I know deep within me that I could never keep Nolan Astor.

"I'm told you know how to break Mating Marks as well. Properly," I add, because obviously the Seer Astor went to as an adolescent claimed that very ability.

The Seer closes her eyes, looking pained. She shakes her head. "He's as much of a fool as he was then."

I blink. "I don't remember telling whose Mating Mark I was wanting you to break."

She levels me with a condescending stare. "I saw the two of you enter together. Who do you think brought about the earthquake that separated you?"

Unease ripples through my belly. I have to remind myself that this woman can't touch me. Though if she can cause natural disasters, I'm not sure I should let myself be comforted. I can only hope that causing the ceiling to cave in didn't use up too much of her magic.

"Why would you want to separate us?" I ask, though there can only be one answer. Predators separate packs because they're easier to trap that way, easier to attack, rip apart.

I take a step back, my foot landing on a rock that scrapes loudly against the cave floor.

"You fear the wrong people, Wendy Darling," says the Seer, unbothered by my retreat.

Indeed, when I reach the mouth of the tunnel, the Seer flicks her hand, and vines sprout from the walls, blocking the entrance.

My heart pounds. *"Astor!"* I scream, hoping my voice will travel by echo through the cave.

"Hush, girl," says the Seer, pacing now, pulling her red hair back into a tail at the nape of her neck with a leather tie she unwinds from her wrist.

"Astor, he—"

The woman is upon me, her hand wrapped around my mouth. I can't feel it there, but something about her being this close startles me enough to silence me. It's one of those moments in time that feels as though it's happened before, like I'm being transported back to a previous version of my body.

Her vibrant blue eyes blink at me in pain.

It's only now that I notice the gash across her throat. The slit of flesh, no longer bleeding in death, but ruined all the same.

My heart stops in my chest.

We took her back home to bury her.

357

"No," I whisper, horror gripping me. I do everything I can to make sense of what I'm seeing, but my mind is whirling in circles.

"Iaso?" I ask, hating how pitifully desperate my voice sounds.

She backs away, placing her hand over her neck to hide her scar. "How much did he tell you about me?" she asks. When I stumble over the words, she snaps her fingers at me. "Quickly girl. Before he finds you."

Fear lances through me, but something is wrong, and I have the feeling that I won't know what until I give her the information she wants.

"I know you are—were—his wife. I know he tried to get rid of his Mating Mark to be with you. You were friends with him, and Peter, when you were a child. I know your blood contains healing properties, and that when the plague struck Estelle, you went to the Darling mansion to heal their daughter. I know..." I fight the urge to shut my eyes, to shield myself from her expression as I recount her death. "I know my mother slit your throat and made me drink your blood to save me. And I know it destroyed him."

"Yes. Yes, it did, didn't it?" Iaso's expression is far off and I wonder if she's remembering her own death or the boy Astor used to be. The boy she fell in love with.

Slowly, she leans herself against the walls, shutting her eyes. Tears squeeze from her lids to her pale-blue cheeks.

"Please," I say. "He just wants to be rid of our Mating Mark. He never stopped loving you, and he never will. He doesn't want to love anyone else. It's his choice."

"You sound thoroughly convinced," says Iaso.

I swallow, shifting on my feet. But I can't talk about Astor now, not when I'm face-to-face with the woman who unwillingly took my place in death. "I'm so sorry," I say. "I'm so sorry about what they did to you. For me."

Iaso flits her hand. "It was long ago."

"But you've been trapped here ever since."

She stares off into the distance, like she's searching through the past. "He won't quite let me go on."

"I don't understand," I say.

She sighs, pinching the bridge of her nose. "That much is obvious."

I would flinch at the insult, except there's no unkindness in her voice.

"Do you love him?" she asks abruptly.

At that, I do flinch.

"That's answer enough," she says with a flit of her hand. She begins to pace across the cave floor with the sort of determination I'd expect from a healer. "And yet you're willing to help him rid himself of the Mating Mark?"

Again, I nod.

A sad smile softens her full lips. "So it's truly love, then. My husband is a fool for not seeing that."

"I think he sees it. He just can't care for me in the same way," I say.

"Clearly not," she says, anger spiking in her tone, though I can't understand why. She runs her hands through her hair at her scalp, pacing again. "Nolan, what have you done?"

Again, the unease settles in my belly. I don't understand why she's so distraught over Astor trying to remove his Mating Mark, unless she fears it will fail just as it did when they were fifteen. Still, that doesn't make sense. Doesn't seem to be enough to inspire the distress, the disappointment I'm witnessing.

It hits me then that it can't be a coincidence that Iaso is the Seer we've been searching for. There has to be a reason Astor didn't tell me we were returning to his home village.

Something as dull and heavy as stone thuds in my stomach. "He's not trying to break his Mating Mark, is he?" I ask.

Iaso's fingers stop running through her hair, frozen in that crazed position as she spins on her heel to look at me. "Just give me a moment to think. I can get you out of here. Or..." She squeezes her eyes shut, thinking. "Keep him trapped long enough to let you escape. You do have a way off the peninsula, don't you?"

I shake my head. "Only on his ship."

"Of course," she says, rubbing her palms together. "Then perhaps if you told him I was begging him not to go through with it. Perhaps he'd still listen to me…"

"Please," I say, tired of being left in the dark. "Just tell me what he's trying to do."

But when Iaso stares at me, mouth half open, apology written on her expression, I think I already know.

"He tricked me," I whisper, filing back through every moment I've spent with Astor. Every stolen glance, every brush of his hand, every almost kiss. My mind screams that it couldn't have all been a ruse to get me to fall for him, to trust him.

To follow him into a dark cave alone.

No. Astor is my friend, if nothing else. Even Maddox could see it. And Maddox is the captain's closest friend. If he didn't care for me, surely Maddox would have been able to tell.

If there was a moment in time when I should have realized the truth, I'm unable to find it. And besides, it's too late.

"I'm so sorry, Darling." His voice is gentle. Genuine. Pained, even. Or perhaps I'm simply hearing what I want to hear.

I turn to find Astor standing at the mouth between the tunnel and the cave, on the other side of the crossed vines Iaso had summoned.

His blade is drawn.

CHAPTER 50

WENDY

*W*hen Astor closes in after slicing through the vines, it's like a predator trying not to spook his prey. He even holds his Mated hand up, placatingly. Apology shadows his eyes, deepens the purse of his lips.

At the sight of him, Iaso lets out a pained sob.

"How long?" I ask. "How long have you been intending to sacrifice me to get her back?" Astor winces, but I don't give him the chance to respond. "That's what this is, isn't it? Some dark bit of magic that makes it so that the living can trade places with the dead?"

My mind races to catch up.

I gasp, realizing it's just like the story I used to tell John and Michael. The one where the man sacrificed his wife so that she could trade places with his dead lover. His dead lover, who had been slaughtered by his jealous wife. The murderer's life in exchange for the victim's. It had been depicted in the Nomad's sketchbook, hadn't it? I'd flipped right by it, immediately distracted by the sketch of the Reaper and the Oak.

I might not have been the one to slit Iaso's throat, but I'm the one who drank her blood. I'm the one who technically killed her.

Except the stories aren't the same. Not really. Because I'm not Astor's wife. I'm not even his lover.

"Wendy—"

"Were you already planning this the night in the crow's nest? When you almost kissed me? What about all those times you practically begged me to fight back? When you locked the faerie dust up to protect me, was it so I'd feel everything about your betrayal when you finally brought me here? How long, Nolan?"

He cringes at the use of his given name, but I'm not done.

"You could have kept me locked up," I almost shout. "You could have carried me over your shoulder, bound and unable to move. You could have been content to let me go on hating you, but no. You went and made me love you. You pretended to be my friend."

Astor shakes his head. "If it's any consolation to you, which I'm not enough of a fool to think it will be, I didn't know until we met with the Nomad."

My mind races back to my private meeting with the Nomad. How he'd offered me exclusive information about the Seer in this cave in order to bargain for Tink. How he'd put it into my head to betray Astor.

"He offered you a deal too," I say, feeling so stupid. "That way, it wouldn't matter if either of us failed. As long as one of us succeeded, that person could retrieve Tink for him. Me with my sway over Peter, you with the brute force of your crew."

"And what was it that you wanted?" he asks.

I stare at the calling stone in my hands. "I was going to free Peter of his curse."

Astor swallows. "Was going to?"

"I decided not to. The Nomad told me the Seer would only have enough magic to break one of the curses, so I was going to let you remove the Mark instead."

Guilt washes over Astor's face. His blade shakes, but he doesn't sheathe it. Doesn't cease his steady approach.

"Peter's cursed?" asks Iaso, though Astor doesn't appear to hear her. Doesn't appear to see her either, likely because I'm the one who activated the calling stone.

"Yes," I say. "He can't feel pain."

Iaso crinkles her brow.

Astor looks confused as to who I'm talking to, but realization soon dawns on his face. "Iaso is here," he says, eyes scanning the room hungrily for his lost wife.

Somehow, I'm the one who's never felt so invisible.

Iaso goes to him, clings to his shoulders. "Please, Nolan," she says, pressing her forehead to his. "Please, don't do this. This isn't you. This isn't the man I love."

But he can't hear her, can't feel the press of her skin against his brow.

"What is she saying?" he asks, staring straight through his wife at me.

I open my mouth to tell him, but something stops me. Maybe it's the emptiness of the cave. The way Iaso's voice doesn't echo. The desperation with which she tries to reach her husband but can't.

She's spent fifteen years like this. Alone. Calling out to those who can't hear her.

I assumed there were more than just her in this cave, and perhaps there are, but I've heard no one else calling out to me. Can she even speak to the others who are dead, or do they wander about, unable to communicate?

She's spent fifteen years trapped, all so I could live. All so my parents wouldn't have to suffer the pain of losing their daughter. Had I died, I would have faded into nothingness or crossed to the afterlife. Iaso hasn't been granted that luxury, that peace.

She's weeping now, screaming at Astor, who still waits for my response. "Please. Please, don't ruin yourself for me. Please, Nolan. I love you, but this isn't you."

My heart aches. Iaso didn't choose to trade her life for mine when I was a child. That choice was thrust upon her. Even so, when given the chance to take her life back, she'd rather be doomed to the shadows than watch the man she loves slaughter me. A girl she sees as innocent.

Maybe that's why my mouth produces the lie with such ease. "She says she misses you," I say, tears bubbling in my eyes, falling down my cheeks. "She says she's been so alone. That she wants to come home."

Iaso goes still, hanging off of Astor's shoulders, her breathing ragged from weeping. Slowly, she swivels her head toward me. "What do you think you're doing?"

My throat hurts, but I get the words out all the same, craning my neck to the side and shrugging. "I wasn't supposed to be here. I wasn't supposed to live. I was supposed to die during that plague, to have spent the last fifteen years at peace. It was wrong, what my parents did to you. I was given years I wasn't supposed to have. Years I squandered in fear, when you would have used them for good. Think of the children you would have healed while I was climbing towers and hiding from the shadows. It's okay that you want to go home, Iaso."

She stands, placing herself between me and Astor. "There are many things I would do to escape this wretched place. But his soul is too valuable a cost."

I offer her a sad smile. "I know. That's why I'm giving him my permission."

Astor goes still, all except for his blade, which is shaking. He paces toward me, straight through his wife, who is back to screaming, tugging at his neck, though to no avail. When he reaches me, he places his warm hand on the back of my neck, pulling me into him. So my body won't fall when my legs give out from underneath me, I realize.

His ivy eyes shimmer under the gleam of tears as he presses the blade to my neck. When he speaks, his voice is hoarse. "Why, Darling? Why is it that you never fight back?"

"I don't have to wield a blade to cut you, Captain," I say with a soft smile, the sting of a tear at my eye.

His blade trembles at my throat, his own throat bobbing. His chuckle is pained. "Is that what this is? Wendy Darling's last revenge? The knowledge I'll see your face every time I close my eyes? Are you intending to haunt me from the grave?"

"Come now, Captain," I say. "You should know better than that."

"Is that so?" he asks. "Because I would hate to think..." He closes his eyes, breath halting. "I would hate to think..."

"That I'm a fool, so hopelessly in love that I'd let you slit my throat as long as I thought it's what you wanted?"

The playfulness has left his expression now. He's desperate. It doesn't suit him.

"Don't fret, Captain." I steal a glance at Iaso, who's crying, though she's no longer fighting him. "I'm not doing this for you."

Astor actually flinches, as if someone's put a blade through his stomach. But it's just me and him in this room, and I've never been all that good at fighting back. When he closes his eyes and brings his forehead to mine, I can't tell which one of us is trembling.

"Thank you, Darling," he whispers.

"An apology and a thank-you in one conversation," I say. "Careful, Captain, or I might just start to believe you care for me, after all."

"I don't deserve the honor of claiming that," he says. "I shouldn't...I shouldn't have been cruel to you."

Something swells in my throat. Not so much the captain's words, but that I already know them. Already believe them. "I know. Now, if you'd get on with it, please. The anticipation is torture."

His ivy green eyes sweep over my face. I can't tell if he's memorizing my every feature, or simply searching for some wickedness in me that will justify what he's about to do.

In the end, he has to close his eyes as he presses the edge of the blade to my throat.

I let out the smallest gasp as the cold blade slices through flesh and a sharp pang eddies at my throat. Warm blood wets my skin, but that's not what really hurts.

I don't want to die. Not any more than I wanted to die when I grew ill of the plague. I want to live a long and peaceful life. I want to taste happiness for longer than a few stolen moments. I want to live, but perhaps not the way I have been used to.

I wish I had let myself be happy.

I wish I had let go of the shadows. Spent more time playing with Michael. Laughing with John.

There's a bit of me that knows I'm betraying them by not fighting back. But no matter how much I hate to leave them, I can't leave Iaso here. Not when she's given so many years to me.

Not when I wasted every one of them becoming more of a ghost than she is.

The blade trembles, digging deeper into my throat. I cry out. It's not going to be a clean cut. The captain can't bring himself to do it swiftly, and he's going to prolong my suffering.

"Darling, please," the captain begs, though I'm not sure what he's asking.

Maybe for me to just die.

"Please. Please, fight back," he says, eyes still closed as he rests his forehead against mine. "Please." He's heaving now, and I don't understand. Pain trickles, following the trail of blood against my neck. "Beg me. One word, Darling, and I'll stop."

"I'm afraid I'm a bit weary of begging you, Captain."

When he flutters his eyelashes open to look at me, I can hardly breathe. Anguish ripples in my chest at the pain in his expression. Leftover magic from the Mark that binds our souls together in a pitiful twine of dangling string, I'm sure.

He lets out a strangled sound.

And drops the dagger.

In a moment, he's on his knees, pulling me to the ground with him, cradling me to his warm, heaving chest as he weeps, before the blade even clatters to the ground. "I'm so sorry," he mutters. "I'm so, so sorry."

His face buried in my shoulder, relief filling my lungs, I don't realize he's not talking to me until Iaso appears behind him, brushing her fingers through Astor's hair, though he can't feel her.

"It's okay, Nolan," she whispers. "I never expected you to hold on this long."

If Astor wishes to hear his wife's response, he must be too ashamed to ask, because he remains quiet, cradling me to his chest. I can't bring myself to embrace him back. To comfort the man who listened to me admit my love for him, while all the while plotting to trade my life for the dead's.

But Iaso deserves for her words to be heard. So I whisper into the captain's ear everything she says, every word of comfort. I let him cling to me as he weeps.

"He loves you, you know," says Iaso, a smile soft on her freckled face as she watches Astor. "In his own, broken way." She's crying now. "It's all I ever wanted for him. I thought...I thought the Nolan I loved was gone." She turns to me. "Do you love him?"

When I don't answer, she grins. "You do."

"Broken love was what got you killed in the first place," I whisper, and Iaso's countenance falls, so I don't finish my thought.

I don't have the heart to tell her that I don't want anything to do with broken love anymore. I could still do it, I realize. I could pick up the blade and bring it to my throat. Trade my blood for hers.

That would be the brave thing to do.

But I only had enough bravery in me for one shot. Now that it's passed, I'm too weary, too cowardly to pick up the blade on the ground.

As it turns out, I don't get the chance.

"What have you done to my Darling?" hisses a voice from the edge of the cave. I shoot my neck up to find Peter, swathed in shadows, his wings taking up the entrance of the tunnel. He stalks toward us, and as I scramble to my feet, Astor turns, placing his back to my front as he covers me by reaching his hands behind his back.

Peter cranes his head to the side. "Oh, so now you're trying to protect her? Tell me, Nolan, why's there blood dripping from her throat?"

CHAPTER 51

WENDY

"Peter," Iaso gasps, her voice almost in a trance as she finally recognizes the boy from her childhood, now lost to the influence of the shadows. "What happened to you?"

He must sense her presence because his ears flick, but he doesn't seem to be able to hear or see her any more than Astor does.

"How did you find us?" asks Astor.

"Your time is up," says Peter. "Six months. This," he says, pointing to the mark of their bargain, still silver against his shadowed skin, "led me right to you."

I reel, confused. We still have twelve days. Twelve days…

Based on the Estellian calendar. But not on the moon cycle.

I check Astor's reaction for any hint of whether he knew Peter had meant six months based on the moon cycle, but he doesn't argue against Peter's timing.

I realize then why Astor meandered a day. He couldn't have killed me while still within the six-month time period. He must have known Peter would be coming after us.

"You didn't return what's mine to me," says Peter.

"I never specified that I would," says Astor.

"Well," says Peter, his teeth pearly and baring. "I'm here now, aren't I?"

When he moves toward me, Astor backs up, spurring me toward the cave wall behind us. His grip on me is too gentle for someone who plotted to kill me. "I'll give her back," says Astor. "But only if that's what she wants. And only if you shift out of that form."

The laugh that echoes through the cave sends chills through my bones. "Are you implying that I might hurt her?" asks Peter. "That I might lay a hand on her? Or is shedding her blood permissible so long as her maidenhood remains intact?"

For the first time, I witness a flush climb the captain's neck, and the way he hesitates to answer tells me it's not from anger. He cranes his head softly toward me, behind him. "Do you want to go with him? Do you feel safe with him?"

In answer, I untangle myself from Astor's protective grip. His hand lingers on my shoulder, his thumb grazing my neck, for just a moment too long, so I shrug him off. As his Mark leaves my flesh, it's as though I've been seared in the gut. "I don't feel safe with anyone," is all I say.

Peter's smile is feral, hungry, as he takes me in. As I cross the cave room to him, Iaso glides in front of me. "Something's wrong," she says.

It's cruel, but I laugh at her. Hurt flashes across her face, but she gets out of my way.

When I reach Peter, he doesn't touch me. Probably doesn't want to shift back into his fae form while the captain is anywhere close. I wish he would. The faster I can get him to shift, the more time for him to return to his right mind before he gets me alone.

My skin crawls thinking of what he might do to me if he doesn't shift. What almost happened in the Carlisles' reading room.

So, for once in my life, I take advantage of the little control I have left and interlock my fingers with Peter's. He flinches as the shadows dissipate to reveal tanned skin and copper hair, though his eyes remain painted black.

Still terrifying, but at least the hand I'm holding is flesh. At least the ink in his eyes will drain. Eventually.

At this point, all I want is to get back to my brothers.

"Come now, my Darling little thing," says Peter, wrapping a possessive arm around me as he leads us backward out of the cave.

"Wait," I say, sliding my hand into my pocket and retrieving the calling stone. I turn back to Astor, who can barely stand to look at me. "You should keep this," I say.

Iaso gives me a grimace, but Astor's eyes land on the stone. There's hope there, but something lost, too.

"Thank you," he says, throat raspy. When he steps toward me to retrieve it, Peter makes a clucking noise and plucks it from my hand.

"Forgive me if I don't trust him," Peter says. "I'll bring it to you, Captain."

Astor tenses, but he waits for Peter to cross the room.

When Peter presses the stone into Astor's Marked hand, he offers the captain a feral grin. "You shouldn't have touched what was mine."

Shadows, silky as ink, drip off of Peter's hand, coating the stone like tar.

"No!" Astor bellows and yanks the stone from Peter's grip, but it's too late. Across the room, Iaso's bluish veins have turned black, jettisoning inky streaks across her face. Her hands go to her throat, and she gags as tar pours from her open mouth, coating her front in black blood.

My hand finds my mouth to cover my gasp, but it's too late. Astor's gaze snaps to me at the wretched sound, distraught recognition overcoming his face.

"What's happening to her?" he snarls.

"Peter, stop. Please," I say, racing over to Iaso. She's on her knees now, and though I try to comfort her, there's nothing I can do when my hands sweep through her. She turns to me, her eyes as black as Peter's, though they're wide in horror.

"Peter, *please!*" I scream, but my pleas are drowned out by the captain.

He's on his knees in front of Peter, begging. "Please, just don't hurt her," he says. "I'll do anything. She's your friend, too," he says, confusion swarming in his eyes.

"What's to say you wouldn't try to hurt Wendy again to bring her back?" asks Peter, staring down at Astor in cruel delight. "What's to say you wouldn't keep trying to take her from me? You can't give a present, then expect it back, Astor. But you never did realize that as a boy either."

"This isn't you," I say, as Iaso's skin starts to fade from silvery blue to gray. She's trying to mouth something, but I can't make it out against the bubbling black foam. "Once you're yourself again, you'll regret this."

Peter ignores me, staring down Astor.

"Whatever you want," says Astor. "Just don't hurt her."

"That's the thing," says Peter, black eyes flashing. "What I wanted was for you not to touch my things."

The stone in Astor's hand explodes in a flurry of shadows, sending orbs of magic shooting across the room. They light the abandoned torches lining the cave walls, casting an eerie burning glow across the cavern.

Iaso screams, a wilting cry of anguish that must pierce through the veil of the dead, because Astor snaps his neck toward where she's kneeling, his eyes wide in terror. He runs to her, but it's too late. Shadows are pouring out of her mouth, her nose, her eyes, ripping through her chest, her fingertips, her belly. They're eating her from the inside, writhing worms of darkness.

They consume her until there's nothing left.

Astor's crying, reaching for a wife who's no longer there. He doesn't realize it until he turns to find the look of shocked horror on my face.

We exchange one last glance. I don't school my face in time.

He looks as if he's been speared in the stomach, and then something in him shifts. He blinks, then kneels, brandishing his sword from its scabbard.

When he fixes his gaze on Peter, there's nothing of the kind man I thought I knew in his eyes. Nothing of the tenderness I was beginning to recognize.

"There," taunts Peter, "problem solved. Aren't you grateful that I put your wife out of her suffering? She'll probably thank me in the next life. I bet she's grateful that you're no longer imprisoning her here."

Astor bellows, then lunges. Sword clashes with shadow as Peter parries the captain's attack with a whip he's conjured of shadows. The shadows curl around Astor's sword, attempting to wrestle it from his hand. But Astor is schooled in combat. Rather than attempt to regain control of his sword, he releases the hilt, spinning and striking at Peter from behind with a spare dagger he unsheathes from his boot.

Peter dodges well enough, sensing the attack without having to see it. When he whips around to face Astor, there's unadulterated malice —the amused sort—in his expression. Astor thrusts his dagger toward Peter, but it's deflected by Peter's shadows. This time, Astor's prepared, and brings the dagger back to his chest before the shadows can wrap their tendrils around it. When he swings again, the tendrils aren't ready, and he manages to nick Peter's shoulder.

The gash cuts through Peter's leathers. It's nothing, really. A simple slice of flesh. The kind of wound someone like Astor or Maddox would likely not even notice during battle.

Not Peter. Peter gasps.

It's a quick inhale, coupled with a flash of shock on Peter's face. He hides it almost immediately.

Not fast enough.

"Thought you said he couldn't feel pain," says Astor, eyes brimming with a hunger for blood.

Peter blinks, stepping backward. He looks unsteady, like the bit of pain he's experienced has rattled him. And why shouldn't it?

Peter's not supposed to be able to feel pain. He likely hadn't remembered what it felt like.

My mind whirls, trying to make sense of it. Slowly, as Astor approaches Peter, backing his shocked opponent into a corner, my attention pivots to the place Iaso Astor withered away.

Spirits only have a limited amount of magic to offer after they die. What you and the captain want—there won't be enough magic for both.

She'd overheard me tell Astor that Peter couldn't feel pain. Not only that, I'd admitted that this was my original intention in visiting the Seer, to heal my Mate.

So when he'd ripped her from the inside out with his shadows, when he'd torn her spirit apart, she'd used up her well of magic to break his curse.

Something tells me she hadn't meant it as a gift.

Grief mingled with renewed vigor propels Astor, all brute strength. Peter, usually nothing if not quick, precise, falters with every dodge.

He doesn't realize he's trapped until his back hits the cave wall.

Something within Astor splinters. All the rigid restraint he usually carries in his firm shoulders, all the rage channeled into purpose—it's unleashed now, the last remaining bolster of the dam snapped.

I remember my alienist telling my mother that when humans undergo more stress than their minds can handle, they revert back to a shadow of who they were as a child. Regress into the comfort of the person they've built the rest of their persona around.

When Iaso was banished from this realm, when her spirit was destroyed, magic had spewed out of her, lighting the abandoned torches on the walls of the cave.

There's one over Peter's head. Astor removes it from the wall, its flame flickering in panic, as if it knows its end is near. Astor snuffs it out.

Then steers it toward Peter's chest.

I gag, though I don't know if it's from the scent of burning flesh that hits the cave air, or the way Peter screams, his body writhing in agony. Perhaps it's the way watching Peter, my Mate, suffer feels as if Astor has taken the brand to my own chest.

Or maybe it's just that as Astor tortures Peter, I don't see Astor, but Nolan. And I see the little wraith who ran for help in the village. The little boy who was concerned not for his own safety, but the newcomer's. The child who, after being tortured, forgave, knowing it wasn't Nolan who'd hurt him—not truly.

It can't end like this. Not between the two of them. Peter had been kind once. Forgiving. He'd befriended little Nolan Astor, even after being tortured by him.

This can't be how it ends.

As I make my way toward the garish scene, I kneel, retrieving Astor's abandoned dagger—the one he dropped after slicing my throat —from the ground.

They start out pure, my intentions. When I go to fasten my fingers around the hilt, I intend to save both of them. Peter, from the torture and the death surely to come at Astor's hand. Astor, from murdering his oldest friend, the boy who had shown him kindness.

But when I stand, the weight of the dagger in my hand, I realize I'm already holding something else.

Astor was right, that night in the crow's nest.

I'm so very angry.

I think perhaps I've never recognized it, because it doesn't match the anger I've seen in others. It doesn't burn hot, only to consume itself quickly, fizzle out because it's guzzled more oxygen than its environment contains.

No, mine's been fed slowly. So slowly, I hadn't noticed it growing. And as I've never attempted to put it out before—why put out a fire you don't know is burning?—I find I have no way of containing it. No blanket to throw over it. No basin of water nearby.

With the dagger's icy hilt in my hand, I feel Astor's betrayal over again. Except this time, I let myself feel it. Iaso is gone, so there's no use in tempering my feelings on her behalf.

Astor slipped Peter's ring on my finger, knowing exactly what it would do to me as he kneeled. Then he used the very same hand to pick up this dagger with the intention of killing me. The same hand he used to cup my cheek the night in the crow's nest.

It happens in a flash, but my mind slows it down. Possibly because of where I've been fixating.

I watch as Astor's desire to make Peter suffer burns out. I can see the moment it changes in his face—when his face falls and he just wants it to be over.

I watch as Astor brings his dagger down with his Mated hand.

Later, I'll tell myself all sorts of reasons for why I did it. I'll tell myself I was saving my Mate, that my Mark drove me to it. I'll tell myself I was keeping the captain from killing his first friend, saving the little boy Nolan from growing up to murder the one person who showed him forgiveness. Later, when my dreams torment me by replaying this moment, I'll convince myself it was because I wanted to get back to John and Michael. That Peter was my only way back to Neverland, to my brothers.

For now? For now I know the truth.

When I bring the dagger down, I know exactly what I'm aiming for.

And it's not the captain's blade.

The cut is so clean, I hardly feel it reverberate against the hilt. Barely get to feel the satisfaction of a perfect hit.

Astor's hand goes flying.

I sever it from his arm just in time for Peter to scuttle out from underneath his dagger, dislodged from its target. By the time Astor's hand hits the ground, the gold of his Mark has already shriveled to gray, matching the deathly ill skin of his forearm.

His blood drips from the edge of the blade I'm clutching.

He's so shocked, so stunned, he doesn't even cry out. He just stumbles, falls to his knees, and stares at the stump at his wrist, bleeding profusely, covering the dead tendrils of his Mark with blood.

Now that the Mark is gone, now that there's nothing tying me to Astor, I wait for the pain to drizzle away.

It seems I'm going to be waiting for a very long time.

The captain's gaze slides up to me, his mouth barely agape. There's betrayal written all over his face, grief and loss, too, but there's something else. Something I can't quite place.

The captain swallows. "Well done, Darling."

CHAPTER 52

WENDY

What happens next is a blur. At some point, I must have dropped the dagger, because as Peter leads me through the tunnels, hand gripped on my shoulder, I notice that my hand is empty. Except for Astor's blood, which stains the folds of my palm, my knuckles.

We'd left him there, bleeding and grasping his wrist in shock. Peter had already begun to heal from the burns, aided by the fact that he was still transitioning from his shadow self to his fae form.

He's still trembling, though. Even as his fingers dig into my collarbone.

I don't have the energy to tell him he's hurting me.

I hear little else except the pounding of blood in my ear, the sound Astor's flesh had made as it split. Sickly. Like the last pig carcass I had cut through. But something else taps through the buzz in my head. Footsteps.

Charlie and Maddox round the corner, hair windswept, breathing hard. Upon seeing Peter, they instantly draw their swords.

"Saw you swoop into the cave," says Maddox, steely gray gaze pinned on Peter. "We were keeping an eye out from the ship."

Peter doesn't seem to hear them. All I know is that his hand tightens at my shoulder.

It's not quite fear that lances through me. I think I'm in too much of a state of shock for that. But my mind eddies into focus. Somewhere deep down, I know that these are my friends, and that I need to protect them, Peter still not himself.

As Charlie approaches, keeping her eyes fixed on Peter as she extends a hand to me, the other on the holster at her belt, I shake my head. "I'm going with Peter."

They hesitate and Charlie gives Peter a suspicious look. "So you're choosing him after all?" she asks, not bothering to mask the disappointment in her voice.

I continue, nodding toward where we came from. "The captain's injured. He'll be needing the two of you."

Charlie and Maddox exchange concerned glances, then run off after their captain. Before they turn the curve, Charlie turns back to me. "Are you sure?"

I nod, because that seems like the only thing to do. She frowns. "Take care of yourself," she says.

And then she's gone.

THE FLIGHT back to Neverland is cold.

Even with Peter's warm arms wrapped around me, I can't seem to fight off the chilled spray of the ocean surface below. Or maybe it's just my heart turning to stone, refusing to beat blood to warm my limbs any longer.

I keep waiting for the agony of Astor's betrayal to melt away. Keep waiting for my body to remember that there's no Mark binding my soul to his anymore. No reason for his claws to cut so deeply into me.

I wait and wait, silence washing over me, but never relief. Just the rain, cold and cruel and pelting.

I wait for my feelings for Peter to return in full force. For the thrill I used to feel when he flew me through the air to billow underneath my skin, cascading me in light and joy and adventure.

But I'm not flying. Peter is. I just happen to be attached.

And what about you, Darling? Do you soar?

At some point in the journey, it dawns on me that despite everything, I still love him. Love Astor.

In an attempt to detach myself from that love, that pain, all I accomplished was severing the last of the threads binding his heart to mine. The only reason he felt anything for me in the first place.

I should have known better. Hadn't I told Astor the day I confessed my love for him that it might not have been real for him, but it was real for me? The real seems like it plans on staying around longer, an unwanted house guest chipping my favorite pieces of dinnerware.

"Wendy Darling," Peter whispers when my tears have finally dried up. When I peer up at him, his blue eyes stare down at me. I guess it's been long enough for the effect of his shadows to wear off. That's why he hasn't touched me in the way his shadow self so desires. "You're safe now. I'm taking you home."

I repeat those words over and over to myself. I don't have a home, not really. But John and Michael are the closest thing to it. Charlie was almost a home. Maddox too.

But their loyalties are to their captain, not to me. I wonder then if they knew his plan. If they wanted Iaso back, too.

No, Charlie wouldn't have betrayed me like that. Besides, she didn't even know Iaso. And the conversation I overheard between Maddox and Astor would indicate that Maddox knew nothing about Astor's betrayal. It's cruel of me, but it makes me feel better to know that Maddox will feel a twinge of the betrayal I do when he discovers what Astor hid from him.

It occurs to me that when I'd asked Astor to go alone with him into the cave, that's what the three of them had been arguing about. Astor had already planned on leaving them behind, not wishing them to be around to stop him once they realized his intentions.

Lost in my thoughts, it takes me a while to realize it's no longer raining. Yet moisture still drips into my hair.

Tears.

Peter is crying.

Finally, that at least seems to stir my heart. Makes it move from where it's slumped, frozen up. Like a sore muscle refusing to extend after being overworked, finally giving in to a stretch.

"Wendy," Peter says, his voice soft, broken. "I..." The words seem stuck there, in his throat as it bobs. His blue eyes are so beautiful, shimmering as he cries. "I don't know why I..." His gaze flits back and forth, like saying it aloud will make it real.

I wonder now if it's just the regret over Iaso's second death that's hit him, or if it's all of it. Every bit of pain he couldn't feel before now, all cascading down on him in angry waves, greedy to get what was due long ago.

He keeps gripping me with one hand, the wind whistling through my tangled hair as he grasps his chest with the other. "It hurts," he gasps. "In here."

I nod, brushing my forehead against his chest as I do. "I know."

"She was my friend," he says, like he can't believe his own words. "When we were children. I don't know why...why did I...? It wasn't me," he says, breathy now, almost shaking me, like he has to get me to understand.

I imagine that's what I'll tell myself when I look back on slicing Astor's hand from his wrist. It's such a pleasant lie.

But for now, I entertain it for Peter. I'll have more pain to divvy out to him once we reach Neverland. Once I tell him I'm taking my brothers and leaving for home, though I don't know where home is.

"The night in the Carlisles' library...it wasn't me," he breathes again.

"I know," I say, numb.

He nods, relieved that he thinks I understand. He thinks that because I forgive him, I won't leave him. But I can't go back. I can't return to Peter's arms, knowing what I confessed to Astor on the ship. Knowing that I love another man.

Knowing that had it been my choice, I would have never left Nolan Astor's side.

· · ·

379

WHEN WE LAND on the beach, my feet hitting the familiar sand, I can't help but feel that I'm sinking into it. That the ground is unsteady, about to crumble underneath me.

"Wendy," says Peter, shaking as he turns me to face him. "I'm so sorry for...for him. For the person I've been. I couldn't..." He rubs at his chest, and I nod.

"I know," I say, sighing. "I forgive you. You weren't working with all your inhibitions."

Peter nods, a panicked smile overcoming his features. Like he thinks maybe my forgiveness is too good to be true.

It is.

But I'm weary, and I want to see my brothers.

"I'm so glad to have you back," he says, sliding his fingers over my ring and twirling it tenderly. "Now we can finally start our life together."

My numb heart gives a lurch at the hope in his expression. Is that how I looked every time I stared up at Astor? Like he had crafted the very world I inhabit? Like he was the only source I could count on for my next breath?

I'm not sure who that thought makes me hate more: Astor or myself.

I wince, and Peter blinks, confused.

Slowly, I slip my hand away from Peter's. I don't want to talk about this right now. Don't want to ever have this conversation, but I can't bear for him to cling onto that stupid, desperate hope. Can't stand to do the same thing to him that Astor did to me, stringing me along for his own benefit.

"I'm not staying," I say.

Peter blinks. "You don't want to stay in Neverland?"

I furrow my brow; saying the words actually hurts, but I don't know how else to get him to understand. "I don't want to stay with you."

Peter flinches. And I realize it's the first time I've ever seen him make that expression. The first time he's ever felt that kind of sting in my presence. It looks unnatural on his usually carefree face.

"But we're Mates," he says.

That, at least, stirs a bit of annoyance inside of me. "I'm aware. But I'm also aware that our being Mates wasn't the original plan."

Peter goes still, his familiar blank expression returning. "You're mad because I didn't tell you about Astor."

"No," I say, running my hand through my hair. "Well, yes, but that's not the point, Peter. The point is that I don't know who I am. The point is that, my whole life, my soul has been split in two, and I've been unknowingly making decisions based on the two of you. The point is that if I had the choice..."

Peter's face turns to stone. "You would choose him."

This time, I don't back down from Peter's pain. His discomfort. "Yes."

"Even after everything he did to you? Even after he chose her over you?"

I take a breath in, frustrated that he doesn't understand. "No. No, of course not. But before I knew that, I chose him, Peter. I chose him, not knowing if he'd choose me. Fairly sure he wouldn't choose me, honestly. And I'm not tossing you the leftovers just because he didn't choose me back. I'm not marrying you when I..." I let out a tiny sob. "When I still wish he'd made a different choice."

"Is that what your plan was, then?" Peter asks, backing away. "Did you go to the cave to break the Sister's blessing just so when you crushed me I could actually feel it?"

"What? Of course not," I say. "And it's not a blessing, it's a curse."

"I don't remember asking you to break it," he says through gritted teeth.

"Do you even hear yourself?" I hate how my voice spikes as shrill as the wind howling around us. "That curse was turning you into a monster. Or have you forgotten what you almost did to me at the Carlisles'? What you did to Iaso?"

At that, Peter actually blanches. Guilt immediately pierces my ribcage, but I refuse to let it master me.

"Tell me the truth," he says. "Were you really breaking it for me?"

I open my mouth to tell him, "Of course." But my tongue stops me, and I shake my head, wrapping my hands around my waist.

Peter approaches, softly this time, taking my cheek in his hand. "You wanted me to love you," he says. "You wanted all of me; I know you did."

"Of course I did," I say, glancing away. "I meant it when I said I loved you, Peter."

"And now you have me," he says. "All of me, my heart on a platter. Ready for you to run it through."

"Peter..."

"Things will be different, I promise," he says. "I won't let you go again, not like I did on the beach that day. I couldn't bear to see you go again. Wendy Darling, I could be everything you've ever wanted. Just give yourself some time."

He takes my cheek, brushing my Mark. My Mark that belongs wholly to him now. He means it to be romantic, but all it sparks in me is resentment. He's right, that I still feel a pull toward him, a tug deep within my heart. But if I've learned anything from Astor, it's that we don't have to follow the paths our hearts mark out for us, not even when there's magic involved.

We can always fight back.

It would be easier, to succumb to the comfort of Peter's arms. Easier than leaving.

I've been letting the current take me wherever it will for so long, my muscles have atrophied. I've forgotten how to swim against the resistance.

But if I don't want to drown, I'll have to start remembering.

"Peter," I say, taking his hand in mine and removing it from my cheek. "I've made up my mind."

I think it might be the first time that sentence has ever left my mouth. It should hurt, but it doesn't. It just feels powerful.

I watch him break, and it cracks me on the inside, but not my will. He closes his eyes, like he sincerely believes that when he opens them again, I'll have changed my mind.

"You've changed," he says when he finally looks at me through those long eyelashes again.

I'm not sure how to respond to that, so I nod. "Goodbye, Peter."

When I go to pull from his gentle grip, he tightens it. At first, I think he's just squeezing my hand.

But then he doesn't let go.

"Peter..." I say, warning in my voice, though I carry no threat.

He pulls me into him, pressing his forehead to mine, cradling my back as he pulls me into a gentle embrace. I let myself melt there, into my friend, just for a moment. But then he whispers in my ear. "Stay," he says. "Choose me."

Something on the crook of my arm burns, at first a gentle tingle, but it escalates as it deepens. For the briefest of moments, I don't know what's happening.

No.

"No," I gasp, pulling away, but even now, my resolve is dwindling, coming apart at the seams. Glancing down, I catch the remnants of our bargain—the blank check I gave Peter the night in the tower, scalding my skin.

I try to pull away from him. "Peter, no! What are you doing?" I ask, panic overtaking my body. I watch as a third oval forms on my skin, filling the empty space between the other two as it forms a link. A chain. With each passing moment, my muscles do less and less to resist him.

"Peter, please," I say, my voice high. Begging. But he's not letting go, and I'm no longer fighting him. "Please don't do this."

His blue eyes go bright, tears glazing his eyes, but not falling. This is hurting him, too. Just not as badly as he'd hurt if I left.

"Don't choose him, Wendy," he says, then with an exhale that feels like death's breath against my cheek, he says, "Choose me. Always. No matter what."

The sob gets strangled in my throat—the lock clicking, the door shutting. The last bit of burnt flesh falls away, leaving smooth pink skin surrounding the now-completed bargain on my forearm.

"Okay." The word comes out without my permission. "I'll stay."

No, no, no, no.

I want to scream, but it won't come. It's pent up in my throat, tied and wrangled and stuffed down. I want to beg him to stop, to let me go. For a moment, I fear my mind will leave me, that I'll blink and my feelings for Astor will vanish away.

I cling to them like a safe harbor.

But they remain. I take in a breath and consider Peter's words. The bargain only affects my actions, my choices. Not my feelings. I'm a slave to Peter's will in body, but not in my mind.

"Okay," I whisper, hating how my limbs betray me. How I fall into his arms. "I choose you. It's you, Peter. It'll always be you."

That fool. When he pulls away, there's nothing but joy in his eyes. Like he's so relieved at not having to suffer the pain of me leaving him —the same pain I felt the first time I was separated from him in the captain's ship—that the fact that it wasn't my decision to choose him is inconsequential.

"I'm going to take care of you from now on, Wendy Darling," he says, bouncing on his feet. "I'm never going to hurt you again."

"I know," I say, and I actually smile, eyes and all. Because that's what choosing Peter means, choosing to go along with his dreadful games of pretend. His insane commitment to happiness at the cost of all else. Choosing Peter means being happy.

Or, rather, acting like I am.

My smile must be convincing enough; he must think the wording of his bargain has changed my feelings, because his face lights up, relief washing over his features.

When he links his fingers through mine, I can't breathe. It's not like the first time he held my hand, my heart hammering with excited tremors. No. I know what's coming next. My stomach turns over in my gut, and I can hardly breathe. When he leans in, I sigh against his kiss.

"Peter," I say as he leads me across the beach, toward the Den, where he'll take me to his rooms and have me at last. Where, to him, I'll seem as though I'm adoring every graze of his hands against my flesh.

I wasn't me—wasn't that what Peter had said once the pain had been taken away?

Now I'm not myself anymore either. Peter and I—we're just two imposters playing at love. Play-actors on the stage, except my strings are in Peter's hands, his in the Sister's.

There's a scream bubbling up within me, but there's nowhere for it to go, so it just burrows within me, building the pressure behind my eyes and hollowing out my organs as it slams them up against the wall of my interior.

I want to go home, but my feet dance across the sand like that's exactly where I'm going. Without me telling them to, my hands find themselves clinging to Peter's arm, my cheek pressed against his shoulder as we walk.

When he looks down at me, it's with the most devastatingly genuine smile. It's the kind of smile that would have floored me once. I suppose it does now, just in the slamming me to the floor and holding me by the throat sort of way.

Halfway to the Den, I've resigned myself to my fate. At least I'll get to see John and Michael. At least I'll get to be with them, keep them safe.

And they'll think that I'm happy.

It will take John years to believe it. But no one can act like I'm acting, put on a show like my body is putting on, for that long. Not without magic helping them along. And John won't suspect magic.

Manipulation. A foolish girl following her own foolish whims, perhaps.

But he'll find that believable.

And he won't worry about me anymore.

And we'll all be together.

And it will be okay.

It. Will. Be. Okay.

I've almost convinced myself by the time we make it halfway to the Den. Fairly impressive, though Astor wouldn't think so. He'd tell me I've given in too quickly, granted Peter the power to lead me around like a pet on a leash.

But Astor would only be manipulating me if he said such things, so I choose to ignore his voice inside my head. He lost his right to my mind, anyway.

"Peter," someone calls through the brush. Footsteps pound toward us, breathing labored. "Peter, you have to—"

Victor comes into view, his black hair disheveled, his eyes blood-shot, red coursing through the whites. I haven't seen him like this since the day we found the man we assumed to be his brother's killer. Even then, he wasn't this distraught.

He swallows his words as soon as he sees me. "Wendy." There's no welcome home in his voice. No excitement to see me, despite the fact we're friends. He tries to compose himself, stand up straighter, calmer. "I'm glad to see you home safe."

It doesn't matter how calm he tries to force his voice, he can't hold the evidence that something is terribly wrong.

Because Victor's holding Michael's hand.

My brother hums under his breath, unaware of my return. His voice is high, sharp. I don't need to hear what he's singing to know he's upset. Distraught, even.

The Lost Boy won't look at me.

"Victor, where's John?" Fear for my brother grips my chest, slicing through the love-struck exterior my bargain has me under. It's still there, compelling me to choose Peter, but my love for John is something separate. Something I can cling to while I hold my choosing of Peter in the other hand.

Victor doesn't answer. He just squeezes Michael's hand tighter.

Peter goes quiet, but his voice is commanding, concerned. "Victor? What happened?"

Victor glances back and forth nervously between me and Peter, like he's tiptoeing around a minefield, trying to find the right words when there are none.

Michael's singing gets louder. "Last one to the top's dead meat."

My heart stops in my chest.

I drop Peter's hand and run.

CHAPTER 53

WENDY

The forest is sinister, the shadows enveloping where there should be a faint outline of the trees in tonight's bright moonlight. There should be light, and there is none, and it seems the shadows are doing it on purpose. They jump from the brush and obscure my path, holding their fingers over my eyes like I'm a frightened child.

They don't want me to see. Don't want me to find what's at the end of this path. But my feet propel me ever onward.

I run, skirting by trees, slamming into bark when the shadows obscure my vision too fully, but I run all the same, allowing the forest to beat my body to a pulp.

All the while, I hear John's laugh.

I hear it as he yells, "Last one to the top's dead meat," in the middle of our tutoring sessions. I hear it as he grabs Michael and throws him over his shoulder as we race toward the clock tower, Michael's giggling contagious. I feel John's spindly fingers around my ankles as he lunges for me in our hallway manor, doing anything he can to keep me from winning.

At least, I think I feel it. But it's just the thorns on the forest floor grasping at my ankles, begging me to turn around.

I can't just turn around. I run, and with every step, I leave an imprint of my heart—torn in two—on Neverland's floor.

And then I'm back to the day John, Michael, and I raced through this forest back to the Den. The day John had pretended to lag behind, just so he could tease me about how he could still outrun me.

How he would still get there first, despite being younger.

I only know I reach the clearing with the reaping tree in the center because there's no longer any tree trunks to slam into, nothing else to block my path.

The shadows stay firmly wrapped around my eyes, nothing deterring them now that my blood is clean of faerie dust.

"Please," I tell them. "Please, you have to let me see. I have to know. I can't bear not knowing."

Still, nothing but darkness.

"Please," I beg. "You can't protect me from what's real."

There's a hesitation, and I wonder if the shadows intend to blind me for the rest of my life. But then they dissipate, slowly leaking from my eyes. It's the glow of the bulbs on the reaping tree that sneak through the darkness first, a gentle beauty as deceptive as the reaping tree itself.

The shadows slink back into the forest, leaving me alone, though not entirely.

They're still obscuring the face of the dead boy hanging on a noose from a branch of the reaping tree, its lights backlighting his form. I don't need to see his face to know that it's him. I recognize his lanky frame, his long limbs.

When I take a step forward, something crunches underneath my feet. Pain and blood flow against the soles of my feet.

Glass from round spectacles litters the forest floor.

It takes me blinking the tears away, limping closer to the body, before I can make out his features.

John's face is sallow. His neck bruised with purple blotches that creep up around the noose.

I hear the cause of death matter-of-factly, in John's voice. Like he's standing next to me instead of dangling above me. *"Victim's neck must not have snapped. Bet he was too thin for his weight to do it for him. He probably struggled up there for a few minutes before he lost consciousness."*

I'm faintly aware of Peter's approaching presence. I think he and Victor were arguing in the forest. They must have been because when they rustle out from the trees behind us, Peter snaps, "Ever get between me and Wendy again, and I'll—"

I only turn to face them because I'm aware Michael was with Victor. It's like there's a checklist in my head of things that have to be done.

What to do when your brother is dead.

Number one. Make sure Michael doesn't see.

But Michael has already seen. That's why he was chanting earlier. Why his voice was high, strained. Why he sang the song that led me here. That way I could see it too, make it make sense to him.

But I can't make it make sense to Michael.

Not when it doesn't make sense to me.

Victor has tied a scrap piece of fabric over Michael's eyes. A gamble, but Michael seems not to mind the darkness. I whisper to the shadows to watch after my brother for a while.

And then I look at Peter. He's staring up at John's body, pure shock on his expression.

So that's what it looks like when Peter's in pain. There's none of the familiar indifference left. The cool apathy. Peter's blue eyes have watered over, his breath going labored.

When he looks at me, he's distraught. I think it might be on my behalf.

When Peter approaches me, I let myself melt into him, then have to remind myself that it wasn't my choice to do so.

It feels easier to pretend it's my choice. I don't have the energy to resist any longer. Who cares if my life is tied to Peter? John is dead.

John is dead.

My brother is dead.

I open my mouth to ask…but then realize I don't have a question in my mind. So Peter asks for me. "When did you find him?"

Victor pauses, Michael's hums filling the space. Peter's chest is warm against my cheek. It's the only reason I'm still standing. "Only just now. I was taking Michael out for a stroll—he was getting antsy inside. I tried to shield his eyes, but…I think he saw."

There's another question there, but my mind can't process it, my lips can't form the words.

I cling tighter to Peter. My brother is dead. His spectacles are glass shards at the bottoms of my feet.

I think I understand now why Michael likes to step on sharp things sometimes.

"Get him down," I whisper into Peter's chest.

When Peter pauses, I snap, "GET MY BROTHER DOWN."

Peter pulls away from me, a bit stunned. But he does as I say, wings batting as he flies up to the branch. For a moment, it seems as if he doesn't know how to go about it—cut the rope or untie it.

In the end, he takes a dagger to the noose, then holds John's body as it slumps in his arms. When he touches back down, he lays John in the grass.

"Who did this to him?" I ask, falling to my knees before my brother and wiping his hair from his forehead. It's grown even longer since I last saw him. Our mother would have had a fit.

"Wendy Darling, why don't we—"

My voice is calm. Like I'm the dangerous one here and I'm brokering a deal with an enemy turned business partner. "I want to find who did this." I pivot to Victor, my voice sounding far off, even to my ears. "Victor, when was the last time you saw John?"

Peter takes my hand. "Wendy, you're in shock. You need time to process—"

"Don't talk to me about processing," I snap, anger fueling me. Confusion warps Peter's face.

I want to laugh at him. To ask him what he expected choosing him to look like in practicality.

I can choose Peter all day long. I can let him hold me. I can kiss him and bed him if that's what he's after.

I can choose him and make him miserable at the same time. I wouldn't be the first.

Peter and I stay locked in a stare-down, but he folds first. It takes me a moment to understand his hesitation is because he can't stand my pain. "I don't think you're going to like the answer that you find."

"I didn't like finding my brother's corpse hanging from the reaping tree," I say, vaguely noticing how hardened my voice has gone. "Somehow, I doubt the answer to my question of when Victor last saw him will be more painful than that. I don't think finding his killer will be worse than that."

"And if there's not a murderer?" says Victor.

"Victor?" Peter asks as we both turn toward the Lost Boy.

Victor nods, almost ashamed. "John stopped eating the onions a few days ago."

Peter curses under his breath.

"What does that have to do with how he ended up dead?" I ask.

"Because," Victor says, "Simon stopped eating the onions too."

My heart doesn't have it in me to fear anymore. "And what happened to Simon?"

LATER, when we bury John, I have Victor help me remove his coat. I can't bear to do it myself. Feel the weight of John's body without any of the resistance that would normally indicate life. Can't bear to wrestle it off of him. Victor helps by keeping John's body stable, sitting it upright as I tug the coat off my brother's arms.

The process makes me sick, but I make myself push through. I want Michael to have John's coat. Something to wrap around himself that reminds him of his brother.

Still, once John is buried, I find I'm the one who's wrapping myself in his coat, cowered in the corner of Peter's bedroom—my bedroom now. It's a pitiful excuse for John's embrace, but it's all I have left of him.

My hands haven't stopped shaking since I found John's body strung up in the tree. I'm so tired of seeing my fingers tremble, witnessing my body's reaction to the agony it's been through over the past few days, so I hide them in John's coat pockets.

My fingers brush against something cold. Wooden. I remove my hand to reveal a tile, much like the ones John and I used to make for Michael to help him communicate. My heart aches as I turn it over in my hand. John must have been working on a communication board for Michael to use in Neverland. This one says "PETER" and is inscribed with an icon of wings. I can see Michael now, bringing it to John on one of the nights Peter was out on an errand for the Sister, or out looking for me. His way of asking John where Peter was. John trying to explain that Peter was out. That he'd be back soon.

Michael doesn't understand either of those concepts.

It's this thought that breaks me most of all.

EPILOGUE

WENDY

*A*t night, I speak to the shadows. I ask them if that's why they hid my eyes from John's body. If it was because they were ashamed of what they did.

They don't answer back, of course.

They can't.

Not with the faerie dust flowing through me.

Peter doses me twice a day now. Every time he brings it to my lips, I hear Astor's voice, his grating condescension mocking me for my weakness. But his words can only reach me for a moment at a time before they're silenced by the taste of honeysuckle and a whirl of lights.

Even when the first rush dissipates, I can hardly hear him.

But I can still hear John. Sometimes he's alive, laughing with his morbid sense of humor, making jokes about his death like he did the deaths of our parents. I laugh with him until I cry.

And then he comes again, but this time it's his corpse, and it's clawing itself out of the grave I insisted on digging for him with my bare hands. He's groping at the ground above him, unable to get out.

When that happens, Peter gives me another dose of faerie dust.

I spend my few sober hours of the day with Michael, playing with the train set, spinning its wheels as my brother hums dirges. I'm not sure where he picked those up. I'm fairly sure my parents never brought him to a funeral. But he heard them somewhere.

At night, I sleep in Peter's bed, though he doesn't touch me more than to wrap me in a cocoon. I'm not sure what would happen if I didn't insist Michael sleep on a cot in the room with us. I still can't tell how much of my outward reaction to Peter he's delusional enough to believe.

Sometimes I believe it myself.

It's easy, when you're going through the motions, to slip into believing.

I fight it for a while—the bargain, the curse.

I scream on the inside, but only during my sober hours, and those are becoming less and less bearable. My muscles grow weary, whether from grief at the loss of John or the toll of the faerie dust, or being tugged around at the end of the strings of my bargain, I'm unsure.

But eventually, my mind stops screaming.

The smile on my lips forced upon me by the magic of our bargain eventually strains so hard, it hurts more not to smile than it does to just give in when Peter teases me and flashes me that adoring smirk. It's easier to let the laughs fall from my lips than it is for them to scrape against my throat trying to escape.

It's easier to let my heart flutter at his kiss than it is for the magic in my body to fight the urge to vomit.

It's easier to forget than it is to remember.

And so, slowly, over the weeks or months or however time works in this chasm of a realm, choosing Peter turns into wanting Peter. Which turns into loving Peter.

And by the time it's happened, I've forgotten why I ever bothered fighting it at all.

CAGING DARLING

THE LOST GIRL SERIES BOOK THREE

T.A. LAWRENCE

BONUS CHAPTER

TALAWRENCEBOOKS.COM

Wondering what was going on in Captain Astor's head the night he met Wendy?

For a *Losing Wendy* bonus chapter from Captain Astor's perspective, as well as a bonus prologue from Peter's perspective, sign up to my newsletter at talawrencebooks.com

ACKNOWLEDGMENTS

I hope that in dedicating this book to myself, I haven't come across as thinking I've done any of this on my own. It's more that if I had access to a time machine and could gift my younger self one of my books, I would pick this one. I like to think I'm not nearly as unkind to myself as I once was.

That being said, I couldn't have gotten to a place of being gentle with myself without the tremendous love that's been outpoured on me by my Lord and my God, who loved me before I loved Him.

Jacob, you know me better than anyone on this earth, which means you get to see all the ickiness I can't hide from you like I do everyone else. Thanks for knowing me and loving me still. It's funny how I get in my head about all the reasons I'm a bad wife, only for you to tell me you actually like the qualities I'm giving myself such a hard time over. Thanks for being the buoy to my tether, babe.

Dad, I'm sorry for making you mad with this one. Just kidding; I'm not that sorry. Thanks for being so supportive of my writing from the beginning. I can't tell you how much of my confidence that I can actually do this comes directly from you.

Mom, thanks for taking me to see the world when I graduated high school. I'm so thankful to be able to draw from my own adventures as I write made-up ones. You gave me stories of my own to tell, and that's such a gift.

Rachel Bobo, thanks for loving this imaginary world, possibly even more than I do. I was in such a creative rut before you kept me on the phone for more than an hour gushing about these characters.

Alyssa Dorn, as someone who is not detail-oriented, I'm so

thankful that you are. Also, my official standard for whether my plot twists are good enough is whether I'm able to get them past you. Morgan Cari, you have such a gift for communicating the emotional journey of the reader. It's so nice as an author to be able to gauge those reactions throughout the book.

Christine, thank you so much for your kind feedback and for being so easy to work with and dependable.

Maci, your illustrations are beautiful. As much as I enjoy the final product, I love getting to watch your process. Thanks for bringing an element to my storytelling that I can't do on my own.

C. F. E. Black, thanks for being my author friend. It's so nice having someone I can talk business and writing with who tolerates my voice message rants.

Rachel Broadway, thanks for the name Darian Maddox. It didn't fit Nolan, but I liked it enough to make up an entire character based off of it. Coulter, thanks for giving me the idea for the first line of John's POV. Aimee, you send the absolute best post-publication texts. Thanks for always giving me a confidence boost while my ego is in a vulnerable state. Logan, thanks for the scurvy joke that's hidden in this book. Mattler, thanks for making me feel like being an author is a real job. Preston, I'll never be able to write a pirate sub-plot without thinking of canoeing on Emerald Lake. So thanks for that. I think?

Kyliegh Romine, thanks for hyping my books to the closed-door community. I love getting to see the pictures of my books on your shelf.

To all my lovely readers, if it weren't for you, the voices in my head wouldn't be nearly as socially acceptable.

ABOUT THE AUTHOR

T.A. Lawrence spent her childhood lost in a daydream. She was fond of her imagination, despite its annoying tendency to torture her with rather detailed nightmares. As an adult, nothing has really changed, except that she's learned to turn daydreaming into her job and nightmares into idea-fodder. Crafting a chilling twist is her favorite pastime, but she puts out the occasional fantasy rom-com to convince her friends and family that she's not *that* twisted.

ALSO BY T.A. LAWRENCE

The Lost Girl Series

Losing Wendy

Freeing Hook

Caging Darling

The Severed Realms

A Word So Fitly Spoken

A Tune to Make Them Follow

A Bond of Broken Glass

A Throne of Blood and Ice

A Realm of Shattered Lies

A Swoony Solstice

Of Tangles and Tinsel

The Astoria Chronicles

The Keeper of the Threshold

The Secret of Atalo

Printed in Great Britain
by Amazon